Praise f

Karen Kay is a wonderful storyteller, and if you have never read an Indian romance, make sure this is your first. I, for one, have always wondered what would happen if a Plains warrior was suddenly thrown into the midst of England's high society. Now I know. Now you have the chance to find out.

Geralyn Fine, *The Time Machine*

This graphic historical transports you into the lives, loves, and customs of the plains Indians during the turbulent 1840's. This stirring romance is action-packed, remarkably touching, and extremely informative. If you enjoy a good, spicy western romance, this one is definitely for you.

SI *Rendezuous*

This novel, part fable and part historical fact, is mixed with vivid imagination. Karen Kay presents interesting characters and a sweet, yet sexually charged love story with elements similar to those in Jude Deveraux's *Remembrance*.

Gerry Benninger, Romantic Times

Look for these titles by Karen Kay

Lakota Series
Lakota Surrender
Proud Wolf's Woman
Lakota Princess

Blackfoot Warriors
Gray Hawk's Lady
White Eagle's Touch
Night Thunder's Bride

Legendary Warriors
War Cloud's Passion
Lone Arrow's Pride
Soaring Eagle's Embrace
Wolf Shadow's Promise

The Warriors of the Iroquois
Black Eagle
Seneca Surrender

The Lost Clan
The Angel and the Warrior
The Spirit of the Wolf
Red Hawk's Woman
The Last Warrior

The Clan of the Wolf
The Princess and the Wolf
Brave Wolf and the Lady

The Wild West Series
The Eagle and the Flame
Iron Wolf's Bride

Gray Hawk's Lady

Blackfoot Warriors, Book 1

Karen Kay

PK&J Publishing
1 Lakeview Trail
Danbury, CT 06811

Gray Hawk's Lady

ISBN 979 8 54370 0 259

Dedication

To the two Gennys in my life: my mother, Genevieve Wilson, who brought music to my life; and Genevieve Johnson, my neighbor, who gave me a sense of drama and her own unique view of life.

And to Paul, my husband. Your presence, my love for you, fills this book. I love you.

Acknowledgment

Special acknowledgment to L. Ron Hubbard: in his book *Buckskin Brigades,* he has documented the Blackfoot viewpoint of the Lewis and Clark incident, the only place where I have found it, and he first brought home to me the dignity and wisdom of the Native Americans, especially the Blackfeet.

It only goes to show that in all things, there are always two sides to a story.

Note to the Reader

At the time when my story takes place, there were three different tribes of Indians that, together, comprised the Blackfeet or Blackfoot Nation: the Piegan, or Pikuni—their name in the Blackfoot language; the Blood, or Kainah; and the Blackfoot proper, or Siksika.

The Piegan, which is pronounced Pay-gan, were also divided into the Northern and Southern bands.

All three of these tribes were independent and were known to the early trappers by their own individual tribal names. But because the three shared the same language, intermarried and went to war with the same enemies, it became more common, as time went on, to call these people under one name: the Blackfoot, or Siksikauw.

At this time, the time of my story, the names "Blackfoot" and "Blackfeet" were used interchangeably, meaning one and the same group of people.

However, during reservation days (the story goes, as I was told it), the US government utilized a misnomer, calling the tribe of the Southern Piegan, or Pikuni, the "Blackfeet." This designation stuck, and to this day, this tribe resides in Northern Montana on the Blackfeet reservation and is referred to by the government as the "Blackfeet" (although they are really the Southern Piegan or Pikuni).

Consequently, when we speak today of the Blackfoot tribes, or the Siksika Nation as a whole, we talk of four different tribes: the Blackfoot, Blood and Piegan bands in Canada and the Blackfeet in Montana. Thus, when referring to the "Blackfeet," one is speaking of the band of Indians in

Montana, whereas the name "Blackfoot" refers to the band of Indians in Alberta, Canada.

If this seems confusing to you, I can assure you, it baffled me.

Thus, in my story, because the Blackfeet and Blackfoot names were interchangeable at this moment in history, I have used "Blackfeet" as a noun (I went to visit the Blackfeet) and "Blackfoot" as an adjective (I went to Blackfoot country). I did this for no other reason than consistency.

I am also including some definitions of common Indian words that might be unfamiliar to the reader, which I hope will help toward further understanding.

Algonquin—"member of a group of Indian tribes formerly of the Ottawa River valley in SE Canada. Also, Algonquia—Widespread American-Indian language family spoken from Labrador westward to the Rockies and southward to Illinois and North Carolina." *The Scribner-Bantam English Dictionary*, 1977. Some of the tribes that spoke this language were the Cheyenne, Blackfoot, Arapaho, Shawnee and Ottawa.

The Backbone of the World—term used by the Blackfeet to indicate the Rocky Mountains.

Coup—a term in widespread use by the Indians to mean a deed of valor.

Crow—a tribe of Indians that inhabited that part of the northern United States around the upper Yellowstone River. They were at war with the Blackfeet.

Gros Ventre—a tribe of Indians that neighbored the Blackfeet.

Kit Fox Society—all Indian tribes had different societies for men and for women. They denoted different social strata and were graded by age.

Medicine—described by George Catlin in his book *Letters and Notes on the Manners, Customs, and Conditions of North American Indians*, "'Medicine' is a great word in this country;... The word medicine, in its common acceptation here, means *mystery*, and nothing else; and in that sense I *shall* use it very frequently in my Notes and Indian Manners and Customs. The Fur Traders in this country, are nearly all French; and in their language, a doctor or physician, is called *'Medecin.'* The Indian country is full of doctors; and as they are all magicians, and skilled, or profess to be skilled, in many mysteries, the word 'medecin' has become habitually applied to every thing mysterious or unaccountable..."

More-than-friend—in most Indian tribes, a more-than-friend refers to friends of the same gender who have made a pact to fight together and hunt together, etc., in an effort to increase both persons' survival. Such was a friend, but more. It was expected that if one of them had troubles, so too did the other take on those troubles as his own, helping to find solutions.

Parfleche—a bag fashioned out of buffalo hide and used by the Indians to store clothing, food and other articles. An Indian used parfleches much as the white man uses a chest of drawers. They were often highly decorated, and some were sewn in patterns "owned" by a particular family, thus easily recognized.

Sits-beside-him-woman or -wife—in Indian tribes which practiced polygamy, this referred to the favorite wife, usually the first wife. She directed all the other wives and had the right to sit next to her husband at important meetings.

Snakes—this refers to the Shoshoni or Snake Indians. They bordered the Blackfeet on the south and west and were traditional enemies of the Blackfeet.

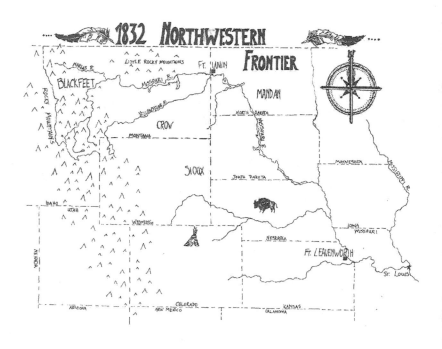

Prologue

St. Louis

January 1832

*L*ady Genevieve Rohan's laugh reverberated throughout the parlor, filling the atmosphere with a gaiety that might have been dispelled at once had anyone taken a good look at the young English heiress. While it was true that Genevieve's brown eyes sparkled, one had only to observe the circles beneath them, the paleness of her skin and the pinched-in quality of her cheeks to know that the lady was distraught.

The facade she presented this cold morning in January, however, could have fooled Satan himself.

Suddenly she grinned. "Why, Mr. Toddman," she said after a short deliberation, flicking her ever-present fan open and bringing it to her face to hide all but her expressive eyes. "Our manservant informs me that you are here to see me this morning, not my father. I am flattered by your attention, but I am most curious to learn what you have come here to tell me."

The young man flushed, his gaze not quite able to meet that of the young lady. He cleared his throat, and, looking away, brought up a hand to pull at his collar. Finally, he said, "Please excuse me, Lady Genevieve, if it seems improper to you. It is only that I must see you urgently. There are some matters that have come to my attention, and I feel it only right to ask you about these things now. After all, there is no need for me to carry tales to your father—nor to mine."

Genevieve smiled, while impishly peeping out over her fan. "You are thinking of carrying tales? And what matters are these that have you in such a dither this fine morning?" she inquired.

13

The young man hesitated. He pulled at his collar yet again, making a face this time as he made to stretch his neck. At last, though, he said, "I have been to the bank this morning, and I have discovered that the management there is under the misapprehension that *you* are now in charge of your father's finances."

"Ah, I see."

"Do you? Jolly good, then. Well, you would certainly understand that I would appreciate your every expediency in clearing up this matter with the bank. Why, I came away from that institution this morning with nothing more to show for my efforts than empty pockets, and this after I have done so much for your father's project."

"Yes," she said, "I can understand your confusion. It is your project, too, is it not?"

"Well, certainly." He cleared his throat. "Yes, by Jove, of course it is. It is only — "

"Then you were able to procure that which we need?"

"That which we — " Non-comprehension turned to quick understanding as the young man's coloring went from pale to a deep crimson. He looked away. "Oh," he said. "You mean the Indian."

Genevieve nodded.

The young man shrugged his shoulders and smiled. "All in good time, Lady Genevieve, all in good time. You should not be worrying about such things. I have the matter well in hand."

Genevieve scrutinized the young man sitting before her, her gaze direct, forthright. She sighed. At length, she drew her silky fan closed, and, setting it in her lap, said, "Mr. Toddman, you do realize that my father's work is due in no more than a year's time?"

Again the young man shrugged. "Yes?"

"Then you must also realize that my father needs a considerable amount of leisure in which to outline all of his facts so that he can consolidate and categorize all that we have learned here."

"I fail to see — "

"There is only one tribe of Indians that we have not yet studied, and only that one tribe remains before my father can assimilate his notes and begin work on his thesis of the American Indian culture. It is this singular fact alone that keeps us from realizing my father's accomplishments. And, sir, it is my understanding that it has been your duty to procure this Indian. I believe you have had access to my father's account in order to finance such an expedition."

The young assistant shrugged.

"Mr. Toddman, my father still has no Indian from this infamous tribe to complete his studies."

"It is not so easy as it would appear."

"Yes, I do realize that. So my father has told me. It is why he has allowed you such a free hand with our account. But it also came to my attention the other day that our money in that account has been dwindling at an incredible rate. And, while this might be expected on such an expedition as ours, there is nothing here at the moment to show for such expenditures of funds."

"Nothing to show for it?"

She nodded. "The project remains unfinished."

The young assistant came to his feet, and, presenting his back to Genevieve, paced toward the fireplace, which stood at the opposite end of the room. At last, he turned to stare back at the lady. He shook his head. "How can you say such a thing? There is more than enough here to account for all the exchange of funds."

"Mr. Toddman, the work is not—"

"And after all I've done for you. Did I not produce all the Indians you desired? Wasn't it I who introduced you to William Clark, who is now Superintendent of Indian Affairs? Wasn't it I who brought you delegates from the Sioux Nation, from the Omaha, the Cheyenne? How about the girl who was sent here from the Arapaho? Why, I even managed to bring you someone from the Crow and Pawnee tribes, and all this despite the fact that we were supposed to go and visit these tribes, not have them sent to us. And now you—"

15

"My father needs a representative from this last tribe to complete his studies. That's all. You know this—probably better than I do. And, Mr. Toddman, we had all three of us agreed to study Indian tribal languages this way. We had all decided this would be more efficient. It wasn't just my father and I. You know this. Why are you arguing about this with me?"

"I am not debating the point with you, Lady Genevieve. But don't you see? Your father doesn't need this tribe of Indians. He could complete his work without procuring one more tribe. He has more than enough material to finish it now."

Genevieve sighed. She closed her eyes for a moment, looking as though she wished she were somewhere else, or failing this, that there might, at least, be someone else she could trust to handle this particular subject...and this man.

But realizing, perhaps, that there was no one else, she breathed out deeply, and, opening her eyes, carefully studied the man before her. "Mr. Toddman," she began, "if you feel my father has enough material for his studies now, why have you spent over twenty thousand American dollars these past few months trying to obtain a representative from this last remaining tribe?"

"Your father wanted this—" the young man uttered quickly before he halted, his gaze coming up to catch the lady's glance. Quickly, though, he looked away as he croaked, "You know...?"

She cleared her throat. "Yes, I know all about it, Mr. Toddman. But what I do not understand is, if you felt so deeply about the manner in which we were going about this, why did you not just talk to my father and let him be done with it?"

The assistant paused. He opened his lips to speak, but when no words came, he closed his mouth. Several minutes ticked by before he tried again. At last he said, "I have had other matters that required my attention."

Genevieve looked away. "Yes," she said. "I know. Creditors have brought me notice that there are many gambling debts that you owe. I had to pay one just last week." She sighed. "Please understand, Mr. Toddman, that while I know my father has condoned such behavior from you, I cannot. Not when our funds are so low."

The young man twisted around to confront the lady. It took him a moment before he could utter, "What are you saying?"

Genevieve looked up toward the ceiling. "It is not the bank that has made the error, Mr. Toddman." She drew a deep breath. "It is I who put a stop to your drawing funds from the account. I know it will be an inconvenience to you, but until we complete our studies here, we can no longer afford the luxury of the gaming tables. I would have told you earlier; it's only that—"

"How dare you!" The assistant started forward, stopped; then, in a flurry of agitated pacing, threw up his hands. "You have no right!" he snarled. "Why, my father is helping to finance this project, too."

"Yes, I know, but—"

"He did not give you leave to stop my financing, I am certain."

"Mr. Toddman, I—"

"The money is not yours."

"Yes, I know, Mr. Toddman, but my father—"

"This has nothing to do with your father, and you know it. This is *your* decision, isn't it?"

"Yes, it is," she said. "And until my father recovers and is able to deal with these matters himself, you will have to settle them with me."

"Oh, you think so?" he asked, his words almost a sneer. All at once he stopped his striding, and, almost too quietly, said, "I will send word to my own father in England about this, and then we will see with whom I will deal."

Genevieve lifted her chin. "That will make little difference to our situation."

"We shall see."

"Mr. Toddman, both your father and mine are enamored with this project, and you know it. Neither of them wants this study sabotaged, and that is exactly what you are doing by continuing to visit the gaming tables.

17

At the rate you are losing money, there would soon be no further funds available to finish this project."

It was here that Mr. Toddman, sixth son of the Earl of Tygate, drew himself up to his full height. One would have thought that the man had been physically injured, so great was the air of his distress. At length, however, he deigned to look down his nose at the lady before him, and in a haughty voice said, "You dare to criticize me, Lady Genevieve, and yet look at you. You, who must always look the height of fashion. You, who must always appear the proper English lady."

"Mr. Toddman, I fail to see what—"

"Expense, Lady Genevieve. Expense. You take me to task, yet you reserve for yourself only the best that this godforsaken town has to offer."

"Mr. Toddman, you are talking about clothes, a necessary expenditure. I am speaking of gambling, a habit in which only the very rich or the extremely lucky can indulge. I fail to see—"

"Only for yourself or your father." The assistant carried on as though she hadn't spoken. "Nary a thing for me."

"Mr. Toddman, you go too far. We are speaking of twenty thousand American dollars, spent by you, for you, and nothing to show—"

"That is not true. Why, only yesterday I found another couple of trappers who are not only willing, but who are able to go and capture for us your precious Blackfoot Indian."

Lady Genevieve paused. There was no denying the lady's quick look of relief. But it was short-lived. There was something else easily espied in her glance: some emotion, a distrustfulness, perhaps. Or mayhap she was only wary.

Letting out a sigh, she said, "I am so glad to hear this. Did you say you did this only yesterday?"

"Yes."

"And what were the names of these men, that I might go and tell my father?"

The young man hesitated, his face drawn in and his cheeks filling with color. "What difference does that make, Lady Genevieve? Isn't it enough that I have done it? We will find out more about the two men when they return with your Indian."

Genevieve hesitated. Clearly, she wanted to believe the man, but still she delayed in speaking for several moments. "Mr. Toddman," she said, her voice unable to disguise her apprehension. "How much did you have to pay these trappers this time?"

The man shrugged, his hand again coming up to reach for his collar. "Now, Lady Genevieve," he said, "is that something you should be worrying about?"

"I believe so. As I have already said, since my father has become ill and I have of necessity taken control of the financial matters of the family, I think I should be apprised of exactly how much you paid these men, if only so I can make an adjustment to the account."

Mr. Toddman hesitated, but at her continued regard of him, he uttered, "Five thousand American dollars."

"Five thousand—" Genevieve stopped, unable to restrain a show of emotion, which revealed itself as a quick flush upon her cheeks. She cleared her throat. "Five thousand American dollars, Mr. Toddman? Such is an exorbitant fee, of which I'm sure you are aware. Were the men you paid surprised that you were willing to part with such a price?"

"Hardly."

She tilted back her head. "And of course you paid it all in advance."

"Of course."

"And you pledge me your word that none of the money went toward the gaming tables?"

"Milady! How dare you!"

She didn't respond; she just looked at him. "Mr. Toddman," she said at last, "might I remind you that my father is allowing you to draw on his account only those sums of money of which he approves?"

"And you think he did not approve this expenditure?"

19

"I am fairly certain of it."

From across the room, the assistant surveyed her for innumerable seconds while Lady Genevieve held his gaze. At length, the young man said, "My father will hear of this at the utmost possible speed, believe me. And when he does...you might find, Lady Genevieve, that you will be in need of revising your opinion of me and my work. You might find," he said, smirking, "that you will need to come and beg me to help you. And, milady, how I look forward to that day. Until then," he started forward, "unless you give me further funds, I will stop all my work for you." He laughed. "And won't your precious project be in jeopardy then? Go try to engage a trapper or trader without my help, and see for yourself how easy it is."

"But you said that you had just hired —"

"So I did, Lady Genevieve, so I did. But that was before our little talk. Did you really think I would help you when you refuse to finance me —"

"Mr. Toddman, you go too far! I am not refusing to pay you any wages you are due, only the money that you spend —"

"Without complete financial support, Lady Genevieve," the assistant straightened his shoulders, "I somehow find myself in the position of being unwilling and perhaps unable to offer any further assistance to this project." He smiled. "Might I suggest that you go and find your own Indian?"

Genevieve coughed. "Mr. Toddman!"

"Or perhaps," the young man said as he paused, leering, "mayhap if the trappers do come back with your Blackfoot Indian, I might be the one to interview the savage, and then it will be I who will have the pleasure of finishing this much-needed book."

"Mr. Toddman," she said, presenting to the man a demeanor that looked, to all appearances, quite calm. "You cannot do that. You are under contract with my father, and —"

"A contract that you have broken, not I. Can I help it if you choose to let me go?"

"I —"

"Our meeting is at an end, Lady Genevieve...unless you are willing to renegotiate the bank notice."

Genevieve looked away. She stared at the wall for innumerable seconds before finally, as though defeated, she uttered, "I cannot."

The young assistant drew his lips together until they looked more a thin, painted line than mere lips, rife with outright hatred. He said, "Then we have nothing further to discuss, do we, Lady Genevieve? No," he continued as she made to rise. "I will show myself out."

And with these parting words, Mr. Toddman propelled himself forward and quickly left the room.

"Excuse me."

Genevieve glanced over toward the door, her gaze troubled. "Yes?" she asked abstractedly. "What is it, Robert?"

"It's your father, milady. He—"

"My father?"

"Yes, milady. He's had a fall. He tried to get up from bed, and—"

"Where is he now?"

"He is back in his bedroom, milady, and I—"

"Summon a doctor at once, Robert."

"It has been done, milady."

Genevieve had already risen and was most of the way across the parlor room when she paused mid-stride, looking up toward the domestic who stood beside the entryway. "Thank you, Robert. Bring the doctor upstairs as soon as he arrives."

"Yes, milady. Will you require anything else?"

"No, Robert, except..." Genevieve took a few more steps toward the hall. She gave the man a shy smile. "Thank you again, Robert. I don't know what my father and I would do without you. You're probably the best friend we've ever had. I hope you know that we will always appreciate your loyalty to us."

And to Robert's "Yes, milady," Lady Genevieve fled from the room.

****

"Father, what have you done this time?" Genevieve practically flew across her father's bedroom to Viscount Rohan's side. "You know the doctor told you to stay in bed until you are fully healed of this gout."

She stopped and bent down to place a kiss on the man's forehead. "If you will only heed the doctor's advice, it will not be that much longer before you can be up and about, and doing all the things you need to." She stopped when she noticed that her father had barely even heard her. She glanced downward to find a letter in his hands.

"Blackfeet" was the only word she caught in the letter before her father's hand fell toward the floor, the paper dropping at the same time.

"What is it this time, Father?" she asked, kneeling down to pick up the letter.

"Blackfeet," was all he muttered.

Genevieve spared a quick glance upward. Not again. First Mr. Toddman, and now her father. Was there to be no end to the problems this tribe presented them?

"The Blackfeet again, Father? What has happened now?"

Her father didn't answer, and Genevieve darted a quick look at the viscount.

He made no response.

She sighed. How could one ignorant savage tribe cause them such havoc?

"Father," she said, "I know the Blackfoot Indians have caused us some problems, and believe me, I am aware of the difficulty you face. I, too, have heard the legends of these people. I've listened to the stories the trappers tell of them; I've heard of how no one can go into Blackfoot country and live to tell of it, of how this tribe guards their territory so well that only the foolhardy will venture into their realm. How could I not? It's all anyone ever talks of, if I so much as even hint at their name. But really, Father, we have to come to terms with them if ever we are to finish this project."

Her father hadn't heard a word. He just stared away from her, the paleness of his face, the dejection in his manner, a testimony to his distress.

She frowned. "Father?"

Still, he didn't answer.

What *were* they going to do about the Blackfeet? They needed a study of them, and yet...

"Is it possible that we could finish your manuscript without an account of this tribe?" she asked. "Especially since the Blackfeet appear to be more savage than the rest? Oh, I've heard the whole story, of course: that the trouble with the Blackfeet originally started when the Lewis and Clark expedition ventured into their territory, killing two tribe members. But the killings had all been done in self-defense. Everyone knows that. Surely the Blackfeet wouldn't hold a man guilty for defending himself, would they?"

Or would they? It was a common fact that from that incident forward, the Blackfeet had vowed to kill any further intruders into their land.

Genevieve glanced at her father. He still stared straight ahead of him.

She grimaced. "It's hard to believe." She spoke to her father quietly, taking his hand in her own. "The incident with Lewis and Clark took place almost thirty years ago. What sort of people would harbor a grudge for thirty long years?

"Is it possible, Father, that your publishers might extend your deadline? There has been a fort close by to their country now for three years. Why, even last week I read something about a steamship that will be sailing soon on a voyage up the Missouri River to that outpost. I think it's called Fort Union. Surely no land will remain savage for long, or a people continue to be so antagonistic when there are a great many civilizing influences coming into it. If we could only have more time."

She closed her eyes and drew in a deep breath.

That was the problem. They had little time left to complete this project. And with her father ill and Mr. Toddman in rebellion, she was afraid the bulk of responsibility for the project was now going to fall upon her.

Was she up to handling it?

23

Was it possible that she, a mere woman, could succeed in seeing the manuscript finished when the men in her life had so far failed?

"Genny?"

"Yes, Father?" She opened her eyes.

"Did you read the letter?" Viscount Rohan gripped her hands as she leaned over him.

"No, Father, not yet. But I—"

"Read it, then...oh," he said, as Genevieve picked up the paper, "never mind." He glanced at the ceiling. "It doesn't make any difference now. It's impossible, I tell you. Can't get the bloody Blackfeet here. Can't go to them. But I need to, Genny; I must...or else..."

"Father, what—"

"Look at the letter. It's from the publisher. They won't even consider the project finished without a study of every major American tribe. And they specifically include the Blackfeet. But that's not all. Oh, Genny, what can I do but get out of bed? I must go there, and I must leave here at once."

As the viscount made to get up, Genny gently pushed him back onto the pillows. "You'll not be going anywhere. Not until the doctor says you're able."

Viscount Rohan flopped back against the bed. "Oh, what am I to do? What am I to do?"

"It may not be as bad as you think. I just this morning had a talk with Mr. Toddman, and he believes it might yet be possible to get someone from the tribe to come here. He's hired another couple of trappers."

"Won't do any good."

Genevieve frowned. "What do you mean? Isn't that what we've been trying to do these past few months?"

"Read the letter, Genny. Read the letter."

"Yes, Father, but I..." Her voice trailed off, her gaze already skimming the paper in her hand. "I don't see what—" She sucked in her breath, barely managing to keep her grasp on the letter. "Oh my...how can this be? It's not possible."

24

"It's what I would have thought too, Genny, but as you can see, it's already happening."

"I don't understand. I thought Mr. Catlin was merely painting the Indians' portraits..."

"It happens all the time. Haven't you noticed how, the moment you get a project in mind, you have to act on it right away or someone else steals it from you?"

"No, I haven't...well, perhaps—"

"And without so much as talking to you about it?"

"I suppose—"

"Someone has to go there, Genny. There's no longer time to hire another to do it." He sighed and glanced over toward the window. "You'd best bring young William Toddman to me, Genny. It's the only way now."

"I don't understand. How can this be?"

Her father didn't answer, and his lack of response told her, more than anything, that the situation of which she read was, indeed, just this serious.

"Father," she said, "it still states here that George Catlin is merely painting Indian portraits. He is not doing an anthropological study as we are. Surely that's not truly competition. Our projects are worlds apart. They can't drop our studies just because someone else is interested in doing something similar to ours. It's not done. It's..."

"The publishers haven't stopped their support. But with Catlin actually visiting the Indians in their own country and painting their portraits, we stand to lose our project. We aren't holding as strong a position as we once did. We haven't been there. He has—he is."

"Still," she said, "it can't be as bad as it seems. Catlin is, after all, American, and your publishers are English. Perhaps we should talk to Mr. Catlin and see if we can collaborate on this project, since we are both interested in the same thing. Maybe we could persuade Mr. Catlin to publish his works with ours. It's possible. And if, after we talk to him, we still can't... Well, Father, you have nothing to fear. Our publisher is

English...English. Now, I ask you, would an Englishman take an American's story over one of his own? Really, Father."

The viscount sighed, leaning his head back against the pillows and closing his eyes. A long moment followed, the silence between father and daughter somehow echoing their mutual distress. At length, Viscount Rohan opened his eyes, staring out the window as though something of great interest lay just outside. He said, "There's more to it, Genny. I made a foolish mistake. I admit it now. Wish I could take it back...can't. Too bloody cocky, I was." He shook his head. "But it's too late now, much too late, and I...I'm so sorry, Genny."

Genevieve took her father's hand in her own. "Don't worry, Father. We'll find a way out of this. Haven't we always done so in the past?"

"Not this time, Genny. Not this time. Too much at stake." He gritted his teeth. "How could I have been so stupid?"

"It's not so bad. It's not as though *all* of our wealth is tied into this project. We still have our home, our lands. In truth, though I want this project to succeed as much as you do, what would be the worst thing that could happen if it didn't? We'd go back to England, find some other project, and off we would go once again. Oh, I know your reputation would suffer because of it, but really, Father, such a thing is so easily remedied. Perhaps we could study the Indians of South America and their languages instead."

"Oh, Genny, no. It's worse than that. Should have told you, I guess. Didn't think I'd ever have to. Too damned arrogant for my own good is what I was."

"And with full, good reason." She smiled. "After all, you are England's leading—"

"Genny, no." He withdrew his hand from her own. "It's more complicated than that. I've done something I haven't told you. Something that will make you hate me. Something—"

"Never!"

The viscount shook his head. "Listen to me. I must tell you this now. I should never have withheld this from you. It's just that...I never dreamed I would get so ill. How could I have known?"

26

"Exactly, Father. Whatever it is, we'll see our way through it."

He breathed in deeply. "I don't know, Genny. I fear… It happened back in England, a few weeks before we were to set sail…"

"Before we…? What are you talking about, Father? What happened?"

"He came to me late one night."

She shook her head. "He? Who is he?"

"The Duke of Starksboro."

"The Duke of Starks—" Genevieve paused, a wave of foreboding coming over her. "Father," she began, "why would you even see the man? I don't care if he is a duke. He has meant you nothing but the utmost harm ever since you beat him to that African project so many years ago. Plus, he is the most terrific bore when it comes to this sort of work—thinks he knows all about it while he displays his utter stupidity. Why, do you know that he told me that he thought the American Indian was no more human than the ape? That it was pointless to study such a person? There's something quite evil about the man, Father. I think you should have no further contact with him."

He sighed. "I have to, Genny."

Her stomach dropped. She raised her gaze to his. "Have to?"

He slowly nodded. "And so do you."

"Stop it! How can you say such a thing?"

The Viscount Rohan closed his eyes, a gloom appearing to descend upon him that had nothing to do with health, or the lack of it. "Should have told you sooner."

"Told me what, Father?"

He swallowed, a noisy affair, set off as it was against the silence in the room. "I made a bet with the man."

Genevieve sucked in her breath.

"I know, I know," he said as though she had spoken. "I just couldn't suffer his gloating any further."

"But Father—"

"Bet him is what I did," he continued. "Bet him that the Indians were human, real people. Bet him I'd bring back evidence of their civilization, of their intelligence. I wagered all that we have, Genny. Everything. Our home, our land. And something more."

He paused, and Genevieve, squaring back her shoulders, sat up straighter in her chair. She thrust out her chin, trying to ignore the feeling of dread settling over her.

"You have to understand, Genny," Viscount Rohan went on. "I didn't see how I could fail. It was such a fantastic bet to make, and so easy to win. Or so it seemed. Of course these Indians are people. Of course they have their own civilization. How could I fail? And he had challenged me with double what the publishers are paying me, plus he threw in a good-sized portion of his land as well. How could I resist? Or more importantly, how could I lose?"

Genevieve looked at her hands in her lap. "I understand. What else did you bet him, Father?"

The older man sank back farther into the pillows, if that were possible. "I gambled…" He paused. "Genny, please try to understand."

She cleared her throat. "What else did you bet?"

Viscount Rohan squeezed his eyes shut. At last, he muttered, "My work, Genny."

"Your work? I don't understand. I… How could you —"

"I…I gave the duke my word of honor that if I fail, I will quit doing these studies on my own. I promised that I would work only for him —"

"No! Father!"

"But I promised this only if I fail, Genny. And it just didn't seem possible at the time that I couldn't manage this simple project."

Genevieve Rohan sat in silence for a short while, her gaze focused downward. At last, though, without lifting her head, she said, "Perhaps there is still a way out of it. You could always put your work in my name. I haven't —"

"Won't work, Genny."

"Why not?"

"You're a woman."

"What does that have to do with it? I'm your daughter. I have seen other women carry on in the names of their fathers."

"That's just the point, Genny: in the names of their fathers. Besides, the duke must have anticipated this. He made me promise him your work too."

"Father!"

"But look at what I had to win."

"Or lose."

"Genny…"

She sat still, her mind in a whirl, though conversely, she couldn't seem to think at all. Suddenly, she frowned and looked up. "We have very little time, then, don't we? Perhaps you had best forget the Blackfoot Indians and the studies of their culture and language. If we begin work right now, we have barely enough time to catalogue and put onto paper all we have learned. Perhaps it is best, then, if we set sail back to England at once."

Her father slumped his shoulders, his head down. "I can't, Genny," he said. "You read the letter. Without a study of that tribe, I can't even begin to submit the manuscript for publication, especially not now that Catlin is making ready for a trip into Blackfoot country himself."

Silence. "I see," Genevieve said at last, although she wasn't certain that she did. She scowled. "Father, I'm not quite sure that I understand. How does your finished manuscript fit into this? Did you merely bet the duke that the Indians were people, or does this somehow relate to the finished work of this project?"

He gulped. "To the finished work."

Genevieve gasped, her breathing becoming more pronounced, more difficult. She said, "Tell me exactly how it is that this wager is based on your work."

Her father shrugged. "Since I had to finish the project anyway, and you know what an 'authority' the duke is on anthropology, I wagered that I would find the Indians with culture, language and a way of life of which to be proud, each and every tribe, and that he could use the completed work as his proof."

She nodded her head. "I see. And there is only this Blackfoot tribe left to study, and then the whole project is finished—at least from a research standpoint?"

"Yes."

"And you have all your notes and observations already written about the other tribes?"

"Yes."

"Are you sure this Blackfoot band is the only major tribe left for you to study?"

"Certainly."

She rose slowly, pushing down at the material of her skirts as she did so. Her hands shook, and she found herself unable to meet her father's gaze. At length, though, she said, "I will have to think about this, Father. It seems as though we are in an unsolvable dilemma. I will have to see if there is some way for us to resolve this. In the meantime, I would not rely on William Toddman for any more of your projects. There is something wrong with the man, more than just his wasteful gambling, but I can't quite ascertain what exactly. While it's true that he has spent most of our money at the gaming tables, I fear there is something undisclosed that is driving him...something I can't quite..." She lifted her shoulders slightly. "I do not trust him, Father, and I do not believe you should either... I—"

A knock on the door interrupted her, and a few seconds later, the local doctor stepped into the room.

"Hello, Dr. Gildman," Genevieve said, extending her hand toward the man. "I'm so glad you were able to come and see my father." She turned then, and gazing down at the worried countenance of her father, she smiled, even though it was a wary smile at best. "Don't worry, I'll think of something. You just concentrate on getting better." She bent down to press a kiss to her father's forehead. "I'll be up to see you tonight, Father. Dr. Gildman," she acknowledged, and, shifting away from the two men, she quietly left the room.

****

Stunned. No, that wasn't quite the word: numb, startled, jolted...that's how she felt. Genevieve sat in her room some hours later, having not moved from this one spot in all that time. She stared straight ahead of her.

This couldn't be happening to her...to them. It was all so dramatic—so histrionic. And yet...

How could her safe, secure world have turned stark in such a small amount of time?

Her father was a wealthy man. Surely he hadn't needed the money the duke offered. So why had he done it? Had the duke pressured him somehow?

The Duke of Starksboro? Why the Duke of Starksboro? The man was old, decrepit and...

A shiver of pure revulsion swept over her. When she thought of the man—

No. She could not let this happen. There was something evil about this, about the duke...

Certainly, the man was her father's most vocal rival, jealously seeking to acquire the same sort of fame that her father enjoyed—a fame her father rightly deserved, a fame the Duke of Starksboro did not.

It would be different, she admitted, if the duke would take the pains to explore the world, as she and her father did, before commenting upon it. But he did nothing of the sort, seeking instead, time and again, to buy his way into prominence...literally.

And now the duke was trying to do the same thing to her father.

She shivered.

She had to do something about this.

She couldn't ask her father for help anymore—he was part of the problem. And Mr. Toddman? Out of the question.

She puzzled over it. What they needed was a Blackfoot Indian. One mere Blackfoot Indian.

What they really needed, what *she* really needed, was to ask someone she trusted to go into Blackfoot country, to go there and make notes on the habits and customs of the people, then to come back.

But who?

They had already tried to hire men to do it. For ten long months, she and her father had been trying to do this.

Certainly they had found people to hire. But those men had disappeared, along with the money paid to them, never to be heard from again.

Besides, she had several times talked with the trappers and traders in this area. Most could barely even speak proper English. What made her think such men could write it?

Perhaps if she appealed to Mr. Catlin himself?

She groaned. George Catlin had his own people supporting him — and one of those people had gone to a rival publishing house with news of Mr. Catlin's project.

Kind though she knew Mr. Catlin to be, she doubted he would be willing to give her father the necessary information to finish his book. Although —

An idea took hold within her. Her head came up, and suddenly she swung her weight up onto her feet.

She began to pace back and forth, over and over, finally padding over toward her window.

She touched the cold pane of the window there as she stared unseeingly out into the garden, whitewashed now with snow. Her moist breath, shown at first as a fog on the glass, began to crystallize even as she watched it, and suddenly an idea materialized before her. All at once, she knew what she had to do.

It was a whim, a flimsy, stupid idea, most likely impossible…and yet this might be her only chance. *Their* only chance.

She would go.

That a steamship was traveling there soon made it all the more imperative that she leave. It was almost as though she were destined to go there.

True, she might be a novice at survival along the frontier, and certainly she held a healthy respect for her own life, but what sort of life would it be if she and her father failed at this project?

She would rather die than return to England defeated, there to lose reputation and worse, to have to cater to the Duke of Starksboro.

She shuddered. Yes, she knew what she had to do.

Turning, she stepped toward her door to ring for their servant, Robert.

Robert would help her. Of this she was confident. In fact, she was counting on it.

Chapter One

Fort Union
Northwest Territory
Mid-June 1832

*F*ort Union lay on a high bank, nestled between the Missouri and Yellowstone Rivers. To the east, across one river, rose hills and mountains, while a forest of cottonwood trees lined the river's eastern shore, and the sandy banks glowed golden under the sun.

On the western side of the river, the fort stood proud, surrounded by a beautiful, open plain, stretching northward for some distance. Encircling the fort were tepees, some of them white, some yellow and brown, all painted in multicolors of reds, blues and yellows. They looked grand, these primitive dwellings, lying in a field of green grasses that was itself surrounded by hills, valleys and dales. Off in the distance, to the north and east, ran a deep ravine, appearing to drop off where sky met land.

Indians traversed back and forth from their encampments into the nearby fort. Several tribes had come to this place to do business—a very healthy business for the fort, the Indians trading a wealth of furs and hides for the steel blades of the white man, for the pots and pans he offered, the blankets, the beads and trinkets.

Lady Genevieve had stood upon the fort's rampart the previous night, looking out over the Indian encampments, hoping to obtain some insight, from a distance, into the character and life of the tribes present. It had been her first night at Fort Union, and, gazing out over the encampments, with the dry wind upon her face and the grass-and pine-scented air smelling more foreign than anything she had ever imagined, she had felt enchanted.

It was an unusual and wonderful sight—the primitive dwellings, the fires lit both inside and out, the music of the drums and singing from the camps below playing accompaniment to the very sounds of the night: the crickets, the locusts, the nighthawk, the wind itself.

This is what her father lived for, what he had longed to see, and she'd wished last night that he could have been there. But it was just not possible.

She had traveled here on the steamship the *Yellow Stone*, it having taken almost three months to complete the journey. She and Robert had made the trip together, leaving her father back in St. Louis to recover from his illness.

Her father had objected to her coming here, of course, but he'd had no sway over her. She'd made up her mind what had to be done; nothing would stop her.

But now, in the light of day, she was discovering much about this place that she could barely tolerate.

"Mr. McKenzie," Genevieve said to the heavy Scotsman who seemed to be in charge, "is it necessary that all these trappers and traders remain here in my quarters while I try to do my work?"

"Aye, lass, that it is. That it is. If ye'll be needing to talk to the Indians, then ye'll be obliged to have the protection of these men."

"Protection?"

"Against the savages, lass."

"I see. And will the savages protect me from *your* men?" Genevieve fanned her face with one of her gloves. "Truly, Mr. McKenzie, the looks your men give me make me feel uncomfortable. I require only the interpreter that I have hired from you. My manservant, Robert, will give me all the protection from the Indians that I will need, I promise you."

McKenzie had only laughed at her, at what she'd said, but it appeared she had made her point. Within only a few moments, he had taken his leave of her, and he had grabbed most of his men to go with him.

She breathed out a sigh of relief. "Robert," she called, "please ensure that none of those men come in here without your knowledge."

"Yes, milady."

"Good. Now let's see what can be done to these quarters to make them more...livable. If I am to work here for the next few days, I will require a few things. Is there a maid I can hire?"

"I will see to it, milady."

"Good, then," Genevieve said. "Notify me as soon as this room is clean, so that I might interview the Indians."

And to Robert's "Yes, milady," Genevieve strode out the door, her umbrella held just so over her head to shield her complexion and her hair from the glaring rays of the savage summer sun.

****

Why didn't the savage look away? And why didn't he join in the laughter? Laughter the others in his tribe were enjoying...at her expense.

Genevieve shuddered and glanced away from the window, her gaze catching on to and lingering over the simple, hand-carved furniture that had been given to her for her "use."

The room was clean, but that was all it was.

There was nothing in the room to recommend it—no feminine touches here and there, no lacy curtains to cushion the windows, no crystal or china to brighten each nook and cranny, no tablecloths, no rugs...no white women, period. Except for her.

She groaned.

She had thought, when she and her father had reached St. Louis, that she had come to the very edge of civilization, but she had been wrong. At least there, she and her father had been able to rent a house where they had enjoyed all the comforts to which they were both accustomed.

But here, away from any sort of civilization, she felt destitute.

Genevieve sighed, her white-gloved hand coming up to bat at a fly hovering around her face.

"Robert," she spoke out. He bent toward her where she sat at the crude wooden table at one side of the room, and said, "Go ask Mr. McKenzie if there is any truth to the rumor that these Blackfoot Indians are leaving today. Oh, and Robert," she added as her manservant rose to do her bidding, "please ask Mr. McKenzie if those two half-breed trappers I met yesterday are still in residence at the fort, and if they are, please tell him that I wish to see those men at once."

Robert nodded, and, as he set off to carry out her wishes, Lady Genevieve turned back toward the window and looked out at the Indians, her gaze riveted by the dark, ominous regard of that one mysterious Indian man, but only for a moment.

She averted her glance, a certain amount of healthy fear coursing through her.

And why not? These Indians, though dignified enough in their savage appearance and dress, wielded enough untamed presence to instill terror into the hearts of even the most stouthearted of trappers and traders.

A shiver raced over her skin, the sensation bringing with it...what? Fear? Assuredly so. She had been gently raised. And yet...

She lowered her lashes, again studying the Indian in question, her head turned away and her hat, she hoped, hiding her expression. The man stood there among his peers, all ten or eleven of them. All were here at the fort to trade; all had come to this room to see — what the interpreter had said they called her — the mad white woman.

But none of the other Indians affected her like this one Indian man. He, alone, stood out; he, alone, captured her attention. Why?

Perhaps it was because he was too handsome by far, primitive and savage though he might be.

Was that it? She concentrated on him again. Perhaps it was the energy that radiated from him...maybe....

She tried to look away, to fix her gaze on something else, someone else, but she found she couldn't. No, she examined *him* more fully.

He wore a long skin tunic or shirt, generously adorned with blue and white geometric designs. His leggings fell to his moccasins, and everywhere, at every seam and extending down each arm and the length of his tunic and the leggings themselves, hung scalp locks, hair taken from the human head. Though black was the main color of those locks, now and again she saw a blond or brown swatch of hair: white man's hair. It made her shiver just to think of it.

The Indian's own black mane hung loose and long, the front locks of it extending well down over his chest. His eyes were dark, black, piercing, and he seemed to see past her guard and defenses, peering into her every thought. In truth, she felt as though he glimpsed into her very soul.

Genevieve tossed her head and looked up, the brim of her fashionable hat sweeping upward with the movement. She tried to pretend she hadn't been staring, hadn't been inspecting. It was useless, however.

Had she but known, the sunlight, pouring in from the open window right then, caught the green chiffon of her hat, accentuating the color of it. And her hair, the auburn-red locks of it, glowed with a health and vitality equally appealing, and there wasn't a savage or civilized gaze in the place that didn't note the lady's every move, her every expression. She, however, tried not to notice theirs.

She forced herself to look away…from *him*. She didn't want to think about him. She needed to concentrate on her own purpose for being here. She hadn't made such a long, grueling journey to sit here and gawk at one Indian man, compelling though he might be.

She had to find some Indian child or maiden here, now, today, willing to come back with her to St. Louis. She must.

She would not accept defeat.

It should have been a simpler task than it was turning out to be. Hadn't she made it plain that she meant no harm to these people? That she and her father would only detain the person for a few months?

Hadn't she told these people that she would return the person who volunteered back to their tribe at the end of that time, handsomely rewarded?

She had thought, back there in St. Louis, to lure one of the Indians with a trinket or two, a gown, a necklace for the women, money — anything, but some treasure no one could ignore. It should have been simple.

She had reckoned, however, without any knowledge of the dignity of the tribe in residence here at the fort: the *Piegan* or *Pikuni* band of the Blackfeet. It was a grave miscalculation on her part.

If only she had been more prepared to offer them something they might consider valuable. But how could she have known this?

Wasn't this the problem? *No one* knew the Blackfoot Indians. It was this fact and this fact alone that made her father's manuscript so valuable.

Genevieve sighed. It got worse.

She had such a short time in which to work, too. Only today and perhaps tomorrow.

She had tried to convince Mr. Chouteau, the part-owner and captain of the steamship, to stay at Fort Union a little longer. She had argued with him, using every bit of feminine guile that she possessed, but to no avail. He had remained adamant about leaving on his scheduled date.

The river was falling, he'd said. He had to get his steamship, the *Yellow Stone*, back to St. Louis before the Missouri fell so low that the ship would run aground.

It was not what she wanted to hear. It meant she had only a few days to accomplish her ends. It also meant that she might be facing failure.

No, she would not allow herself to fail.

"Milady." Robert materialized at her side, his large frame blocking out the light as he bent down toward her. "Mr. Kenneth McKenzie says the Indians are preparing to leave on a buffalo hunt and will most likely be gone by tomorrow. I have taken the liberty of arranging for the two trappers that you seek to come here to see you." Robert seemed to hesitate. "Milady, might I offer a word of caution?" he asked, though he went on without awaiting her reply. "The two men that you seek are known to be scoundrels. It has also been said of them that they have often been dishonest in their dealings with the trading post here as well as with Indians. It is my opinion that you would do well to—"

"What else am I to do?" Lady Genevieve interrupted, though she spoke quietly. "Robert," she said, not even looking at him, "you know the dire circumstances of this venture. How can I possibly go back to St. Louis with nothing to show for my journey? And worse, how could I ever face my father again? You know that his condition is even more delicate now. If I were to fail…"

"But, milady, surely there must be another way besides dealing with these trappers."

Genevieve raised her chin. Focusing her gaze upon Robert, she said, "Name one."

Robert opened his mouth, but when he didn't speak, Genevieve once again glanced away.

"You see," she said, "even you know it is true, though you won't say it. There is no other way. Mr. Chouteau keeps telling me that the steamship is to leave tomorrow or the next day. I must be on it, and I must have an Indian on board, too. I wish it were different. I truly wish it were. You must know that if I could change things, if I could make them different, I would." She paused. "I cannot."

Robert stared at her for a moment before he finally shook his head, but he offered no other advice.

Genevieve said, "I will see the two gentlemen as soon as they arrive. Please ensure, then, that they are shown to me immediately."

"Yes, milady," Robert said, rising. He stood up straight, and, as Genevieve glanced toward him, she was certain that her trusted bodyguard stared over at *the* Indian, that one Indian man.

But the Indian's menacing black gaze didn't acknowledge Robert at all. Not in the least. No, the Indian stared at *her*. Only at her.

Genevieve rose to her feet, averting her eyes from the Indian, although in her peripheral vision she noted every detail of the man. She shook her head, intent on shifting her attention away.

And then it happened. Despite herself, she turned her head. Despite herself, she slowly, so very leisurely, lifted her gaze toward his.

Her stomach fell at once, and the two of them stared at one another through the panes of glass for innumerable seconds.

She knew she should look away, but she couldn't. She watched the man as though she wished to memorize his every feature, as though she needed the memory for some time distant, to be brought to mind again and again. And as Genevieve kept the man's steady gaze, she felt her breathing quicken.

Suddenly he smiled at her, a simple gesture. It should have had no effect on her whatsoever.

But it did, and Genevieve felt herself go limp.

All at once, as though caught in a storm, her senses exploded. Her heartbeat pounded furiously, making her bring her hand up to her chest.

And, even as she felt herself beginning to swoon, she wondered why she was reacting so. One would think she had never before caught a man's smile, had never before seized the attention of one simple man.

She heard Robert calling her name, and she breathed out a silent prayer of thanks for the interruption. She shut her eyes, which proved to be her only means of defense, and, taking as many deep breaths as she could, tried to steady the beating of her heart.

"Lady Genevieve." She heard Robert call to her again.

"Yes, Robert, I'll be right there." Her voice sounded steady, though she hadn't been certain she would be able to speak at all.

She opened her eyes, but she didn't dare glance at the Indian again. She couldn't risk meeting his gaze even one more time. And so she turned away from him, walking as swiftly as possible from the spot where she had been so recently seated, her silky gown of lace and chiffon whispering over the crude wooden floor as though it alone protested her departure.

She would never see the man again, never think of him again; of this she was certain. But even as this thought materialized, another one struck her with an even greater force: she fooled herself.

She would think of him, perhaps too often, over and over again, and in the not-too-distant future. She wouldn't be able to help herself.

She knew it. Truly the Indian was a magnificent specimen of man. Yes, that was the right word. Impressive, splendid.

Utterly, completely and without question magnificent.

****

"Whatever Indian you convince to return with you will not come to harm in any way because of this, do you understand?"

"By thunder, Genny-girl, 'course we understand."

Ignoring the trapper's crude form of address, Lady Genevieve nodded and took a step backward, if only to escape the stench of the two men who stood before her. She said, "You will receive your money only when I am assured that the deed is done, and not before then. Do you have any questions about this?"

Neither man uttered a sound.

"You are certain you understand what to do?"

"That we do, Genny-girl, that we do."

Genevieve didn't like what she heard, didn't like what she saw and certainly didn't want to acknowledge what she feared about these men, but she had no other choice than to hire them. None.

For good or for bad, she had committed herself to this.

She raised her chin and, in the haughtiest voice she could muster, said, "Robert, my manservant, will be there on the steamship waiting for you." She nodded to her side, indicating her bodyguard. "When he tells me you have met your side of our bargain, then I will pay you—and only then. Do I make myself clear?"

"Yes, ma'am."

"Good then," she said, and turning away, dismissed the two men, who left unhurriedly, though Genevieve spared them no further attention.

She wished she could put aside her doubts of what she was about to do, and she hoped for the umpteenth time that what she did was the right thing.

She closed her eyes, drawing in a deep breath. It had to be right. It just had to be.

Somehow, in some way, she would make it work. She had no other option. If she failed, not only would her father face ostracism and ruin, so too would she.

Genevieve let out her breath. If she could only convince herself that her course of action was justified, she might sleep better.

Oh, well. Squaring back her shoulders, she set about packing up the belongings she had brought with her to Fort Union, preparing to board the *Yellow Stone* for the long journey back to St. Louis. And though the memory of a certain pair of dark, intense eyes haunted her every thought, she chose to ignore it, to ignore them, though at the thought of him, nothing could quite still the rapid fluttering of her heart.

Chapter Two

The Northwest Territory

Aboard the Steamship Yellow Stone

Mid-June 1832

"Milady, they have an Indian."

Lady Genevieve grabbed her dressing gown from the foot of her bunk aboard the steamship. "Take me to her, Robert. Is she all right? She isn't scared, is she? I'll go and sit with her so that she knows we mean her no harm."

"Milady, I...I don't believe that will be necessary. I will attend to the matter—"

"Nonsense!"

"Milady, I—"

He didn't have a chance to say more. Genevieve had hurriedly wrapped her dressing gown around her, had already opened the door of her compartment and was even now scurrying down the steamship's corridor.

"Milady, don't—"

Genevieve didn't seem to hear him. She had already flung open the other cabin door, had already stepped inside, had already—

He heard her ladyship's gasp, and, casting a quick glance to the heavens, set out after his mistress, if only to protect her. And the Lord knew she would need that protection now.

****

It was a mistake. It had to be.

It was the only thought that came to mind, and Genevieve gasped, drawing back closer to the cabin door.

This was no Indian maid. This was...

A human growl sounded from the interior of the room.

Genevieve, her hand clutching her throat, jumped backward.

"As you can see, milady." Robert's voice sounded from behind her. "It is no Indian maiden here. I will return this man first thing in the morning."

Genevieve paused, several minutes ticking by as she struggled to find her voice. At last she said, "There is no time. It is the middle of the night, and we both know the *Yellow Stone* sails in no more than a few hours. We... I—"

"What is it you require me to do, milady?"

"I...I don't know yet, Robert. Leave me for now. I wish to speak to the—"

"Milady, I must protest!"

Genevieve shook her head, the movement causing the locks of her hair to sway and fall downward toward her waist, the mane of it appearing more a cascade of spun copper than human hair.

"Leave me," she said. "I wish to speak to the Indian alone. But Robert," she threw a quick glance over her shoulder, "stay by the door, please."

"Yes, milady. I will remain here. You have only to call if you need me."

"I know that, Robert. And thank you. Now, leave me with the Indian. I guess he will have to do, don't you suppose?"

"I don't suppose anything," Robert said, taking up a stand just outside the cabin door. "And if you want my opinion—"

"I shall ask for it," Lady Genevieve said, though in truth, she spared her servant little more of her attention. How could she do otherwise? What lay before her compelled her to move forward into the room, her whole being engulfed by the magnetism she felt inside.

She left the door open, if only for the security of knowing that Robert stood close at hand.

The Indian was tied standing up, his hands held at his sides, his feet bound. The man couldn't really hurt her. Still...

She stared at the Indian in the darkness of the cabin, her gaze guided only by a small stream of moonlight shining in through the porthole. She tried to scan the man's features, but it was impossible. He looked more phantom than real being at this moment, the silvery light from outside casting an unearthly glow all around him.

Was he the one? The thought kept recurring to her as she stood in place, reluctant to move any closer. *Was he the one from the fort, the one who had captured her attention?*

It couldn't be, and yet... Surely fate wouldn't deal her such a wicked lot as to bring that same man into her presence now. Surely...

She didn't want to think about it. That Indian at the fort, that man she had seen there, had stirred to life something deep within her, something... She sighed.

She couldn't quite place it. She didn't know what had happened back there; she only knew she did not wish to explore such matters now.

Was he the one?

She was almost certain it was so.

She began to pace toward him slowly, one careful step after another, until at last she stood not more than a few feet away from him.

Instantly the savage allure of him—a uniqueness that was part American Indian, part male—set her senses to spinning, and Genevieve, unused to such intense sensation, took a deep breath. At once the musky scent in the air engulfed her, making her feel as though she stood in a silken cocoon, and she recognized the pleasant aroma of buckskin and sage...and something else...some other scent not quite...

A candle lay on a table next to her, and she picked it up, lighting the wick of it quickly.

She held up the small flame toward him. She looked into his face, he into her eyes. All at once, Genevieve sucked in her breath.

He was the one.

Their gazes held. Something elusive passed between them, an emotion that Genevieve could hardly explain.

Excitement? Was that it? Excitement combined with what? Fascination?

Puff...

He blew out the candle.

Genevieve let out her breath and closed her eyes, feeling as though she might swoon at any moment. What was happening to her? Why did she suddenly feel so giddy, so light-headed?

She would have to relight the candle, for her own sanity as well as for the more practical reasons. She would have to talk with this Indian. And that required light, since she would have to communicate with him via the Indian sign language she had been learning.

She began to move her hand toward the table when—

"If white woman had only let me know what she wished, she could have obtained what she required from me without abduction. I might have been willing...then—"

"You speak English?"

"Have I not proven just now that I do?"

"But how is that possible?"

The Indian didn't reply, only looked away, and Genevieve was immediately presented with his profile: strong, foreign, handsome. She drew in her breath as a shiver raced over her skin, and she wondered, was she frightened, or...?

Her breasts swelled against the chiffon material of the gown that she wore beneath her robe, and Genevieve was reminded that she was hardly dressed to receive a man — even if that man be an American Indian.

She gazed up at him, and at once a tremor swept over her, bringing with it with an unusual sensation all over her body, especially there in the junction between her legs.

Genevieve shifted her weight uncomfortably. What was happening to her? Why did she feel this way? What was it about this man that brought on excitement, this feeling of...craving?

Briefly she pondered such questions. None of this made any sense.

This man was hardly what she would call a *man,* someone she could physically crave. He was an American Indian — a savage, a person reported by the best authorities to be more animal than human. Such "people" were beneath her. Weren't they?

Hadn't the whole of her education so far taught her this? It was true, wasn't it?

Or was it?

Her body didn't seem to think so. Her body responded to the Indian as any other twenty-year-old woman might when in the presence of a handsome, half-naked and virile man. Genevieve felt her stomach twist. She whispered, "You are not hurt, are you?"

The Indian swung his gaze back toward her. "Hurt?" he repeated, his stare, or rather his leer, never leaving her. "And where would I feel this hurt? In my heart, which weeps to learn that the white woman has no honor? Or in my spirit, which promises the white woman revenge? Or do you mean my flesh?" He paused. "It is nothing."

"You *are* hurt!" So that was the other scent she had smelled earlier...blood.

The Indian lifted his chin, and though he stared at her as if she were a small quarry he stalked, he said nothing.

"If you are hurt," she said, "I will attend to your wounds at once."

"You will not." The Indian raised his chin another notch. "I will not have your touch upon me. The white woman's medicine is tainted. I will have a medicine man, if I require anyone at all." He paused; then, barely over a whisper, he ordered, "Now."

Lady Genevieve ignored the order. "There is no one else." Her voice, too, seemed to be strangely quiet, though authoritative.

He raised his wrists, the rope around them halting the movement halfway up. He stared down into her curious gaze. "Release me and I will find a medicine man."

"I can't do that," she murmured. "Where are you hurt?"

The Indian looked away from her as though he could spare no further conversation with her, while she took a dangerous step forward.

"I could help," she said, her motion bringing her ever closer. "Please believe me. I intend you no harm. Truly." She gained yet another step in his direction.

He didn't say a word. He didn't move. He might have been as unmovable as stone.

She paced forward, each step as treacherous as if she were crossing a swift stream.

She gazed up at him, studying him while his attention was diverted. So close was she to him, she could smell the combination of sweat and blood mixed with the musk-sweet scent of sage. She could see the sweat upon his brow. She lowered her inspection of him to his chest, noting the moisture that covered him there, the blood all over his side. Blood?

She surveyed his chest as best she could while standing here in the dim, silvery light. Vaguely she noted the strong chest and upper-arm muscles, the slim, tapering stomach, the gash to his side…gash? She stared at it. She reached out a hand toward it. "How did you get this?"

She touched his skin above the wound, her fingertips seeking out the warmth of his skin. All at once he shivered, and she had no more than registered the fact when a heated charge tore up her arm.

She pulled her hand back as though to escape, but it was too late. The damage had been done. She was more than aware of him, of his physical, male appeal, and the air fairly crackled with the knowledge.

He swung his attention back toward her, eyeing her as if she were prey rather than a woman of flesh and blood. And though Genevieve knew she should move away from him as far as she could, she couldn't make her body respond to the command to do so.

Slowly, feeling caught in a trap, she positioned her body closer to his.

"How is it," he asked, his voice oddly soft, "that the white woman with no honor does not know how I came to be hurt? Was not she the one who commanded this? Was not she the one who wished me into this state? She who wanted to see me again, she who had me practically stripped, she who plans to use me for her own ends?"

"No."

"White man lies easily. So do his women. Look at me when you deny this so that I might see the truth or lies of your words."

She sighed, though dutifully she brought her gaze up to meet his. "Truly," she said after a moment, "I did not know something like this might happen. I only meant to take someone from your tribe for a short while. I would treat them well and return them to the tribe as soon as possible. No injury, no stripping, no degradation. None of that was commanded by me. I'm so very sorry."

He stared down at her, and Genevieve wondered how it seemed that his head had come so much closer to her own. She looked away.

"Then set me free, white woman of no honor—"

"Do not call me that." She brought her gaze back to him. "And I cannot let you go. For all that I regret doing this to you, I need you. But I promise you that if you let me attend to you now, there will be no further harm to you." She was more than aware, as she gazed back up at him, that during her speech his face was no more than a few inches from her.

She should back away. She tried to make herself do it; she couldn't. His head gradually descended toward her. And her reaction? She leaned in closer.

Then it happened. His head came fully down to hers. She didn't even have a chance to think before all at once his lips crushed down on hers, and in that moment Genevieve thought her world might surely end.

It was a savage kiss...and yet it wasn't.

Her stomach twisted in response to him, her limbs refused to move, and she couldn't think to question why this Indian would be kissing her.

In truth, there were a thousand things she should have done, a hundred things she should have uttered. She neither said nor did any of them. Instead, she stepped in closer toward the Indian, and if anything, he leaned farther down.

The kiss deepened, going from savage to sensual, and Genevieve became unable to think of anything else but those lips on her own: their feel, their warmth, their...arousal. She responded in an odd way, too, as though she had known this man all her life, as though this man were some titled English gent, as though this man belonged to her and she had every right to—

He broke off the kiss, and Lady Genevieve stood still for a moment, not able to move, not able to produce one coherent thought.

She noted that somehow her hands had found their way onto his chest, that somehow she had drawn in even closer to him, that—

"You see," the Indian broke into her thoughts, "I was right. This white woman is a woman with no honor."

She stared at him for several moments. It was a long time before she could speak, and then she only uttered, "Oh!"

She backed up then, but her gaze never left him, and she wondered what she should do. She felt suddenly as though she should return the insult with cutting words of her own or, failing that, at least shove him away. But she did neither.

Glancing down, Lady Genevieve lifted the hem of her dressing gown. Taking one step back, she pivoted away, fleeing the cabin in a fluidity of motion that would have rivaled the swift descent of a hawk, the swish of her dressing gown the only echo of her distress.

But one thought kept coming back to haunt her as she fled down the steamship's corridor: she had never been more excited in her life.

Not in all of her twenty years so far on this earth had she ever felt more exhilarated, more alive. And she was terribly afraid it all had something to do with the Indian. In truth, she was certain of it.

Chapter Three

It was embarrassing.

*T*hat was all it was. Certainly nothing more. To think she had actually allowed that Indian to kiss her. She held her fingertips up to her lips, intent on wiping away the trace of him. But she didn't. Instead she found herself closing her eyes, remembering the feel of him, the taste of him, the…

She pulled her thoughts up short. What was wrong with her?

She wouldn't think of it. She wouldn't allow it. It was embarrassing. That was all. Period.

She paced back and forth within the perimeter of her small quarters on the steamship, her emotions unsettled.

Male…a man…she and Robert had stolen away a man. Never had she imagined they might take back a male member of the Blackfoot tribe. She'd always reckoned it would be a woman, or mayhap a child. But a man…

What was she to do with him?

She had thought to help her father by starting his studies for him on the journey home, by beginning a communication process with the person, by learning the Blackfoot language, by teaching the other person her own. But now?

It would be impossible. How could she go back into that man's presence again? After tonight? Besides, he already knew English, which raised another question. How did he know it?

"Yes?" She answered the knock at her door.

"Milady?" It was Robert.

"You may enter, Robert."

Her servant opened the door, stepping in only far enough to close the door behind him. He didn't say a word, awaiting her question to him first. But Genevieve found it difficult to do more than stare at the man, and at length, Robert, perhaps sensing her mood, said, "What is it you wish me to do with the Indian? There is still time for me to take him back to his people."

"And replace him with another?"

Silence. Robert didn't utter a word, and it was his reservation more than anything else that bothered her.

"You see," she said after a while, "there isn't time to get someone else. We will have to keep him."

"Milady, surely there is another way. I suspect the man will be trouble."

"Yes," she said, "I believe you are right. The man will be trouble. But what other choice do we have? The ship is due to sail in a few hours, and the Blackfoot people are, themselves, leaving as soon as day breaks."

"I understand, milady, but how can we keep him? We would not even dare to take him on deck at any time during the journey for fear he might jump overboard and swim ashore, tied or not." He paused. "Did you know I found him practically untied after you left?"

"Did you?"

The servant sighed. "I believe he may require more effort than either you or I can handle."

She nodded. "I agree, but what can we do? There must be some way to keep him here."

"Milady, it is a three-month journey back to St. Louis, and, as you might remember, there can be delays due to storms, sandbars, even floods. It would be easy for the man to escape, and I fear we may not have him long anyway." Robert paused. "The man does not wish to be here. He will find a way to escape."

Genevieve turned away, the dim light from the candles silhouetting her profile as she did so. She paced toward the porthole at the other end of the room, then back, her nervousness almost a tangible thing. She chanced a glance up toward Robert before saying, "Perhaps we could make him want to stay?"

"Milady," Robert frowned his disapproval, "I hardly think—"

"We could teach him our ways, introduce him into English society, be kind to him. We could make him want to stay, couldn't we?"

"Milady, I don't believe the man will want to stay anywhere tied—"

"Then we will untie him, but watch him carefully."

"Milady, the man is Indian. He is a savage, a wild man. And as such, there are items of interest within our room that he could use as a weapon and still escape. It would be much too dangerous."

"But necessary. See if you can bribe the two trappers who brought him to us, or anyone else with experience, into making the trip down the Missouri with us. They could help us guard the man."

"Milady, might I remind you that those trappers are renowned for being untrustworthy."

"Then don't use them. Find someone else. Surely there are people for hire here who will do nothing more than watch a man in a locked room and keep him from escaping."

"Milady, I must protest—"

"Robert, please. I am desperate." She paused dramatically before looking over toward her servant, and at last she said, "You know that."

Robert sighed. He looked away, clearly unwilling to give in too easily, though at last he said, "Yes, milady," letting out his breath as he said it. "I will see what I can find at this early hour of the morning, though please do not expect much. I fear most of the trappers will be too busy sleeping off the effects of last night's whiskey to clearly understand what it is that I ask."

Genevieve looked toward her servant, an expression of gratitude in her gaze. She smiled at the man. "Thank you, Robert," she said. "I realize you do not wish to do this, and I am once again in your debt. I could not ask for a better friend than you."

Robert shrugged, letting the compliment flow over him as though he were stone and it a mere puff of wind—although Lady Genevieve could have sworn, as she watched him back away, that there might have been, if only for an instant, a glimpse of happiness there within the glint of her servant's eye.

****

The Indian's room was too small, much too small.

And it didn't help to remember her resolve of only a short while ago: that she couldn't face this man any time soon for fear of what he might do, what she might do....

She stopped her train of thought. She *had* to be here now, she *had* to watch over the man while Robert went ashore to recruit more help. It was only for a little while longer, and then she could escape. But by Jove, these close quarters heightened the effect this man had on her.

Genevieve tried to glance away from the Indian, to look anywhere but at this very real man who stood not more than a few feet away from her. She shifted uncomfortably, aware that she had dressed too quickly in her haste to get to this room while her manservant went ashore. She had failed to don her shift beneath her dress, and the knowledge made her feel vulnerable, almost naked.

Naked. She glanced at the nearly nude man who stood before her. He wore only a breechcloth, moccasins, and a necklace. She studied the strings of bone beads that hung down over the man's chest in a series of loops, creating a breastplate of sorts. Fascinating.

She continued to look, unaware of exactly when her attention turned from the necklace to the man's chest, all bronzed skin and muscle. Without full awareness of what she did, she allowed her gaze to inspect the man everywhere, her glance traveling down to his stomach, flat with defined, hard muscles. Lower still she stared, downward toward his breechcloth, toward his...

She pulled her glance up short, admonishing herself, forcing herself to gaze away from the man.

It was too late. Already her stomach, her nerve endings, her heartbeat fluttered out of control, and Genevieve's knees buckled under her, forcing her to take a seat in the only chair available in the room—a chair, of course, closer to *him.*

She gulped and looked anywhere in the room but at *him,* certain she could make herself realize that it wasn't the Indian who made her feel all weak and giddy inside. It was only natural that she would have such a reaction toward him, she told herself. After all, he *was* handsome, and she was a young, healthy woman. What woman wouldn't swoon at seeing so much of a man's body exposed?

You see? she scolded herself mentally. *It's not the Indian at all.*

He moved then, and Lady Genevieve, despite herself, couldn't control her gasp or the shiver of reaction that raced over her skin.

She looked away. "I won't harm you," she spoke at last, breaking the silence of the room. "I promise," she said, not daring to bring her gaze back to survey the man.

The Indian didn't say a word in response, and she chanced a quick glance at him. She gasped. Such hatred emanated from him that it made her pause. With a shake of her head, she said, "I promise you that I will return you to your people at the end of a few months' time—at the most, a year—and I will do all that I can to see that no abuse befalls you."

The Indian didn't utter a thing, looking away from her as though he had lost all interest in her, in his situation.

"I promise."

He turned his head back toward her sharply. But still he didn't speak, just glared at her.

"Truly, I do."

He narrowed his eyes at her, his expression saying more clearly than words could have what he thought of her and any promises she might make.

"I know you understand me, and I know you are angry with me, but isn't there anything I can do to make your stay with us more comfortable? I cannot let you go. Believe me, if I could, I would."

No response whatsoever, just a glare.

She shook her head, raising her chin. "What more do you want from me? Haven't I just promised to care for you, to ensure your comfort and your safety? I cannot change the reasons why I must take you back with me. If I could, I would. Can't you just make the best of it?"

Again nothing, no response.

"Please," she said after a moment. "Won't you speak to me? I know you can. I honestly mean you no harm, and I do promise to protect you in any way that I can until this incident is behind us." She paused. "Please?"

She heard a quick intake of breath then, and raising her gaze to his, she saw him frown at her. It seemed to take forever, though at last, still glaring at her, he said, "Do I look like a woman, that I need your protection? I would rather be harmed than remain here…" he raised his wrists, "tied."

She didn't say anything back to him right away. What could she say? That he certainly didn't look like a woman? That she'd had no trouble realizing his gender? That she meant to untie him later?

Yes, she did mean to give him more freedom later. But not now. There was no one else here to prevent this man's escape. And she was afraid that if she told him this now, somehow she would find him gone within so short a span of time that she would be left wondering exactly what had happened.

And so she did nothing, merely looked over toward him, until at length she said, "Thank you for speaking…I think."

He grunted, his only response.

A moment passed, then another, Genevieve feeling more awkward than she could ever remember feeling. At length, though, she asked, "How is it that you know English?"

The Indian squinted his eyes, his lips pursed as he scowled at her. He didn't say a word.

She continued, "Did you learn it from the traders? I wasn't aware they had been in your country for long. At least not long enough for you to learn the language so well."

Again his look pierced hers, the venom in that glance a very real, palpable thing.

But she chose to ignore it, feeling a safety in the knowledge that he was tied and could do little about it. Besides, she never looked at him directly, happy to stare somewhere between his collarbone and his chin. So she carried on. "Or have missionaries been in your country? Or perhaps the French, although they would speak French, wouldn't they? Maybe the English? Oh, well, that would be quite impossible, wouldn't it? Maybe you learned it from—"

"The Black Robe."

"I beg your pardon?"

"Go ahead."

"What?"

"Beg, *okamanii*," he said, no expression whatsoever on his face. "I would like to see you beg."

"Humph!" She threw a lock of auburn-red hair over her shoulder, the action reminding her that she wore neither hat nor headgear of any kind as would have befitted her station. "You misunderstand," she said, daring to look toward him, though her gaze didn't quite reach his eyes. "I did not mean that I will actually beg you. 'Tis merely an expression that says 'I did not understand what you said; could you please explain it more fully?' You see, I did not comprehend what you said about the black robe, and so when I said 'I beg your pardon,' what I was—"

"*Ha*'! I know what the white woman means. I understood it then." His dark gaze cut into her own. "Still, I would like to see my own enemy, the white woman, beg." A corner of his lips turned upward. "It would bring me pleasure to see this."

Genevieve sat in silence for a moment, her glance finally encompassing the whole of the man who stood before her. "I am not your enemy." It was all she could think to say.

His smile at her, or rather his smirk, widened. "*Saa*, no," he said, "your race of people does not call it this, as I recall. Yet, with my people, anyone who forces another into an act against his own will is an enemy to that person. You may call it 'lovemaking,' what you intend to do to me, but I will never see it as that. I am not willingly here. You might make my body respond to you, as you did earlier when I kissed you, but *I* will never respond to you — not willingly — ever."

Genevieve choked, her face filling with a deep red color that she had no way of controlling. She opened her mouth and closed it several times, able to do no more than sputter, "You...think...that...I..." She couldn't finish it. Her head suddenly reeled as though she had spun around the room several times, and she came to her feet, where she swayed before she was able to back away from him toward the door.

Whatever was wrong with the man? How could he suggest such a thing?

She brought a hand to her chest, trying to still the throbbing of her heart, endeavoring to prevent herself from collapsing.

Where was Robert with the other men who might help watch over the savage? She wouldn't stay here any longer; she couldn't, she mustn't....

She had to.

Her back against the door, she darted a look over toward the Indian, her gaze inspecting him as she had never done to anyone else. What, she wondered, possessed the man to say such a thing to her? He was a savage indeed.

She instantly felt contrite that she had once thought him good-looking and worthy of attention. Well, no more. She would spare him not more than another moment's thought — as soon as she left here.

Why then, she wondered, couldn't her body agree with her? Why was her body reacting to his words as though the man had suddenly declared his undying love for her? Why, for goodness sake, did she feel warm all over?

She wanted to leave. Yes, that was what she wanted to do…what she had to do. Her hand fell to the doorknob. She turned it. She wanted to; she had to… She dared not. The man might escape.

At last, realizing she had no choice but to remain where she was for the moment, she took strength from somewhere within, and, looking straight at the Indian, said, "You again misunderstand." Her voice was quiet, soft, so barely audible that even she could hardly hear it.

He smiled a cold, unmerciful grin. "I think not," he said slowly. "Your intentions were made more than clear to me."

She swallowed. "No, it's not true. I only bring you to my father, who is completing a work on the cultures and languages of the American Indians. We lack a study of your tribe. That is all we need. That is all I am doing. Nothing more. When the study is done, we will return you to your people. I promise you."

The Indian shrugged and gazed away.

"Did you hear me?" she asked, his lack of response causing her to grow angry. She sighed. "I promise you, I am doing no more than taking you to my father…that is all."

Again, the Indian shrugged.

She grimaced. "Sir, Mr…. What is your name?"

"*Ha!* Do you now request that I give you a part of me?"

"No, I…" Her mouth fell open. "I ask only your name, that I might address you properly."

"*Hánnia,* how is it," he asked, "that you want to learn about my people's culture, and yet you do not know what you ask of me?"

"I…have I somehow insulted you? If I have done something wrong, could you tell me?"

He jerked his head to the left, and, looking away from her, sighed. "How is it you do not know these things?" He seemed to address the wall as he spoke. "How can it be that you do not know that if I tell you my name, I

61

give you a part of all that I am, a part of me that your people call the soul, *ksissta'pssi*? Is that what you want, white woman of no honor? Do you wish to own my soul?"

"No, I...I... You are right. I did not know. It is not that way in my culture. In my society, a name designates your family; that is all the meaning we attach to it. Beyond that, a name has little significance to us, except perhaps for its beauty."

The man nodded. "I have learned this of the white man. *Ha'*, is it not strange that I should know more of your culture than you do of mine? Yet *I* do not wish to 'know' yours."

"I..." She paused, taking time to close her mouth. "Yes, that is quite strange, and I would like to learn sometime how it is that you have come to know what you do about my culture. Will you tell it to me?"

Again he presented her with silence, glancing away from her and ignoring her as though he were alone in the room.

She sighed. "Very well. But I feel I must call you by some name. Would you perhaps be offended if I were to assign you a name?"

No response.

"I could give you a name like—"

"Hawk," he said, shifting to bring his glance back toward her. "You may call me Hawk. The Great Gray Hawk that squeezes the life from his prey, *ikkitsinaattsi ayinnima*." He smiled, or at least it appeared to her that he did. "And do not doubt, white woman with no honor, I always, always, corner my prey, playing with them as a hawk might, unto their death." He paused. "*Aisskahs.* Always."

She swallowed, her eyes opening a fraction of an inch wider. "Very well, Mr. Great Gray Hawk," was all she managed to say. She tried to grin, but the action was lost to her. At last, after biting on her lower lip, she said, "I do not know from where or from whom you received your information of what I intend to do to you, but I promise you that I have no intentions toward you other than delivering you to my father, where I am hoping that you will help him with his studies. Then, when those studies are complete, you will be free, and I will more than compensate you for your time. You will be handsomely paid. You see? You are no prisoner…"

He held up his hands, which were, at that moment, bound.

"That is necessary only in order to keep you here."

"I am a prisoner, then."

She sighed. "You are being difficult."

He actually smiled at her, really smiled, though she noted that the expression had little to do with humor. A long moment passed, during which he held her gaze, before at last he said simply, "*Iniiyi'taki*. Thank you."

She felt her mouth drop open, and her throat worked as if she intended to say more, but at that moment Robert shoved at the door, the action throwing her slightly forward. And without so much as a hello or good-bye to the Indian or to Robert, Lady Genevieve picked up the long skirts of her gown, and turning, fled from the room.

Chapter Four

"*Why*, Mr. Chouteau, what a great pleasure it is to see you."

"Ah, *Mademoiselle* Genevieve. You are sight for these poor eyes this day. And please, please, I am to take a walk. You are to walk with me?"

"I'd be happy to," Genevieve said to Pierre Chouteau, who, in addition to being part-proprietor of the boat, was acting as their zealous navigator. Turning toward him, she contemplated the man for a brief moment. Of medium height, with black hair and black eyes, he stood only a little taller than she.

But he was a handsome, charming Frenchman, probably about forty years of age, who, dressed in his suit and waistcoat, somehow looked out of place in this wilderness. He was married, and his wife and two daughters had accompanied them on the voyage upriver as far as St. Charles.

Grateful to Mr. Chouteau, Genevieve had long ago dubbed him a genius. In truth, she couldn't imagine how the boat could have survived this, its maiden voyage into Blackfoot country, without the perseverance and doggedness of this man.

Never before had men navigated the swirling, muddy Missouri by steam. And no one at the start of this journey had thought the venture would be successful. The terrible nature of the river had discouraged other, less ambitious men.

But Pierre Chouteau was not a man who recognized defeat. In truth, it was due mainly to Mr. Chouteau and his belief in her cause that she was here right now.

It was odd how quickly she had become accustomed to the daily routine of the steamer. It was still with some awe and a little bit of fear that she had watched these riverboat men pitted against the terrible forces of nature. Rains and floods had washed the debris of falling banks into the river, where the swift current and floating driftwood had made boating a lethal occupation. Nevertheless, these men struggled to map out routes to the outermost regions of this vast country where none had existed before.

And despite her resolve, her fear, her prejudice, she discovered within herself a feeling of affinity for this wild, unconventional journey. There was a freedom to be had here in the openness of the West—a sense of space, of belonging, a feeling that one could reach out and capture...eternity.

She took a deep breath and looked back at the scenic land bordering the river. Here, in the northernmost parts of the Missouri, the shores lay without timber; here the prairie stretched out from the river into forever, the land boasting its beautiful carpet of green and brown grasses and extending outward as far as the eye could see—straight to the horizon.

Here she could feast her eyes upon the dales and bluffs, the ravines and caverns. Here she could watch the elk and buffalo, the wolves and antelope, the mountain goats and bears off in the distance, all eking out an existence on this wild, picturesque stretch of land.

At the start of their journey, she had been apprehensive, not entirely certain she would make it back to St. Louis. Now, on the return voyage, she wasn't certain that once she returned to civilization, she might not crave this sort of adventure again...and again.

She shook back her mane of hair and looked away from the scene before her, sighing, the action bringing her back to the present. Courteously, she smiled at Mr. Chouteau and placed one hand upon his arm. Cocking her umbrella over her head, Lady Genevieve shielded herself from the rays of the noonday sun and began to stroll with the gentleman.

There was so much she wanted to ask this man beside her, but she politely held back, looking away from Mr. Chouteau before she voiced the one question uppermost in her mind. Finally, clearing her throat, she asked,

"How long do you think it will be before we will return to any sort of civilization, Mr. Chouteau?"

The older man hesitated, then shrugged. "I am hard to say. In the first place, I am seeing the river ahead of us, and I am seeing so many sticks that I must steer boat around. *Et,* I am saying, could be a month before we come to St. Louie, maybe two."

Genevieve nodded her understanding, following the man's broken English as well as if he were speaking to her from some formal English tea room.

And it was no pretense on her part. She had learned some of the "river talk" on the journey up the river and knew that what was referred to by Mr. Chouteau as "sticks" were actually floating trees in the river. These "sticks" sometimes covered the entire surface of the river, making it almost impossible to navigate.

"And do you believe we will have any trouble on this return journey? I mean, because we are now floating with the currents rather than against them, could we possibly return home in even less time?"

"*Oui, mademoiselle. Et,* I am to say is possible that we will get there sooner. But troubles? This is the Missouri, and it is difficult to understand. In the first place, I am to navigate against the forces of nature. There is always the sticks that are trapping us. But do not fear, *mademoiselle.* I am to getting you back to St. Louie soon."

She smiled. "Thank you, I am happy to hear your reassurance." She looked away from him. "But please tell me, Mr. Chouteau, I am curious—do you know what has happened to Mr. Catlin? I know he arrived with us when we reached Fort Union, and I remember him painting several portraits of the Indians there. But I notice that he is not on the steamer going home. Do you know why?"

"*Oui, mademoiselle,*" the handsome Frenchman said. "He is, how you say, floating downstream with Ba'tiste, the trapper who has come in from the West. Mr. Catlin, he is visiting the other tribes, and he is painting pictures of the Indians."

"I see." Her grip on the man's arm tightened. "Do you know, perchance, how long Mr. Catlin might be gone?"

"*Oui, mademoiselle.* That is, if he is survive, he will be for many months gone, one year perhaps."

Genevieve nodded and looked away. "I am most grateful to Mr. Catlin for introducing me to you. If not for you and your steamboat, I would not be able to accomplish what I must. I wish him well, though I would have liked to have told him so personally. I trust Mr. Catlin will arrive safely home. I believe that he will."

Pierre Chouteau nodded. Then, almost hesitantly, he asked, "*Mademoiselle?*"

"Yes?"

"The Indian."

"What Indian?"

"The Indian, below. The one in your suite. He is…*mademoiselle*, how do I say? I have for many months traveled on the Missouri. I have seen very, very much. I am for living many months with the wild Indian, so I am to think I know them. And I am to tell you that this one, this one on the boat, he is trouble, you understand. I am hearing, as you say, him growl all the night, and I say to myself I am must to tell the *mademoiselle*. She, I am saying to myself, does not know the danger."

"Danger? But Mr. Chouteau, he is no danger to anyone. He is—"

"*Non, mademoiselle,* the Indian, he is wild. He is not liking to be inside a cabin. He is vengeful. He is best to be put to the shore and let loose. We get you another Indian on the way down the Missouri."

Genevieve glanced upward and away before at last saying, "I cannot do that. I need a Blackfoot Indian for my father's studies. It is the only reason I have made this journey. If I don't return home with this Indian, I will have failed." She held up her hand when the older man would have spoken. "Oh, I know," she said, "that it would have been better had we taken away a woman or a child, but what can I do? It's not as though this man were my own choice. As you may recall, I hired some trappers to bring me a Blackfoot Indian. I cannot very well... Mr. Chouteau, the man is all that I have."

Her companion shook his head. "*Mademoiselle, I—*"

A wild scream split the air. A manly scream.

Genevieve and Pierre Chouteau both turned to stare at one another, both voicing the same words at the same time: "The Indian."

Genevieve was the first to recover, picking up the front of her skirts and running to the nearest set of stairs. With nary a thought, she let the umbrella slip out of her hands as she hurried as quickly as possible.

She hadn't seen the Indian in a full week, ever since that first day when she had guarded him while her manservant went ashore. She didn't want to see the Indian now, or even in the future, really. But something in that scream, something frightful, gripped her.

What if the man were in trouble? What if some warring tribe member had found her Indian tied, unarmed, unable to defend himself? Weren't there enemy tribes riding upon this boat, roaming freely even now? Wasn't the boat carrying Indian as well as white passengers? What if her Indian had been attacked? What if her Indian...had died?

The thought was too much to bear. And Genevieve didn't stop to scrutinize the facts: that she feared the man's death, that her fright might come not because of what she needed from this Indian, for herself, for her father, but rather from an innate horror of...her own feelings?

Genevieve shook her head, grimacing as she hurried down the corridor. What had gotten into her of late? That she should be in a dither over the fate of some half-naked Indian just didn't sit well with her. The man clearly didn't deserve the least amount of thought or attention.

Still, she hoped that if the man were in danger, she wouldn't be too late to save him, and she hoped—no, she prayed—she would find the man alive.

So busy was she with her thoughts, she didn't notice that the pink chiffon of her umbrella shimmered in the water where it had landed, sparkling now, again, then once more before the muddy water of the Missouri claimed it, carrying the foreign-looking object away forever.

And perhaps it was for the best.

****

She should have knocked.

It was the first thought that struck her. Well, maybe not the first.

Red-faced, Genevieve could only stare at the scene laid out before her. She knew her mouth gaped open, but there was nothing she could do about it. Suddenly feeling as though her body were made of marble instead of flesh and bone, she stood still, not able to blink, not able to move.

And the men stared back at her.

She tried to utter something, but her mouth wouldn't work. And she couldn't think of a single word or phrase she could have said in this sort of situation, her knowledge of social graces failing her yet again.

"It is the white woman." It was the Indian who spoke, the *naked* Indian *man* who spoke. He grinned at her. "This does not surprise me."

Now, Genevieve had always known that men's bodies differed from women's. She'd even had a notion of what a naked man's body looked like. But never had her imaginings prepared her for this…this very real flesh-and-blood man who stood before her.

And it did not escape her notice that even as the Indian spoke, the part of his body most obvious to her seemed to grow, to expand, to —

She gasped. She blinked.

"Lady Genevieve, I am only trying to dress the young man. There is no need for alarm." It was Robert who spoke, though Genevieve barely noticed the other man. "Our Indian friend here is quite resistant to wearing this pair of breeches." It was only then that Robert seemed to notice, really notice, the state of dress — or rather, undress — of the man. The older man glanced from one young person to the other. "Might I suggest, milady, that you leave me alone with the Indian?"

Genevieve licked her lips, wondering if she'd ever find her voice. At last, she averted her gaze. It was the only thing she could do. She couldn't yet speak.

"*Naapiaakii*, the white woman, does not wish to leave." The Indian leered at her, though he spoke to the man. "*Naapiaakii* has many plans for me; is this not true, my own enemy?"

"No," she spoke at last. "I...I burst in here only because I heard your scream." She turned her head back toward the Indian—a mistake. Somehow that part of his body had grown even larger. She shut her eyes and groaned. "I was worried that you... I thought maybe some enemy tribe had... I had to—"

"*Naapiaakii*, white woman, is my enemy, my own enemy." His gaze at her was steady, direct. "Know that I always seek revenge, my own enemy. *Always.*"

"Don't call me that. I am not your enemy."

The Indian's expression was disbelieving, insolent. "So the white woman has told me before." The Indian lifted his arms, his wrists still clearly tied. "The Great Gray Hawk does not believe white woman. Gray Hawk is unwilling captive of white woman. Gray Hawk will obtain great pleasure from taking revenge on white woman." He leered at her, his lips turning upward in a smirk. "And revenge will come soon."

"Don't be ridiculous!" A chill ran down her spine as she backed toward the door. "There is no need to seek revenge upon me. As soon as my father is finished, I *will* return you to your people. I give you my word of honor on it."

The Indian sneered. "White woman of no honor expects me to believe her when lies roll easily off her tongue—"

"Nonsense! When have I ever...?" She didn't finish the sentence. Gray Hawk turned his back to her, presenting her with a clear view of his backside, of his tight buttocks. And Genevieve couldn't help but look. "I..." She retreated toward the door. "I am sorry that I disturbed you. It's only that I—"

He looked back at her just then over his shoulder, a smiling jeer accompanying that glance. That he had caught her scrutinizing him did not bear critical thought on her part.

With a gasp she spun away from him, presenting him with her own posterior view, though hers was thankfully clothed. She reached for the door, and, jerking it open, fled out into the relative safety of the corridor.

Someday, she thought to herself, *I will have to stop ending our conversations by running away.*

Still, even as she thought this she rushed back to her own quarters, not pausing to look at anyone, nor to talk with anyone along the way. And she quite convinced herself it was better this way.

****

The young man who called himself Gray Hawk watched the white woman from over his shoulder. And despite himself, he continued to observe her until she disappeared through the door of the big medicine canoe. He jerked his head to the left, his only expression of emotion.

Ha'! He was disgusted with himself—with her. He hated her, this female enemy, which made the reactions of his body all the more unwelcome. Truth be, though he had taunted her with the image of his nudity, he was amazed that he reacted to her the way he did.

He thought back to that first night of his capture. From the moment she had stepped into his presence that night, he'd not been able to believe what he saw.

Shock. Yes, that was what he'd felt.

And with reason. He'd been prepared to hate the person responsible for his capture, for the manner and cruelty with which he had been taken. He'd been alone, of course. Alone, and close to the medicine canoe. Otherwise, he would have been able to overwhelm his enemy, no matter that they had struck him from behind. But never had he dreamed at the time that his enemy would be the white woman...at first.

Truthfully, he'd been attracted to her at the fort, admiring her persistence, her beauty, her courage in the face of his peers, who had laughed at her. Certainly, like the other members of his tribe, he knew what she asked, knew that she was seeking to take one from among them back to a place she called St. Louis. And though, like the others, he'd known that what she asked was outrageous, a thing no one from the Blackfoot tribe would do, her quiet persistence had gained his admiration.

If his tribe had not been at peace with the white traders at this fort, Gray Hawk might very well have stolen her, perhaps to make her one of his wives…perhaps not.

But his tribe *was* at peace with these particular white people, and Gray Hawk could think of no way to take her away and still keep the peace.

Yes, he had admired her, though after that first momentary shock of seeing her, Gray Hawk had realized his error in doing so. This person, this woman whom he had come to admire, did not deserve such respect.

Where he had endowed her with a quiet strength, now he had learned she was weak, giving in to demands of the flesh. Where she had, at first, looked sweet, virginal, he'd now come to understand that she was experienced—a temptress.

He'd gazed at her then, as she'd stood there before him, and he'd understood that this was the woman the kidnappers had spoken of; this was the woman those men had been joking about, saying it was *she* who had demanded that the Indian be beaten and then stripped, telling him in lurid language what *she* would do to him after the capture, not only in physical body, but in soul.

Yes, it was she who had taken away his freedom, she who enslaved him now, she who intended for him the utmost in degradation.

Hatred had filled his mind even as he had stood there watching her.

Malicious thoughts, however, breed malicious words, and he had used many on her, knowing her to be an enemy and deserving of such treatment.

And then she had come close to him, and good sense had fled him.

His body had reacted to her, and it hadn't mattered what he'd thought. He'd wanted her—not out of love, he'd realized, but with lust, and that lust had controlled him, if only for a short while.

The kiss had occurred spontaneously enough, although he congratulated himself on being clever enough to turn the embrace into a weapon, taunting her with the force of his own will.

What he hadn't counted on was his body's reaction to her, the stiffening in his groin needing no interpretation but the obvious.

He frowned. None of this mattered now. What he'd felt then, what he felt now, was unimportant. He would escape; it was only a matter of establishing when.

And he would get even. No one—particularly a woman—would treat him in such a manner without cost. And in a land where it remained up to the individual to hand out deserved justice, it had become more than the thirst for revenge that drove him: it was his duty.

In truth, there had been several times these past few days when he could have escaped—the man they called Robert did not guard him well—but Gray Hawk was determined that he would have his revenge upon this white woman.

If he left, he would take her with him, and then let her see who was captive and who was not.

And so Gray Hawk waited for a more enticing opportunity. He, a member of the prestigious Kit Fox Society, the most honorable of warrior societies within his tribe, would dignify that name by seeking the revenge that was rightfully his. He would delay his flight for a while; he would observe his environment, observe the white woman, her habits, her movements, until he could escape and bring her with him. Yes, he would emerge victorious.

"You shouldn't speak to milady that way."

Raising one eyebrow, Gray Hawk glanced over toward the manservant. He understood this man to be no more than a slave to this white woman. And in such a position, the man deserved no attention from Gray Hawk.

"She is a good person, and she has reason for doing what she does."

Again he raised that eyebrow. It was his only response.

Robert snorted. "I know that you understand me, so if you have something to say, speak it; don't just look at me."

Gray Hawk shrugged and turned his face away from the man.

"It is true that she is doing what she is doing for her father."

Gray Hawk didn't move, didn't react or indicate in any way that he had heard the man.

"She has risked much to come here. And I can promise you that you are in no danger from her. There is no reason for you to be afraid."

Gray Hawk turned his face back toward the older man. Afraid? Who was this slave to insult him? No man, and particularly no slave, mocked him without cost. Gray Hawk tilted back his head. Again he studied the man, then said, "You are brave for a slave. But then I would be, too, if I were in your place and the man I insulted was tied and unable to wreak the justice that such words deserve. Afraid?" asked Gray Hawk. "Take away these ties, and I will show you how afraid I am."

"Yes, I suppose you would at that," said Robert, a half smile hovering around his lips. "However, I am not at liberty to take away the ties, and," Robert pinched in a bit of material in the breeches he held up toward the Indian, "I am no slave."

Gray Hawk turned his head away. "Words and labels mean nothing to me. You do the white woman's bidding. You are a slave, no matter the title you put to it."

The other man smiled. "Yes, I can see how it would appear that way to you. Feeling a little indignant that a mere woman has not only captured you, but continues to hold you?"

Gray Hawk shrugged; it was his only answer, though at length he asked, "What is this 'indignant'?"

Robert held the breeches up to his charge. "A blow to your pride."

Gray Hawk glanced casually toward the older man, smiling smugly. "Yes, slave," he said, "you could say Gray Hawk is indignant. But know, slave, that there is no enemy alive who would treat me in such a way and would not fear the sting of my revenge. Do not doubt that I will have it."

"She doesn't deserve it."

Gray Hawk looked down his nose at the man. "That is for me to decide, slave. To take to heart the words of an enemy is certain death to the one who would listen. Do I look such a fool?"

"She is not your enemy."

"*Ha'*! There is no enemy that I have who would treat me worse."

"What?" Robert shook his head at the young warrior. "How old are you that you would even know what worse treatment is?"

When Gray Hawk didn't reply, Robert asked, "Twenty-four, maybe twenty-five years?"

"I am twenty-five winters old."

"Too young to know, my good lad. Too young." When Gray Hawk's eyes narrowed, Robert continued, "Look around you. I ask you, look around. What has she done to you that is so bad? Yes, you are tied; yes, you have lost your freedom, but only temporarily. As soon as she has accomplished her purpose, you will be freed, your passage on the steamboat paid so that you can return to your people. What is so bad in that?

"Can you tell me that you are denied food, sleep, shelter?" Robert went on. "No, you cannot. You are given all that you desire. Why, lad, look at what we are doing. Am I not even now fitting you with new clothes? Am I not treating you well? I can promise you that as soon as her father is finished with the studies he is doing, you will be restored once more to the same sort of freedom that you have enjoyed in the past, and you will have much more to show for your time than any one person in your tribe."

"I do not understand what this 'studies' is. But..." Gray Hawk held up his hand when the other man would have spoken, "...you say I have food, sleep and shelter here? Did I not already have that when I was free and with my people? You say that I will have my freedom back when she is finished. Did I not already have my freedom before she took it from me? You say that I will have much to show for the time I spend with her. Did I not have all that I desire before I came into contact with her? When I come to the fort, I see the white people keeping birds in a thing called a cage. The bird has all that he wants, and still the bird longs for freedom, will fly away as soon as

75

the cage is opened. Do not mistake what you do for me. A cage is still a cage, no matter its comforts.

"I put a question to you now," Gray Hawk continued. "You say that she treats *me* well? Now I ask you how you know this. Will you promise me here and now that she will feed and clothe my family while I am gone? Can you say that she will attend to their needs as well as to mine in my absence? Will she stay behind now and hunt many buffalo so that my family's bellies will stay full through the winter? So that my women will have many skins to make more clothes, more shelters? Will she do these things while I am gone, so that my family will survive the harsh winters of the North? So that there is no death in my family?"

The older man paused in his work and did nothing more than stare at the young warrior. He said nothing.

At length, however, he swallowed and said, "Yes." He cleared his throat. "Well now, I don't suppose she considered that. But come, my good man. There's no use thinking about it. What will be is what will be. Meanwhile we have to get you fitted into these breeches. It would be the utmost of bad fortune if milady were to catch you again with your pants down." The older man tried to effect a chuckle, though the action was lost on the younger man.

Said Gray Hawk, his gaze penetrating the other man, "You speak with the foresight of a child. And I am not uncertain that you also speak with crooked tongue."

"I beg your pardon."

Gray Hawk scowled. "What is this begging? I do not see you begging."

Robert grimaced. "I do not mean that I am begging."

"Then why do you say it?"

Robert exhaled noisily. "Merely an expression, lad. Merely an expression. What I am really saying is that I am not sure I heard you correctly. Could you please repeat it?"

"I would rather you beg." Gray Hawk stuck out his chin and looked down at the other man.

"Yes," the white man said, "I suppose that you would."

The atmosphere in the cabin turned to silence. And though no more words were spoken, Gray Hawk allowed the man to fit him out in breeches.

No one, though, could stop the Indian when, the breeches fully in place and the young man gazing at himself in the mirror, he broke into a fit of laughter that continued on throughout the rest of the morning.

Chapter Five

*G*ray Hawk couldn't believe his eyes.

He stood within the four walls of a room the white people called a "ballroom." And he could barely credit what he saw.

He shook his head. Was the white woman so shameless that she would flaunt herself in public? Despite his own opinions of the woman, he had never thought to see her parade herself in such a manner as he was witnessing — and with all to see.

Gray Hawk frowned and looked away from the woman.

Almost a full moon had elapsed since his capture and containment aboard this boat. Out of necessity, Gray Hawk had come to a mild truce with these people. Having grown tired of his confinement, he had given his word that he would not try to escape so long as the white people allowed him to walk the decks outside, untied and unencumbered.

That he was bound back up when he reached his room suited him fine. It meant the white people did not trust him in his own room; it meant he could escape from there when an opportunity presented itself. It meant there was still a chance.

But these walks had given him the freedom to observe the boat, the people on it, and he had gained insight into the society and customs of these people who invaded his country, although there was more here that puzzled him than enlightened him.

For instance, gently raised and bred as a Blackfoot scout and warrior, Gray Hawk could not understand why the white men insisted on carrying

78

and displaying their weapons, while those same men divested the Indian of any guns, bows and arrows, even knives, while aboard the boat. Always, among his people, an enemy was given a fair chance in a fight.

The white man said he did this for the Indian's own good, that this stripping of arms acted as a "protection" of the Indian, to prevent warring tribes from taking one another's lives. Gray Hawk, however, keenly observed that this was not the case.

So far one Indian had lost his life because of it, that man being unable to defend himself against a drunken trapper who had taken it into his head to shoot bullets at the Indian's feet.

To make him "dance," the trapper had said.

The Indian lay dead.

Personally, Gray Hawk believed the white men were cowards, taking away the Indians' weapons only so that the trappers and other white men could intimidate the Indians without fear of recourse. Hadn't he already seen those white men shouting insults and degradations at them? Laughing at the Indians and calling them cowards because the Indians had no choice, under such unequal odds, but to stand and take the abuse?

Hadn't he witnessed the taunting of the Indian wives and maidens at the trading posts? Hadn't he wondered what happened at night when their men, weaponless, were unable to defend their homes?

He snorted. Such measures were the actions of men who lacked confidence and courage.

Scowling, Gray Hawk swung his attention back toward the white woman.

She and several of the trappers and other white men circled the floor to the strains of several instruments.

Gray Hawk didn't understand either the dancing or the music. For one thing, the white woman partnered with the men, not dancing separately as was the Blackfoot custom. For another, she danced here completely unchaperoned.

To his own mind, when she did this, she flaunted her respectability. How could she hold on to her pride after she had touched and had been touched by so many men?

And though a part of him wanted to reason that perhaps the white man's custom was different from his own, he still couldn't quite credit it.

Women were, after all, women, weaker in strength and easy prey to men. Therefore, to his own way of thinking, a woman should consider her own vulnerability. If she truly took pride in herself, she should be looking to the men in her family for protection.

He thought back to his own tribe, the Pikuni. There, a similarly-aged woman, faced with the same situation as he saw here, would have called upon her male relatives to protect her honor, her virginity.

But this white woman didn't. Why? Was she beyond respectability?

The thought was oddly disturbing.

There was also something else that he had observed here that he didn't understand: why did the white men cater to her? Waiting upon her as though she were distinguished, as though she were a warrior recently returned from a successful raid?

Never had he seen such a thing. And he wondered if this were a common practice among the whites, and if so, why the white men preferred to treat their women so badly.

All his life Gray Hawk had been taught that women had a rightful place in society, along with the men, but as women. Women possessed skills and emotions a man was often at a loss to explain. A stupid man might negate such things; a wise man valued them.

Even as a young boy, Gray Hawk had observed that men did not exercise their will against women, nor did men cross the line and do the work of a woman. For to wait on a woman when she was well enough to care for herself would be as to declare to that woman that she was not worthy of the man's attention or affection. And no man who valued his woman would stoop to such a thing.

There was more. There was a certain protocol that men observed around women. And so far Gray Hawk had yet to observe this in the white world.

That a man would cower to a woman, that a man would fear her wrath, that a man would risk anything—even that woman's respectability— to gain her favor, made Gray Hawk seriously wonder if the white men in this country had any backbone.

He had actually asked Robert to turn around one time so that he might see the white man's back. But Robert had laughed and walked away, leaving Gray Hawk to ponder in silence the strangeness of this white society.

Robert sewed; Robert cleaned the room; Robert brought in the meals; Robert saw to the Indian's comfort, providing him with blankets and other articles of warm clothing. Robert even took orders from the white woman.

Gray Hawk didn't understand it. Gray Hawk didn't appreciate it.

How could a woman take any pride in herself if the man in her life did all of her work? Did the white men think so badly of their women that they would take away the dignity and respect that came from a project well done, that was rightfully a woman's?

The more he watched and observed, the more confused he became.

He had again asked Robert about these strange customs, but Robert had only shaken his head and laughed again, leaving Gray Hawk to draw his own conclusions as to the oddities he saw.

A movement out of the corner of his eye caught his attention.

She stood there in the middle of the floor, surrounded by five or six adoring men, and, despite his antagonism toward her, Gray Hawk couldn't help but admit that she was probably the most beautiful woman he had ever seen. In truth, he had thought so from the first moment he had seen her.

"She's quite a sight, isn't she?"

Gray Hawk didn't spin or in any way turn about to acknowledge Robert, who had come upon him from behind. Indeed, Gray Hawk did nothing more than scowl, though he did note to himself that Robert had read his mind correctly and had commented on his thoughts as if he'd heard them.

"She's a true English heiress, my good chap."

Gray Hawk merely raised an eyebrow. He didn't know what an English heiress was, nor did he care, though he realized it must mean quite something to Robert, to these others, if their adoration toward her were to make sense.

"You could join that circle."

That had Gray Hawk doing a slow about-face. He was about to comment when—

"Why, yes," he heard the white woman's lilting voice, "I do know quite a bit about the American Indian…from my father's studies, you understand."

Gray Hawk glared at her over his shoulder.

"Would you like to hear some of what I know about these savages?"

Savages? Gray Hawk narrowed his eyes at her, to the accompaniment of five to six male voices, all muttering agreement. All except the Indian stared at her in worshipful wonder.

"Well," she commented, and Gray Hawk could hear the smile in her voice, "all American Indians on this continent wear tanned animal skins, the fine art of producing silk and other materials being wholly unknown to these indigenous people."

Gray Hawk looked down at his own clothing of breeches and waistcoat, something Robert had fought hard to get him into; indeed, the servant had succeeded in doing so only by hiding the Indian's own breechcloth and moccasins. And, though he hated the white man's clothing, for the first time Gray Hawk was glad he was wearing it.

Gray Hawk smiled and turned around so he faced the woman. She had her back to him.

"All American Indians sit upon the ground. Chairs and other furniture of the civilized world are not known to them, nor would the savages know what to do with them if they even saw such articles."

Gray Hawk immediately sat down in a nearby chair.

"Nor have the American Indians any china: no cups, no saucers, no plates, no silverware. In fact, my father has found that most American Indians eat with their fingers, a most disturbing habit."

Gray Hawk picked up a cup of tea from a nearby table, and, balancing it, saucer and all, on his knee—behavior he had seen Robert and other white men perform—the Indian took a sip from the cup.

Someone in the audience chuckled.

The white woman cleared her throat.

"All American Indians, except for a few Mandan Indians, have straight, black hair, and most braid or tie their hair in a bunch on each side of their face."

Only that morning Robert had shown Gray Hawk a white wig which had once been worn by the "elite" of their society. That wig still lay close at hand.

In a quick movement, Gray Hawk scooped up the wig and plopped it onto his head.

He sat back down.

Someone in the audience coughed. A few more chuckled.

"All of these savages rarely speak, and most scowl almost continually—and they have, as a people, very little cheerfulness. Why, even their women are given to the dour and humorless life of the plains Indian."

Gray Hawk grinned widely, and, putting his hands behind his head, leaned back in the chair.

"All Indians wear moccasins, a type of shoe that wears out much too readily."

Gray Hawk crossed his legs, the action showing off his booted feet.

A tiny ripple of laughter came from the audience.

"They have no knowledge of smoking, except their clay pipes..."

The Indian lit a cigar Robert had given him only that morning.

"They all eat a diet of only buffalo meat..."

The Indian picked up a scone from a nearby table and took a bite.

"They all—" She stopped. Too many in the crowd were chuckling.

She gazed into her audience, then over her shoulder; then gradually, she turned all the way around. Gray Hawk grinned at her as he caught her eye, watching as the realization of what he had been doing came to settle upon her face.

She didn't gasp. She didn't faint. In truth, she did little more than stare.

And Gray Hawk met that look of hers unflinchingly.

Slowly, with great dignity, she turned back around to face her crowd of adoring fans. She didn't utter a sound for many moments until at last she murmured, "Excuse me."

And with that simple phrase, she swept out of the room while Gray Hawk settled back in his chair, a quiet sense of satisfaction settling upon him.

Score one.

Chapter Six

The beat of the drum and Gray Hawk's voice raised in song could be heard in all parts of the boat. It was a strange tune with an alien melody. Sung in a minor key, it tugged at some inner part of her soul. It made her ache.

"I cannot wait to reach St. Louis."

Genevieve stood at the railing on the main deck of the steamboat. She spoke to Robert, who reclined not more than a few feet behind her.

"I can't help but worry," she continued. "I keep telling myself that it is only two more months. I know I need to hold on for only a little longer, but I keep worrying."

"The Indian's song is sad."

"Yes."

"He has people at home that depend on him for their food and shelter. I think he worries about them."

Genevieve looked back over her shoulder. "How do you know this?" she asked. "Did he tell you?"

"Yes."

She gazed back out at the grass-carpeted land bordering the river. On one of the hills in the distance, an elk raised its head, seeming to stare straight at her. Overhead, the sun peeked out from behind a gray cloud, its momentary brilliance blinding her—if only for an instant. She wet her lips before replying, "I'm sorry."

Robert sighed. "I know. I knew how you would feel if you understood that he had family at home to care for. I didn't tell you for some time because I didn't want to upset you. He told me about this on one of the first days he was here.

"But I do not think you should feel too badly," Robert continued. "I spoke to some of the traders, and they told me not to worry, that the Indians take care of themselves. They said others in the tribe will care for his family while he is gone. It is their way."

Genevieve remained silent, her gaze settling upon far-distant hills. She sighed. "I wish I could do something about it all, but if I let him go…"

"I know," said Robert. "It is why I haven't mentioned anything before. I only bring it up now by way of explaining his melancholy."

Genevieve nodded her head.

Suddenly the drumming stopped, and the boat descended at once into silence. She felt herself holding her breath. For what?

The drumming started again. Then the singing, this time a different song, but equally sad. She let out her breath.

"Is he bound when he is drumming?"

"No, but he is watched carefully when he is not tied."

"Then I needn't worry?"

"No."

"He hates me."

"I know."

"I shudder to think what would happen to me if he were ever to get loose."

"It should not happen, milady. We keep a close watch on him when he is in his quarters, and when he is out walking on the deck, he is bound by his own word."

"Then you believe he will not try to escape?"

"Not while he is walking on the deck. He has given us his word, and from what I understand about these people, an Indian would sooner die than break his trust, once given.

"No," Robert continued. "I do not worry about him when he is walking out on deck, only when he is in his room. We have no promise from him there, and he is careful not to give it."

Genevieve inclined her head, her thoughts far from the conversation.

She held up a hand to shield her eyes as she stared off across this wild land. Over a month had passed since the Indian's capture, and still the man hated her.

It didn't matter how well she treated him, nor how many times she approached him in friendship. Their conversations always ended the same way: he, insinuating that she was somehow lax in her morals, and she, frustrated, giving up and running away.

She had hoped for so much more. She had hoped to befriend him. She had planned to learn his language and to start the studies for her father. It would save precious time.

It was useless.

She still remembered her embarrassment of a few days earlier, when Gray Hawk had mocked her in front of her friends. She had been mortified.

But her feelings then and now had gone beyond embarrassment. She'd realized for the first time how very little she knew about the American Indian. She'd come to see that there was more to learn of these people, of their way of life — more than she and her father had ever suspected.

It was depressing. Her father had a book due in less than a year. Unless he could come to understand these people soon, all would be lost.

But this wasn't all that concerned her.

Gray Hawk did not act submissive, as she had expected, and this didn't make any sense at all. Never had she encountered a native who did not bow or cower to her, to her father. But this man...

She grimaced. Why, he had altogether too much pride. In fact, she would credit him with the kind of mind that seeks independence, the sort of spirit that makes laws, that changes societies.

But that wasn't possible, or was it?

She'd assumed that she knew all about these people. Hadn't she accompanied her father on several expeditions? Hadn't he commented on, and hadn't she then witnessed, the childlike quality of most native peoples?

Didn't the politicians in the eastern regions of America call the Indians "children of the forest," or "of the plains?"

Certainly her father was correct in believing these people to have their own civilizations, but like all indigenous peoples, they lacked the ability to have mature emotions: those of compassion, of charity, of understanding. Or did they?

She closed her eyes and sighed. Something here made no sense. Her father was a learned man. Surely what he proclaimed must be true. Mustn't it?

The alien voice, raised in song, grew louder, invading her thoughts and her peace of mind.

And Genevieve, turning away from the steamboat railing, knew what she had to do, knew what she had to accomplish if she were to save her father.

She would have to talk with the Indian. She didn't like the idea, and she despaired of the final outcome of such an action, but it had to be done.

She would have to set aside her prejudices; she would have to grant him all the rights that she would an Englishman. And, most of all, she would have to elicit the Indian's cooperation.

Somehow.

****

"You may go. I will watch over him."

Gray Hawk missed a beat in his drumming, though he kept on with his song. He glanced over toward the spot from which he'd heard the feminine voice.

He scowled. He hadn't imagined it. There she stood, at the entrance to this room...alone.

He hadn't been alone with her since the first night of his capture. He didn't want to be alone with her now.

He continued to sing, ignoring her presence, though he was painfully aware of her.

How could he not be? She was the most beautiful woman he had ever seen.

He thought back to the first time he had beheld her. Up until then, he'd never imagined there was such a thing as a white woman, never completing the thought that where there were white men, so too must there be white women. Though perhaps he should be forgiven this oversight. Factually, he had never been interested enough in the white society to draw the conclusion. Besides, as a lad he had once been detained at a trading post for over a year, and not once had he ever seen a white woman.

But there she'd been, and Gray Hawk hadn't been able to look away. She had made the small trading room come alive, her reddish hair, her perfectly oval face, her chipmunk-brown eyes and her blushing cheeks seeming to add sunshine to the gray interior of the spiritless trading room. Her strangely sweet scent had filled his lungs until he seemed to sense her even as he slept.

And he'd thought then that because of her presence, his whole journey to the trading post, a trip he'd been reluctant to make, had been worth it. He'd known then that he would have many tales to tell when he returned home, though he feared few would believe his description of the very real beauty of this woman.

Why, with just describing the woman's clothing alone, he would be thrown out of many camp circles, the reality of it too foreign for most Pikuni to credit.

Gray Hawk took a deep breath before continuing his song.

He had joined the trading party as a last resort, and only then at the urging of his mother and sisters. Gray Hawk himself had been intent on

89

leading a war party against the Snakes, a tribe of Indians whose territory bordered the Blackfeet on their southwestern border.

But his sister was soon to marry a prestigious warrior from the allied Bloods, a tribe of the Blackfeet who lived to the far north, and all the women in Gray Hawk's family had been anxious to obtain a new assortment of beads to use as decoration for the wedding gown.

And Gray Hawk, after much cajoling, had consented to do their bidding.

It was his duty.

So he had joined the trading party. And the rest of the story…

He disliked thinking that he would not be able to return home with the beads. Worse yet, he realized that the women in his family would be reliant upon friends in the camp for their winter stores of food and clothing.

It was not good, and he felt his anger rising toward this white woman. But he would have his revenge. He would ensure it.

He gave no outward sign, however, of what he felt. He continued to sing.

On and on he continued, giving no notice at all to the woman who stood just inside the entryway, even making up new verses, until at last he had no choice but to end the song.

"May I have a word with you, Mr. Gray Hawk?" she asked at once.

He looked up reluctantly. *Ha'*, but he wished he hadn't. Dressed in deep forest green that extended from her hat at the very top of her head straight down to her feet, she dazzled him with her beauty, and he thought at this moment that if she asked for anything, he might very well give it to her.

Luckily, she didn't ask.

She waited patiently for his reply, and Gray Hawk wondered if she knew that he wasn't bound, that he had convinced the guard to untie him.

She apparently hadn't noticed. And he had already noted that she was not the most observant of people. Again, he wondered that she would trust herself with him, even if she thought him to be tied. It was unseemly for a woman.

"I cannot help but notice," Gray Hawk said, "that white woman dares much to come and see me, especially when there is no one with her to act the chaperone."

"I wish to speak to you alone."

Gray Hawk raised his brow at that. A woman seeking out a man who was not her husband? To speak to him? Alone?

Gray Hawk said, "You dare much."

She gazed away from him then, looking around her nervously. She murmured, "Yes, I know. But I really must speak to you in private."

This puzzled Gray Hawk even more, but stoically, he showed nothing. He merely sat in silence, awaiting whatever communication she had to make.

He stared at her.

"I... I..." she began, "I wish to come to some sort of truce with you, if I might."

Gray Hawk nodded. "*Aa*, yes, this is good. My freedom for —"

"I cannot give you your freedom."

He didn't even delay a second. "Then there is no truce."

She bowed her head, and Gray Hawk wondered at what game she played. He shifted uncomfortably on the floor.

"Robert tells me that there are people," she began, "women in your life, a mother, sisters, a wife, that are dependent upon you for their winter supplies."

Gray Hawk nodded his head. "*Aa*, yes, it is true, except that I have no wife."

Genevieve's head came up. She gazed at him as though she didn't quite believe him.

She said, "I thought that all male Indians of your age were married."

"Then you were wrong."

"Why are you not married? Is there something wrong? Some reason?"

"Did you come here to discuss me? My reasons for not marrying? And if you did, has the white woman of no honor cause for her interest?"

"No, no. I…it's just that I thought—"

"I am often at war," Gray Hawk interrupted. "I lead and I follow many war parties. Why would I marry when that woman might become a widow much too soon? Better that I wait until the desire for warring is over within me. Better then can I become a good husband and give to my wife all that a man should."

"Yes," she said. "That makes perfect sense, I suppose. It's only that… Mr. Gray Hawk, I wish to apologize. I did not think to inquire as to your family when you were brought to the boat. It was not a proper thing for me to do. And I wish to know what I can do to make it up to you."

He paused. "White woman could let me go."

"I cannot."

Gray Hawk shrugged. He looked away.

She took a step forward. "Mr. Gray Hawk, please try to understand. Just as you have people you are responsible for, so do I. I cannot let you go. Not yet, at least. My father needs you. I have been truthful with you about that. Isn't there some other way I could make this up to you…send one of the trappers back to hunt for your family, perhaps? Please, if you tell me what it is, I will do it."

Gray Hawk paused. Though he realized the sincerity of the white woman's plea, she had overstepped the boundary when she had taken him captive. He could neither forgive her nor see her point of view.

He said, "The white woman offers many things grandly when there is little for her to lose. The white woman still remains free while I am captive. No, white woman of no honor, there is nothing you can do."

She jerked her head away from him then, but instead of running away as she so often did at the end of their "conversations," she took a step forward.

"I could make your stay with us shorter, so that you could return to your home sooner."

Gray Hawk frowned, and picking up his stick, he began to drum. He ignored her.

"I could learn your language, if you will teach it to me, and I wish to learn your customs."

He continued drumming. "For what purpose do you wish to discover so much about my people?"

"I..." She smiled and swept forward, coming down to kneel before him. "It is for my father. He has been commissioned to set down on paper and preserve all the customs of the Indians, so that all peoples of the world might know about them."

He raised his gaze to hers. "Would all Indian tribes come to know of these customs?"

She grinned. "Yes, it is possible. Isn't it wonderful?"

"Tribes like the Snakes, the Sioux, the Crow?"

Genevieve paused. "Yes, I believe in time that they might come to be interested in these things."

"And the white woman wishes me to tell her of my people so that my enemies might hear of it? So that they might gain victory over us?"

"No, that is not the way of it. I—"

"Now you are on both sides of this thing. First you say yes, and then you say no. It cannot be both ways. I think you lie."

She sat back, her skirts flowing around her on the floor, and Gray Hawk made the odd observation of noting that they both wore the white man's clothing: she because it belonged to her, he because Robert had forced it on him.

"No, you don't understand," said the white woman. "I can explain..."

The look he gave her did not allow for explanation.

"Wait, I can show you." She sat up and was rising to her feet when the boat suddenly jerked to the right and to the left. Then, hurtling forward, it came to an abrupt halt.

She pitched forward.

Gray Hawk reached out to steady her, but both of them were thrown across the floor, she landing on top of him once, then twice. She began to rise, but the boat started again and then stopped so suddenly that they were flung forward, first one, then the other, rolling over one another.

"*Hánnia!*"

He landed right on top of her.

"What's happening?" she asked.

He didn't bother answering. He sprang to his feet and raced to the door. Amazingly, it opened to him on the first try.

People hurried down the corridor, and no one paid any attention to the Indian who stood at the doorway.

Gray Hawk grinned. Trained as a Pikuni scout, he had the ability to look at and note everything in his environment with no more than a solitary glance, that data to be remembered in perfect recall even up to several weeks later. It was expected of a scout, and it certainly was considered no unusual feat among his people.

Deciding that the white woman would not get far, Gray Hawk left her behind in the cabin while he sprinted down the corridor to where he saw the gathering crowd.

In a simple glance, he observed that the boat had become caught up in a jumble of river debris: logs and sticks and washed-away tree roots. He also estimated the time it would take to free the boat, noted the position of the sun and how many hours of daylight were left, checked each of the white men's firearms and calculated the distance necessary to dodge bullets. In addition, he evaluated the state of the river for escape.

With a final glimpse, he noted that all the crewmen plus all the able-bodied men, including Robert and his bullies, were involved in handling the problem. He determined as well how long the men would remain occupied to the extent that they were oblivious to their surroundings.

He decided he had a chance. That was all.

Darting back to the cabin, he found the woman.

She backed away from him as though she knew his intent.

But it didn't matter. He would have his revenge.

Ignoring her protests, he scooped her up in his arms and flung her over his shoulder.

She kicked out. She hollered.

It didn't matter. No one was there to hear.

Stepping to the entry, he checked the corridor for traffic. There was no one; everyone had gathered to one side of the boat.

Gray Hawk fled in the opposite direction, up the corridor to the railing, onto the railing itself, and then, with a final jump, down toward the swirling, muddy river. And never once had the white woman ceased her screaming.

Splash! Thud!

They hit the water, their fall taking them far below the surface.

A current tried to take hold of him. He fought it at first. Then, he let his mind merge with the river as he became a part of the water. Soon, he was swimming away, kicking out to gain distance from the boat.

The woman had stopped struggling, and he wondered if she had remembered to hold her breath. He glanced at her. Her eyes were closed, and she appeared to be unconscious.

Ha'! What trouble.

He surfaced.

"Breathe," he commanded her.

She opened her eyes, choked, sputtered, and, taking a deep breath, looked as though she were about to scream.

He ducked back underwater, gliding through its murky depths to the shore.

95

He didn't know how much time he had until they discovered him gone. And he knew that when he made it to the shore, he would have to keep moving.

They would send scouts after him.

He hit the shore and surfaced. She screamed.

It didn't matter. Pulling her back over his shoulder, Gray Hawk emerged from the water and sprinted up the shoreline.

Luckily for him, this part of the river boasted a tree-lined shore, and he was able to seek temporary cover, if only to catch his breath.

He paused a moment; then, with one final glance in the direction of the boat, he darted out from his cover and climbed to the top of the bluff. Never once did he stop. Never once did he falter because of the woman's resistance, nor her screams.

On and on he ran, the woman still slung over his shoulder. He could have run without stopping for several days, but that was under normal conditions. Gray Hawk was encumbered.

His feet hurt him. The white man's clothing restricted him. The woman's kicking annoyed him. But he kept going.

He knew he dared not pause until evening, and even then he would stop only for a moment to refresh himself and tie a bit of cloth around the woman's mouth.

He grinned. That last thought brought him a great deal of pleasure and helped spur him on.

Score two.

Chapter Seven

*D*rums kept pounding in her ears.

It was the savage. He was drumming; he was singing. Then he was running, sprinting toward her, then grinning at her.

She awoke with a start. She was being rattled all about; blood rushed to her head.

She opened her eyes. Dry brown prairie grass and dirty white shirt were all she could see.

And then she remembered: she rode on Gray Hawk's shoulder, slung there and kept there by his superior strength. She squeezed her eyes shut, too numb even to weep.

A cold fear swept over her. This savage hated her, believed that she had heaped upon him the utmost in degradation. What, then, did he intend to do to her?

She lifted her head, if only to halt the flow of blood rushing there.

Dusk was upon them, red and pink still clinging to the western sky. How long had it been since the accident, and more importantly, how long had he been running?

Had the others yet discovered their absence? And if so, when would she be rescued?

Rescue. It was her only salvation.

She only hoped the others were fast upon the savage's trail. After all, how far could one man go, burdened down as he was with her?

She glanced up again at the western sky. She was certain it had been much earlier in the day when she had sought out the Indian aboard the steamship. That meant he had been running for quite a bit of time.

He had to be tired.

It gave her hope.

Letting her head flop back down against the savage's back, she began to make some plans.

****

"*O'ksoyi vai*! Eat the raw food!"

Genevieve stared down at the dirty brown roots that Gray Hawk had dug up for dinner. Did he really expect her to eat this?

Gray Hawk bridled. "I do not have any weapons for killing fresh game, and I do not know when I will be able to stop again to dig roots for food. Eat now."

She glanced up at him, the fear she felt a very real and live thing within her.

He caught her glance. "*Mopbete*! Behave! If I had wanted to kill you, I would have done so by now. Eat! There may not be food for some time."

Genevieve said without thinking, "But it's dirty." She immediately bit her lip.

Gray Hawk rose to his feet. He meandered toward her, squatting down directly in front of her.

He picked up the root and wiped it off. He looked at it, then at her, and at last, clearly annoyed, he got to his feet and ambled down toward the stream.

With his back to her, Genevieve entertained the idea of leaving, but thought better of it. For one thing, she'd not get far, not after having witnessed the speed with which this man could run.

But also she remembered looking out from the boat, there witnessing wolves and bears roaming these plains—not to mention other Indians who

98

might be out there, Indians who might be more hostile to her than this man. Better she stay with Gray Hawk until she could formulate some other plan for freedom.

"*Annisa*," he said, coming to stand over her. "It should be all right for you now. I perform for you a woman's task in washing off this food. I do it only because you are new to the prairie and do not know its ways yet. Know that I will not do so again. Now, eat."

Genevieve reached up toward him for the root, her gaze not quite able to reach his. The root still didn't look edible to her, but she took it from him anyway and said, "Thank you."

"Eat the small bulb you see here at the bend. It tastes sweet."

She nodded, and again, not quite able to look at him, said, "Thank you."

Silence fell between them until, after a while, gathering her courage, Genevieve said, "I do not understand why you bring me with you, Mr. Gray Hawk. Do I not burden you?"

He nodded. "*Aa*, yes."

"Then why not leave me here? I'm sure a rescue party will be by soon, and if you leave me, you can get away so much more swiftly," she said, not adding that she would ensure their coming after him when they did rescue her. She *had* to get this Indian back to St. Louis.

He shrugged. "You are not very heavy. I have often carried over my shoulders deer that weigh more than you. Besides," here he sent her a gaze reeking of menace, "I have plans for you."

She swallowed and opened her eyes a fraction of an inch wider. "I... Mr. Gray Hawk, didn't you say you had no intention of killing me?"

"*Saa*. None," Gray Hawk said, seemingly engrossed in eating his own food. "At least, not yet."

She gagged.

"Why should I kill you when there is always the chance for torture?"

Genevieve gasped and dropped her food.

Gray Hawk chuckled. "*Saahkayi*," he said, not feeling kindly enough to translate the Blackfoot, which meant, "I jest." Nor did he bother to tell her that the Blackfeet, as a nation, did not engage in torture. He shook his head. "Come, come now, captive, if you throw away your food, how will I ever fatten you up?"

"Fatten me up?"

"*Annisa*, that is right." Gray Hawk grinned. Getting to his feet, he began to peel away his shirt. "No one likes a bony captive. Come now, you had best sit up and eat before we prepare to go. We will leave here soon."

"Leave? But I thought..." She chanced a quick glance in his direction, though she saw nothing more than the man struggling to rid himself of his shirt. She quickly looked away. "Aren't we going to sleep here?"

"*Saa*, no," he said, "too dangerous. Maybe not tomorrow night, either. The grandfather of all bears lives in this country. He is the kind of bear that eats up all white people who trespass over Indian hunting grounds." He made a gulping sound. "And he eats them up in pieces, a little bit at a time, just like this—"

She snorted. "Don't be ridiculous."

"Do you think I would make up such a tale?"

"Yes, I do."

He grinned. "Perhaps I do...perhaps. But know that I speak true when I say it is not safe to sleep here.

"Now," he continued, having just mastered the secret of the buttons on his shirt. He shrugged the whole thing off and then held out a hand toward her. "*Poohsapoot*! Come here!"

Genevieve gazed over toward him, and her eyes grew wide. She turned quickly away, although her mind insisted on replaying that image of his naked chest: those muscles, all that skin, his masculine nipples shimmering under the starlight. It all seemed to haunt her, though she looked elsewhere. And then there was his long hair, gleaming in strands over his shoulders...

She drew in her breath, and her pulse raced.

Gray Hawk noticed it at once. "What is it you fear, captive?" he asked. "Is it the grandfather bear? Torture? Me? Or," he grinned, "does the white woman of no honor have other, more pleasurable things on her mind?"

Genevieve bridled and looked away from him. How dare he?

Yet what could she say, after all? All of the above? Of course not.

She remained silent.

She heard the sounds of tearing cloth, and, gazing back at him, she beheld him shredding his shirt, making neat, long strips out of it.

"What are you doing?"

He smiled. "I am making sure that my captive does not escape."

She snorted. "Where would I go?"

"It makes no difference. You could do most anything, go most anywhere, and," he paused and grinned, "I would make certain of your whereabouts. Now, come here. *Poohsapoot!*"

"No." She folded her hands in front of her and sat her ground.

"*Poohsapoot!*"

"Humph!"

He grabbed her, pulling her up; all the while she wrestled against him, but in the end his strength won out over hers, and Genevieve found herself tied, bound and gagged. She couldn't take a step, she couldn't speak and she couldn't pick up a thing; her hands were tied behind her back.

She swore the most unladylike oaths, but unfortunately they could not be appreciated. Her words came out only in mumbo-jumbo.

He smiled. His only reaction to her struggles was amusement.

Oh, what she would do to him.

She thought about it over and over, the contemplation of it pleasurable.

And just when she was beginning to gladden at the prospect of planning what course her revenge would take, she remembered that this was exactly what *he* was doing: seeking revenge. Oh, dear.

She quieted.

And this time when he slung her over his shoulder, she didn't struggle.

She would conserve her strength. At least for now. She would need it.

****

This had not been such a good idea.

With her hands tied behind her back and her body flung over his shoulder like a sack, her hair teased his buttocks and her breasts rubbed against his back—his naked back. And in the dress she wore, with a good portion of her breasts most daringly exposed, it was the same as flesh meeting flesh. Hers all soft and feminine, his—

His body reacted accordingly, and he grimaced as his pants became too tight.

This would never do. This was not his intention. He must do something about this. He couldn't even walk in a straight way at the moment.

He stopped and, pulling the woman off his shoulder, settled her onto the ground, her green dress flowing out and her hair falling to her waist like a cascade of fiery liquid.

She sat stiffly, as though any other position but this would cause pain, and he stared at her for a moment, finally squatting down beside her.

"I am going to untie your feet and let you run behind me. It is not good to have blood rushing to your head so much."

She didn't reply, but then he hadn't expected her to. She was gagged. She just stared at him with her large, doe-brown eyes.

"I am going to tie one part of this strip around your waist and the other part around mine. I will need you to run behind me, not walk. We are in the country of my enemies, the Sioux, and we must hurry through it or risk death. We cannot travel during the day, only at night. Do you understand? There is also a party behind us. Therefore, we must hurry. Can you do it?"

"*Hmmmmmm.*" She shook her head and stuck out her chin, indicating the gag.

"*Saa*, Little Captive. I cannot take away the gag. I do not trust you not to cry out to gain attention from your people if they should come close to us. Nor would I expect you to act calmly and be quiet if another warrior were

102

near. I have no weapons with which to defend myself or you. I cannot allow you to make a 'mistake' or to make a sound, however intentional or unintentional that mistake might be."

"*Ahhhhh*," she groaned.

"Come, we must hurry. Soon the moon will be rising, and then we will be exposed again. I cannot allow that." He stood then, and, tying the cloth around his waist, he motioned her up.

And, though he set a pace that might have been a little fast for her, he noted with some grudging admiration that she kept up with him all through the night.

Chapter Eight

$\mathscr{S}$he awoke to a sound of scraping.

She glanced around her with a start, not sure at first where she was.

The bed beneath her felt stiff, grassy and unyielding; the wind whipped across her, making her shiver, bringing with it the smell of…blood? Rawhide?

She sat up quickly.

He was there before her, not paying any attention to her, engrossed in…woodcraft?

What was the man doing?

A deer lay to the side of their camp—recently killed and gutted.

Ah, she put a label to the smell of blood. Beside him lay a spear, obviously hurriedly handcrafted. And, though the point of it was of chiseled wood, not metal, it made no difference.

The blood on the end of it, the deer to the side of it, told its own tale. The weapon was deadly.

She wore no gag, and she rejoiced at the simple pleasure of having her mouth free to speak, though she said not a word, lest he become aware of it and take away her pleasure much too soon.

It was dusk. She had slept away the day here in their camp, which, tucked into a hillside, was hidden from even the most scrutinizing of views.

He apparently had not slept at all but had been working the whole time, making weapons, hunting.

"You could be of service by skinning that deer."

She blinked. "Pardon?"

He pointed to the deer at the side of the camp. "The hide needs to be removed from the deer."

She fluttered her eyelashes twice. "Surely you are not saying that you wish me to..."

"Skin the deer? Of course I am. It is woman's work."

Genevieve pouted, but it was all that she did. Had she been back in England, she would have fainted. But here and now, in this place, she had to content herself with a disdainful look at him, as though that alone would put him in his place.

It didn't work.

He didn't notice.

After a while, he gazed up at her and motioned her toward the deer.

She bristled. "Mr. Gray Hawk," she said at last, "I take this as an affront to my womanhood. I know we come from different cultures, and I understand perfectly well that the women in your camp are all slaves, catering to and bending to the will of the men. But this is not so in my society, and I will not stoop so low as to do your bidding. I daresay, if you want the deer skinned, either do it yourself or find some *slave* to do it."

Gray Hawk gradually ceased his work as she spoke, and Genevieve was glad to see that her tirade had found its mark.

She was about ready to congratulate herself on the brilliance of her oratory when he said, "I would not want to hear what my mother and sisters would say to you if they heard you call them slaves. But very well," he said with a smirk that caused her a slight bit of apprehension. "I shall call *you* 'slave' from now on, rather than 'captive.' Now, slave, skin the deer."

"I-beg your pardon?"

"*Aa*, yes, go ahead. I would like to see you beg."

"Sir?"

"You and your kind keep promising to beg, but you never do. What I am saying, slave, is if you do not wish to skin the deer, you will have to beg me to do it for you."

"What? Why, I never heard of such a thing."

He peered at her. "You have now." He motioned her forward. "Go ahead."

"Why, I would never —"

"That's just the trouble."

"I beg your..."

He shook his head, jerking it slightly to the left. "I do not see that you contribute much, if anything, to your society."

"Why, I —"

He held up a hand. "Your menfolk do all your work: sewing, polishing, cleaning, cooking. I see you, the woman, doing nothing. No wonder the white race is a dirty, unkempt race with their men smelling worse than a bog during the hot days of summer. And no wonder they do not bring their women with them when they come here to our home. Who would want to support a woman who does nothing all day long?

"Not that I blame them." Again, Gray Hawk held up a hand when she would have spoken. "How could a woman ever take pride in herself, in a job well done, if her menfolk constantly take away her joy in the creation of the home?"

"Mr. Gray Hawk, you —"

"Tell me I am wrong."

"You are wrong." She said it easily, though she didn't believe it quite so quickly.

She'd never heard such a point of view before, and, though she dismissed it instantly, something in what he said made her stop and think.

It wasn't true, was it? All her life she had been brought up believing it was the right of the upper class to do no work; that to do labor, even the task of something as simple as dressing oneself, meant to lower oneself; that only servants and the lower dregs of humanity toiled.

106

But now that he mentioned it, his words brought back a feeling of puzzlement that she'd experienced several times as a child. And she wondered, hadn't she observed, when she was young, that those men and women who did the least had the most bitter personalities? Hadn't she seen it recently in their own Mr. Toddman? Hadn't she witnessed a change in him that bordered upon criminal?

Could it be because, as Gray Hawk said, these people did not contribute? Was there some connection between lack of doing and no actual worth to society?

Surely it wasn't so. The life of toil was an unpleasant one, at best. The servants, the people who labored, were seldom happy people. Or were they?

She shook her head as though to clear it. Why was she debating such things? Here and now? She, a Blackfoot captive, sitting in bonds of servitude, out on a lone stretch of prairie, had suddenly taken to philosophizing.

She looked up at Gray Hawk and found his gaze still upon her. He nodded his head toward the deer, which caused her to lean forward and say, "I am not dressed to do such a job. I will spoil my—"

She caught his glance as he gazed down at her dress. She too looked down.

She groaned.

Her dress was wrinkled, dirty and torn, and in places it gaped open, exposing to the air, to his view, to anyone's casual glance, a look at her chemise.

Embarrassment overwhelmed her, and she made a stab at arranging her clothing, pulling it this way and that to bring it into order. She moaned. It didn't matter. Nothing she did helped keep the garment in place. The pieces gaped back open.

She hadn't noticed the state of it until now; she'd been too caught up in her own fears to see it, and she wondered abstractedly how the rest of her appearance looked. Gingerly, she brought her hand up to her hair.

She grimaced. She couldn't even pull her fingers through the mass of it for all of the tangles.

What did it matter?

She rose then and discovered that she could barely walk. Her legs, every muscle in them, scarcely obeyed her commands, so stiff were they from running.

She stumbled over toward the deer. "I want you to know that I have never been reduced to such a low state as this," she said to him. "And I would see that you understand that..." She looked to the ground, all around the animal. "Mr. Gray Hawk, I haven't a tool to —"

"Here." He threw her a sharp stone, carefully chiseled. The object landed at her feet.

She picked it up, looking at it as though she had never before seen a rock. And in truth, she hadn't. Not like this. This stone had been carefully made into a knife.

She glanced at the deer, then at the "knife," then back at the deer.

She slumped her shoulders.

"Take a part of the hide in your hands along the backbone," he suggested, "and run the knife under it. It will tear apart from the meat more easily that way."

She gazed at him, then back at the deer.

She picked up a handful of the carcass, held the knife to it, stabbed it under the hide.

Blood ran out.

She shrieked and fell back, her head spinning as though she had twirled around a number of times, her throat raw.

Some of the blood spilled onto her dress. She squealed.

"*Ha'!*" he said, coming over to squat down beside her, a look on his face that said he couldn't quite believe it. "Have you never skinned a deer before?"

"Never!" She sat up.

"A squirrel?"

"No."

"A rabbit?"

"Of course not!"

"*Hánnia!* Do your menfolk do even this for you?"

"Menfolk?" She shifted uncomfortably. "I don't know to what or to whom you are referring, Mr. Gray Hawk, but I can assure you that my father and I have more than enough servants to handle such matters as this, thank you very much."

He shook his head. He looked as though he might like to say something, but with a jerk of his head, he did no more than pick up the stone knife that she had dropped. He gazed at the deer for a long time, his thoughts unreadable, until at last he said, "I will do it for you this time, but you must mimic everything I do so that when next I bring an animal into camp, you will know what to do. Do you understand?"

She hesitated. She glanced at him, down at her dress, over toward the knife that he held, and to the deer, which still lay to the side of the camp. At length, seeing no possible way out of this situation, she nodded.

It seemed more than enough for him. With only a grunt for acknowledgment, Gray Hawk began his instruction.

He showed her the proper procedure for skinning an animal, how to cut the hide away from the muscle, how to preserve the pelt to make it ready for clothing, how to cut up the meat; he even showed her what do to with the sinew that ran throughout the muscle, how tough it was and why his people used it for thread. He showed her the use of several of the bones, the brains—how they were made into a paste for use in tanning skins. And finally, all this done, he demonstrated what to do with the leftover bones and any other remains of the animal so that the wolves and other night creatures would feed on it, the animals then effectively erasing any traces of the Indian camp.

He made her repeat each task and every motion after him.

It took until late in the evening before the whole job was done, so meticulously did he instruct her—even to the making of a fire and how to cook the meat slowly over the flames.

She'd never be able to do it on her own, but she didn't tell Gray Hawk. A camaraderie had built up between them as they'd worked, and she found herself reluctant to break it.

Said Gray Hawk, as they later huddled around the fire, the work finished, "I am taking a chance, lighting this fire while we are in Sioux country. But it is late in the evening, not a good time for warring, and I scouted all around our camp today while you slept and saw no trace of the enemy. But this may be the last time we will have a fire. Take pleasure in it."

She nodded. "I will." She paused. "Does that mean we will remain here the rest of the night? It is awfully late."

"*Saa*, no. We will move on."

"I see," she said. "Where do we go?"

"North."

"Oh."

Silence. An uncomfortable sort of silence.

"What is to the north?"

"My home, my people."

"The Blackfeet?"

"*Aa*, yes."

"Oh."

Silence again.

"Could you take me south to St. Louis?"

"*Saa*, no."

"If I don't arrive home with you, my father will be ruined, as I will be too."

"That is your problem, not mine."

"Please, Mr. Gray Hawk. We have time to go to my father and still come back to your people, I promise you. Couldn't you make the trip south, just for a little while?"

"No."

Silence. The kind that stretched on and on.

In due time, Gray Hawk said, "I might have gone with you willingly once—if you had asked."

"You might have?"

"Once. But you did not ask."

"I'm asking now."

He shook his head. "It is too late."

She sat up straighter. "Why is it too late?"

He shrugged his shoulders. "Do not ask the why of it. Know that it is simply so."

"But—"

"You ask too many questions. And though this is not a bad trait, try to discover your answers by observing the person in front of you, as is the Indian way. Oftentimes, the answers you seek are there for you to see, if you will look."

"That's ridiculous. I've never heard of anything so—"

"Go ahead. Try it."

"Why, I never. I...oh, all right," she said, sitting forward to gaze at him more directly. "I will." She stuck out her chin and examined him. "What I see is..." She suddenly giggled.

"Do not laugh. Look."

She stared at him again, this time surveying him as though seeing him for the first time.

He sat before her in profile, and she took her time inspecting him. High cheekbones; a handsome, though foreign-looking face; a slightly aquiline nose; a clean, straight jaw; full lips, the kind that had felt just right against her own.

111

Her stomach dropped.

He glanced over to her at once, as though he knew what she'd thought. His gaze fell to her mouth while his lips parted slightly.

He whispered, "Do not be discouraged, Little Captive. Just look."

He turned his head back around to profile. "Just look."

Long black hair that fell from a center part; perfect physique; dark, bronze-toned skin; broad shoulders; muscular chest; flat stomach; the white man's black breeches; protruding genitalia —

She gasped and stared away from him at once.

He chuckled. He knew. He said, "Do not worry, Little Captive. You are enemy to me and, therefore, safe from me."

"Why, I never... I wasn't... I..."

"You forget, white woman, that I have practice at this. I can see what is on your mind. Now look at me. Look, and tell me what you see. The answers to your questions are right there, if you will only observe closely."

"All right," she said, bringing her regard back to his face. "I will."

She gazed, she gawked, she peered. Smooth cheeks, she thought, cheeks devoid of facial hair. Her stare touched him gently. Full lips; long, straight eyelashes; dark, dark eyes; thick eyebrows that reminded her of his namesake. He turned all at once to stare directly into her eyes.

Then suddenly it was there before her: his past, his present, his feelings for her.

She knew what he thought, just like that. She didn't want to know. She didn't want to see.

She gasped and turned away.

"What did you see, Captive?"

"Nothing," she said. "I saw nothing."

She felt that he watched her, her own face now in profile to him. And though she tried to hide it, she could sense that he read right through her. And despite her own misgivings, she came to a startling truth: she'd never felt so close to another human being in her life. In that single glance, she'd seen his intentions, past and present. She knew his thoughts. She knew him.

She didn't want to.

He grinned. He understood.

"Come," he said. "Let us end this now and eat this deer meat so that we can start on our way. We have already lingered here too long."

Genevieve nodded. And while she helped him to clean up their camp, it came to her again and again: at one time, he had liked her. He had even wanted her. And in the beginning, he would have come with her had she done no more than ask.

This was more than she wanted to know about him, and she marveled at the reality of her knowledge, just from the simple act of surveying him. Here was a type of knowledge, of certainty, she'd never dreamed existed. And she wondered that the instruction had come from an Indian, a savage.

But there was more. She also knew that he liked her no longer. She had read that meaning just as easily as she had seen the other.

Yes, he wanted her still; but because of his dislike, because he did not feel an affinity for her any longer, she was safe with him.

She sighed and looked up into the star-filled sky, marveling that out here, on this deserted stretch of prairie, she had learned more about humanity in a few minutes than she had done in all her twenty years so far upon this earth.

She bowed her head. Truly, the knowledge was more than she could easily handle.

Chapter Nine

They had stopped shortly before dawn, and she had begged for the privacy to go and wash her body, her dress, her chemise.

He had granted her that right but had made it clear that he would have to stand watch over her…for her protection.

The stream was shallow—not more than five feet deep in the middle—and cold, but refreshing for all that. And as she splashed into it, she was reminded of simple childhood pleasures: of swimming, of romping on a warm summer's day, of England.

But this wasn't a warm summer's day. It was dawn, it was August, she was not in her safe English home, she was not a child and…she was not free.

He had gagged her again while they had traveled through the night. Despite all her promises to him that she would keep quiet, he had tied her, and they had carried on, running most of the time. She was barely able to keep up with him, her muscles protesting at this seeming abuse.

But it was dawn now, time to stop.

She breathed out slowly and ran her hand through the shallow water, the ripples and surges of the current carrying the pinks and blues of the morning sky from rock to rock as it made its way toward some unknown destination. She was glad the night was over.

She closed her eyes, listening to the sound she made in the water, enjoying the racket of her own splashing, while overhead a mourning dove cooed, welcoming in the new day.

"*Omaopii*, be quiet."

Her? Or the dove?

She looked up at him, and he motioned her to silence before turning his back to her.

She sulked and instantly stabbed a glare at him where he sat on the rise just above the stream.

This was too much. He had dragged her, tied and gagged, across the prairie until she thought she'd never be able to walk again, and now that they had stopped, now that she had a moment to herself to tend to her aching muscles and sore feet, he wanted her to be quiet?

She opened her mouth to say something scathing, but was reminded that he might likely tie and gag her again, even during the day as she slept, if she antagonized him too much.

She grimaced and opted for silence, plus a piercing stare at him, instead.

However, it gave her little satisfaction, and so she stomped her feet up and down a few more times before settling down into deeper water, if only to let him know what he could do with his silence.

Ah, the water felt wonderful. She relaxed into it with a smile, though her break didn't last long. She had work to do.

She began to undress, it being no easy task. She was physically drained; she was sleepy. She was also grouchy, but she needed to get this chore done and over with so she could lie down peacefully and sleep the day away.

Yes, she thought as she removed her dress and petticoats and placed them before her for washing. She was tired and cranky, but she was also, conversely, excited.

She didn't know why, but she was.

Perhaps it had something to do with the fact that she had come to understand, somewhere during their flight, that Gray Hawk would do her no harm, other than holding her captive.

He might talk fiercely at her. He might even growl at her for committing some Indian faux pas, but she no longer feared for her life

115

around him. With this new understanding of him had come a measure of comfort, enough that she had been able to take note of her surroundings as they had traveled into the night.

For the first time since her abduction, she had been able to look, really look, at the environment. And she had found it strange, different…exciting.

The prairie sky at night reminded her of being aboard a ship, with stars everywhere. Except here, instead of the sound of water splashing against the boat, one heard the hooting of an owl, the howl of a wolf or the cawing of a nighthawk.

Despite herself, she'd felt an affinity for this place growing within her.

"Hurry, Captive." Gray Hawk's words interrupted her thoughts. "Daylight is almost upon us, and we must be hidden by then."

She scowled up at him, though his back was still toward her.

"I might hurry more if I weren't so weary from having to keep up with you. I'm winded, I'm tired and I'm hungry, and I intend to soak my muscles until they are no longer sore."

He chuckled, a sound she had grown to dislike. "I have seen the way you walk, and I think it is this that is at fault for your weariness. But I think," he said, "that if you will watch the way I walk, with the toes pointed inward and the knees bent, instead of legs straight and toes out, you will not tire so easily and will able to keep up. This is how the Indian walks, and an Indian can travel a long time before he tires."

"Humph!" she said. "A likely story."

"But true."

"What difference could it possibly make? After all, walking with the toes pointed out is quite fashionable. It is the way all proper English ladies are taught to move. I'm afraid my governess would quite faint if she were to hear you speak like this."

"I do not know what this 'governess' is, but I can tell you that walking with the toes pointed out puts strain on the back. The weight of the body is not balanced over the feet where it should be. But if you point the toes in and bend the knees, the weight of the body falls forward, allowing one to walk a great distance."

"Humph!"

"I will show you."

He rose and made to turn around, though he didn't look over toward her.

"Not now," came her rapid reply as she quickly submerged herself in the water. "I am bathing."

He chuckled. "Should that make a difference to me?"

"Yes," she said. "No gentleman would—"

"I am Indian."

"Yes, but...you promised me privacy this morning so that I might bathe and wash my clothes in peace. Do you not remember?"

He sighed. "*Aa*, yes, I do remember, but I also recall that you promised to cease your complaining."

"I have."

"You have not."

"Gray Hawk—"

"*Annisa*, all right now. I will keep my promise, though you have failed to keep yours."

She drew in a breath of relief. "Thank you. I will try to do better."

He laughed. "I hope that you do," he said. "I certainly hope that you do."

She settled down again to do her washing. Thank goodness he hadn't turned around. She had that moment removed her chemise and drawers, and had been in the process of washing the stains from them. She now stood in the water in nothing more than her stockings.

"By the way," she said as she removed the remaining articles of clothing and began to scrub them, "how is it that you know English? I thought that there were no white people in your country."

"From a Black Robe," he replied.

"A black robe?"

"A priest, a medicine man of your people."

"Oh. There was a priest who came to your village?"

"*Saa*, no," said Gray Hawk. "It is a long story."

She looked around her, at the endless stretch of prairie. "I seem to have the time to listen."

"You will not like it."

"That could be, but just the same, I would like to hear it."

He paused. "Very well," he said at last and seemed to settle back against the ground. "It happened many years ago, when I was a child. I accompanied my father to the north and east on a trading mission to a place called Fort William. There, the white soldiers took away my father's weapons. They said it was to help him, to protect him."

"Yes," Genevieve said. "This is done at the post. I saw it done while I was at Fort Union. And it *is* for the good of the Indian. Many of the warriors, if they met an enemy in the fort, would be tempted to commit murder. It is the only way the post can ensure peace."

Gray Hawk grunted. "So they say. But did you observe that the white traders are allowed their guns and their weapons when inside the fort?"

"Well, naturally."

"What is so natural about this?"

"The white traders have no vengeance against the Indian tribes. They would not be tempted to kill anyone."

"Do you think so?"

"Yes."

He bridled. "Well, it is not so. I will have to teach you better how to observe."

"What do you mean? I take offense to that, I think."

Gray Hawk shrugged, but she didn't see.

"So?" she asked, when he didn't seem inclined to continue. "What happened? I don't understand. Other Indians have come into the trading post, but none of them speak English as well as you do."

When he still didn't reply, Genevieve prompted, "Gray Hawk?"

"I am thinking that you may not want to hear the rest of the story. You possibly might not believe it."

"I will try, Gray Hawk; I will try. Won't you please continue?"

Still he hesitated, though after a while, he said, "The white traders, whom you claim bear the Indian no grudge, began to poke fun at my father, there at the fort. They called him bad names, making obscene gestures at him. But my father, because he had no way to defend himself, ignored them. But then they began to make him dance."

"Oh, how terrible. They made him dance when he didn't want to...and in public?"

"No, Captive, you do not understand. They did not make him step to music or to the beat of a drum; they made him dance by shooting bullets at his feet. You must have seen this a few times. It was done while you were aboard the medicine canoe."

"No, I didn't know that—"

"An Indian, a Crow, died on the boat because of it. This man, this Crow, was, along with several other Indians, a guest of a white man who was taking them to a post in the South. These Indians were free to roam the boat at will. One of the Indians came across a trader who had drunk too much of the spirits of the fire water. The trader's aim was bad when he made the Indian dance. He killed the Crow. And so it was with my father too."

"The traders killed your father?"

"*Aa*, yes, it is so."

"Oh, that's terrible. I'm so sorry."

Gray Hawk lifted his shoulders in a dismissive gesture. "I was left alone," he continued, "for no one else from our tribe had come with us to that post. It was almost winter. And so I stayed at the white man's post,

119

under the care of a Black Robe, until others from my tribe came to rescue me. It was over a year before I was returned to my people.

"I learned much about the white trader at that time," he said. "I learned that the white man will say anything to protect himself. He will lie and he will cheat in order to get that thing he calls 'money.' He will do most anything, even kill a friend, if it means he will obtain this 'money' from doing it.

"I learned, as all of our people have learned, to leave the white man alone. All of our dealings with him have brought harm to our people. But I learned something else: no amount of reasoning, no amount of talk, will change the white man in his attitude toward the Indian. He kills all that he encounters, animal and Indian alike. It is a terrible sickness with him, and my people have not yet learned how to deal with this person, the white trader."

Silence. Deadly, terrible silence followed Gray Hawk's speech.

"I'm so sorry."

"Why should you be? It had nothing to do with you, and you did not know my father."

"Yes," she said, "I know, but I can still feel compassion for an injustice committed against you. And the killing of your father was truly an inexcusable injustice."

"*Aa*, yes, that it was. And it is one of the reasons why, when the white man comes into our territory, we kill him."

Genevieve had been gently washing her hair as he'd been speaking, and, having just dipped her head into the water, she raised it again abruptly.

"You would do that?" she asked. "You would kill a white man just like that, for no other reason than that he is in your territory?"

"We must protect ourselves."

"But—"

"The white man, when he comes to us, brings us death and misery. Many times we have asked the white man to refrain from bringing whiskey

120

to our camp. Our people go crazy with the whiskey and sometimes kill each other if they drink too much.

"The white man doesn't listen. He brings it with him anyway."

"But—"

"We ask the trapper not to kill the sacred beaver, the animal who brings to us the presence of the underwater people. But the white man doesn't listen. He comes. He destroys.

"We met the white man in peace many years ago, when he came through our land for the first time. You know these men, Lewis and Clark. But the white man who called himself Lewis tricked us with talks of peace and killed two of us without reason. The white man brought us trickery and death. Is it any wonder, then, that we protect ourselves from him? No. When we see him in our territory, we kill him."

Silence.

"Mr. Gray Hawk?" she addressed him after a while. "If I am not rescued by my own people, will you be taking me into Blackfoot territory?"

"*Aa*, yes. That is my intent."

"Will your people kill me, then, too?"

"*Saa*, no. What makes you ask such a thing?"

"I am white. I am going into your people's territory—"

"You are also a woman."

"Does that make any difference?"

He shook his head. "But being under my guardianship does."

She gulped. "Will I have your protection?"

"If white woman stops asking so many questions, yes," he snapped. "Now, come, it is time to finish your bath."

"No, that is, I...can't..." She stopped speaking and gulped, suddenly panicked. What had she done? Had she been so involved in listening to Gray Hawk that she had lost all sense? She had just washed *all* of her clothes. She now sat in the stream, completely naked, with no dry clothes to wear.

"Captive, it is time for you to come out."

"I...can't. All my clothes are wet. I...I haven't anything to put on. I..." Her voice dropped to no more than a whisper. "I guess I will have to stay here until they are dry. Either that, or..." she shivered, "...I suppose I will have to put on a wet dress."

"*Saa*, no," came his reply. "Wait."

She sank back down in the water. "What is it, Mr. Gray Hawk?"

No response.

"Mr. Gray Hawk?"

"The deerskin. I have not yet made clothing from it," he said, and she gasped. He spoke from no more than a few yards away from her. "It is as big as a robe, and you can put it on while your clothes dry. Here, I will hold it for you while you stand up."

She blinked. "No, Mr. Gray Hawk. I cannot allow that. You would see me in my altogether."

"In your what?"

She heard the humor in his voice. She didn't like it.

"Mr. Gray Hawk, I have on no clothes."

"I understand this."

"No, you don't. I washed my chemise and even my stockings. I sit here with not a single stitch of clothing upon my person. And I will certainly not rise up while you are here."

"Then," he said, a chuckle in his voice, "you will be very cold when this day is through."

"Just leave the deerskin. I can pick it up as soon as I emerge."

No response, no answer, not even the rustle of grass to note his presence.

"Mr. Gray Hawk?"

"I am here."

She bristled. "Would you leave the skin and go away?"

"*Saa*," he said simply. "No."

She looked back over her shoulder. He stood just a few feet away from her, the skin held up in front of him, his gaze on her unwavering.

"Mr. Gray Hawk," she began, "did you not promise me privacy while I bathed?"

"*Aa*, yes," said Gray Hawk. "And I gave it to you, too, until I discovered that you needed my help. I have decided now to help you, much as your slave, Robert, 'helped' me."

"Robert is no slave."

"Is he not?"

"No."

Gray Hawk shrugged. "As you say. Come, Little Captive, I will help you stay warm while your clothes dry."

"Mr. Gray Hawk, are you suggesting…?"

"You are safe from me, white woman. I do not make love to my enemy. I am only suggesting that you warm yourself in this robe."

She raised her chin. "I will not get out until you leave."

"You will be cold, then. For I will not leave until you get out."

She hit her hands against the water in frustration, spraying droplets all around her, hoping that some of the water would hit him.

"If you do that again," he said, "I will come into the water and pick you up where you are."

She bridled. "Turn your head."

Silence.

"Mr. Gray Hawk?"

"Yes?"

"Oh! You are dreadful!" She sprang up all at once, and, splashing to the shore as quickly as she could, she practically clawed her way up the bank until she reached his level. Running forward, she flopped herself into the deerskin robe.

He closed the flaps of the skin around her, surrounding her in the warmth of the robe, though there was one other problem: his arms remained around her.

"Mr. Gray Hawk?"

"Hmm?" His voice came too close to her ear.

"You may let me go now."

He nuzzled that ear.

"Mr. Gray Hawk?"

He nestled himself at her neck, and all at once a delicious sort of sensation tore over her body, making her more than aware that she wore nothing beneath the robe. The junction between her legs felt suddenly warm.

She moaned.

She hadn't meant to.

She turned toward him slightly, and suddenly his lips were on hers, the delicious taste of him upon her mouth.

That did it. She was lost.

She shifted around toward him, little knowing what she was doing, the silly robe forgotten as it fell to the ground.

Flesh met flesh as her bare breasts pushed against the hard wall of his chest.

And then the kiss deepened. His tongue met hers, and she was engulfed by him, he taking, she giving.

She'd never felt this way in her life, as if she belonged to him and he to her.

His hands came up to smooth back her hair from her cheeks, his touch firm, yet gentle and seeming to adore her. He smelled of wood, of smoke, of pure male scent.

And Genevieve whimpered.

That set him off as though he, too, couldn't get enough of her, and the kiss deepened yet again, her body swaying toward him.

Gray Hawk's Lady

His lips left hers to trail kisses down her neck, up to her ear, down one side of her neck, up the other, over and over.

She sighed as sensation exploded within her, the sound of her soft whimpers lost to her own ears.

His hands reached down over her buttocks, and she strained against their feel, wanting more, wanting...

He pulled her in closer while his lips captured hers once again.

She moaned.

He groaned.

He spoke, his breath mingling with hers. "You had best pull the robe back up and around you."

She could barely make out the words, her only thought being how wonderful he tasted.

"Little Captive, I don't know how long I can take this without going further."

She didn't answer, only pulled his head back down to her and snuggled up closer.

"White woman of no honor," he said as his lips trailed tiny kisses over her own, "if you do not back away from me now, you may never again have the chance."

She stopped.

She also didn't go away from him all at once, her lips still hovering near his. She drew back a quarter of an inch.

He breathed out deeply.

And, with their bodies pressed up closely to one another, she couldn't help but notice just how ready he was for her.

She drew in a strangled, shallow breath.

"Gray Hawk," she said, her voice barely above a whisper, "I...please don't call me that again."

"What?"

"White woman of no honor."

"You do not like it?"

"No."

"Then prove to me it is not true."

"Oh!" she muttered. "I..."

Talking was useless, especially considering the state of her undress, how closely her body was snuggled up to his, the state of his arousal.

She really had no choice but to back away, pick up the deerskin robe and pull it quickly around her.

She started to turn, to flee into the shelter of the trees, but before she was able to take a step, he drew her back into his arms.

"There is much passion between us, white woman," he said huskily, his head once again descending toward hers. "You must take the precaution of staying as far away from me as possible. I cannot say that I will be able to let you go if we get into another position like this."

He kissed her then, his lips coming down over hers, his tongue sweeping into her mouth, his scent, his taste overwhelming her.

But before she reacted to it, to him, before she again fell victim to this insane desire, she pushed away from him, and with one last look at him, at the passion so clearly etched there in his eyes, she whimpered.

Then she turned and fled.

Chapter Ten

A week passed in much the same manner as it had since their escape from the boat. She slept through the day, traveling at night; he hunted, worked and rested during the day, guiding their course by starlight. She avoided him, but then she had always avoided him. The main difference was that since their kiss, she now projected sexual meaning into every small chore he did.

It was maddening.

When she watched him light a fire, she remembered the way his hands had felt upon her face. When the firelight shone on him, lighting up his features, she recollected how handsome he had looked under the dawning of a new day.

As he carved away at a piece of wood, she recalled his firm, yet gentle caress. Watching him carry a deer for skinning, she remembered his cradling her, holding her. He spoke; she watched his lips. He ate; she stared at his tongue.

It went on and on, and Genevieve began to despair that she was becoming obsessed. In truth, unless she could get away from him soon, she might likely seek him out and ask for his kiss: a fate she could not allow to happen.

And so she found herself hoping for rescue, wishing for deliverance, longing for freedom—but most of all, *praying* for a change in attitude, an indifference toward him.

It didn't happen.

Karen Kay

But, even worse, she didn't understand her reaction. Yes, the man was handsome, desirable, even beautiful in his own exotic way. But the man was also *Indian*. A mocking, discourteous, ungracious Indian at that. He was also not a man she should be allowing liberties with her.

She had never given much thought to the sort of man who might, at last, attract her, but if she had, it wouldn't have been someone from an entirely different race, a completely alien society.

It would have been someone from her own social set, someone like her father, someone…

How could she be attracted to Gray Hawk? She could make no sense of it whatsoever.

Yet she could not deny the effect he had on her. How could she? She had to fight his allure daily.

She knew, too, from watching him, that he fared no better than she did. And though that should have brought her some measure of relief, it had the opposite effect on her: it stimulated her.

But he avoided her more now than he had ever done in the past. He no longer tied her, and the gag, which she had protested so much, had never again touched her lips. In truth, he did nothing that might lead to his having to touch her, nor get too close to her.

He said few words to her, too, and rarely did he even look her in the eye.

She knew she should thank him for his thoughtfulness in this; she even knew that she should acknowledge his strength of will. She found, though, that she could not.

She felt like cursing him for that strength…then, contrarily, wanting him…then disgusted with him all over again and finally, returning full circle, enchanted with him.

But most of all, she found herself wanting him, his touch, his embrace; and though she was certain she would have rejected him had he made even the smallest of overtures toward her, conversely, she felt slighted when he did not.

Perhaps she was bored. Maybe that was her trouble. Or perhaps she suffered from captive-itis: a condition, she was certain, wherein the captive desired, became obsessed with, and had wicked thoughts about, said captor.

She sighed, smiling and shaking her head. Whatever the problem, she hoped only for a resolution soon. Anything would do: rescue, escape, premature death, *something*. For, in truth, the current state of affairs was driving her mad.

"Why has the white woman not married?"

His question had the effect of striking out at her, so engrossed was she in her thoughts.

She had just awakened, was pushing back the deerskin robe that had been covering her, and was yawning when his question came at her like an arrow upon its mark.

She hadn't expected him to speak, had presumed they would continue much as they had this past week, each of them ignoring one another. If she had envisioned him talking to her, paying her any attention at all, she certainly wouldn't have imagined his bringing up a subject so delicate. Not when they were both trying to pretend they had no effect upon one another.

But then, she was measuring his responses by a set of English standards and sensibilities. She was no longer in England, and even if she were, Gray Hawk was not one to fuss over conventionalities.

She should have realized.

"Sir," she said, sitting up and running a hand through her hair, "I would like you to know that I have a name."

He raised an eyebrow, his only response.

"It is Genevieve, thank you very much."

He inclined his head, then repeated, "Why has the white woman not married?"

She gave him a ladylike sniff. She looked at him but didn't answer.

"White woman is beautiful. White woman is passionate. White woman is resourceful." He stared at her directly. "Why, then, is white woman not married?"

129

"What makes you think that I am not married?"

He shrugged. "I know it."

She came to her feet and, bending down, picked up the deerskin robe. She shook it out, being careful not to disturb Gray Hawk's woodworking as she did so; his crafted arrows, bows and tiny statues were all, in her opinion, works of art.

She folded the robe, and, looking around her, was amazed at the number of Indian articles they now possessed: moccasins, breechcloth, bags, belts, robes—all made by Gray Hawk—all carried, when they traveled, by her.

She shook out her hair, and, with the deerskin robe still in her arms, gazed down at him, noting again his change in clothing. No longer did he wear the black breeches and boots. Those had long ago been replaced by breechcloth and moccasins.

She didn't approve of the change, of course. Why should she? The Indian clothing exposed too much of him to her scrutiny, and his breechcloth did little to hide his natural endowment. She gazed there now.

He was altogether too handsome.

Realizing where she was looking, what she was thinking, she all at once brought her glance up to his. He grinned, and she bristled.

"Why not look at me closely, as you once instructed me to do, and find the answer to your question yourself?" she asked snidely. "Did you not teach me that you needn't ask a person about a matter when the answer is right there before you?"

"I have been trying to do this," he said, his gaze quietly resting upon her. "And I cannot discover the truth of it, though I am certain you are not married, nor are you in love with a man. What I cannot understand is why not."

"Well, you needn't expect an answer, since I don't believe I gave you permission to ask me such a personal question."

He just stared at her. "I need no permission."

"And I need not answer."

She turned thereupon and started to walk away, but Gray Hawk was too quick for her. Springing to his feet, he caught her and locked her in his arms, bringing her up closely against him.

It was the first time he had held her or touched her since that day one week ago.

She shut her eyes briefly, her reaction to his nearness sweeping through her like a tornado of fire.

He brought his head down toward hers. Again he asked, this time with his lips pressed closely to her ear, "Why are you not married?"

She shrugged out of his embrace, and, though every fiber in her skin felt as if it were on fire, she held her head high, her chin out. "That is my affair."

"And I am making it mine," he said, stepping forward and staring at her as though she were quarry. "I ask you again, why?"

She shook back her hair, pushing it out and away from her face. She glared at him. She said nothing.

"Is the white woman running away?" He moved a step forward. "Is she promised to someone she cannot abide? Or does she merely wish a little excitement before she must settle into marriage?"

"Why, none of those." She took a step backward.

"If she wishes to make love without marriage, I can surely accommodate her." He pressed forward. "Is this the reason she has come into Blackfoot country? To play the part she desires without others within her society discovering her transgressions? The white trappers who captured me and brought me to you said this was so. They jumped me from behind. Did you know that?"

She shook her head. She backed away still farther. "No, I—"

"They knifed me in the side, and while two held me down, another one kicked me. And all the while they told me the things that you wanted, things you would do to me, telling me that you would have me this way because you could do no such thing in your own culture, not if you wished

131

to live there in peace. At every kick, they told me what you would do to me. Sexual things. Sensual things. Very stimulating things."

Her eyes wide, she took one more step backward.

"I thought these things that they told me were true. I could see no reason why they would not be…that is, until several days ago. And then it came to me that you had never exhibited any sexual overtures toward me when you held me captive, nor even more recently, when I held you close and you could have had me any way that you desired. And this, despite your own passion.

"It was this," he continued, "more than anything else, that caused me to realize those trappers lied. So now I find myself looking at you in a new way, and I find that I cannot discover why the white woman would come into Blackfoot country. I thought I understood this woman. I did not like her, but I understood her. I no longer do. Most of all, however, I wonder: if the white woman is not the sort of woman who desires many favors from many men, why then is this woman not married?"

He moved forward; she backed away.

She said, "You…you believed that I…?"

He nodded.

"How could you?"

"I did not know you."

"But—"

"Your trappers took me captive. It all fit, or so I thought."

"It wasn't true."

"None of it?"

She shook her head.

"Then why," he repeated, "why are you not married?"

"I…I…you… I do not have the time."

He frowned. He stopped. "I do not understand."

"My father. All my life I have traveled with my father. I have devoted myself to him, to his work. I am his assistant. I do the same work he does. I help him. I have no time for anything else, anyone else."

"And your father allows this?"

"Why would he not?"

"When he dies, what happens to you then, if you have no husband?"

"I..." Of course, she had thought of this once or twice, but she had never seriously considered the possibility. Her father had always been spry, young for his age, full of life and energy...at least, until recently.

Said Gray Hawk, "I think you should consider marriage."

"And I think you should mind your own business."

"What is this 'business' that I should mind it?"

"You know what I mean."

He smiled. "Has the white woman escaped her father and come into Blackfoot country looking for a husband? If so, I should tell her that I am not available."

"As if I would... I thought you were not married."

"So am I not."

"Then why are you not 'available'?"

"I told you once why this is so. Think back, Little Captive, to what I said to you in the past."

She lifted her head, jutting out her chin. "Why should I when I am not interested?"

He took another step forward. "Are you not?"

"No."

She might as well have waved a red flag at him. Without warning he reached out and pulled her into his arms, his head swooping down over hers.

His lips dangerously close to her own, he said, "Tell me again that you are not interested."

She glared up at him. "I am not interested. I could not care less about your marital state."

He smiled then, but she didn't have time to ponder its meaning.

He said, "Your breath is so sweet when you say that."

And then he captured her lips with his own, his tongue sweeping forward to tantalize her.

She pushed at his chest; he pulled her in closer.

She pounded on his shoulders; he took her hands in his own.

His lips left hers briefly to trail kisses over to her ear, down her neck, up to her eyes, back to her lips, his tongue tracing their outline, then to the other side of her face, the action repeated.

"Gen-e-vee."

It was the first time he'd ever said her name. It was the first time she'd ever heard her name whispered with such a note of passion, the sound of it foreign, titillating.

His lips hovered over her ear; then he swept down over her neck, his lips, his tongue kissing every single part of her skin.

It was all too much. It was her undoing.

She shut her eyes as crazed yearning swept through her.

"Gray Hawk," she murmured, little knowing she'd said anything. Her lips seeking his, she turned her head. She touched his lips with her own.

Explosion. It was the only way to describe what happened next.

She leaned in closer, he bent down farther.

They met. They kissed, their tongues seeking each other's as though paying homage to one another.

She gave, her whole being engulfed by him. He took.

His sweet taste filled her mouth; his scent, masculine and musky, enveloped her. His touch, firm yet gentle, aroused her to a point where she had no idea of time or place.

Her arms went around him, and even as he caressed her back down to her buttocks, pulling her in closer, she stroked her hands up and down his back — his magnificent, bare back.

The imprint of his sexuality pressed against her stomach and she nestled up closer to it, glorying in the fact that only a piece of rawhide separated him from her.

And all the while, his lips had never left her own, his tongue stroking inside her mouth, in and out, as though only in this way could they obtain pleasure.

She shivered, desire racing through her blood.

She wanted him. She wanted his bare skin against her own. She wanted more of him, every part of him. And she would give him all that she had to give.

She swooned, arching her back and pressing her breasts to him in open invitation.

His lips left hers, and she smiled lazily up at him.

He said, "Tell me now, Gen-e-vee, that you are not interested in me as a husband."

He shouldn't have spoken. He shouldn't have said a word. He should have just taken what he wanted, anything he desired...

But he didn't. He broke the spell. And worse, he'd made her feel terribly wrong.

Her reaction was strong, if not immediate. And she realized right away what she had allowed to happen.

Embarrassment overwhelmed her.

She gasped. She'd wanted him, yes; she would have made love to him too, without even thinking about it, so lost had she been in his arms. In truth, she'd been his for the taking.

It shouldn't have been. She should have resisted him. But how could she? She would have had to have been a saint to turn him away.

She'd not been able to help herself. Emotion had encompassed her, emotion more forceful than anything she'd ever experienced. She'd always been attracted to him, more so lately. But this?

He'd held her, simply held her, but the sensuality that had coursed through her veins made her realize she'd been awaiting this moment for weeks. And she wouldn't have denied him anything. Not when the intoxicating taste of him was upon her mouth.

She moaned as the truth hit her. She had *feelings* for him—powerful, strong feelings for him.

But with his words and his misplaced humor, all that potency and wonderful, pent-up emotion was turning on him. It was shifting on her, too, her passions mixing up, becoming unsteady and crashing in on her as though she stood in the middle of a lumberjack's forest.

It was all too much for her.

"Oh!" She pushed at his chest at last. "How dare you!"

He grinned. "Easily."

"Oh!" she said again, stepping back. She threw her hair over her shoulders and stuck out her chin. She said all at once, almost in self-defense, "I don't want you."

He raised an eyebrow. He put his arms over his chest. He smirked.

"How could I want you?" she went on, her words and feelings spontaneous, any affinity she'd felt toward him changing quickly to the opposite, to malice. And she could little control herself when she said, "You are a savage, Gray Hawk, a heathen, an *Indian,* and that makes you no better than an animal in my eyes. If ever I were to look for a husband, it would never be among a member of a different race of men, I can assure you. I would sooner die."

The atmosphere around them grew suddenly cool and very quiet.

She should have taken heed.

She didn't. She couldn't. Tender emotion, turned ugly, now raged within her, feeding on itself, tugging at her, dictating to her, holding her in its grip.

"Tell me," she mocked, "how would you deign to support me if we married? Where would we live? How would you even think to raise your head in my society, where it is believed as a fact that the Indian is no more human than a wild animal?" She glared at him. "Do not mistake my words, Gray Hawk," she said, oblivious to the sting of what her words might do to him. "I would never look to you for a husband."

Had Gray Hawk been a lesser man, he might have taken her by force at that moment, if only to prove his point.

He could have. All he would have had to do was kiss her again.

But Gray Hawk was not the animal she accused him of being.

Yes, he might mock her, he might tease, but Gray Hawk knew himself to be a gentleman, within the true meaning of that word. Gray Hawk was chivalrous to a flaw.

He was Pikuni. He was Blackfeet.

He could no more have taken sexual advantage of this woman, despite the fact that she was white, than he could have killed his own mother.

And so Gray Hawk did the only thing he could do.

He grinned. He smirked. He raised an eyebrow and said, "We will see, little Gen-e-vee. We will see."

"Is that a challenge?"

Again he smiled, and, turning his back on her, began to walk away. But before he left her completely, before he began his daily chores, he looked back over his shoulder at her. And he grinned as he said, "Perhaps."

Chapter Eleven

What on earth had gotten into her?

How could she have said such things to him?

Genevieve might have been many things, but cruel was not a word that anyone who knew her would have used to describe her. It never had been. She cared too much about the welfare of others to have earned such a label.

Then how could she have said such things to him? Her words, her meanings, were, by anybody's definition, brutal. And whether they represented the true "thinking" of her society or not, it wasn't up to her to speak them.

She fretted over it the entire evening. She wanted to say something to lessen the damage she'd done by her careless words, wanted anything to ease it, but she couldn't bring herself to do so.

To bring up such a topic now would only stab him again with the realities of what she'd said. And she didn't want to do that. She had caused enough damage.

Genevieve focused her attention on something else. She gazed at the curling hills of the prairie, which lay all around her. Dusk had brought the hues of pink, orange and red to the sky, and the colors were, even now, reflecting themselves upon the hills, the sky's shimmering tints of color painting the brown carpets on those hills as though their rolling character were a canvas.

It was one of the most beautiful sights she had ever seen.

The air was cool, fresh and invigorating, and the wind, which seemed incessant, blew locks of her hair across her face. She inhaled the air, fragrant with sage, and, shutting her eyes, imagined she was at home in St. Louis.

Overhead a nighthawk squawked, breaking into her reverie, and she opened her eyes to the reality of where she was.

It wasn't so bad.

She sat beside a smokeless campfire, a prelude to traveling. She'd even come to think of this time, this meal that they shared at this time of day, as their breakfast, though it must have been close to seven in the evening.

Gray Hawk, she noted, sat across from her, quietly singing, another thing she'd become used to with him. He sang almost constantly when they were in camp—strange songs, with little melody that she could discern, and all in a minor key. She remembered once asking him about the meaning of the songs, knowing this data would make an interesting contribution to her father's works, but Gray Hawk's answer had been so vague, she had chosen to stop trying, and to simply listen and enjoy.

He also chipped away at a stone, making the object into a deadly point. And this was another thing that amazed her: he was resourceful. It was the only word she could think of to explain it. From the hides of animals, the branches of bushes, from trees and stones and the very earth itself, they suddenly had many serviceable items. All handmade by Gray Hawk.

She had tried to help; in fact, she did, her job being to skin the animals he brought into camp. But that was all that she did. She didn't seem to possess the energy or the know-how to do more than this, and Gray Hawk, as though sensing it, hadn't pressed her.

"Gray Hawk," she asked, interrupting his singing, "have you noticed something odd?"

He glanced up at her.

"I have been thinking…"

He had discontinued his song.

"Isn't it odd that we don't run across more animals than we do?"

He shrugged. "This is good."

139

"But I remember seeing so many different animals roaming these plains as I looked out at them from the steamboat. I have seen some deer, some elk, buffalo, and I hear the wolves at night, but not much else. Why are we not running into more of them when we travel?"

"Because," said Gray Hawk, "I am a good scout. I do not want our path to come upon a dangerous animal."

"Dangerous?" She laughed, her tone mocking. "If I remember correctly, I saw some elk from the boat, and a buffalo or two. They were big, Gray Hawk, but hardly dangerous."

He looked as though he were about to say something, but he didn't. Instead, he grinned. "Then you have never experienced the grizzly bear or a pack of wolves. These animals would not only kill you, they would do so slowly and painfully. And you must not yet have experienced the buffalo bull in mating season, who will gore anyone who comes close to him or to his mate. And of course, there is the *ca ca boo*."

"The what?"

"The *ca ca boo*."

She gave him a puzzled glance. "What's a *ca ca boo*?"

"It is a very dangerous animal. It is half animal and half lizard. It has fur to keep it warm, but scales and gills for swimming under water."

"I've never heard of it."

He sat forward. "It is as big as the trees, maybe bigger; it lives at the bottom of lakes, and…it is particularly fond of women."

She snorted, shaking her head.

"You do not believe me."

"Of course not. The trappers and traders would have told me about such an animal."

"You think so?"

"Of course," she said, although she gazed up at Gray Hawk to judge the truth of what he said from his expression.

"During the day," continued Gray Hawk, "the *ca ca boo* lives at the bottom of lakes, and if one is so foolish as to swim in a lake where one exists, it means certain death. But it is most dangerous at night, when it comes out of the water to look for women."

"Oh, pooh!"

He motioned toward her. "You go walking by yourself at night. You see for yourself if what I am saying is true or not."

"I don't believe you."

He shrugged, jerking his head to the left. "It is safe for a woman to walk the plains at night only if she is with a man. You see, the *ca ca boo* hates men, for the *ca ca boo* cannot defend himself against men on the land—only in the water. But women," he shook his head, "he will take them back to his home in the lake."

"That's the silliest thing I've ever—"

"Go on—go walking by yourself at night. You will see for yourself. But remember, a woman is lucky if the *ca ca boo* eats her all up. It is better than a watery home, for he makes slaves of all women."

"Do stop," she said. "I want no more of these fairy tales."

"What is a fairy tale?"

"A story that is not true."

He grinned. "Go see." He gestured off to the hills. "Go take a walk. I do not hold you here."

"You do too."

He looked taken aback. "Where are the ropes that bind you? Where is the gag to make you cease your prattle? You have been free for a long time. Go ahead and leave."

She took a deep breath. "You try my patience, Gray Hawk."

"How is this so?" He made a great show of looking all around their camp. "I see no ties. I see no bindings. How do you say that I do not speak the truth?"

She shook her head. "Where would I go, Gray Hawk? If I knew my way back to St. Louis, I would leave. But I don't."

"I will point the way."

"Yes, and I will get lost and I know it. Do not make a mistake, Gray Hawk. You hold me captive by my own lack of knowledge."

"That is for you to say."

"Would you stop it?"

"What?"

"You are baiting me, first with the talk of a dangerous animal that doesn't exist and now with chatter of freedom, without giving me the means to actually strive for it."

He gestured off toward the distance. "Go ahead." He pointed to the west, toward the sunset. "Go in the direction where you keep the sunset to your right side. If you do that, and if you follow the river, you will eventually find this St. Louis. I do not keep you."

"I would get killed."

"Why do you say that? Are there not only 'big' animals here, not dangerous ones?"

"Now you make fun of me."

He grinned. "Yes, I do. It is unkind of me. I will stop."

A moment of silence passed.

In due time, Lady Genevieve asked, "Then you really do protect me when you walk ahead of me?"

He nodded. "*Aa*, yes, it is so."

"You are not trying to make me feel inferior?"

"*Saa*, no, it did not occur to me to do this."

"Why?"

He drew his brows together, puzzled. He asked, "Why...what? Why do I not try to make you feel this...lesser?"

"No, Gray Hawk, why do you protect me? I thought I was your captive. I thought you hated me."

He glanced at her as though she had lost all sense. "You are my captive, but I do not hate you." He smiled. "Perhaps once I did hate you, but that lasted only a short while. I protect you now because you are female."

"Yes...?"

"You are weaker, and so need me to—"

"If I am so weak, why do you make *me* carry all the supplies? In my culture, a true gentleman would never stoop to such a thing. And a gentleman would never walk ahead of a lady."

He lifted his shoulders. "I do not understand. Are your men cowards?"

"Cowards? Of course not. Why, I never—I—"

"To the Indian," said Gray Hawk, "if I did not do these things, if I were to carry the goods for a woman, if I walked behind her, making her lead the way, I would insult her. It would be as to say she was not worth protecting."

"But I—"

"There are many things on the prairie that could attack an unwary traveler. A wrong step could mean a rattlesnake bite. A bad or careless path could find us in the way of a grizzly. If we were to come upon trouble, would you rather I be prepared for it with weapons in my hands, or would you rather I have my arms full of supplies and be unable to protect us?"

She opened her mouth to speak, but said nothing.

"If we are to survive," Gray Hawk went on, "I must be constantly on the alert to my environment and to anything that might cause us trouble—"

"Wait." She held up a hand. "I'm not certain that you aren't making this all up."

He sent her a disdainful glance. "Do you say that I lie?"

"Not lie," she said, "exactly." Her voice trailed off. "Mr. Gray Hawk, while I can understand why you might walk ahead of me out here—that makes some sense to me—I am at a loss, still, to comprehend why you make me carry all the supplies. I'm not too certain, Gray Hawk, but I think you might be exaggerating, perhaps to get even with me with tall tales of protection, of animals. I think—"

"Would you rather we run into a grizzly bear and have me unable to fight it because my hands are full of clothing?"

"No, of course not. That's not the point I'm trying to make. I—"

"I must travel unencumbered so that I can defend us against danger, against the wild animals—"

"An animal like the *ca ca boo*?"

He stopped. He grinned. He shook his head and said, "Especially the *ca ca boo*."

She smiled back at him. She still didn't believe him, at least not about his reasons for making her carry their supplies, and especially not about the *ca ca boo*.

Still, that night as they made their way across the moonlit prairie, she was glad to see that, unencumbered, Gray Hawk stood ready to defend them, and as she gazed about her, she wondered if perhaps there were a half-furry, half-scaled lizard creature just waiting at the foot of the next hill.

Waiting for her.

It was not something she wished to put to the test.

****

"I want to go and see my father. Won't you take me?"

No answer.

She glanced ahead of her toward Gray Hawk, awaiting his answer.

Several days, perhaps another week, had passed since she had last talked with Gray Hawk about the plains animals. She had hoped to approach him again on the subject, making note that this would add authenticity to her father's book, but the subject had never been broached again, and she had found other things drawing her attention...other things like Gray Hawk himself.

She grimaced as she looked at the man now. Tall and sleek, his walk resembling the prowl of a wary panther, he trod ahead of her, nonchalantly presenting her with the enticing view of his backside.

She frowned. She should look away, and she knew it. But she didn't seem to be able to do it. Or perhaps she just didn't want to. Whatever the reason, she found herself studying the man rather than ignoring him.

He paced ahead of her, walking as though with restrained passion, as if he had to rein in his emotions. And though she knew he was merely being careful of where he stepped, she couldn't help but be reminded of other things about him: of the warmth of his arms around her; of his foreign features, of how he had looked under the golden rays of twilight, the dim light throwing his face into shadows and highlights; of his kiss and how it felt to have his lips pressed against her own, his taste so seductive, so masculine-sweet. And it was all she could do at present to try to focus her attention elsewhere.

It didn't work, of course. The more she tried to put him out of mind, the more she pulled him— mental images of him—into view.

And as if that weren't enough, nature, it appeared, also conspired against her.

There were certain things she did not want to notice about him, things that made her heart skip beats, things that made her stomach turn flip-flops. And nature seemed intent on pushing these observations into her view.

For instance, take his clothing—or rather, lack thereof.

He wore only breechcloth and moccasins. How was she supposed to look away from him when his clothing left all that skin to her perusal? When the prairie breezes blew back his dark hair, allowing her brief glimpses of his muscular back? When even his quiver full of arrows, which fell almost diagonally across his back, gave no clue that it would ever cover over the power suggested there by his muscles?

No, nature presented her with a problem: how to look away.

Her gaze fell lower.

She grimaced. Here was yet another part of him that she found impossible to ignore.

The breechcloth. It revealed more of his tight rear than it covered, and she found her gaze too often centered upon that area, wondering how it would feel beneath her fingertips, how it would look naked, how it would…

She pulled up her thoughts. What was she thinking?

She *had* to reign in her thoughts. She *had* to keep from remembering him, the passion of his response, the hard-rock feel of his chest, the tender sensation of his touch, the…

She shook herself physically.

Enough!

Perhaps her problem stemmed from the fact that they now traveled by day, Gray Hawk having announced only yesterday that they had at last stepped foot into the territory of the Pikuni.

He had been elated. She'd never felt more depressed.

It meant she was even farther from home. It meant any pursuing party from the steamboat would not likely catch up with them, there being very few white men willing to risk the threat of appearing in Blackfoot country alone.

But it also meant that she had to march behind Gray Hawk by day, this presenting her with a new predicament: how to do so and keep her sanity.

"Gray Hawk?"

Again, no response.

"Gray Hawk, won't you please reconsider and take me back to St. Louis?"

"White woman talks when she should listen."

"Gray Hawk, I…listen to what? You are not speaking and I—"

He had stopped, and she ran straight into him.

He held up a hand, signaling her to silence.

She wanted to ask what the problem was, but she dared not. He was suddenly too quiet, his eyes narrowed.

Something was wrong.

She took a glance around her. She saw nothing, but then she didn't know what to look for or how to listen.

They were traveling in a place where fir trees, abounded. The trees were large, and, looking up, she was awed by the natural canopy they created overhead.

The path they had been walking was easier now, too, although a bit noisier since they trod over dry pine needles that crackled with each step they took. She had thought it seemed safer here than out walking over the open prairie.

Now she wondered.

Gray Hawk motioned her away from him and down, behind a large bush.

He stayed out in front, positioning himself behind a tree.

She fidgeted, and again his hand came out to motion her to silence.

What was it? An animal? Other Indians? Warriors?

She began to fret. All this time she hadn't really considered what would happen to her if Gray Hawk were injured...perhaps even killed.

She suddenly realized, however, that as invincible as he seemed, Gray Hawk was, like her, flesh and blood. And although she hadn't been happy about following him, at least he was a predictable companion.

What would happen to her if he were killed? What if this were an enemy tribe of Indians? What if their numbers were too great for Gray Hawk? What then?

At least Gray Hawk had been kind to her...in his own way. At least he was sympathetic toward her...a little.

She closed her eyes. She held her breath.

There was more.

She didn't want him to die.

There, it was out. She'd grown to...well, to like him a little, and the thought of his leaving her, of his never again speaking to her, even if their talks did resemble a sparring match, was most unbearable.

She didn't know why and she didn't know what had come over her, but at the moment she didn't care. All she knew was that Gray Hawk had to survive.

She looked around her at the seemingly quiet environment. Somewhere out there was danger.

Somewhere out there, Gray Hawk would have to confront an enemy.

Somehow she had to keep him alive.

Kneeling down, she began to pray.

Chapter Twelve

*G*ray Hawk had been among the white people long enough to learn some of their more choice, colorful words. He silently said some of them now.

He cursed at his own stupidity, at his nonchalance. Having crossed over into his own territory, he had relaxed his guard. And he hadn't heard, hadn't sensed, another party, hadn't been expecting any, until they were almost upon him.

He might pay for his lack of diligence now.

These were not his own, the Pikuni, who approached him, nor were they Indian.

The lack of care as to where the foot fell, the rattling of bushes, the unconcerned talk, the smell of unwashed flesh—whoever it was stood upwind—all led to one conclusion: the white man.

What were white men doing in Blackfoot territory? What did they want? What were their intentions?

Were they the "Northern White Men" from Saskatchewan, those friendly toward the Pikuni? Or were they the newer, more aggressive "Big Knives," the Americans, famous for their lying and cheating ways toward the Indian?

And if they were the Big Knives, were they looking for the white woman?

He didn't think so, having lost the party that had first pursued them many days, almost one full moon, ago.

149

But if not them, who, then?

He waited. He was at a disadvantage.

He had just recently made his bow, and he hadn't been able to obtain his favorite wood, the ash, for it. He had woven strips of sinew and rawhide around the bow to make it stronger, but it was still too soft, having been fashioned from the willow.

His arrows, too, had only bone or wooden points, not steel. And he had no gun, not even the cheap trading-post issue.

He was clearly handicapped in this situation.

And the woman—her response was unpredictable. Once she saw white men, would she sing out to them? Would she betray him?

He cursed himself for becoming at ease around her; he damned himself for neither tying nor gagging her. If their positions were reversed, Gray Hawk knew which side *he* would take, and it wouldn't have been what he hoped she would do now.

Luckily, the white men didn't know he was here...yet.

He could wait them out, hiding from them, for they were not wise enough to have already spotted his presence.

But he knew this wasn't a good plan. The white woman would betray him. Besides, once the Big Knives picked up his trail, even if they were several miles back, they could easily overtake him if they desired it.

Better to confront them now.

This decision made, he waited until the enemy came into sight. Then Gray Hawk stepped away from the tree, into the open and into their line of view. With his senses alert and his knees quivering, as though ready for action, he waited.

Still, it was several moments before the trappers became aware of his presence.

There were four of them. Each went for his gun— the kind, Gray Hawk noted and as he had expected—that was the cheap, trading-post-issue rifle.

Gray Hawk held up his hand, a sign of peace. He waited for their understanding.

It didn't come. Either the white men were stupid, didn't understand the sign, or just didn't care. They still held their rifles pointed at him. And casually, as though he confronted such men every day, Gray Hawk said, "I am from the nation of the Blackfoot, the Pikuni. You are treading on country that is not yours. This is a warning. Big Knives are not welcome in Blackfoot country."

"Did ye hear that?"

No answer.

"Spoke English, 'e did."

"What's a Big Knife?"

Said Gray Hawk back to them, "What are you doing in this, Blackfoot country?"

All four men, guns still pointed smirked.

"'E says hits 'is country, gen-teel-mon," said one, ignoring Gray Hawk's question. "What do ye say we teach t'is varmint a lesson?"

"Wait, you bloom'n fools. What if thar be more'n 'im? Did you ever think o' that?"

Another said to Gray Hawk, "Whar be t' rest o' yer party?"

Gray Hawk didn't answer, didn't move, didn't even let his features betray his thoughts.

"Answer up, ye 'eathen."

"Careful, Charlie, where thar's one, thar's bound t' be more." Then, to Gray Hawk, "Whar are t' others? What are you do'n 'ere?"

Gray Hawk's features didn't alter one bit as he said, "This is *my* country."

One smiled; then, waving his rifle at Gray Hawk, said, "Well, that don't quite cut it 'ere. Thar's four o' us 'n only one o' you. Answer m' question, 'eathen."

Gray Hawk stood silent, unmoving, seemingly at ease, yet he was ready and in position to grasp his bow and arrows.

One of the men cocked his rifle.

151

"Answer, now. Whar are t' others?"

"Shoot 'im, Charlie, shoot 'im."

"Yea," the man licked his lips, "let's kill o'selves a' Injun."

Silence.

A gun fired.

Gray Hawk dodged, and, pulling arrows from his quiver, shot off a series of missiles faster than a man could load a gun.

One shot, a miss.

Another arrow struck, landing in the man's arm, narrowly missing his heart. He yelled.

Another made its mark. One down.

More yells. Two men jumped forward, grabbing Gray Hawk and wrestling with him, trying to knock him to the ground.

But though they were big and burly, they were also drunk. They were no match for Gray Hawk.

Gray Hawk trilled out his war cry and broke free, plunging his knife into the side of one of them.

A yell. "He cut m'."

"Hold 'im, Charlie."

"Hi's tryin'."

"Hi gots 'im. Shoot!"

Gray Hawk wrestled. He had to break loose. He had one arm almost free.

A shot. A miss.

And as it occurred to Gray Hawk that these men would never win a shooting contest, both men plunged at him, kicking him off balance and knocking him to the ground.

"Shoot 'im, Charlie, shoot 'im."

Gray Hawk wrestled one, broke free and jumped on top of the man. The other pulled him off from behind, sticking a knife at Gray Hawk's neck.

"Shoot 'im. Now!"

"Yea, shoot 'im."

A gun cocked. A deadly silence.

"No!" The white woman suddenly jumped up, out from behind her cover of bushes.

"Lordy be."

"Gawd almighty."

Gray Hawk glared at her, and, watching her look around, he saw that she trembled.

He scowled then, but she didn't see, and Gray Hawk thought he would have gladly wrung her neck at that moment.

She had come to help the white men. She had leapt out from her cover, clearly anxious to see him die. And this, thought Gray Hawk, when he had almost gained the advantage over these men.

"Lordy, it be a white woman."

The knife dug deeper into Gray Hawk's neck. The man said, "Now what be a' Injun doin' with a white woman?"

"He was helping me to return home," came the response.

Silence.

Then, all at once, all three men laughed.

"Thar'll be a story t' bring 'ome, boy, now, won't hit?"

Gray Hawk stared at her—actually glared. What was she doing?

"Gentlemen, I am Lady Genevieve Rohan, recently come to this country with my father, Viscount Winfred Rohan, the famous author and anthropologist."

"A' Hi's the queen o' t' Nile."

All three men cackled.

"I had come here," she crept slowly forward as she spoke, "to help my father with his project, and as you can see, I became terribly lost. This gentleman, this Indian, found me and is returning me home. I would appreciate your letting him go."

153

"Now ain't tha' pretty?"

Two of the white men snickered.

Gray Hawk scowled at her, not understanding her. What game did she play?

"Why would Hi let t' 'eathen go, ma'am? This Injun varmint done kill't m' friend—"

"In self-defense."

"Don't matter. Hi's afraid 'e'll 'ave t' pay."

With the gun pointed at him, the knife at his neck, Gray Hawk struggled to get out of the hold. The knife cut into him—how much, he didn't know.

He heard a gunshot, then another.

He was free, the shots having hit one of the men who'd held him. The other man backed away.

Two down.

Swearing, cursing, the one who held the gun glared first at him, then at the woman.

The woman? Gen-e-vee. She held one of those cheap rifles in her arms, pointed not at him—but *at the white man.*

Gray Hawk gazed at her, momentarily frozen. What was this? Had the white woman really come to *his* defense?

He looked around him, at the men on the ground, at the obvious evidence.

It would seem so.

Had he misjudged her?

He'd hated her, sought revenge upon her, desired her. But he'd never trusted her, nor had he ever thought she would trust him.

Was there more to her character than he'd supposed?

Amazed, he watched as she motioned the remaining man who'd held him back toward the first white man.

This was too much for Gray Hawk to comprehend all at once. He snapped at her, "What do you do?"

"I'm saving your life."

"That is not what I meant."

"Isn't it?"

"*Saa*, no. You were supposed to stay under cover."

"And watch you die?"

"Do I look dead?"

She spared him a glance. "Almost."

"Have you thought what you do? These men are white. Why do you not go with them? They would take you to your St. Louis."

"Would they?" She smirked. "Somehow I doubt it. But it wouldn't matter. Do you think I could watch them kill you?"

"And why could you not?"

"Because I—"

"Ah, ma'am, Hi hates t' interrupt yer interestin' talk with yer Injun friend, but why's you 'oldin t' gun on us? We's yer own kin."

Irritated, she glanced toward the white men. "Be quiet."

"Gen-e-vee." Gray Hawk grinned. "And here I believed the white woman wanted nothing more than my scalp within her hand."

"Ma'am? Ma'am?" one of the men piped up. "What does ye do? 'Ave ye thought about it? This Injun 'ere will kill ye as easy as 'e talks t' ye."

"Be quiet; I—"

It all happened so quickly then, there wasn't a moment to think.

One of the white men suddenly produced a knife, throwing it toward the woman.

Gray Hawk pushed her out of the way while at the same time picking up the knife, which had harmlessly hit the ground. He threw the weapon back at the man in reflex.

He hit his mark.

Karen Kay

The man fell.

The fourth man, the last one still standing, had rushed forward. Gray Hawk met his advance. He wrestled with him for a moment, but the man had the advantage; Gray Hawk having just thrown the knife had put himself off balance.

The man succeeded in knocking Gray Hawk down and now pointed a gun right at him.

Another gunshot sounded.

The white man looked up, startled. All at once, he fell.

Gray Hawk sent a puzzled glance beside him, his scan taking in the fallen man, the gunshot wound and the man's obviously deceased state.

He swung his gaze back around to the white woman.

She held a smoking gun. She said, "My father made sure I was an excellent shot."

Gray Hawk rose to his feet. He came right up to her and took the gun from her hands. He said, "I am very glad of that. I am also very happy you are on my side."

"I have never killed a man before," she said.

Gray Hawk nodded. "It is never an easy thing to do. You are very brave. I honor you."

"Brave?" Her voice caught on a sob. "Honor?" Turning away from him, she hiccupped. Then she gasped. "I don't think so." And so saying, she ran from the scene as though the spirit wind itself were pushing her forward.

Gray Hawk watched her go, and as he did so, it crossed his mind that he did not understand this woman whom he had alternately hated and desired. And it came to him that he had greatly underestimated her.

Narrowing his eyes, he thought about it for a moment. She had this moment saved his life. She, who appeared to hate him more than any other being alive. She, who couldn't wait to be gone from his presence. She, who did not want to accompany him.

He said then, as though to the wind, "You, little Gen-e-vee, are very brave, indeed."

****

He supposed this had been the start of his change of viewpoint, the beginning of his state of indecision.

He no longer knew what to do with the white woman.

No matter his feelings for her in the past, he could no longer look upon Genevieve as his slave, nor could he pretend that she was the object of his revenge.

Not any longer. Not when she had come to his defense, when she had saved his life.

She had now come to that exalted status where he admired her. She hadn't wanted to kill a man; it had made her sick to do so, yet she had done it—to save *him*, an Indian, a man whom she professed to dislike.

What she had done was a braver act than that of a man who went to war to kill or to be killed: braver because it was not what she'd wanted to do; braver because she had set aside her own fears—and for *him*.

Her sacrifice was not something he could put aside easily.

So what was he to do about her? It was a dilemma.

What he had planned for her—to make her a slave, to seek his revenge by bringing her to ridicule within his camp—was no longer possible, nor even desirable.

But if not that, then what? What was he to do about her?

He had to bring her home with him; he had to bring her into his camp, but how to do it without...

If he took her into his village without some satisfactory explanation for her being with him, he would make her the object of ridicule—for in his culture, a woman could not spend time alone with a man and retain her reputation.

And while this scenario had at one time appealed to him as a different means of revenge, it no longer did.

He could take her back to this St. Louis, he supposed, since he had begun to realize it was no idle problem she was trying to solve. Whatever it was that had brought her into this country alone had the power to ruin her life. This he had come to understand.

But to his own way of thinking, to take her back to her home would be to accept defeat for himself.

Wasn't it true? Wasn't it what he had observed in his own, in others' camps, that when a man takes a woman captive, he keeps her...captive? To do anything else would be to label himself a coward. It was the way of things.

He couldn't likely do that.

Of course, there was one other step he could take, one he was reluctant to make, if only because of who he was and who she was.

He could make her his wife.

He snorted.

It was a foolish solution. He was not ready for marriage. He did not want it or a wife.

And though he knew that one day he would find a woman and settle her into his tepee, it was not a step he wished to take now, with a white woman.

He was too fond of the warrior life, too fond of the widows in his camp, too fond of the easy lifestyle of little responsibility.

No, he wasn't desperate enough about the white woman's situation to contemplate making her his wife—although, he thought, gazing over toward her, it did have the appeal of appeasing his attraction toward her.

He jerked his head to the left and scowled. What was he thinking? Once he returned home, there would be a number of women who would be only too glad to accommodate his needs. He didn't have to concern himself about one skinny white woman.

And yet...

Perhaps if he weren't so desperate to ensure the welfare of his mother and sisters, he might have turned around right then and catered to the white woman's wishes, taking her back to St. Louis. Maybe if he weren't so worried.

But he *was* desperate; he *was* worried.

Without enough food and clothing, those he loved most would not be able to make it through the long northern winter of Blackfoot country.

He had to ensure their welfare.

But that didn't mean that he would like what he was going to have to do to the woman...Gen-e-vee.

Many men would then seek her out if he brought her into camp unmarried; these men would believe her to be a loose woman of no honor. And it wouldn't matter how much he defended her. Words would not circumvent actions, and she had spent time with him, alone — unchaperoned.

He stared at her now as she bent over the task of skinning an elk. Slender to a fault, she looked as though a good gale would snatch her away. Her reddish brown hair, he noted for the umpteenth time, was an unusual shade, as were her brown eyes, which at times seemed to match the shade of her hair, appearing more tannish-red than brown.

She had refused the Indian clothing he had offered her, and she still wore the green white–man's dress, now tattered and torn almost beyond recognition. It was a problem, her dress. The bosom of it came down too low, and, in the state of its disrepair, had her practically bursting from its confinement.

She was small, yet full-breasted, and he wondered just what those mounds of flesh would feel like in his hands. In truth, he dreamed about it.

He wouldn't press her, though, to find out. The debt of gratitude he now owed her would not allow him to approach her in a sexual, suggestive way. Not any longer.

But this wasn't all he noticed about her.

Her hair gleamed bright and shining under the sunlight. And it was all he could do to look elsewhere.

She had given in to combing the mane of it with the brush he had made out of twigs tied with rawhide. At present, she allowed the full locks of it to flow smooth and full around her face. Sometimes she looked as though a warm, glowing sunset surrounded her.

He shook his head. What was he to do with her?

He didn't know. He just didn't know.

But he had to decide fast. He had precious few days left before he would come upon his own village.

He watched her, trying to read her thoughts. But because he no longer played a game of chase with her, he found himself less interested in breaking into the privacy of her thoughts.

He admired her, too. She had learned to skin an animal quickly, just as she had taken to smoking the meat, even to cooking. She was bright and intelligent, and he wondered that he had never credited her, nor others of her race, with much intellect or humanity.

In truth, he had never been given reason to until now. He had considered the white man a coarse, unrefined and ill-mannered race.

After all, what did the white man know of this country? Very little that Gray Hawk could see.

The white man became lost more times than he could find his way; he knew nothing of woodworking, of the making of useful articles and fine weapons; he could not remember even twenty days ago in perfect recall, which was a point of survival upon the plains.

He knew nothing of sign language, of scouting, of using a network of runners as a means of communication—and the white man was more often drunk than sober. Besides that, he seemed intent on fixing the Indian into that intoxicated state, too.

No, to Gray Hawk's point of view, the white man would not even have made a worthy opponent, let alone become the object of admiration.

"Gen-e-vee?"

She stopped her work and glanced at him.

His attention seemingly on the tiny statue he was carving, Gray Hawk said, "Tell me again of your father and his work."

"Are you thinking of taking me back to St. Louis?"

"Quiet, white woman. I am merely curious."

"Please, Mr. Gray Hawk, if you would take me back, I would be forever in your debt."

He held up a hand. "I tire of hearing this same prattle. I think you must say this to me more times a day than I can count. Now tell me what he does and why it is so important for you to return. I do not understand, white woman, how a man can be so dependent upon a woman for his own livelihood."

She turned around in full, sitting down upon the ground. She said, "That is not true, Gray Hawk. Are you not dependent upon your women? Who keeps your home for you? Who makes your clothes, your food, your bags? Who cares for your children?"

He nodded. "Yes, I can see that you could say that. But these works that you mention are those of a woman, and it is a fact that a man cannot live without her. But he lives with her as a woman, not in competition with her as a man."

"Mr. Gray Hawk, do you suggest—"

"Do I make a woman hunt food for me? Do I require her to defend me? Do I ask her to make my weapons, to ensure their strength? These are my responsibilities. I might listen to her suggestions. I might even seek out her opinions on some matters, for she has many emotions I do not feel, and these emotions, these loves of hers, are her strengths. But hunting, warring and defense are a man's domain. I am not in competition with her."

When Genevieve opened her mouth to speak, he again held up his hand.

"What you do in your world," he continued, "from what I can comprehend, is a man's work. I can see, because I have had to teach you these things, that you did not cook before now, and I have not observed that you have talent toward the making of clothing or other items that are, in general, the woman's sphere of activity. From what I understand, you do the same work as your father. How does he allow this? Does he not know that, to do so, he takes away the qualities and creativity of a woman, which are her beauty?"

She hesitated. She looked as though she might say a great deal, but she held back, gazing away as though she studied something in the distance. At length, her attention still seemingly elsewhere, she said, "I have never heard such a viewpoint before, and, I must say, Gray Hawk, it startles me a bit— yet I can see that it makes perfect sense to you. I must tell you, however, that in my society, for me to do such work as you describe would be to lower myself in the eyes of my peers."

"Who are these peers, that they should judge you?"

"They are people of the elite status in my society."

"Elite?"

"People who are…above…other people."

"Above? You mean people of distinction within your tribe? People who have proven themselves to be able to provide, able to share their treasures with others?"

She frowned. "No, Gray Hawk. By 'peers' is meant people who are the children of great men, people who by birth are raised in status above others."

"Just because they were born to a man of worth?"

"Yes."

Gray Hawk paused, weighing what she said against what he knew. "How can this be so? Just because a man is a great chief does not mean his sons will be also."

She sighed. "Let me see if I can help to explain this. Do you not have slaves in your society?"

He shrugged. "Sometimes we keep a captive and she becomes a slave to the one who captured her, doing much-needed tasks for the household. But she is not kept a slave. She often will marry into our tribe and thus become an equal to all others."

162

The white woman brought her gaze back to him. "Well," she said, "it is similar in our society. There are people who are servants who do the work of the household. By reason of birth, these people come from a lower class of people and so are hired to do our work. It is considered most degrading if a man of any higher class, and especially if a woman, were to do actual physical labor. Such would mean dismissal from the upper circles of our society. It is unseemly to do so."

Gray Hawk paused. He took his time in trying to understand what this woman said, for it all seemed incomprehensible to him. Men and women who did no physical labor? He asked, "Are these 'peers' old people, then?"

"No," she said. "They are all different ages. But by reason of birth, they are held in higher esteem than others."

He frowned. "And these 'peers,' what sort of work do they do?"

She hesitated. "Sometimes they will run an estate that their father has left to them. Sometimes they will go into the same business as their father. But most often they are not required to work. To labor, to *have* to work at all, is considered a weakness."

"And these slaves—"

"Servants."

"And these servants do—"

"Most of the work? Yes."

Gray Hawk shook his head. "Do your people not think of the life of the servant? Do they not consider that the servant, too, desires to enjoy life?"

"I do not believe it crosses many people's minds."

Gray Hawk gazed deeply at the woman to observe the truth or deceit of her words. Seeing her sincerity, he said, "I do not understand how this can be so."

"Perhaps because there are people who do not observe as you do. Perhaps, too, because our towns are so big, it is easy to ignore the strife and suffering of other people."

He nodded. He still didn't understand, but he would leave the subject for now. "So tell me," he said, "about your father, and why his work is so important to you that you would risk coming into my country alone."

"It is complicated."

"I will listen."

"No, I mean, there are so many things for me to describe to you, so many different things about it, that even if I tell you, you may not understand."

"This could be so. There are many things about your society that I do not understand. But I will try."

She sighed. She looked away for a moment as though collecting her thoughts, and then, at last, she started to speak.

"Very few people in our society hunt for food or clothing anymore. Our society is so complex that it is no longer necessary to do that. We exchange things for our food. We barter with others with something called money," she said, going on to explain in detail, telling him little by little about money, about the written word, about what sort of work people did for this money in order to trade with others for the necessities of life.

It took her hours to get it all out.

He listened quietly. Some concepts he readily understood, but some he asked questions about, over and over, until he at last had an idea of what she said.

When it was all said, Gray Hawk sat forward, commenting, "So that is why the white man lies and cheats—in order to get this 'money' without having to do work. I had seen that this was so in the past. But I did not understand it until now."

She didn't say a word.

"Better is the Indian way," he said. "At least within our village, a lazy man is never admired, while those who provide, those who share with others, those who are wise, are listened to and exalted with many songs and stories told of their generosity. Better that the white man throw away his money and learn to live more honestly with himself."

She said nothing, just quietly observed him.

"So your father will not get this money that is promised to him if he does not deliver to the people who guaranteed him this money for the work that he is doing on the Indian tribes? And he cannot finish his work until he studies someone from my tribe?"

"Yes," she said. "That is it."

"How did he know of our tribe to bargain for such a thing?"

"The Blackfeet are well known among the white man for being both ferocious and difficult to bring to civilization. My father was already paid a good sum of money for this book because of his promise to seek out and learn about other tribes, and especially about the dreaded Blackfeet."

Gray Hawk grinned. "Is that what the white man thinks of us...'dreaded'?"

"Yes," she said. "That is your reputation."

"It is good," he said. "It is good." He gazed at her.

"So, you will take me back there now that you understand?" she asked.

"No," he said. "It is not my problem. I have my own to see to. I only wanted to know what had driven you here."

"But Mr. Gray Hawk, if you will only—"

"Enough said. We go now. We break camp. We are close to my people, and I wish to find them before the best hunting season is over. Come, I will help you with that elk. We need to be on the trail soon."

"But Mr. Gray Hawk—"

"I have spoken."

He watched as disappointment came over her features—her eyes were downcast, her lower lip pursed. He set himself against feeling too much compassion toward her.

He had matters of his own to attend to, and, until he had completed his own responsibilities, he could not consider hers.

At least not for now.

But come spring... No, it was not something he would tell her. He might change his mind.

Chapter Thirteen

*C*ooler winds blew here.

She had taken to keeping the deerskin covering around her shoulders nowadays, even as they walked.

She had grown used to thinking of this journey as a curious adventure, one she would write about if ever she returned to civilization. She only wished she had a journal with her so she might jot down her observations of the Indian, of the wilderness, of this land.

She had never seen anything so beautiful as these plains, these valleys they traversed, nor had she ever seen anything so wild.

The wind blew incessantly, though it was fragrant with the smell of wildflowers and sage. It whistled around stone-carved hills and whispered across the fields. Sometimes it blew cold, seeming to freeze her to the core; sometimes it felt warm, blowing her hair back as though it were a lover's caress.

The fields were brown here, summer coming late to this prairie. The grass was dry, brittle and crunchy beneath her feet; the hills were rolling, seeming to stretch out forever against a wide blue sky; and always in the distance now were the mountains—snowcapped, majestic mountains.

It was all foreign to her—alien, yet strangely enticing—the feeling of space, of freedom, which was suggested by the vast expanses of this land. It seemed now as comfortable and as pleasing as if she had been born to it. She actually had the feeling of her thoughts gaining room, spreading out, giving her the opportunity to think clearly.

Gray Hawk, too, seemed to be pretty much at ease, and she noted that he no longer bore haggard circles under his eyes, an obvious sign that Gray Hawk had rarely slept on the earlier part of their journey.

In the beginning, she had never actually seen him sleeping; he had always seemed on guard, alert, watching. Always he had been busy doing chores, making weapons, fashioning clothing. She could never remember him resting.

But now that he was in the territory of his home, he at last appeared more relaxed and not obsessively concerned about setting up guard.

She remembered back to their talk when she had explained the nature of her father's work and the hierarchy of her society.

His comments upon it all had been spontaneous and curiously insightful.

It was odd, she thought. Not only did his viewpoint make more and more sense to her, but there was a wisdom about him, about all he said, that went beyond the instructions of her own schooling.

What he'd told her came to him not only from his own people and customs, but from his own observation of life as he knew it. And despite herself, Genevieve began to accept his point of view more and more. And she realized just how alien she must have seemed to him at first—alien and lazy.

It was an impression she meant to correct.

"Gray Hawk," she said, pacing along behind him, "I am sorry for what I said about you earlier. It was wrong of me."

He chanced a brief glance over his shoulder. "What was it that you said?"

"I was merely repeating things I'd heard without observing for myself the truth of the statements."

"I am glad that you want to talk about this now. What was it that you said?"

"Oh, it makes no difference. I only wanted you to know that I am sorry."

He suddenly stopped and pivoted around to confront her. "I would like to know what it is that you feel is so wrong that you must say something about it now."

"Surely you must remember."

He shrugged. "There have been many things you have said to me that were not complimentary. You have been a captive. I understand, and I have not thought much about it. Will you enlighten me now as to which one is not correct or shall I guess at one?"

She looked down at the ground. "I was ashamed the moment the words left my mouth, but I couldn't bring myself to tell you."

"And now you can...say it to me?"

"I would rather not. I would rather just let you know I am sorry."

He grinned. "And I would like to know what it is that has you acting so..."

"Stupid?"

"I do not know what this 'stupid' is, but perhaps it fits. What is it?"

She sighed. She lifted her shoulders. She said, under her breath, "I am sorry I called you a savage and a beast. None of what I said was correct. It was wrong of me to say it."

He shifted his weight from one foot to the other. He gazed at her thoughtfully for a moment before at last bringing up a hand to touch her cheek. He said, "Think nothing of it. I, too, have had opinions of the white man that are not flattering. Perhaps we can say that we both have been ignorant. People are people, good or bad, but still they are people."

She nodded, her glance still directed downward. He touched a finger under her chin to bring her face up toward him.

"There is much about you, Gen-e-vee, to admire."

She smiled up at him, her gaze meeting his. She said, "Do you think so, really?"

He grinned. "*Aa*, I do."

She closed her eyes, the smile still on her face.

And suddenly he was there before her, not more than a scant inch away. She could feel the movement of his head downward toward her; she smelled the fragrance of his skin.

His lips touched hers.

"Gen-e-vee," he whispered, his breath warm and fresh upon her own.

"Oh, Gray Hawk."

His arms came around her, and she fell in toward him.

"This is madness," she said, and he nodded.

Still, his lips came down upon hers once again. And she leaned in even closer.

His kiss was a lingering sort of kiss, the sort that demanded more.

He took; she gave gladly. His tongue swept forward, parting her lips, and she welcomed him in by returning the caress with all the passion of her own kiss.

"Gray Hawk." His lips had left hers to trail kisses down her neck, up to her ear, back to her lips.

"Gray Hawk. I want... I..."

"I know," he murmured. "I can feel the desire within you."

"Why do I feel this way with you?"

"I don't know, but I too—" His lips had made a path to her ear.

"I have from the start."

That brought his head up so that he gazed down into her eyes. "You have?"

She nodded. "Only I didn't know what it was. I'm still not certain I do."

"Gen-e-vee. It is lust, desire, sexual sensation—and we must fight against it."

"Yes," she said as his head bent lower, down over her chest toward her breasts. "We must fight against it." She drew her shoulders back to allow him better access.

"*Aa*, we must not allow ourselves…" His lips, his tongue, teased the upper part of her breast where it lay exposed to his glance, to his caress. His fingers teased the nipple that lay hidden just below the cut of her dress.

"Gray Hawk." She arched her back. "Please, I—"

He released her breast from the shabby confines of her dress, and she moaned. Never had she felt such sensation, such release.

"Gen-e-vee, I want more," he said, his head still bent, his lips teasing her nipples. "I cannot seem to have my fill of you. I must ask you to make me stop if you do not want more. I do not—"

She had loosened the top of her dress so that it fell to her waist.

He stood back and stared, his gaze warm, dark, sensual.

His fingers came up to tease, to play with her breasts, her nipples. "You are so beautiful," he whispered. "Do you know what you do? Do you realize what this does to me?"

"No." She shook her head, and he groaned.

He glanced around him suddenly, at where he was, and then he was leading her toward a cluster of trees. "It is not a wise man," he said, "who does not keep his guard during the day. Much could happen to him…"

He drew her in among the trees even as he spoke. The spot he chose was well hidden within the timber. He dropped to his knees, bringing her with him.

"I have dreamed of this; I have wanted you for so long. I lust for you, Gen-ee."

These were not the words she had dreamed of hearing on such an important occasion as this, but somehow it was enough. They sounded as music to her ears.

He tried to remove her dress, but his fingers stumbled over the buttons.

She helped him with it until, shivering, she knelt naked before him.

"Gen-ee."

And then his lips captured hers, his hands on her breasts, his fingers ranging lower, down her stomach, down farther.

It was naughty, it was forbidden, it was sinful; yet as he lowered her to the ground, his fingers there between her legs, she found it also exhilarating, wonderful...beautiful. It felt right. It must be right. Nothing that felt this good could be wrong, could it?

"Gray Hawk?"

He'd leaned over her as he brought his hands up to make a pillow for her from her discarded clothing. Her fingers were at his chest, up over his face, tracing the outline of his high cheekbones.

"Gray Hawk?" she asked again, and his gaze sought hers. It had been on the tip of her tongue to ask him to slow down, to warn him that she was scared. But she didn't.

She drew in her breath instead. The look in his eyes, the passion there, the intensity, the look of love there on his face, made her want...a sensation tore through her, and she noticed the area most private to her, there between her legs, began to ache.

"Gray Hawk, please love me."

"*Aa,*" he said. "It is what I intend to do—and perhaps, too, it is what I have intended from the start."

His lips captured hers again, his tongue playing inside her mouth. But only for a moment.

Down lower he bent, his lips, his tongue, kissing her neck, her chest, then each of her breasts.

She arched her back, inviting him to do more. And he did.

His hands massaged, kneaded the soft mounds of her flesh while his lips and tongue caressed her nipples.

And then he kissed her lower, his lips making a trail over her chest, her ribs, her stomach. His hands still massaged her breasts.

Down lower even still.

"Gray Hawk?" she asked, suddenly afraid. "What...?"

She couldn't say more. He had parted her legs, his lips even now teasing her there between her legs.

"Gray Hawk, I—"

He gazed up toward her, though his lips never ceased creating their magic.

"Gray Hawk, I can't... I mean...surely we can't..." She had meant to protest a bit more, but somehow the words died in her throat. She'd never felt anything like this, and though she knew this couldn't be right, all thoughts of modesty, of stopping him, evaporated as water did to dry air, replaced instead with raw desire.

She groaned. "Gray Hawk?"

His only answer was more kissing, his tongue doing things to her of which she'd never dare speak.

And it was all rather confusing, because Genevieve, having been taught by the "best authorities," knew that sex, although a necessary part of a commitment between two people, was something to be endured, not enjoyed.

She'd learned thoroughly what lay ahead of her in the marriage bed if ever she were to commit. And the more learned the "authorities," the more it had been brought home to her that the sexual act was no more than a painful experience, something to be tolerated and suffered in silence while the man fulfilled his needs.

A "good" woman, she'd been told, felt nothing. A "good" woman would never respond to a man.

There was no enjoyment to be had.

Well, she thought, they had all lied.

She *was* a good woman; she lived a clean life, one filled with good intentions toward her friends and associates; and never, not ever, had she felt anything more resembling rapture, anything so sensual, so arousing, so...beautiful.

Yes, she knew without hesitation, there had been no truth in what she'd been told.

173

Truth?

Suddenly it came to her—what it was between them, herself and this wild Indian. She knew all at once the meaning of it.

It had been there all along, of course, but because of the wide gaps in their cultures, in their beliefs, the knowledge would never have materialized had they not been thrown together as they had.

She loved him.

She wasn't sure how it had happened, or even when it had first started.

But she knew she loved him.

And it didn't matter that he was Indian or that she was white.

He was a man and she was a woman, and she loved him, that love as deep and as strong as if they had known each other all their lives.

She ran her hands through his long hair, and he looked up at her briefly, though he never paused in his ministrations.

"I love you," she said, and, closing her eyes, she gave him wider access for what he was doing, not noticing his slight hesitation.

It began to build then, the feeling, the ache down there, and she moved her hips against him that she might feel it better.

Her breathing became shallow, the pleasure becoming more intense, increasing to a crescendo—and all at once it happened, a crazy, overpowering sensation, a culmination of all this mad desire.

She'd never known anything like this, never dreamed such excitement existed. She whimpered, she moaned, suppressing the desire to scream. But from somewhere, perhaps far away, she heard herself repeating, over and over, "I love you, Gray Hawk. I love you."

But Gray Hawk didn't say a word.

In essence, her declaration had shocked him, and it was all he could do at the moment to lie still and feel the depths of her pleasure, her emotion.

He would not seek his own pleasure. Not this time. It was enough to contemplate hers.

Besides, Gray Hawk thought in the aftermath, as he laid his head upon her thigh, breathing in the delicious scent of her, he had never experienced anything quite like this himself.

He had felt a part of her, somehow. It was not something that had ever occurred to him in all of his affairs in the past.

Something was different here, and he couldn't place exactly what it was. But perhaps, if he were honest with himself, he might have admitted to feeling a touch of love toward her as well.

But Gray Hawk was not quite so open, nor so keen at appraising his own feelings with regard to this woman.

All he knew at the moment was that he felt wonderful, completely and utterly fantastic.

And...he wanted more.

Chapter Fourteen

"*We* will have to marry. It is the only way."

"What? What are you talking about?"

"Do not be upset because of what has happened to us. I will do the honorable thing; I will marry you."

Genevieve gulped. "But why?"

He gave her an annoyed looked. "Must I teach you everything? How is it that you do not know that when a woman submits to a man as you have to me, there are only two choices left to her? If she is lucky, the man will marry her. If she is not, then she will have to live with the disgrace of what she has done all her life. I am offering to marry you. I will ensure your reputation."

"I see," she said. "And what happens to the man?"

"What do you mean?" He gazed at her, puzzled.

"The man who 'disgraces' her. Does he, too, live a life of humiliation thereafter?"

"Of course not."

"Well, why not? He was a party to the action too."

"*Ha'*, you are a difficult woman."

"But truthful."

"I do not make the rules that my people follow. I have not caused these things to be. I only know it is the way of things. The woman will be disgraced if she submits; the man will brag. Perhaps it is not how it should be," he conceded, "but it is the way things are.

"In my camp," he continued, "the man is not a man if he does not try to make a conquest of a woman. If he succeeds with her, her reputation will be tainted for the rest of her life."

Genevieve gasped. "Even a young girl who does not yet understand the way of life?"

He nodded. "Young girls, after reaching a certain age, are taught never to be alone with a boy. It is also understood that there are sometimes mistakes and that a man will try to mislead a woman. It is also why a woman is never alone with a man."

"Never?"

He nodded his head. "Not if she wishes to safeguard her reputation."

"And a man?"

Gray Hawk chuckled. "He will have a better reputation if he succeeds."

"Why, that's terrible."

He shrugged. "For the woman, perhaps."

"I don't understand. Have you done this? You seem to have an extensive knowledge of…" She felt blood rush to her face. "…of things of a carnal nature. Have you, then, taken advantage of a young woman?"

He shook his head. "It has not been my interest. Some young boys make a habit of trying to ruin young maidens. I have not had the same desire. There are too many widows in our camp only too eager to please a man. And these widows, I am told, know many more ways in which to enjoy the act of lovemaking."

"Gray Hawk!"

He smiled and tilted his head toward her. "Why make trouble when I have wished to remain unmarried? It has happened that a man is sometimes caught by the maiden's relatives—and that he is forced to marry her. I have not wished this to happen to me, nor has there been a girl with whom I might want to take a chance."

177

Karen Kay

"If that is so, then why did you...with me... you—"

"We have been alone on the trail much too long, and you have been too tempting."

"But I—"

"Understand this, Gen-e-vee. When we get to my village, you will have to live with my people. If we come there without my taking you as my woman, you will be disgraced—and perhaps, if I do not make a move to protect you, you would be expected to perform with others that which you have given me."

"No!"

"It is why we will marry."

"But I cannot."

"And why can you not? Do you think I offer this to you easily? Do you think that I yearn for this?"

She didn't answer.

"It is not an easy thing for me to do, to offer you marriage. I have enjoyed my unattached state. I like it very much. It has given to me a great deal of freedom, and that makes me reluctant to end it. But if I do not do it, you will be dishonored or worse."

She cocked her head to the side and gave him a curious glance. "Why should you care?" she asked.

"Do you forget so soon that you came to my defense when I least expected it? Do you not remember that you perhaps saved my life?"

She stared at him for a moment. "So that's what this is all about. Because I saved your life, you feel that..." She lowered her voice, speaking as though to herself, though he heard every word. "It doesn't have anything to do with what happened between us... It—" She raised her voice. "I thought you hated me."

"No," he said. "Perhaps once—"

"Ah, so you admit it."

He sent her a gloomy look. "I had once thought that it was you who had captured me, who'd had me stripped, who'd intended to use my body to pleasure her. It was only right that I seek revenge upon such a person. And it is true, I would have cared little for this person."

"But I never —"

"I know this now."

"You do?"

He nodded. "*Aa*, yes, it is so."

"And you want to marry me?"

"Understand me, white woman. Not want. Must."

She crossed her arms over her chest and pouted. She said, "Well, I cannot."

He felt like shaking her, startling her, throwing in her face the declaration of love that she'd made to him in the throes of passion. But he would not.

Such an action would be considered cowardly, as well as unmannerly. And the Blackfoot Indian was anything but ill-behaved.

"Besides," she was saying to him again, "how would anyone know what has happened between us unless you tell it?"

He gave her an exasperated look. Did the white woman know nothing?

"We are on Blackfoot land. Scouts are all around us. Some could have seen us."

She gasped.

"Not that I believe any did. But that is not the point. Just by your presence with me — unchaperoned — others will think that the worst has occurred. They will also ask me about it, for all will want to know of your virtue or lack of it. And I cannot lie."

"Why not?"

"I am not the white man, that I —" He stopped himself. It would do no good to berate her race. No, she was his responsibility now, and it was up to him to teach her about the honest, Indian way to live. He said, "Because to my people, to lie is to be labeled a coward, and worse. For a man to lie would be to disgrace himself, as well as to tempt bad luck for himself and for his family. This, no Blackfoot Indian would do. The Blackfoot beliefs are not like the white man's. The Indian does not only live his religion for a few days out of the moon cycle. The Blackfeet are with their god always. Everything they do is connected to their beliefs. And above all, an Indian must be truthful with himself and with others. There can be no deceit when one lives his beliefs constantly."

"But we also—"

He held up his hand. "You forget that I have lived a full year with the white man. I have known the Black Robes and I listened well to them—and I observed. The white man mutters to his god about truthfulness, but lies behind the backs of his friends and his enemies. I saw white men cheat; I saw white men lie. I saw white men promise strict behavior and then betray it all."

"But the men you are basing your opinions on," she said, "are frontiersmen, and many of them are the thieves and scoundrels of our society who have come to the West to escape punishment. Surely you have such people among the Blackfeet."

"Yes," he said, "but not many. Those who do such things are cast out of the village and do not survive long on their own."

She nodded. "It is the same in our society. The men you are meeting here have been cast out of our society, but instead of dying off alone somewhere, they come to the West where, if they are able, they survive."

He breathed in deeply. He considered her words for a long time. Perhaps, he thought, he had passed judgment without having a full understanding of the entirety of what was occurring within the white race. Perhaps not.

At length he said, "Our talk, Gen-ee, while it is interesting, takes us too far from the point, which is this: we will marry."

She sighed. "You do not understand, Gray Hawk. I cannot."

He sat looking at her for several moments, until suddenly he rose.

They had been talking to one another while the blackness of night fell all around them. He had built a small fire for them earlier in the evening, and they'd been sitting around it, conversing, speaking of many things.

And in all this time, they hadn't moved away from the place where they had made love only a few hours earlier, when they had been content merely to find out about one another.

He needed to get away now.

Didn't she know the enormity of what he was offering her? Didn't she realize the sacrifice he made? For her?

Most likely not. She knew so little of his society, of him.

But such understanding didn't help to cool his anger. Rejection was still rejection.

He needed to be gone from her, if only for a little while. He started away.

"Gray Hawk," she said, her glance staying him for a moment. "I must ask you something."

He planted his feet apart and crossed his arms over his chest while he looked down at her. He said, "I am listening."

"Gray Hawk, I... It isn't as though we actually *had* sexual intercourse, is it?"

He didn't say a word as he stood over her. He just looked down upon her.

Her voice lower, she asked, "There's more to it...isn't there?"

Didn't she know? Stunned, he frowned. He asked, "Are you truly so innocent?"

"I guess...I must...we didn't, did we?"

He bristled. "If you really don't know this thing, then it is even more important that we marry. I will see that we—"

"Gray Hawk, I cannot marry you."

He breathed out heavily. "Cannot or will not?"

"Both," she said.

He could make her agree with him, he knew, if he were to take her into his arms again and make love to her. It would be an easy thing to do, and it would have the advantage of easing the ache inside him.

But Gray Hawk was Pikuni, a chivalrous man. He would not push her toward such passion, nor would he remind her of how easy it would be for him to convince her to agree. To do so would be to take advantage of her.

He would not do it.

And so he did no more than glare at her. Then, taking a step away and spinning about on his toes, he sprinted from their camp.

****

Gray Hawk lay next to her, not touching her, his even breathing telling her that he was asleep, or at least close to it.

He was upset with her, and she could understand why. But there was little she could do about it.

She could not marry him. She had to make him understand this.

Perhaps if she didn't have a father to think of, perhaps if she had grown up within his society, perhaps if he could fit into hers — maybe then she could marry him.

But not now.

There were too many matters to consider, too many things in the way.

Yes, she had determined she loved him, but was this enough reason to build a life around him?

She didn't think so.

Besides, the love she felt toward him was too new, too fragile, to construct any hopes around it.

She undoubtedly hadn't been thinking with her head when she'd declared her feelings to him.

But now that they were apart, at least physically, she could think more clearly, more logically, and she began to ponder some important questions.

For instance, if they were to stay together, where would they live? She was certain she could not abide staying in his world. Could he live in hers?

And if he could, what sort of work would he do? His main job in his world, as she could see it, was that of hunter and defender. Not much call for that in her culture. Could he adapt to her society? Take up a trade? Would he even want to?

Or would he expect her to give up everything she knew, loved and owned to live with him? Probably.

And she was certain she could not do that.

Besides, what would her father say? Her friends back in England?

And how would she raise any children that might be the result of such a union? Would they be considered Indian or white by her society? By his?

Genevieve was a realist, if nothing else, where this issue was concerned. She couldn't expect Gray Hawk, who had been brought up in an entirely different culture, to be able to reside in her society without great change to him, and she would never begin to suppose that he might have the means to support both her and their children as any other Englishman might do.

He knew nothing of her society. Mightn't it take him the rest of his life just to learn the intricacies of the English culture, her world?

And this would be his fate, were he to agree to live in her world, which she doubted he would.

Besides, she wasn't sure she wanted him to change all that much. Here, in his environment, he was magnificent. In hers…?

There would also be the ever-present prejudice, which they would have to fight for the rest of their lives. No one would sympathize with a white woman who had taken an Indian husband, particularly when most frontiersmen did not even consider the Indian quite human.

The situation, if they were to live in her society, would be unbearable. How long could they keep a marriage alive under such conditions?

Would it be any different in his culture?

But there was even more. She had only moments ago discovered that Gray Hawk had asked her to marry him so that he might preserve her reputation among his people, and this because she had saved his life. He spoke nothing to her of love, nothing of his feelings toward her, only of lust and now of duty.

Would it have been different if he had declared his undying devotion to her? Would she have felt more inclined to accept his proposal?

Maybe. But she didn't think so. Not when she had her father, his life and his reputation to consider, as well as her own.

Which brought her full circle. She needed to get home.

Focusing on her past rather than her future, Genevieve considered the possibility that if she married Gray Hawk, she might be able to convince him to take her home. It was also conceivable that Gray Hawk, having married her, would keep her shut off from the white world, knowing that contact with them could cause her to run away.

In truth, he might have asked her to marry him only because he had no intention of taking her back to her own home—thus his overwhelming concern for her reputation, since she would have to spend the rest of her life in the Indian camp.

But she had to return home. She could not allow it to be otherwise. Without her, her father stood to face the degradation of losing all he had spent a lifetime accumulating, plus his reputation.

She could not even admit to herself the possibility of this happening. Not to her own father.

And so she *had* to return. She *had* to make Gray Hawk see this, and she had to convince him to take her there.

She really had no other choice.

A chilling wind blew over her suddenly and she shivered, glancing at the same time over to where Gray Hawk lay with his back toward her.

He looked warm.

"Gray Hawk?"

He didn't answer.

"Gray Hawk, I'm cold. Do we have another robe?"

She heard him draw in a deep breath. "There is only mine."

"Gray Hawk, I don't suppose that we could...that you—"

He turned over to face her, his dark gaze seeking hers. She could almost feel his breath, his anger upon her.

She said, "I was thinking...that we could share the—"

"Do you know what will happen if I come over there now?"

"I—we would—"

"Make love."

"Not necessarily. We could just share one another's body heat and robes and—"

He snorted. "After what happened between us today? Do you honestly believe I could take you in my arms and lie with you all night without kissing you, without caressing you, without loving you?"

She felt as though something had hit her in the pit of her stomach and all at once a warmth spread through her.

She said, however, "Do you think we would really make love?"

"*Aa*, I do."

"And if *I* objected to your making love to me?"

"Then it would not happen. Do you think that you would...protest?"

"I believe so. I—"

"Do you forget that I did not meet my satisfaction today?"

His satisfaction? Did he mean that same sort of feeling she'd had when he had taken her to the culmination of—

She pulled up her thoughts.

No, she honestly hadn't known. She gazed at him in the darkness, trying to interpret his look. She said, "You didn't?"

"*Saa*, no, I did not," he responded. "And it is all I can do right now to hold myself back from seeking you out again. If I come over there, be assured that we will spend the night as lovers."

185

Karen Kay

Emotion surged through her. She wanted him, wanted his touch, his embrace. But she mustn't, she shouldn't...

She ran her tongue over her lips, and she felt his attention shift there, to watch.

What she did next, she could never really explain or justify to herself — especially after logically analyzing her situation only a few moments earlier.

Maybe it was because she felt herself to be in the grip of more sensation than a person had a right to, or perhaps she simply needed his comfort. Whatever the reason, she could barely contain herself as she said, "I want you to come over here, Gray Hawk. I... Gray Hawk, I want you to hold me."

She could feel the intense look he gave her, but he paused for probably no more than a second.

And then suddenly he was there, taking her in his arms, bringing to her his robes, his warmth...his passion.

"If I make love to you now, we cannot go back to the way we were. I will demand that you marry me, for you will no longer be a virgin."

She just looked at him.

"Do you understand this?"

"I—"

She meant to object. Truly, she meant to say no.

But he kissed her then, and she could no more think logically than she could have scaled the moon.

He said, "Oh, Gen-ee, how I need you. Do you know how much?"

She shook her head.

"I will show you."

186

Chapter Fifteen

He held her, just held her for a long time, his hands running up and down her spine.

She breathed in the musky aroma of his skin, savoring the smell of it, the texture of it, the salty taste of it, storing all the perceptions of it away in her memory in case she wished to bring it back to mind in the future.

The northerly wind blew upon them, and over them, but neither one of them seemed to notice, both too caught up in the awareness of one another.

She felt the evidence of his arousal against her, and she wanted nothing more than to reach out and caress him, to hold him, to look at him.

But she dared not do it, feeling too shy to initiate such a thing. Oh, how she wanted to, however.

When they had made love earlier this day, she had been the one who lay naked under him. He had been clothed, at least in a breechcloth, and she had not seen him —

"Go ahead."

"What?" she asked.

"Do you forget that your thoughts are quite plain to me?"

"Oh."

He took her hand in his, and slowly brought the touch of her fingers down toward the juncture of his legs.

She drew in her breath. She touched him, and she had the pleasure of hearing him sigh.

She whispered, "Do you like that?"

"*Aa*, yes. Do you?"

"Yes," she said. "Very much."

"*Aa*, Gen-ee, there is much good between us, much pleasure."

"Yes."

"We will have a happy life together, my beautiful sits-beside-him-woman."

Thoughts of denial didn't even occur to her. She smiled. "What is a sits-beside-him-woman?"

His lips nibbled at her ear. "It is a man's first wife."

His first... She suddenly could barely breathe. She mumbled, "First...wife?"

"Yes," he said. "It is the highest place of honor for a woman, and I will give it to you. You will have a voice, a say in all things that pertain to me, to our life. You will direct any other wives I might take. You will always be first in my affection."

She physically backed away from him.

"There will be no other affection, no other wives, because there will be no marriage," she said.

He took her back in his arms. "There will be after tonight."

"No." She struggled away, out of his embrace. She said, almost to herself, "I don't know what came over me. I was all ready to bed you, even perhaps of a mind to marry you. I... Thank goodness you told me all this before..."

He lay back, staring at her. He asked, "All what?"

"Wives, sits-beside-him-woman, other women. I could never, I will never —"

He paused for a moment. "That is right. I had forgotten. The white man takes only one wife."

"Yes," she said. "Naturally."

He grinned at her. "It is not so natural as you might think. Because of this way of reasoning, I have observed the white trader making a slave of his Indian wife, requiring her to do all the heavy work of the home with no one else there to share the workload. There is much work for the woman; it is only right that there be other women—other wives—to help with the load."

"I would never—"

"It would be your place to direct all the other wives. You would not be required to—"

"There would be no other wives."

"You wish to take on all the work for yourself? You would become burdened down and haggard. Better it is that I get you help."

She scooted away from him even farther. "There will be no other wives because there will be no marriage. I don't know what came over me. How could I have even considered something so foreign, so primitive, so—"

"Natural?"

"No. I will not do it. I will not marry you."

"Even if I take no other wives?"

"You... I...what do you mean?"

"Perhaps my mother and my sisters could help you with the workload so you would not become too old before your time. Maybe, too, there will be orphans within the camp who could help you. If a sits-beside-him-woman does not wish her husband to take other wives, then he does not. I would not force you to break your own custom."

"I could never... I would not... You wouldn't?" She gazed at him.

And he shook his head, saying softly, "No. You have my promise."

She didn't want to feel it; she didn't want to compromise her own ideas about such things, her own convictions. But what he'd said, the way he'd said it, made her feel as though she was the most important thing in his life. He was giving up the way he believed—for her?

Suddenly her objections to him, to what he proposed, seemed petty and silly compared to what he was sacrificing, and she felt her reasons for

189

denying him start to melt, slipping away from her as though they had never been there in the first place.

She said, "If we were to marry, you would take only me?"

He nodded. "*Aa,* yes."

Perhaps she shouldn't have felt what she did. And maybe she should have remembered her resolve of earlier. But it was just not to be.

All at once, if only for a moment, she forgot about her heritage, about her father, her home, her society, her objections. The only thing of importance to her right now was this man who lay beside her, not more than a few inches away, this man who was disregarding his own custom to accommodate hers.

She smiled at him then, and, scooting up closer to him, she said, "Oh, Gray Hawk."

And he grinned back at her before taking her fully into his arms.

"Gen-ee, my sweet Gen-ee. How great is my desire to make love to you."

"Yes," she said.

"Then you want it, too?" he asked, his lips just barely touching hers.

"Yes."

"Then you wish to marry me?"

"Oh, Gray Hawk. How I wish it could be."

She could feel him smiling, though at last he said, "Do not worry, my Gen-ee. If you wish it, it is done, then."

And Genevieve, barely knowing what she did, grinned.

****

"You are so beautiful," he said as he began to strip her dress away. "I have always thought so."

"Even when I had first captured — "

"Even then. I did not like you at that time, but I have always thought you are beautiful." He kissed her lips. "I did not know it then, but I will always hold close to me the day I first saw you."

190

He began then to kiss his way down toward her breasts, from where he had just removed the upper part of her dress.

"Gen-ee," he whispered against her skin. "I think of you as Woman-with-Many-Stars."

"Woman-with-Many-Stars?"

He lifted his gaze to hers and grinned.

And she said, "That's quite a beautiful name. Why do you think of me in that way?"

"Because," he said, "when you smile, I see many different lights in your eyes." He looked up and gestured above him. "Like the stars."

She smiled at him. "You are very poetic, Mr. Gray Hawk."

"Perhaps," he said. "But I speak the truth."

He gazed down toward her breasts, and, bending, kissed first one, then the other soft mound. He said—muttered, really—against her skin, "I believe that I should tell you that Gray Hawk is not my true name."

She went all quiet and started upward, but he held her back.

He raised his head, resting on one elbow over her, while with his other hand he played with her hard nipples. He said, "It is what I called myself when I lived with the Black Robes, because I had caught and tamed a hawk that looked more gray than brown. But now that you are my sits-beside-him-woman, you should know that this is not really my name. It is also unlucky for me to speak it to you, but because we are married, it is a belief we can put aside. I am known in my tribe as White Wolf, but do not say the name aloud, for my people believe that to do so takes away a part of my spirit."

"Do you truly believe that?"

"What?"

"That for me to speak your name would take away a part of you, that it is unlucky to do so?"

He rose up a little on his elbow. "I have seen bad luck fall to a person who did such."

"I see," she said. "Do all Indians believe this?"

He shrugged. "I do not know. It is the way of things with my people."

"I still don't understand. Do all your people have two names, then?"

"Some have more."

"What?"

"When a man demonstrates greatness, he is permitted to take on a new name in honor of the coup he has claimed, no matter how many times this happens. But he never speaks the name if he is wise, nor would anyone call him by that title."

"But how do others address him, then?"

"A man sometimes has another name which he permits to be spoken, as I have. But more often we call one another by our relation: brother, uncle, friend."

"I think I understand. And so you would call me Genevieve, although my name would be Woman-with-Many-Stars to the Blackfeet?"

"No. Women have only one name, which they use throughout their lifetime."

"But you just said…"

"That is for men only."

"But you gave me—"

"You are an unusual woman. Enough of this."

He returned his attention to her breasts, and she sighed. "Gray Hawk?"

"*Aa.*"

"Say it in your language."

"Say what?"

"Woman-with-Many-Stars."

"*Kakato'siiksiaka Ohpnaapiaakii.*"

"*Ka-ka-to…*"

"*…siiksiaka Ohpnaapiaakii.*"

"It sounds very pretty."

He grinned. "As you are."

She breathed out deeply. "Gray Hawk," she said huskily, "please love me."

"*Aa*, yes, my sweet Gen-ee." He raised himself up to kiss her lips. "I will."

His tongue opened her lips, sweeping into her mouth, caressing her, loving her as though only in this way could he get close enough to her.

His hands traveled lower, past her breasts, and on toward the juncture of her legs.

"Oh, Gen-ee," he muttered against her lips.

"Gray Hawk, I've never felt like this before," she said as his head moved lower, kissing her neck, her ear.

"I have not either. We make good medicine together."

"Is it supposed to be like this?"

"I have heard that it can be." He had lowered his head, his lips even now kissing her breasts.

Genevieve sucked in her breath. "Oh, Gray Hawk, don't stop."

He grinned as his lips made a path down over her stomach, lower still, kissing her navel. He said, "It is not my intention to stop. Not until we both wish it. Gen-ee?"

"Yes?"

"I wish to kiss you here." His fingers played with her, there where the short, springy hairs hid her womanhood. "Do you want me to?"

"Gray Hawk, yes, but I—"

His lips were already there.

"Gray Hawk, I should visit the river first so I could make it more pleasant for you. I—"

"It is already pleasant." He kissed her again.

"But I could—"

"Why do you keep talking? Are you afraid I might not like your taste, your scent?"

"It has occurred to me."

"It is not true. I like it," he murmured. "In truth, Gen-ee, it drives me mad with wanting you."

"Gray Hawk!"

They ceased to talk then, both content to do nothing more than feel the incredible excitement they created in one another.

Gray Hawk never hesitated in what he was doing. He kissed her, he played with her, bringing her to release once, and, to her amazement, again before he at last raised his head to grin at her.

He sat up.

It was only then that she caught sight of his body, all smooth muscle and hard contours. In response, the pit of her stomach turned over.

He looked magnificent, beautiful, handsome and...immense.

Only on very rare occasions had Genevieve ever seen a man in the nude — in actuality, only once, and that had been Gray Hawk. But he hadn't been fully aroused that one time — at least, not like this.

She drew in her breath. "Gray Hawk, you are...big."

He chuckled. "Do you mean to compliment me?"

"No, I—"

He gave her a curious glance. "Do you worry, Gen-ee?"

She nodded.

He grinned. "It is still a compliment." He came down over her. "You are a virgin, Gen-ee, but I think your body can still take me. It is made for this." He kissed her.

And Genevieve, snuggling up to him, to his warmth, forgot all about her apprehension.

"It will hurt at first," he said, "but the pain will go away. I promise you."

She nodded her head.

And he entered her.

"Oh, Gen-ee."

He moaned, and she stifled a scream.

He didn't move for a long time as he lay cradled within her; he just kept kissing her lips and her cheeks, his lips trailing down farther to her ear, then back to her mouth.

She liked what he was doing with his lips, but the other...was this why she had been told that the woman felt no pleasure? Was it the woman's lot to feel pain while the man took his pleasure? Surely something so wonderful could not also be so unfair.

She whispered, "Will it be like this all the time?"

He shook his head. "No, sweet Gen-ee, only this once."

"Truly?"

"Truly."

He began to move his hips slowly, coming up onto his forearms over her.

The second thrust wasn't so bad, she noted, nor was the third, the fourth, the fifth. She lost count.

Actually, it began to feel soothing down there, his movements and hers seeming to fulfill that ache she'd been experiencing there for so long.

She began to move with him, and he rose onto his hands, holding his weight away from her.

He smiled down at her, and her stomach, her legs, the very core of her womanhood responded at once, the whole of her body filling with sensation.

"Oh, Gray Hawk," she murmured. "I believe that I truly love you."

He stared at her then, just stared at her, his hips never ceasing their movement. No smile lit his face; no feeling at all did he show as he said, "*Hánnia*, Gen-ee, *Kitsikakomimmo*."

And Genevieve needed no translation to understand what he said. He loved her, too. He didn't need to say it in English. She *knew* it.

It happened then.

He had never ceased his movements. She had never quit hers.

It built there between them, the pleasure, the wonderful sensation.

Both staring at one another, they met their crescendo together, both releasing their happiness toward each other at the same time. They moaned and they whimpered, their sound resembling more a song of music than one of pain.

Their pleasure went on and on until at last, exhausted, Gray Hawk fell over her.

"Oh, Gen-ee," he murmured against her ear.

She grinned and drew her legs more firmly around him. "Oh, Gray Hawk," she said, "I love you."

But she was never certain he heard her. He'd fallen asleep at once, her arms still around him.

Chapter Sixteen

"*You* belong to me now."

"I beg your pardon?"

"You are mine now."

"I'm sorry, but I belong to no one."

It was, perhaps, a moot point to argue, since she lay nude within Gray Hawk's arms. But she couldn't let such an all-encompassing statement fall without comment.

He said, "From this moment forward, you will lie with no other but me. You are now my sits-beside-him-woman."

Was she? She tried to think back to what they had discussed earlier. She remembered him saying something to this effect a little while before they had made love, but she couldn't recall her own response.

Had she agreed?

Surely not. Besides, there had been no ceremony—even in crude form—that would have united them as husband and wife.

"Gray Hawk," she said, "to be your sits-beside him-woman would mean that we are married, and I do not remember any ceremony that has bound us."

He chuckled. "You do not recall this?" He touched her breasts. He squeezed them.

She moaned just a little.

"Or how about this?" He ran his fingers down to her womanhood.

"Gray Hawk, you tease me."

"*Saa*, no," he said. "Only a little. What we did is one of the oldest ways in the world to unite a man and a woman. Be glad that I told you before I took you that I would make you my sits-beside-him-woman. With no gifts presented to you, I could easily walk away from you and brag of it to my friends." He touched her nose with his finger. "Be happy that I claim you."

"Humph!" she said as she snuggled into the shelter of his arms where they lay beneath a canopy of wooded forest. Gray Hawk had brought them here the day after they had made love, saying that this was a secluded spot, one not easily detected by other tribes, nor by a scout from his own Pikuni.

They had lingered in this camp now for two days, alternating between making love and sleeping, more often involved in the former.

She didn't know why she argued the point with him. She had come to understand that she loved this man more than she could remember loving anyone. And it seemed that in any society, white or Indian, when a woman felt the way she did about a man, they married.

Yes, there would be problems. Yes, there would be heartaches to face and to overcome in the future, but it all seemed so far away from her now.

All she wanted at the moment was to enjoy the present. The present with Gray Hawk.

She asked, "How long do we stay here?"

He drew a deep breath. "I do not know. I do not wish to leave, and yet I know that we must. I have things I must see to in my village—"

"And I have my father."

"*Aa*, yes," he said. "Your father."

"Gray Hawk—"

"Not now. Let us enjoy this just a little longer. Too soon we will have to face our problems. Let us have this time together now."

"But—"

"*Ánniayi*." He held a finger to her lips. "Not now. Soon."

She opened her mouth, but he gave her such a stern look that she found herself chuckling at him instead of scolding him.

She stretched, and, glancing away, looked above her to where the blue sky peeked down through the boughs of long, spiny pine and balsam trees. She could see puffs of clouds up there, the white dots in the sky the only thing to be witnessed in an otherwise unmarred blue perfection.

Below her, Gray Hawk had placed fir tree branches. Their cushiony softness, with the buckskin robe beneath her, acted as a mattress for her. The fragrance was enchanting, reminding her of Christmas, and though the pine limbs made a crunchy sound each time she moved, it was not an altogether uncomfortable bed.

She gazed off to her right, where there stretched more of the forest, dark green as far as she could see. She turned her head in the opposite direction to catch an occasional glimpse of snowcapped mountains through the rustling tree boughs.

It was cool, too, in this country, but she barely felt it, wrapped up as she was in Gray Hawk's embrace.

"Where are we, Gray Hawk?"

"We are in my country, Pikuni country."

"But where is that exactly?"

He shrugged his shoulders. "It is north and west of the white man's fort where I first saw you. Our country is marked on the west by the Backbone."

"The Backbone?"

"The Backbone of the World, what the white man calls the Rocky Mountains."

"Oh, I see. We are that far west?"

He nodded.

And she sighed. The knowledge was depressing, all out of proportion, especially in the wake of her recent awareness of Gray Hawk.

But there was nothing for it. Their location only served to remind her of how far away she was from St. Louis. And she feared that all might be

199

lost. Even if a miracle occurred and she was able to persuade Gray Hawk to turn around and take her back home, there might not be enough time now to salvage her father's project.

It was odd, she thought. Although she had just discovered her love for Gray Hawk, a love that brought her feelings of joy and happiness, another part of her was as despondent as she was happy. And her fears seemed always there, just slightly out of view until a memory of her father or her home came to mind, replacing with anxiety any enjoyment she might feel.

In truth, Gray Hawk's continued disregard for her predicament did much to anger her.

There must be something she could do. She thought for a moment. There was one....

"Gray Hawk," she began. "I have a proposition to put to you."

"What is a pro-po-si-tion?"

She stared at him. "It is a like a suggestion. It is an idea I would put to you in an effort to bargain with you."

"You wish to barter with me?"

"No, Gray Hawk, bargain."

"Is it not the same thing?"

"No, I... It doesn't matter. I would like to present something to you and see if I might reach an agreement with you."

"For something that you want?"

"Yes," she said. "But also for something that you seem to want, too."

He rose up onto his elbow next to her. "I am listening."

"Well," she said, her words coming quickly, "as you know, I worry over the fate of my father's work. You must realize that I was desperate to help him with his project, otherwise I would never have come to this country."

He nodded.

"I propose this to you: take me home, back to St. Louis, but you accompany me there. There, you and my father can talk; he can learn all he wants about your people from you; and in return for this, I will gladly marry you and return here to this country with you."

He didn't even hesitate. He said, "You are already married to me."

"I did not agree to it, though."

"You did when you lay down beneath me."

"I did not know that."

"It matters little to me. The result is the same. You are my sits-beside-him-wife, and I already have you in my country. You try to barter with things that are already mine."

"That is not true."

"Is it not? I see you here before me. We are in Pikuni country. I—"

"I will fight you, Gray Hawk. I could make your union with me unbearable, and believe me, if you do not help me, I will try."

He gazed at her for several moments before he rested back against the ground, bringing both hands up behind him to cushion his head. He said, "Yes, I can see that you might do this. It is within a wife's realm to make her husband either rejoice in his decision or regret it. I will not interfere with you in this matter. But I do not think, little Gen-ee, that you can carry this all the way through our marriage."

"What do you mean?"

"The marriage bed," he said, grinning. He slanted a glance off to the side, toward her. "It is there in the marriage bed that I think you would have little opposition to me."

"Oh! Of all the..." She turned over, presenting him with her back.

He came up behind her, fitting his hard curves against her soft ones. She scooted over farther, away from him, but he put his arm over her to prevent her from going too far. Picking up her hair and nuzzling her neck, he said, "I cannot take you to your St. Louis right now, beautiful Gen-ee. I have my own problems that I must see to as soon as I get back to my village. If I didn't have those, maybe I would do as you ask, but it is not to be. I cannot pretend that I do not have responsibilities in my home."

She leaned back against him. "Nor can I, Gray Hawk," she said, turning her face slightly toward him. "Nor can I fail to remember that I must help my father."

He nodded his understanding, and, taking her in his arms, he kissed her.

"I am sorry," he said. "I wish it could be otherwise. I wish I could grant to you all that you desire, but I cannot. I have to take all matters into consideration, and that includes my own people."

"But—"

"Not now. Later you can yell at me and say bad things about me. Let us have this one last day together without fighting."

"I'm not—"

He kissed her again, this time sweeping his tongue into her mouth, and she responded to him at once, meeting him with an immediate passion of her own.

And as the day wore on, as he had predicted, so, too, it happened: he met no opposition from her within the marriage bed.

****

They left the next morning, packing up their few belongings and setting to the trail before the sun had even touched the horizon.

Their way became more difficult, since they were no longer traveling over the prairie. They had started to ascend a small mountain, and now their trail was marked by luxuriant forests where the trees grew tall and splendid, where the weeds and flowers sometimes grew high enough to touch the shoulder, and where the cool, fragrant smell of pine, of grasses and of crisp autumn air assailed them.

The earth beneath her feet was blanketed with undergrowth, giving Genevieve the impression that the ground was not quite solid.

There were lakes, too, hidden here in the mountainous forest, the pines and firs growing right up to the water's edge. And even she couldn't fail to notice the tracks of deer, of moose, of bears, which crossed their path and disappeared within the forest.

They stopped at one of the lakes to drink of the cool, clear water. It was refreshing, invigorating and cold, and Genevieve realized that this lake must be fed by icy mountain streams. She could also make out the distinctive sound of waterfalls splashing into the lake.

"Where are the waterfalls that I hear?" she asked Gray Hawk.

"To the east." He pointed. "We will go by one of them soon."

"Really? Will we stop there?"

He grunted. "We can, but only for a little while. We are close to my village, and I am anxious to arrive."

"I see," she acknowledged, and again they fell into silence.

She began to recognize some things, like the birds. She identified the call of a loon, the songs of many thrushes, of the robins and the doves. In truth, there were so many different birds here, she could barely keep count. She had already taken note of sparrows, chickadees, and even some tree swallows.

"What is the name of the bird that sings such a pretty song?" she asked Gray Hawk after a while.

He stopped. He listened. "That?"

"Yes." She nodded.

"That is the *atsiinisisttsii*, the bobolink. It is the bird we call the Gros Ventre bird, because he talks good Gros Ventre, the language of a neighboring tribe."

She smiled.

On they went, and once, when she chanced a peek up at the snowcapped mountains to their left, Genevieve saw a band of mountain goats traversing the difficult peaks. Here, too, she got her first glimpse of a glacier.

She mentioned this fact to Gray Hawk, who only shrugged and said they would see many more before they came to his village.

The wind blew a warm breeze upon her, brushing back her hair and bringing with it the fragrance of summer, of lush green grasses and balmy days.

203

She'd never seen anything like this breathtaking landscape, and she wondered how many other white people had ever experienced it.

Not many, she guessed.

But soon they were descending from the mountainous terrain, and the air became warmer, even hot.

They camped for the night in a glade of long grass and wildflowers. Surrounding them were more forests of pine and of balsam.

She fell into Gray Hawk's arms that night and gazed up at the multitude of stars overhead. Something within her reached out to the big expanse of space, and she felt an unusual sensation, as though she were as boundless as the open sky.

In the distance, a lone coyote howled into the night, begging a sweetheart to come out and play. And it occurred to her that she was remarkably content here. Here with her Indian lover, with nothing on her back but her ragged green dress; here, where she owned nothing more than the buckskin robe she had placed beneath her. She had never felt so invigorated, so happy, nor so much at peace.

Her last thought that night before she drifted off to sleep was one of wonderment. She could probably not count even one person back home who, in the frenzied pace and constant strife to pay bills, could attest to sleeping so soundly as she did here.

Was it the air, she wondered, or was it the expansive feeling of being one with yourself and with the environment?

And it was while pondering that philosophical question that she fell asleep.

Chapter Seventeen

Her first view of the Indian camp was from the crest of a hill.

She stared at it for a long while, unable to believe the beauty of what she saw.

Set in a lush expanse of brown meadow, the village stretched out in a circle over what must have been an acre of land. There were well over a hundred tepees down there, some of the structures bleached white, some painted with blues, yellows and reds, the entire effect creating an illusion that the encampment was encircled by a rainbow.

The whole village sat next to a small lake, in which was reflected the deep blue of the sky. And though there were no trees nearby to mar this stretch of prairie, everywhere surrounding the camp were yellow sunflowers and an array of blue, violet and gold wildflowers.

To the south of the camp grazed a huge herd of horses, comfortably munching on the rich buffalo grass. To the north sprawled several rolling hills; to the east, a great expanse of brown prairie.

She and Gray Hawk stood downwind from the camp on its western side, and the smells of campfires, of cooking foods and the fragrant scent of the prairie wildflowers, made her stomach growl. She inhaled the aromas deeply, and, at the same time, she heard the shouts of children at play, the sounds of men's and women's voices in conversation, and of dogs barking.

The wind tousled her hair while it blew back the rags of her dress, and, as she stood there with the sun beating welcome warmth upon her, she felt strangely as though she had stepped onto another planet.

"They know that we are here."

She could only swallow, unable to respond. Words deserted her. And an unbidden fear coursed through her.

She did not know these people; she did not understand their language, and she could not envision what sort of reception awaited her.

She was suddenly glad Gray Hawk had insisted she marry him.

"Isn't it beautiful?"

She nodded her agreement.

He pointed to the north, toward the hills. He asked, "Do you see those slopes?"

Again, she nodded.

"Old men of the tribe sit there on lookout for the village. My grandfathers may even now be there."

She smiled and he gazed at her, his glance lingering on her face.

"There is no reason for you to fear," he said. "You are with me, and you are my sits-beside-him-wife. No harm will come to you."

She wished she could have responded to his words, but she could only smile, and even that was a strain.

"Come." He took her elbow, but she held back. He looked down at her. "I promise you that no harm will come to you. Now, come."

She could see no way to avoid what had to happen, and so she let him lead the way into the Indian camp, fear causing her to stay close to Gray Hawk's heels.

A multitude of brown, curious faces greeted her and Gray Hawk as they made their way into camp. Genevieve gazed down, afraid to look up and witness whatever looks were thrown their way.

All at once there were voices shouting, where before it had been quieter, and dogs ran up to them, seeming to single her out to bark and growl at.

Drums, which had been beating when they'd entered camp, stopped, and children, shrieking, darted toward them. Many of the youngsters reached out to touch her, though Gray Hawk shooed them away with the flick of his hand and a sternly spoken "*Mopbete*, behave!"

Gray Hawk spoke to many people, reaching out to touch a hand here, a palm there, but Genevieve barely noticed. She was too afraid to do more than follow.

Finally Gray Hawk stopped, and Genevieve, almost running into him, heard the sound of a woman's voice.

"*Oki*." Genevieve listened to the woman, despite the words being completely meaningless to her. "*Tsa kaanistaopiihpa ohko? Nomohtsitsinikooka kiistoyi. Nitsikohtaahsi'taki kikao'toohsi.* How are you, my son? Others have told me about you. I am glad you have arrived. I have prayed that you might return."

"*Oki Na'a*, hello, my mother," Gray Hawk responded. "I have returned to you as quickly as I could."

"It is good that you have. I have worried."

Other Indians had gathered around them now, and Genevieve noted that much attention seemed to be centered on *her*, not on Gray Hawk and the woman.

Genevieve stepped closer to Gray Hawk.

"I have many things I wish to ask you, my mother, for I have worried about you and my sisters, but first I should tell you that I have married this woman who has walked into camp by my side. I have made her my sits-beside-him-wife."

The older woman spared the white woman only a momentary glance. "*Hannia! Naapiaakii!* A white woman!"

"*Aa*, yes," he said. "And I would ask that you and my sisters assist her in learning our ways. But first I would request that you help me to settle her into a lodge. As you can see, her clothing is torn and dirty; she has holes in her shoes, and she is tired."

The older woman gazed more closely at Genevieve, scrutinizing her. She said, "She can stay with one of your sisters while we prepare your lodge. I hope that she gave you many gifts for this marriage. For if not, I fear you have made a bad choice. She does not look strong enough even to bear children."

Gray Hawk grinned. He said, "Believe me, my mother, she has much strength."

The older woman nodded, although her look remained doubtful. "Come inside, my son," she said. "I wish to know more of what happened to you and why you have taken such an unusual wife."

Gray Hawk gave an acknowledgment with a single motion of his hand and then turned toward Genevieve. "I am going inside this *niitoyis*, this tepee, with my mother. You stay here and wait for me."

Genevieve grabbed at Gray Hawk, fear causing her to look wide-eyed at the gathering crowd. They all seemed to be staring at her and pressing in upon her. "Please, Gray Hawk, couldn't I come inside with you? I do not feel safe here."

"You will be fine," he said. "Custom does not permit you ever to talk to your mother-in-law."

She pulled on his arm. "Never?"

He shook his head. "You are not allowed to be in her presence alone, either."

"Not ever?"

"No."

"But you would be there."

He signed. "It does not matter. Wait for me here. You will come to no harm, and I must speak with my mother."

She forgot her fear for a moment. In her anxiety, she hadn't really registered his words. She asked, "That was your mother?"

"*Aa*, yes." He looked up to the crowd then. Giving the assemblage a frown, he said, gesturing at the same time, "*Mustapaaatoot annoma*! Go away from here!"

He sent Genevieve one last scolding look before he bent to enter his mother's lodge.

But no one there had ever before seen a white woman, and the novelty of it was too much for a fun-loving, curious people to resist. And so it was that very few people heeded Gray Hawk's warning, most crowding around Genevieve at once.

Some of the women reached out to touch the rags of Genevieve's dress; some fingered her hair, and Genevieve, convinced these people meant nothing more than to scalp her, sank farther and farther back toward the tepee.

****

The savory smell of blood soup wafted up to Gray Hawk as he entered his mother's lodge.

He settled himself down on the men's side of the tepee, and his mother handed him a bowl of the soup that, in Indian villages, was traditionally kept stewing all day long.

"Scouts spotted you several days back," his mother said. "We have been awaiting your return."

Gray Hawk nodded while he wiped off his chin. It was his only form of acknowledgment. "I had to get home and see to your welfare and to that of my sisters."

"*Aa*, yes, but I expected you several days ago."

"I have just been married, my mother." Gray Hawk gave his mother a half-smile.

And, the older woman grinned in response. "I suppose I can understand your delay, then. The woman is pretty, if puny."

"*Aa*, yes, she is pretty."

"What happened to you, my son? Reports came to us that you had gone out late one night and never returned. Your *napi*, your more-than-friend, said that he found tracks that indicated there had been a scuffle and that you had been dragged into what he calls the white man's medicine canoe. But by the time he realized you were gone, the canoe had left, and they despaired of ever getting you back."

"*Aa*, yes," Gray Hawk said. "It is true. And I will tell you all about it, but first I must ask how you have fared in my absence. With my father gone and your deciding you will marry no other, I have worried over you and all my sisters."

His mother gazed away, toward the tepee entrance. She said, "We have done well. Your more-than-friend, as well as an old widower in camp, have kept us well supplied with meat. When I first learned that you were gone, I worried, but friends have ensured that we have not gone without."

"This is good." Gray Hawk said, then again, "This is good. I will have to give a pony to my more-than-friend, and I will give one to the old widower, too. Who is this man who has been so kind to you?"

A haunted look came over his mother's features, and Gray Hawk stared at her. What was this he saw? Modesty? Excitement? He said, before his mother could answer, "Do I know this man?"

"He is one of your uncles," his mother replied. "He had once been married to your father's sister."

"You do not mean Black Calf?"

"*Ha'ayaa*, do not speak his name."

"I am right? It is Black Calf?"

"My son, please do not speak his name."

"But my mother, he is…a…"

"Handsome man."

"He is younger than you."

His mother gave Gray Hawk a considering glance. "Should that make a difference, my son?"

Gray Hawk gazed off to the tepee entrance, then up to the lodge poles and back down to the fire, his glance taking in everything he could find that was familiar: the old tepee lining, the willow backrest, the family robes, the rugs, the parfleches, the gun cases, his father's old bow and arrows, the household utensils. He felt the buffalo robe underneath him, cushioning his seat.

A woman taking a younger man?

"Black Calf?" he spoke aloud. "I would never have thought of you with him, and... Forgive me, my mother. You have shocked me."

"As you have me." The older woman sat forward to bend over the stewing food. "Let us forget about me and your uncle for a moment. There will be time enough to go into it later."

"*Ánniayi*, all right." Gray Hawk nodded.

"Tell me what happened to you."

Gray Hawk hesitated, pretending complete interest in his soup. At last, though, he said, "The white woman captured me."

His mother, who had been in the act of scooping up more soup, dropped the whole thing, fresh bowl and all, into the stewing pot. The older woman turned slowly to face her son. She said, "The white woman is a warrior woman?"

"*Saa*, no, my mother."

"If she is a warrior woman, then...did she force you to marry her, too?"

"Do I look the sort that she could force her will upon me?"

"But if she —"

"My mother, listen to me. The white woman did not capture me to mate with me. The white woman captured me to take me home with her to present me to her father. Her father apparently has taught his daughter the ways of being a man. But that is not important. The white woman came to get me or someone from our tribe to bring back to her father, who is interested in the customs of our people."

"Wait, my son. You confuse me. Are you saying this woman's father is interested in our people?" His mother raised her eyebrows.

"*Aa*, yes."

"And you believe this?"

"*Aa*, yes, my mother. I do."

"Have we ever known this man before? Is he one of the traders?"

"*Saa*, no, he is not, my mother."

"No?" She gave her son an odd glance. "Why would a man we have never seen be interested in us?"

"It is hard to understand, my mother. The whites have many strange customs, but it appears that her father makes his living from telling others stories about tribes such as ours."

"*Aa*," she said. "Her father must be the camp historian, the storyteller. But just as easily not. These whites have been known to speak with a deceitful tongue. She could mean to make a slave of you. Remember that we have heard stories of how the whites captured some of the people of the far south and west, only to make slaves of them."

Gray Hawk heaved out a deep breath. "She is my sits-beside-him-wife, my mother. Do I look to be her slave?"

"One never knows, my son. You must be careful."

"She treated me well when she captured me."

His mother gave him a questioning glance.

"She gave to me my own slave, who did everything for me, who made new clothing for me, who bathed me, who even prepared and cooked my food."

"Did you mate, then, with this slave, and that is why the white woman—"

"The slave was a man, my mother, and I am not a woman in man's clothing."

His mother's eyes opened a fraction of an inch more. She had just scooped the bowl out of the soup; she promptly dropped it again.

"Do you speak the truth, my son? Does the white woman truly keep men as slaves?"

"That is what it appeared to be, my mother, but the white woman says the man is not her slave. She says the man is a friend of her father's who had only accompanied her on her journey into our country."

"A woman traveling with a man who is neither her father nor her husband? And you tell me that she...and that her father somehow allowed this?"

212

"It is hard to understand, my mother. As I said, the whites have many ways that are strange to us. She said the man was not a slave, yet he worked in the capacity of a slave. She said he wished it to be this way."

His mother hesitated, her gaze fixed on her son. At last she said, "The white woman must be a woman of great medicine if she can make a slave of grown men who willingly do her bidding. This man who cared for you was not a boy?"

"No, my mother." Gray Hawk sighed. "He was not a boy. But I think you do not understand it all. The man—"

"Perhaps I was wrong to have judged this woman so harshly if she has truly done these things, if she has counted such a great coup. It is only that she looks so puny. But enough of that. I will have your sisters prepare a lodge at once—"

"My mother, you misunderstand."

"Maybe you have made a wise choice in a wife after all, my son."

"My mother, I..." Gray Hawk lifted his shoulders, completely baffled as to how to bring his mother to a correct understanding in regard to his wife, the whites, their ways.

Although perhaps he should let it go. Gaining his mother's approval of his marriage was, after all, what he had intended when he had entered his mother's *niitoyis*, her lodge. He certainly had obtained it now, although...

Someone screamed from outside—Genevieve—and Gray Hawk, who had jumped to his feet in an instant, was already at the tepee's entrance when the flap suddenly opened and Genevieve fell inside.

"Please, Gray Hawk," she pleaded, her eyes, her face, her whole body, even its scent, ripe with raw fear. "Please, someone is trying to scalp me. Someone reached up and grabbed my hair, and—"

Gray Hawk held up a hand. He opened up the flap; he scanned the outside. He closed the flap, glancing after her, back toward her. He said, "Look behind you, Gen-ee."

"No, I can't, Gray Hawk, I—"

"Look behind you."

"I—"

His gesture toward her this time was stern enough that Genevieve raised her head, darting a quick glance behind her.

A naked toddler sat at her feet.

Immediately, she turned her gaze to Gray Hawk, to his mother, and then back to him. She said, "I…"

He motioned back toward the child.

"Truly, Gray Hawk," she began, "I was certain that someone… I thought that—"

Again he held up his hand. Looking at his mother, who stared openly at the woman, Gray Hawk lifted his gaze upward.

"Come," he said, stepping toward Genevieve. "You must leave here at once. It is unseemly that you have spoken to your mother-in-law."

"But I—"

"Enough!"

He opened the entrance flap and stepped out of the tepee, ensuring that the white woman followed him.

As he had expected, there was a crowd around his mother's lodge. All the people had seen her, had witnessed her fear.

"*Ha*," he muttered to himself. He had better start praying harder, because he was definitely going to need the above ones' help if he ever intended to tame this woman.

****

"Really, Gray Hawk, how was I supposed to know it was a child who had pulled on my hair?"

"You were told to await me while I finished talking with my mother."

"But, Gray Hawk, so many people were pushing in on me—trying to touch me, my dress, my hair. I thought someone had reached up toward me to scalp me."

"I told you that you would be safe here."

"But I—"

"Enough! There are other matters I need to tell you."

"Oh," she said and glanced around her. They were seated in what Gray Hawk had said was his sister's lodge. There was a delicious-smelling soup stewing over the fire as well as several slabs of meat hanging on sticks over it, and all about the tepee were the scents of sage and sweet grass, which, combined with the aroma of the food, made for a foreign, if intoxicating, fragrance.

Genevieve had recently finished two bowls of the soup; Gray Hawk's sister had served the meal before leaving the lodge to the use of her brother and his new sits-beside-him-wife.

There were all sorts of items here that Genevieve would have liked to examine in more detail, but she was afraid to ask the permission to do so.

She did note that all the tepees here were painted, this one's design clearly seen from within. And there was a sort of lining, perhaps five feet high, that stretched all around the tepee. It was sewn into patterns and designs with different colors of rawhide and paint.

This lining's design was a crisscross pattern of reds and blues all laid in strips and underlain with rawhide. The whole effect was bright, original and homey, and it made Genevieve feel more relaxed.

Robes and trading blankets were scattered all around the interior, too, and in the center of the tepee, a ring of stones had been placed around the fire, the blaze appearing to be always burning. Several backrests leaned against the tepee lining, and Gray Hawk sat back upon one right now.

Her gaze fell to him, only to find him staring at her. Unnerved, she looked away.

He said, "My sisters will put up a lodge of your own for you as soon as they can sew it together."

"That is very kind of them. However, Gray Hawk, I need to return to my father. I cannot stay here long."

He held up a hand. "I know. Later we will talk of it."

"But Gray Hawk, we never seem to have this conversation, and it is so very important, and I—"

215

"Silence, woman."

"Gray Hawk, I—"

"We will talk about it, I promise you, but I—"

"When?"

"You dare to interrupt me?"

"You interrupted me."

"But you are a woman."

"Yes? So? What has that got to do with it?"

He sighed. "It is a woman's job to listen to her husband and to quietly—and I mean quietly—advise him. Do I need to teach you this, too?"

She bristled. "It is a man's job, just as importantly, to listen to his woman. And no, you don't. Do I?"

He gave her another stern look.

"Gray Hawk, I'm sorry to argue with you, but this is very important and I—"

"Silence, wife. I know how much you need to see your father, and I said that we will speak of it later."

She sighed. She didn't want to anger him, yet... "When, Gray Hawk, when will we talk about it?"

He, too, breathed out deeply. "We will speak of this problem as soon as I have seen to the welfare and safety of my mother and my sisters."

"All right," she said. "And how long will this take you?"

"It will take me as long as it will take me. And each moment we spend arguing keeps me from performing this duty."

She frowned and peered over toward him. Something in his tone, not his words, made her curious. "Do you worry?" she asked.

He grunted.

Interesting. She watched him carefully as she asked, "What is it? What has you so worried? Is it your family? They seem fine to me, but then I don't understand all that happens here in your camp. Is it me? Have I done something to offend them—you?"

"*Saa*, no, you have done nothing." He hesitated. "I worry because I do not want to be absent from the big buffalo hunt in the moon when we prepare food."

"Why?"

"Because it is from this hunt," he said, "that my people obtain most of the food that will see them through the winter. If I am not here, I will worry about my family."

"But why wouldn't you be here, unless… Does this mean that you are thinking of taking me back to—?"

"Quiet, woman. I am thinking."

She bridled. "I was only trying to—"

"It is a very sorry diet when all one has to eat is dried meat and berries."

"Yes, that would soon grow to be unbearable, but what does that have to do with—"

"I am all that my family has."

"What do you mean? Have I missed something?"

"There is no one else to see to them."

"I am afraid I still don't understand."

He frowned. "I believe I once told you about my father's death."

"Yes, I am so very sorry."

"I also have no brothers, and my sisters are all still unmarried."

"Yes? But—"

He held up a hand. "In our society, the burden of the family's survival sits with the men. While it is true, as you have pointed out, that men cannot survive well without women, so too, women depend upon their men. Is it not up to the man to venture out each day in search of food? Is it not for the men of the tribe to see to the winter stores, their duty to see that all their families have enough food, enough furs and hides to see them through any harsh times…through the winter?"

She sat still for a moment, unable to move. A thought had only now occurred to her, and she wasn't certain what it all meant. At length, however, she said, "So are you trying to tell me that without you, your family could die this winter?"

"I would not like to say it could go that far, but it could happen. They could starve, or they could be very uncomfortable. I would not like to see either happen."

"I see," she said, and it was odd because she really did understand.

"And when I captured you, it was this that caused you so much worry?"

"Mostly."

She stared off ahead of her.

Had she been blind? Why had she not realized until this moment how truly worried this man was about his family? Why hadn't she seen that he was as concerned about his responsibilities to his family as she was about her own?

While it was true that she had known he had a problem here in his village, she had never before been concerned about how he felt. Not really. She had mouthed the words, but...

Why hadn't she?

Had she still, despite all she had learned about him, all that she felt for him, seen him only as a foreigner? An Indian without any feelings or emotions?

Had she?

She grimaced, facing perhaps for the first time an unsavory truth about herself: she simply hadn't cared.

It was not a pleasant thing to realize about oneself.

She lifted her head. Well, she cared now.

She was seeing this man as if she looked at him for the first time. He loved his family. He worried about them. He was trying to do the best he could for them. The least she could do was lend a hand while she was here, if she was able.

218

And so it was, for the first time in her life, Genevieve Rohan felt compelled to ask, truly interested, "What must you do in order to support your family?"

Again he hesitated, giving Genevieve an odd look, but at last he said, "I must see that the women have many food stores, and if they do not, I must hunt many buffalo so that they do."

"And how could I help?"

He looked at her curiously and said, "You could assist me in discovering how much food my mother and sisters have stored. You could also help my sisters with the drying of the meat I bring in; perhaps, too, with fixing the food and with tanning the hides. That would allow me more time to hunt and to find someone who will provide for them throughout the winter."

"I see," she said. "You know, of course, that I am not very skilled in doing any of these things."

"Anything you could do would assist them. Also, you could prepare my things, and yours, too, in case we need to move. There are certain ways of making moccasins and leggings and robes for the cold winters. My sisters will gladly teach you this so that you can prepare."

"All right," she said. "I didn't know that the making of clothing was different."

He nodded. "It is the same in the white man's culture. You wear heavier clothes in the winter. So, too, do the Pikuni. We long ago observed that the best furs for warmth are those that we catch at the beginning of winter. Then the animals have a thick hide and heavy fur. These are the skins and furs we use for warm robes, for winter moccasins, and for bedding robes. My sisters will show you."

"But Gray Hawk, I am not so certain that I—"

"I want to tell you how proud I am of you that you have decided to help." He suddenly grinned at her. "I knew you would make the best sits-beside-him-wife that a man ever had."

"I—" She meant to deny it, but truly, what could she say after such a sweeping and, yes, a flattering statement?

Besides, he had surged to his feet and was already standing at the tepee entrance. "I must go now to see *nitakkaawa*, my friend. I will also send my sisters to you that you may get started."

"I—" Again, she froze. And so when she heard herself saying, "I'm only happy to assist," she decided she would do just that...try to help.

After all, these were a primitive people, and she lived in a much more advanced civilization than they did. She could probably show them a few things....

Chapter Eighteen

*B*y the end of the day, the entire camp was buzzing with the news.

Not only had their elusive Blackfoot brother married, but this same warrior, who was feared by their enemies, who had already counted over twenty coups though he had barely reached twenty-five winters, had been captured.

Not by an enemy tribe, not by a brave warrior. No, he had been captured by a white woman.

Gray Hawk heard the stories and chuckled. Let them think what they wanted. It was good, the people accepting his wife so readily. It was what he had intended should happen.

That she had also done such a brave act when she had captured him, would only add to her credit. Rarely did a man undertake such a deed, an act that might claim his life, and that a woman had set out to do it—and had accomplished it—would be told of in this camp and in many others for years to come.

In truth, many men in the village were already singing songs of her praise, and, for the first time, those same men were allowing women into their circle to sing with them.

It was remarkable.

He didn't tell anyone of his own escape nor of his capture of *her*. There would be time enough for that later.

He sat now inside his more-than-friend's lodge, having been invited there to smoke.

He had given his friend a pony for his part in helping Gray Hawk's family, but there was more assistance needed and another horse to offer if his friend, White Eagle, would aid him once again.

Not that he expected White Eagle to refuse. Being a more-than-friend meant just that. White Eagle was a friend, yet more.

The two of them had given their vows long ago to act for the other, to each one lay down his life for the other, if need be.

It was a custom shared by all the different Indian tribes. More-than-friends went into battle together, hunted together, went on raids together, helping one another and ensuring each other's safety. If one was ever injured, so too did the other take on the injury as though it were his own.

When Gray Hawk had lived among the whites, he had looked in vain for just such a tradition, but he had found none. In truth, what he had discovered had startled him.

Among all people, there are those who deal in lies, who backstab, who pretend help while bringing misery and death. Among all races of men are those who make their own lot "better" by tearing down the good deeds of others. Such people are few.

But while in the white man's camp, Gray Hawk had never witnessed so many of these kinds of people in one place. There he had seen so much lying, cheating and murder — and by those reported to be best of friends — that he had become leery of ever trusting a white man.

He wondered how the white man would ever survive. How could he live and not know that friendship was a matter of life or death? That to live alone always courted disaster? In this country, the more friends one had, the longer he might live.

But a more-than-friend went even beyond all this.

A more-than-friend shared in the other person's happiness as well as each other's misery; they shared one another's adventures, their triumphs, their very life itself. If one's lodge was full with food, so too was the other's.

The only thing a more-than-friend did not share was one's wife, although it sometimes happened that if there were a death, a more-than-friend might be expected to take on the other's family, to care for it and see to its welfare, as White Eagle had done for Gray Hawk's family.

Still, such unselfish giving, whether expected or not, never went unrewarded.

It was why Gray Hawk had offered his friend a horse. It was why he was prepared to offer more.

"My brother," Gray Hawk started, "I have a few more ponies to offer you and a favor to ask of you."

White Eagle's expression didn't even change. "It was what I anticipated when I first saw you walk into camp. It is because of the white woman, is it not?"

"Yes," said Gray Hawk. "I have taken her as my sits-beside-him-wife, and so her problems have become as my own. And she has worries."

"I remember," White Eagle said. "At the white man's trading post, she was trying to persuade one of us to accompany her back to her home. Anyone would assume that a woman who would offer such a thing must have many problems. What are hers?"

"I don't know them all, but the one that worries her most is her father."

"What? Surely he must approve of you. Does he know of your excellent war record? If not, I could go to him and tell him...or perhaps, because you were so far from home, you did not have plenty of horses to bring to him? Other gifts?"

"It is nothing like that," Gray Hawk said. "I did not meet him. We did not travel all the way to her home. I escaped the white man's medicine canoe long before that."

This news had White Eagle sitting up and leaning forward. He asked, "Did you have the Cree love medicine with you, that the white woman came with you willingly? I have heard that theirs is a powerful medicine."

Gray Hawk grinned. "She did not exactly accompany me of her own free will."

White Eagle looked up quickly. "You stole her?"

"*Aa*, yes."

White Eagle grinned. "What a great coup. Why have you not said anything about this?"

"I decided it was not as important as my sits-beside-him-wife gaining acceptance among our people."

White Eagle looked into the fire a long time before he said, "I think you are wise to consider this. Did she truly steal you?"

"Yes, she did, with the help of some others."

"Then she is an unusual woman."

Gray Hawk only nodded his agreement.

White Eagle said, "What is it you need from me, my brother?"

"I must take my wife back to her father for the winter. Her father has some trouble that bothers my wife greatly, and so I must take her to him. She thinks that I can help the man. And so I must try."

"*Aa*, yes, *nitakkaawa*, my friend, you are right. You must try, otherwise your wife might be forever unhappy. You wish me to care for your mother and sisters, then, in your absence?"

"*Aa*, yes. I will also ask my uncle, Black Calf, to help, since you also have your own family to support."

White Eagle nodded. "It is good. There are many buffalo in our country this year. Our chances of success in the moon when the leaves change color are great. Do not worry. I will see that your family has enough meat to see them through the winter. And I will ask Black Calf to help."

"I am very happy to have your help, my friend, and I am prepared to give you two more of my ponies, plus my best buffalo horse, for all these things that you will do for me."

White Eagle stared at his friend. He said, "Your buffalo horse is known to be the best-trained pony in our camp. Many times has he ridden you in close to the herd to make the kill, and never once has he fallen or made an error in his judgment. You are certain you wish to give me such a fine animal?"

Gray Hawk grinned. "I am certain."

"She must mean a great deal to you, this white woman. I can see by your actions that you hold her in great affection."

"*Saa*, no — well, perhaps a little. It is only that — " He stopped himself. Somehow his words didn't ring true. A little? Was that what he honestly felt in his heart?

He changed the subject. "I have heard," Gray Hawk said, "that the geese are flying high."

"It is true."

"Also, I noticed on my journey here that the skins of many animals have thickened already; I saw several rabbits that have turned white before their time, and I observed that the songbirds are all gathering into flocks."

"So it is. We have seen these things too."

"Then you must understand that because these things are all signs of an early winter, I feel I must do this thing quickly: take the woman to see her father, lest I strand myself and my wife in a blizzard. It is why I will have very little time to spend in the camp. I hope you will excuse my hurry."

"*Nitsikksisitsi'tsii'pa*, I understand." White Eagle took a puff on his pipe before passing it to Gray Hawk. "Do you know where this town is that you must take her?"

"No. I know only that it is south and that it sits on the Big River. But I also learned that the big medicine canoe made the journey upriver in a little over two moons. And since I can travel as quickly as it does, I think it might take me that long."

White Eagle nodded. He said, "This is all good. You have considered that you will be traveling through much enemy ground?"

"*Aa*, yes, my friend. But soon autumn will be here, and it is not a time of many war parties. But I will be cautious all the same."

"*Aa*, yes, there is no better scout in all of the Pikuni than you. I believe you will keep away from our enemies. But there is one more thing that I hope you have contemplated, my friend. And that is that if you take your woman back to her people, she may not want to leave them to come home with you."

"*Aa*, yes, I have thought of this, but she has given me her word that she will return with me."

"And you believe the vow of a white woman?"

"*Saa*, no, my friend. I believe *her*."

White Eagle nodded and smiled. "You are wise," he said. "You are wise."

White Eagle then took his pipe, and, holding it out away from him, tapped the bowl of it, the Blackfoot signal that their meeting was at an end.

And Gray Hawk, bidding his friend a good day, arose to go and start his preparations.

****

Genevieve awoke to the musical notes of a bobolink, the bird Gray Hawk previously described to her on the trail. She listened sleepily to the song and gazed up toward the tepee poles, catching sight of the small bird sitting atop the poles, where he was apparently relishing the first few rays of the morning sun.

Genevieve stretched and snuggled deeper into the warm buffalo robes. She was alone in the tepee, Gray Hawk having awakened long ago to go out on the hunt.

It was the way it had been since they had arrived in camp. She rarely saw Gray Hawk.

Up before the rise of the sun and home after it had long set, he managed to get in only a few words with her each day before, exhausted, they both surrendered to sleep.

It must be a custom, she decided. She had noticed that, here in camp, men kept company only with men, and women with the women. Only rarely did one see a couple together, and this was usually at the end or at the start of the day.

And perhaps it was this, more than anything, that had caused her to relent in her requests upon Gray Hawk. Rarely had she brought up the subject of her father this past week, and with Gray Hawk acting the part of a devoted husband, she found herself slipping more and more into a new role: that of a wife.

She stretched again.

She knew she should arise, but here in the Indian camp, she had soon learned that life was not so strict nor so driven, and no one seemed to take notice of whether she dozed an extra hour or two or all day.

In truth, no one seemed inclined to criticize her at all, something she couldn't understand. Or perhaps she simply didn't know their language well enough yet.

Still, she couldn't remember ever having slept so well, so soundly or so long.

It was odd, she thought. After the first week in camp, she had taken so readily to the Indian life that she felt as if it were almost natural to her. She was relieved to have come to understand fairly well the language of those around her. Funny how, when one couldn't communicate, one quickly learned the language.

She couldn't yet speak the Blackfoot tongue, but she could at least tell what was being said to her.

She had met Gray Hawk's sisters that first day in camp and had been startled to learn that the name they had called her, *insst,* meant "sister" or "older sister," although none of his siblings was more than sixteen years of age.

She had been both flattered and pleased when Gray Hawk told her that this was their way: that, for the rest of her life, his sisters were now her own.

She couldn't believe the incredibly warm feeling this knowledge had given her. She'd never had a large family. It now appeared that she did.

She had discovered, too, that Gray Hawk's oldest sister was to be married soon and actually would have been married even now, had it not been for the entire family's grief over what they had thought was the loss of their brother.

But now that Gray Hawk was back in camp, preparations for the marriage had begun once again, both families apparently needing to send one another gifts to secure the marriage contract.

Genevieve sat up, pulling the buffalo robe around her to hide her nudity. Another new thing for her: sleeping in the nude. But nightclothes seemed unheard of here, and she was becoming used to the feel of Gray Hawk's warm body curled up next to hers at night.

It might not be approved of back home, but here, she didn't even try to fool herself. It was heavenly.

She let her gaze scan the contents of the tepee. This was their own lodge, hers and Gray Hawk's; his sisters, his mother, his aunts, his cousins and practically all the women in the entire village had turned out to sew the tepee together. Amazingly, the whole process had taken less than a day.

Her glance came to a willow backrest inside the tepee.

This was another thing that had astounded her: the generosity of her new neighbors. It seemed that the whole village had learned of her marriage, and before the day had finished, she'd been presented with gifts of robes, parfleches, hollowed-out wooden bowls; a tepee lining, two different sets of clothing and moccasins, hair ties, feathers, brushes, backrests and more.

On that first day, Genevieve had stood outside the newly erected lodge, dumbfounded, unable to believe such open generosity, especially when no one there knew her, nor did she have anything to give them in return.

It was only later that she had learned from Gray Hawk that these were the most precious gifts of all: those that could not be returned.

She stretched her arms over her head, the robe falling down around her waist.

She picked up her new dress of white elkskin, lying close by, and pulled it on over her head. The material felt smooth against her skin, like soft butter, yet warm against the morning chill.

She glanced to the center of the tepee, noticing that the fire was no more than a few hot cinders.

She would have to bring in more firewood, and soon.

She sighed. Despite the tribe's acceptance and friendliness toward her, she was still reluctant to venture outside of the lodge, and no one, it seemed, felt this should be different. No one came to get her or to force her out.

In truth, there was little need. Each evening, either one of Gray Hawk's sisters or his mother would ensure that the newly-wedded couple had plenty to eat, both for the morning and in the evening—another custom, Genevieve had discovered.

Oh, what she would give to have pen and paper.

She suddenly heard a scratching noise at the entrance flap, and, recognizing this as a "knock," called out automatically, "Come in."

Nothing happened.

Again a scratch.

Darn! She'd spoken in English. How did one say "come in" in Blackfoot?

She called out, "*Oki!*" No, that wasn't right. That meant—what? "Let's go"? "Hello"? Maybe "okay"?

Well, it was some short word. She just couldn't remember it right now.

Another scratch.

Darn! She jumped up, pulling down her dress in the process as she hurried to the flap, opening it just a crack.

One of Gray Hawk's sisters, Shoots-the-Enemy-Woman, stood outside.

Genevieve opened the flap a little wider and gestured the young girl inside.

Shoots-the-Enemy-Woman bent and stepped inside, saying at the same time, "*Ipii,*" with the same gesture that Genevieve had made.

"Oh, that's right," said Genevieve. "*Ipii,* that's the word I was trying to remember. That means come in, enter, I believe."

The young girl looked puzzled, but when Genevieve repeated the word and the gesture, Shoots-the-Enemy-Woman grinned.

"*Nee dawk seasts. Gittah sto pook kome ma.*"

Genevieve stared at the young girl. *What?*

Again, the girl repeated,"*Nee dawk seasts.*" And she made motions of washing herself, her hair.

"You're going to take a bath?" Genevieve repeated back the motions, and Shoots-the-Enemy-Woman nodded happily, grinning. Genevieve tried to repeat the words back, "*Nee...dawk...seasts?*"

Again, a nod from the young girl. "*Nee dawk seasts.*"

"Well, I'd be happy to," Genevieve said, nodding and grinning back, a gesture of acceptance in any language.

"*Poohsapoot! Nee dawk pook gee ewe.*" The young girl smiled, and, taking Genevieve's hand, pulled her out of the tepee.

The first thing Genevieve noticed as she stepped outside was the incredible number of dogs running freely through the camp. And it was interesting to note that just as the people lived a happy, carefree life, so too did their animals—their dogs, their horses and any other animals they had cared to catch and train.

Shoots-the-Enemy-Woman led Genevieve not to the lake where the camp was pitched, but rather to a more distant and secluded river. The Indian girl carried with her in a buckskin bag some sweet grass, or what the Indians called *se-pat-semo.* Genevieve had noted that the Blackfeet braided this grass and that it seemed to have a number of uses, including a hair wash, a hair tonic and perfume. Also, Genevieve saw some sweet pine in Shoots the Enemy Woman's bag, and some leaves from the balsam poplar, all of which were pleasingly fragrant.

This was the first time Genevieve had visited the women's quarters of the river. Gray Hawk had led her to the lake late each night when no one else was about, but these baths had been quick for modesty's sake, plus icy cold, making them less than enjoyable.

Genevieve could tell that Shoots-the-Enemy-Woman planned a leisurely morning. And Genevieve smiled as she followed behind the younger woman.

Life seemed suddenly good. There was a fragrance of summer in the air, and that, along with the scent of the smoke from the morning fires, the feel of dew in the air, the songs of the birds flying so high above and the sensation of the warming rays of the sun, gave Genevieve an unusual feeling of happiness, as though she were in affinity with the rest of the universe.

All of a sudden, life felt highly pleasant. And to think, she was experiencing it all in an Indian camp.

She beamed. Who would have thought it could be?

Chapter Nineteen

"*po'taki?*"

"*Om-wa naapiaakii yaak-a 'po'taki-wa?*"

"Work." Genevieve resorted to English, pointing to herself. "I wish to work."

One of the older women wagged her finger at Shoots-the-Enemy-Woman, repeating, "*Om-wa naapiaakii yaak-a'po'taki-wa.*"

"*A'po'taki,* work?" Genevieve knew this was the Blackfoot word for work, and she repeated it, intent on making herself understood. She had decided to help the others as best she could — if she could. It would not only assist Gray Hawk, she'd reasoned, it would enable her to enlist his aid in taking her home. And so she said again, "*Nit-a'pa-o'taki,* I work." She smiled.

The older woman gestured again toward Shoots-the-Enemy-Woman, who looked doubtful, and Genevieve was startled to see Shoots-the-Enemy-Woman cast a glance toward the skies.

Was something wrong?

"*Poohsapoot, nit-aak-ahkayi.*" Shoots-the-Enemy-Woman grabbed Genevieve's hand, motioning her to follow.

The Indian girl led Genevieve to the back of a row of tepees. And there, scattered on the ground, were several bundles of rawhide in various stages of tanning.

Also on the ground nearby was a recently-killed bull.

Shoots-the-Enemy-Woman motioned Genevieve to the latter. "*Ooyo'si*," she said. She gestured toward the dead bull.

Genevieve looked at the animal as though she had never seen one until now. She glanced back toward the Indian girl.

"Are you asking me to cook a meal from this? *Nitsoyo'si*?"

Her companion nodded her head and bent down toward the bull. "*Ooyo'si*."

The animal had already been skinned, and Genevieve could see that someone had been there earlier and had cut out the liver, the heart, even the lungs. Gone, too, was the tongue.

Shoots the Enemy Woman gestured toward the intestines and Genevieve felt her stomach drop. They wanted her to cook the intestines?

Were they mad?

However, Shoots-the-Enemy-Woman, after starting the procedure of cutting away the intestines, wiped her hands on the ground, and, looking back toward Genevieve, gestured her forward.

"*Oyiistotoosa!*"

She wants me to prepare a meal of this for Gray Hawk. Genevieve thought she might faint right there. Did the Indians eat intestines?

That was bad enough to consider, but what did they do with the manure within the guts?

Surely they didn't eat it too, did they?

No, that couldn't be right.

But what did they do with it? She wasn't expected to empty it, or—

"*Kika!* Wait!" Genevieve trod over toward the bull.

Shoots-the-Enemy-Woman glanced up at Genevieve. The Indian girl grinned.

Genevieve said in English, "You surely aren't expecting me to empty those guts, are you?" She wasn't quite sure how to say it in Blackfoot, and so she made hand gestures. Genevieve pointed to the guts, making a slitting motion and then a pretense of emptying the intestines.

Shoots-the-Enemy-Woman shook her head.

And Genevieve just stared. Good! She was happy to discover that she didn't have to clean the manure from the guts, but then, too, if she didn't clean out the manure, just how was she supposed to make an edible meal out of this?

Shoots the Enemy Woman made a whole series of hand motions in response, ending with gestures of putting the guts over the fire. Shoots-the-Enemy-Woman smiled.

And Genevieve thought she would be sick right there.

This couldn't be right; Genevieve hadn't understood the hand gestures correctly. That must be it. Because it looked like... No one ate manure, did they?

But Shoots-the-Enemy-Woman was smiling up at Genevieve, getting to her feet, and the Indian girl put her hands on Genevieve's shoulders, as though in a gesture of good luck. And Genevieve was too stunned to do more than stare at the girl.

Shoots-the-Enemy-Woman, however, didn't seem to notice. After smiling, she turned to leave.

No, Genevieve thought, she wouldn't do it. She...

She stopped. She was determined she would help. Did it matter what, exactly, they wanted her to do? If this was what they wanted...

She glanced over her shoulder to watch the girl walk away. Briefly Genevieve shut her eyes before bending down to work over the bull.

She would take only short, quick breaths, she decided, the smell of the innards and manure surely more than a lady of her standing and birth should ever have to endure.

And if she died in the process of doing this, at least she would have the satisfaction of knowing she had helped.

****

Shoots the Enemy Woman, whom Genevieve had begun to call Shoots, giggled.

"What's wrong with it?"

Shoots didn't answer. Her hand over her mouth and her head down, she just giggled until she outright laughed.

"Well, the darn things are cooking, aren't they? But oh, what a smell. What do you people do this for?"

Shoots the Enemy Woman didn't answer, but then, she was too busy laughing.

Genevieve bristled. Did this Indian girl know how long it had taken her to get these intestines cut out without leaking the manure out, and to set them to roasting over the fire?

Apparently not.

Shoots, still laughing, one hand over her mouth, picked up a nearby stick and pulled the whole thing, intestines full of manure and all, off the fire.

One of Gray Hawk's other sisters, Looks-Long-Woman, joined them.

"*Kayiiwa*? What is it?" the other sister asked.

"*Aooyo'siwa*," Shoots said. "She is preparing a meal."

"*Kayiiwa, ipisttsi*? Of what, intestinal gas?"

"*Aa*, yes," Shoots said. And both girls burst out laughing.

"What?" Genevieve wanted to know. "What's wrong with this? Isn't this what you asked me to do?"

Both girls seemed to be able to do no more than laugh, and Genevieve, taking offense, bridled.

Genevieve looked at the intestines, now lying in the dirt and muck on the ground. All that work, wasted.

At last, Shoots picked up the guts lying there on the ground, her sister taking hold of the other end of them. Motioning Genevieve to follow, the two girls headed down to the lake, skirting the village as best they could, both girls giggling as each walked with a hand held over her mouth.

"*Anniistopiit*! Sit there!" Shoots commanded Genevieve once they had arrived at the lake.

Genevieve sat.

Both Shoots and Looks-Long-Woman turned the gut upside down, and, holding the intestine toward the water, emptied the manure into the lake.

Genevieve at once understood. And though she groaned, she was secretly glad.

Thank goodness Indians did not eat this.

The two women were already carefully washing the intestine clean of all traces of manure.

And then, standing up, they began to walk back to camp, again motioning Genevieve to follow.

Once back at camp, the two girls laid a strip of buffalo meat alongside the clean intestine, and, turning the gut inside out, completely covering the strip of buffalo meat, they made a long show of tying the ends of the whole thing together with sinew.

Grinning at Genevieve, the two girls set the intestine, beef and all, to roasting over the coals.

Looks-Long-Woman patted Genevieve on the shoulder while Shoots looked pleased.

Shoots said, "*Iimai'taki-yi-aawa kit-a'pistotsi-'s-yi kit oom ki itakkaa.* Your husband and his friend will believe you did this." And with this said, both girls left, still giggling, it taking Genevieve much too long to translate their words to say anything back.

Funny, Genevieve thought, mulling over the translation, something about their language, the way they said it, seemed familiar…something.

Suddenly, it came to her.

Algonquian. Their language seemed very similar to the Algonquian dialect, a tongue she and her father had studied a few years ago. Could it be an offshoot of the same language?

Was it possible that these people could be of Algonquian origin?

What a discovery!

She would have to test it and see. She could speak a little Algonquian.

And if it were true, it would be a major breakthrough—something she would have to tell her father…if she ever saw him again….

****

As the days passed, Genevieve's life developed into a pattern of work, play and humorous nights spent around a fire. She hadn't become a better seamstress or a cook, but then no one seemed to care, nor even to notice, the people going out of their way to compliment what she did well, even if they had to stretch things a little to find something.

"I don't cook very well," she said in the Blackfoot dialect to Shoots, who sat beside her in Genevieve's lodge, the both of them sewing moccasins.

"No, but you have much medicine."

"I do?"

"*Aa*, yes, you do."

Genevieve gave Shoots a scrutinizing glance. "What does that mean, that I have much medicine? What is this 'medicine?'"

"You do not know?"

"*Saa*, no. I have heard many people speak of this, but I have not understood it well."

Shoots-the-Enemy-Woman sat forward. She said, "The people try to live always in harmony with all that surrounds them. This includes the land, all the animals, the sky, the clouds…everything, including the spiritual world."

"Yes, I have seen this."

"To say that you have great medicine is to say that you have been given power over something—spiritual power—power to heal, or to know the future, to do great things. Do you not have something like this in your world?"

Genevieve thought for a moment. At length, she said, "Not really. Not as you know it. We believe there is only one Creator and that only He has power. But, Shoots, what is it that I have done that makes you think I have great medicine?"

"You do not know?"

"I don't think so."

Shoots-the-Enemy-Woman grinned. "It is talked about all over the camp. I am surprised you have not heard this."

"I haven't."

"Our men have even been singing songs of your praise, for it is well known that you are a great warrior woman."

Genevieve choked. "What?"

"*Aa*, yes. You are thought of highly. It was you, was it not, who captured my brother?"

"Well, yes, but I had the advantage of all my civilization to..." How did she explain this?

But Shoots seemed to have become suddenly hard of hearing. "You see," Shoots said "this is a great coup, to have captured a brave warrior, a deed that some of our best men would not even attempt, and yet you did it."

"But I—" What did she say to this? "Shoots," Genevieve said. "I am afraid I am not the great warrior that you portray me to be."

Shoots-the-Enemy-Woman just smiled. "You do not have to be modest. You are already well thought of."

Genevieve scowled. She said, "Do you know when my husband will return? Perhaps he can explain this better to you. I keep looking for him, but he has been gone already many days."

Shoots-the-Enemy-Woman looked woefully at Genevieve. "I am so sorry that he is gone. You have not been married long, and already he is gone for a long time hunting, and all for what? For my sisters, my mother and myself. We feel bad that we have taken away your husband so soon after your marriage, but if the two of you are to start on your journey, he must do all these things quickly. There are signs already of an early winter, and so you must be on your way soon to avoid getting caught in a blizzard."

Genevieve glanced up from the pair of moccasins she'd been trying to mend. "Journey?"

238

"*Aa,* yes."

Genevieve waited a moment. "What journey?"

"The one you and my brother will be taking as soon as he returns."

"Shoots, I know nothing about a journey. What are you saying?"

Shoots-the-Enemy-Woman smiled and glanced down. "My brother has kept this from you. He must wish to surprise you."

Genevieve sat there, hardly patient. "Shoots, what is it you know?"

"I would not wish to spoil my brother's surprise."

"Shoots? Please, what is it?"

Putting her hand over her mouth, the Indian girl giggled. She said, "He is taking you back to see your father when he returns. It is why he has been in such a hurry to hunt, so that we will have food all winter. It is also why he is with his more-than-friend much of the day. He is making sure that his more-than-friend can provide for us while you two are gone."

"He is?"

Shoots-the-Enemy-Woman nodded.

"Oh, Shoots, this is wonderful. I hadn't known that he was—"

"You must not tell him that I told you. I would not wish to spoil your surprise."

Genevieve smiled. "I won't say a word."

Shoots-the-Enemy-Woman beamed, and, taking the moccasins from Genevieve, said, "I must go now. I will finish these for you. You will take your evening meal with us, will you not?"

"I'd be happy to," Genevieve said and smiled.

****

Gray Hawk trod into camp with White Eagle the very next day.

Genevieve could barely contain her joy, and she would have run up to him right then, but a stern look from Gray Hawk, as he caught her eye from across the camp, kept her where she was.

She beamed at him, but he didn't return the look, going instead first to his mother's lodge and then on to White Eagle's without even another nod in her direction.

Was he ignoring her? Why?

She bridled.

They hadn't seen one another for a few weeks. Shouldn't he be as anxious to see her as she was him?

She waited near White Eagle's lodge for a few more moments. Perhaps Gray Hawk would only be a short while there with his friend.

She waited. She watched.

Nothing.

She paced casually toward White Eagle's lodge, looking around as she went. No one seemed to be paying her any mind.

Good. She had the same sensation she used to have as a child, intent upon some mischief. As casually as she could, she strolled right up to White Eagle's tepee and glanced once more around her.

Did she dare to scratch on the entrance flap to let them know she was here?

She wanted to, and yet... What was the Pikuni etiquette of being in the company of one's husband's best friend? Was it allowed?

She tossed a section of her hair over her shoulder; her hair, as was the custom of the Blackfoot women, was now braided.

Perhaps she should go ask Shoots-the-Enemy-Woman about the proper protocol. Genevieve was about to turn and seek out her sister-in-law when—

"What do you intend to do about your wife when you get there?" It was White Eagle who spoke.

Silence. No response from inside...and Genevieve strained forward. What did he mean, "do about your wife"? She glanced around her again, to ensure she wasn't being watched, and then, kneeling, she huddled in closer toward the tepee.

"I do not understand your concern, *nitakkaawa*, my friend." It was Gray Hawk who spoke. "There is no cause for alarm that I can see."

A pause, then, said White Eagle, "It is always a wise man who prepares for a crisis. If there is no need, one has lost little, but if trouble arises and one is not prepared, one can lose much."

A moment passed; then Gray Hawk responded, "There is little that I can lose, as I see it."

Little that he could lose? If he took her home? He had nothing at all to lose. What could the two friends be referring to? Gray Hawk's freedom, perhaps?

"You trust her, then?"

There was a pause before Gray Hawk answered, "Yes, I believe she will keep her word to me. I know the whites have many unusual ways, but in this I think she speaks true."

What promise had she made to him? She tried to think back quickly. She could remember none. At least none that...oh, yes, she had once told him, when they were still aboard the steamship, that if he would accompany her to St. Louis, she would ensure his eventual freedom.

Was that it?

It seemed there was something else she had told him, but she couldn't think of it at this moment.

"How long do you imagine it will take you to make the journey?" It was White Eagle who was speaking, and Genevieve leaned in closer.

"A month, maybe more. I do not know with a certainty where this village is."

"I have heard that it is in the country of our enemies, the Pawnee."

"Yes," said Gray Hawk. "I have heard those rumors too. I must be careful to guard my wife well, so that the Pawnee do not steal her to try to make the Morning Star ceremony with her."

"*Aa*, yes, my friend," came White Eagle's reply. "I do not believe that you would want your wife sacrificed so soon after your marriage."

She heard Gray Hawk chuckle. "*Saa*, no, my friend, I do not."

241

"What will you do when you get there, *nitakkaawa*?"

"I will take her to her father, I will help him, and then I will leave and return home."

It was a simple enough statement to make, yet for all its simplicity, it had Genevieve straining to hear more. He'd said "I," not "we."

Perhaps she had it wrong. In the Blackfoot language, as in Algonquian, one had to be very careful of their pronouns. Words like "we" and "you" were not used as they are in the English language. Each pronoun was pronounced differently in Blackfoot to distinguish if the speaker was including other people in the "we" or "you," or if the speaker was being exclusive: singular or plural.

Genevieve was sure Gray Hawk had said "*Nitaakahkayi*" or "I'm going home."

"Are you certain, my friend?" It was White Eagle speaking. "Once you take her there, you will help her father and then you, *kiistowa*, alone, will leave. And you do not anticipate any trouble from her over this?"

"*Saa*, no," Gray Hawk said. "I think she will be so happy to see her father that she will not think too much about what will happen with us. I will leave when the time is right. She has promised me this."

Genevieve sank lower onto the ground as she finished the translation. It is said of those who eavesdrop that they never hear well of themselves. Perhaps this was all that was happening here. Maybe she should just leave it now and ask Gray Hawk about this conversation later. Then she might possibly laugh about it. Perhaps she had the translation wrong.

"I still think that you risk much, *nitakkaawa*, my friend."

"Perhaps you are right, and there is something here for me to consider." It was Gray Hawk speaking. "But whether I decide against going there or not does not matter. Until this thing is done, I will have no freedom. And I crave the carefree life I used to have before she came here. I grow tired of this constant worry."

Freedom? Carefree life? He didn't mean freedom from her, or did he?

It was then that something struck her. Gray Hawk had once told her that he enjoyed his freedom — but he'd been speaking of his independence as a bachelor at the time. He'd been explaining to her why he had never married.

And now that she was remembering it, other memories came back to mind. He'd plainly told her that he wasn't happy about marrying her, saying that he was sacrificing much to take her as his sits-beside-him-wife. He'd said it quite plainly: *he did not want her.* She just hadn't really listened.

As though momentarily haunted, Genevieve stared off into space.

"Once you take her back to her father, *nitakkaawa,*" White Eagle was saying, "you will have your carefree life back. Therefore, I would agree that it is well worth your time to take her to her home."

"*Aa,*" said Gray Hawk. "And it will be better if I do it right away. I have already delayed too long."

That was it, then. Gray Hawk really meant to leave her.

She didn't know why the thought of it should make her feel so desolate. But it did.

Genevieve got to her feet as quietly as possible and turned away, not waiting to hear more.

Well, at least she knew. *He means to abandon me...after he's helped my father, of course.*

She wasn't certain why she should feel so sarcastic, or so despondent about the whole thing. That was what she had intended from the beginning, wasn't it? To find and take an Indian back with her for her father, and then to let the individual go?

Her stomach began to twist almost painfully, and she felt as though she might, at any moment, cry.

Well, it wasn't that way anymore; she didn't want to let Gray Hawk go. She didn't care what she had planned at the start; she didn't feel the same way now. She'd come to know him.

She scoffed at herself. Know him? Who was she fooling? She loved him. She'd do most anything for him.

Even live here in this camp with him.

She caught her breath. That was a truth she hadn't quite realized.

Never, in all the time she had been in the Indian village, had she ever consciously decided she might want to stay. Always had been in the back of her mind the idea that she must go home.

But look at what she was doing, at what she had been trying to accomplish in these last few weeks. Wasn't she learning to live here? Making friends, discovering, trying to please? Why?

For Gray Hawk. Why?

She reached her own tepee at last, and, pulling back the buckskin flap, stepped quickly inside.

She glanced around her, at all the items she'd been given here, at those things she'd made herself. And for what?

She'd never come back here.

She shut her eyes and fell to her knees.

How was it possible? When had she started to regard the Indian camp as her home? She, who had always had the riches of the world to surround her? How had this happened to her?

When she had tried to make that pact with Gray Hawk almost a month ago, she'd promised him that she would return here with him if he would only take her to St. Louis. And though she'd meant it, she had felt as if she were sacrificing her very life to do so.

But now, here she was, knowing she would be going home to her father, never to return, and not only did the thought of it bring her pain, she felt as though her life might suddenly stop because of it.

How was this possible?

Love. She moaned.

Of course it was love. She wanted to be near Gray Hawk always. Coming to live here, beginning to know the people, their ways...and seeing it wasn't all so bad...

In truth, there was a freedom here that she would be hard put to find back home. Factually, she couldn't remember ever being so happy, or so at peace with herself, with the forces of nature all around her.

Maybe she should have known that it would come to this...maybe.

But how could she have realized that love would make her want to give up everything: wealth, her country, even her work with her father?

Her father. She groaned.

What was she to do about her father?

She didn't want to return, and yet...

She suddenly looked up. She had a crazy idea...or maybe not so crazy. Why hadn't she thought of this before?

There was a solution right here. How had it escaped her for so long?

She knew enough about the Blackfeet to write her father's thesis for him. *She* had lived with the Blackfeet; she even knew their language and its roots; she was familiar with the Blackfoot customs, their beliefs.

She could write it down and then *send* it to her father. With the steamship traveling up and down the Missouri, there were regular mail passes between Fort Union and St. Louis.

She could *write* to her father. She didn't *have* to go and see him.

Of course, there was always the problem of how to get to Fort Union, but that was a minor problem. The main thing was that she didn't *have* to return to her father, to England.

Could she convince Gray Hawk to take her to Fort Union?

She dismissed the idea immediately. If he meant to leave her in St. Louis, he might not relish the idea of her finding a way to stay here...with him.

She thrust out her chin. How dare he think that way!

One thing was certain: he had to get used to the idea that when a man takes a sits-beside-him-wife, he had better be ready to keep her with him for the rest of his life.

She was going to see that he did.

But first she needed to get to Fort Union. Perhaps she could do it on her own. Could she?

How difficult could it be? After all, the Blackfoot trading party had managed it once before.

Could she?

She wasn't exactly a novice anymore. She had *some* knowledge of how to survive on the prairie.

Hadn't she watched Gray Hawk when he'd brought her here? Hadn't he taught her well? And hadn't she been learning from his sisters? Couldn't she trap her own food now, skin it and cook it?

By goodness, yes. That was it. She could and she would do it on her own. She would go to the trading post alone; she only needed to know what direction to take—well, maybe a few more precise directions—and a little help from her friends or, rather, her new "sisters."

And then wouldn't Gray Hawk be proud of her? He'd better be.

She raised her head and squinted her eyes. She'd make that man see he was making a mistake by wanting to dump her in St. Louis…somehow…some way, she would do it.

But there was more. It wasn't fair that she loved him, and that he only…well, did he love her? Exactly what were his feelings toward her?

Yes, she knew she had his passion. But, she decided all at once, it wasn't enough. She was going to make this man come to *love* her.

By goodness, this was what she'd do.

And it all depended upon her ability to get to Fort Union.

Well, she'd do it. Just watch her. It was a crazy scheme, a white woman going off alone to do such a thing, but didn't a person have to pay attention to dreams sometimes just to get anything done?

She lifted her head. She felt better already.

Chapter Twenty

"*She* what?"

"Your sits-beside-him-wife was asking me many questions today about the white man's trading post, seeking to find the path to take to reach it."

Gray Hawk barely gave the orphan boy a glance. "And what did you tell her?"

"I did not see the harm in pointing out the way to the Big River, and from there to follow it to the fort, at least not at first. But now I wonder."

Gray Hawk, who was still lounging against a willow rest in White Eagle's lodge, peered steadily at the boy. The youth, who had probably reached only ten winters, had come to White Eagle's tepee only a few moments ago, seeking an audience with Gray Hawk. Gray Hawk asked, "Why do you now wonder?"

The young boy stared at his feet. "I worry."

Silence ensued while Gray Hawk waited for the lad to continue. At length, he prompted, "You worry?"

The young boy swallowed. "*Aa*, yes, I do."

"Why?"

The youth looked away. "Because your sits-beside-him-wife left the camp."

"*Ánniayi*, I can understand it, then, your worry. Did she go to bathe alone? You are wise to have come and told me this." It was the only thing

Gray Hawk could imagine Gen-ee would do that might upset this boy. To bathe after dark, without a chaperone, was to take risks, even here in camp.

Gray Hawk started to rise, determined that he would speak to his wife at once about the dangers of bathing alone. He said to the boy, "You have done well. I have a new knife I will give you for observing with such diligence."

The lad shifted, looking down at his feet. "Perhaps I do not deserve it."

Gray Hawk had gotten to his knees when he glanced up sharply at the boy. "What do you mean?"

Again the boy fidgeted, and even White Eagle sat forward. "I am not certain that she went to take a bath. I saw her lead your best pony out of the herd today…"

A long pause. "*Aa*, yes?"

The boy shuffled his feet. "She rode out of camp early this afternoon, and she had with her several parfleches that looked full, plus she took with her a robe around her shoulders and an extra one for warmth. Do you see? I fear she may be going to this fort, and that is why she asked me about it."

Gray Hawk couldn't speak for several moments. He just stared at the boy.

"Why did you delay coming to us with this information?" It was White Eagle who finally put the question to the lad.

"I did not see the harm in it before now. She is, after all, a warrior woman, and as such I have no right to question her movements. Yet, something about what she did seemed strange to me, because she kept looking around her, as though afraid that she might get caught doing something. It wasn't until a few moments ago that I remembered her asking me the way to the white man's fort." The boy suddenly looked up. "I have done the right thing in telling you, have I not?"

Gray Hawk nodded. He cleared his throat, but still he said nothing.

"Do you say that she went out alone?" It was White Eagle who spoke.

"*Aa*, yes. I saw no one else leave with her."

"And she is definitely gone?" Again White Eagle questioned the youth.

"*Aa*, yes. I checked her lodge before I came here. I was hoping I was wrong."

Gray Hawk met White Eagle's glance, but still Gray Hawk did not speak. Something had hit him hard in the pit of his stomach, and Gray Hawk was uncertain how long it would take him to recover.

His Gen-ee, gone? How could it be?

She had looked so happy to see him today, and he had...ignored her.

Perhaps he shouldn't have, but it seemed to him that this was the way a man was supposed to treat his wife. Hadn't he seen other men in the tribe, well-respected men, handle their women this way?

Gray Hawk sighed. Such behavior had certainly gained him nothing.

Perhaps he was wrong to have ignored her. It wasn't the way *he* would treat a woman if he were alone with her. A woman, as far as he was concerned, should be handled with respect.

Something he hadn't done today.

Had his Gen-ee rebelled and gone off without him?

It was something he would never have predicted she would do, but then she had more spirit than most, a spirit he did not wish to crush.

He would go and find her, of course. There was little else he could do.

Not because it was expected of him. No, he would go to her because...why? Why did he feel as though the earth had suddenly slipped out from beneath his feet? Why so...empty?

It couldn't be that he...cared for her, could it?

Well, of course he *cared* for her. He had made her his sits-beside-him-wife. But his feelings for her didn't go beyond a need to protect her, did they?

Or did they?

He stared at the young lad before him. At length Gray Hawk repeated, "She is not in our lodge, you are certain?"

"*Aa*, yes. She is not there."

Gray Hawk acknowledged the youth with a mere look and a flick of his wrist.

"And did she tell you anything about where she went or why?"

The lad shuffled his feet again, looking down. At last, though, the boy said, "Your mother and your sisters were with her when she left. They waved to her."

"My mother?"

The boy acknowledged.

"My sisters?"

"Yes. Your sisters gave her the extra buffalo robe."

Gray Hawk glanced over toward his friend, who seemed unable to do more than give Gray Hawk a puzzled glance.

"Come here, boy," Gray Hawk said, drawing from around his waist a new, shiny knife, beautifully sheathed in white, beaded buckskin. Taking it firmly in hand, he held it out toward the boy. He gave the young orphan a smile. "I will be leaving here soon. I will need someone to watch over my ponies while I am away. I would ask that you do this for me. And, young man, if you do this well while I am away, you may call my lodge your own."

The boy's face suddenly lit up.

"My more-than-friend here will see to it that you are taken care of in my absence. And yes, you have done the right thing."

The quick, bright grin on the lad's face was quite something to behold, and Gray Hawk was glad he had made the offer. Later, when he had retrieved his wife, he knew that his Gen-ee would thank him. Besides being winsome, the boy could provide that extra helping hand he was certain his Gen-ee would need.

"What do you think your wife does?" White Eagle asked after the boy had left.

Gray Hawk shrugged, and, jerking his head slightly to the left, he tried to keep his expression blank. "I do not know," he said matter-of-factly. "When I saw her in camp today, she looked happy. Perhaps she grows tired of my delay and wishes to go and find her father on her own. But I am now ready to leave on that journey. I have seen to all that I must in our village. I may as well start off this night as any other."

"Relax, *nitakkaawa*. I am sure she is all right. She cannot go far in the dark, and there is no sign of rain tonight. Why not get a good night's rest and pick up her trail in the morning?"

Gray Hawk didn't even hesitate. "If she is on the trail, so, then, should I be. Besides, *nitakkaawa*, you do not know this woman as I do. There is much trouble she can get into. I had best leave tonight. She already has many hours of travel ahead of me."

White Eagle nodded. "Do you wish me to accompany you only as far as she is?"

"*Saa*, no, not this time. You already do much for me."

White Eagle grinned. "Or perhaps you do not want me there when you find her. Maybe you would like to spend the night with her alone?"

Gray Hawk didn't return the grin, nor did he do anything else to show an acknowledgment.

"*Nitakkaawa*." White Eagle looked at his friend. "What is it?"

Gray Hawk stared at the tepee poles. He said, "I worry. What if something happens to her? I don't know what I would do if... There is so much trouble that she could cause."

White Eagle frowned. "She is a warrior woman. She—"

"Is not. She could no more defend herself than she could make the wind blow."

"But she captured you."

"Yes, it is true that she did. But not alone. She paid others to do it for her. She paid others to guard me, but she did not actually take me captive. I have let the camp rumors stand without comment because I wished her to be accepted. My friend, when I captured my wife, she did not even know how to cook, skin an animal or build a fire, let alone know how to defend herself against a hungry animal."

"Then she could be—"

251

"In danger now."

"You had better go quickly, *nitakkaawa*."

"Yes," Gray Hawk said. "I fear that if I do not leave immediately, it might be too late."

White Eagle emptied his pipe and, tapping it on its bowl, signaled the end of their meeting. "May the spirits that protect you see your wife and yourself safely on your journey."

Gray Hawk smiled at his friend, and, getting quickly to his feet, stepped from the tepee into the night.

****

"What? You are telling me that you will not allow me to go and search for my wife?"

Gray Hawk's mother gave her son an irritated look. "She has a wild spirit, that one. You must be careful not to squash it."

"Why would I want to squash it?"

"You are a man, are you not?"

"What has that to do with it, my mother?"

Gray Hawk's mother sighed. "Sometimes, my son, I am not certain of you. Where is your power of observation? Are you helpless?"

Gray Hawk grinned. "Only when I want to be."

One of Gray Hawk's sisters, who was pretending to be asleep, giggled. The older woman cast a sharp look at her daughter.

His mother turned back to stare at Gray Hawk. She said, "Your wife would not have left if you were more of a man."

Gray Hawk narrowed his eyes at his mother. No one else would have ever said such a thing to him. No one else would have dared. He said, "There had better be good reason why you speak this way to me. If you were a man, you would no longer be living."

"*Ha'*! We helped her to leave," his mother said. "We thought she had good reason."

"I know that you did, my mother. What I do not know is why. Why did you help her?"

"Surely you must know."

"If I knew this, my mother, I would not be asking you now."

"You must forgive us for siding with her, but we have grown quite attached to her since she has been with us. She does not know how to do many of our chores well, but she tries so hard. And she is, after all, a warrior woman. Maybe she just never learned these things. And she seems so intent, so much in love with you, to be attempting this. And we thought it would not hurt to help her. And, too, because she is a warrior woman, we could not see that much harm could come to her going off by herself."

Gray Hawk drew a deep breath, keeping a hold on his temper. It was not a good thing to do, to show anger to a woman, since a female was unable to defend herself physically against a man. Such things, even anger, only intimidated a woman and ultimately killed her spirit, a thing a man must always guard against, since a woman represented the love and the beauty of the race, their future.

He said, "My mother, my wife is not as invincible as she might seem. She could come to harm out there at night since she does not know the prairie. She has been raised differently than our women." He gazed at his mother, but seeing that she still had the same stern look upon her face, he said, "I worry."

"You should have thought of that before you decided to leave her."

"Leave her?"

"*Aa*, yes, my son. She told us all about it."

Gray Hawk drew back as though slapped. So that was what had happened to his Gen-ee. She thought that he... A spark lit within him. Ah, there was hope.

He suddenly grinned, noting that his mother bristled. He said, "Perhaps you should tell me about how she came to this conclusion, since I have no intention of leaving her."

"Maybe not now."

"Maybe not ever."

His mother gave him a shrewd look. She said, "Prove it."

"I should not have to; I am your son."

His mother sighed.

Now, while it is true that in the more "civilized" world, a mother might still have reason to disbelieve her son, this was not true to the Indian mother. An Indian man, particularly a son, never lied. To do so would be to court death.

And Gray Hawk's mother, knowing this, said, "She overheard you telling your more-than-friend that you were going to leave her with her father once you took her to her home."

Gray Hawk raised his eyebrows. "This is an odd thing for her to have overheard, since I did not say it."

"She was certain."

Gray Hawk shrugged. "I did not say it."

"She must have… I do not believe that she lied. She truly thinks that you mean to leave her."

"Perhaps she overheard someone else speaking."

"Your wife not recognizing your voice?"

"Or perhaps she mistranslated something I said. But this is unimportant. Where is she going?"

"It is true that she might have misunderstood your words."

Gray Hawk could barely contain himself. "Where has she gone?"

His mother sighed. "To the white man's post on the Big River."

So the boy was right. Gray Hawk thought for a moment. "That is a long journey to attempt on her own."

"She is a warrior woman."

Gray Hawk groaned. "Even for a man, that would be a long journey to make alone."

"*Aa*, yes, you are right. But it seemed harmless when she told us of it. And she is doing it for you."

"How can she be doing this for me? Can you not see that I am still here in our camp?"

His mother looked doubtful. "I do not understand it all, but your wife said that she could contact her father somehow at that fort."

"He is not there."

"She said there was still a way. And she explained that then you would not have to take her back to her home...that she could stay here. Do you not see how attentive she is to you? She will make you a good wife."

"I am glad that you think so, but I must get her back before she can do that. Now, I need you and my sisters to prepare my things and hers, because I leave this night to go and find her. And when I get her, I will take her to her village, just as I said that I would."

"But you do not intend to leave her there?"

"I never have."

His mother nodded. "Then we will help you."

No sooner had his mother said the words than all three of his sisters threw off their coverings and sat up, all three of them still fully dressed.

Gray Hawk shook his head when he saw them and glanced at his mother, a half smile on his lips. He said, "Not even my sisters were going to help me?"

His mother grinned. "Not even your sisters."

Gray Hawk laughed. He said, "I am glad that you all like her. I am truly glad. But come now and give me your assistance. I must leave here at once."

And quickly, just as his mother had said they would be, all his sisters were ready to help.

Gray Hawk left within the hour.

****

Genevieve hadn't actually realized how frightening it could be out on the prairie, alone, at night.

Why hadn't she noticed before how dark the sky was, how vast the stars, how quiet the wind, how noisy the steps of her pony?

She glanced behind her. She led the pony by its buckskin bridle since she was afraid it might stumble into a hole under the cover of darkness.

She wasn't certain she should be traveling at night. But she remembered that when Gray Hawk had been in danger, he had always made his moves after dusk had fallen.

It seemed a safe and fast rule.

But what if she stumbled over something: a snake, a bear, a...*ca ca boo*?

Oh, that's silly, she told herself. Gray Hawk had just made up that stupid animal and the story to frighten her. Still...

She raised her head to look ahead of her, being very careful to keep the Rocky Mountains behind her.

There was a moon tonight, almost full, which meant she was quite visible out here on the plains. She had better stay alert.

She gazed off to her left.

What was that?

Had she seen a movement?

She stopped. She slunk back toward the pony, who whinnied at her.

"Shh..." she said, and the pony rubbed his head against her hair.

Had she imagined it? Was it only the wind?

She heard a noise; she saw something move again.

Oh, Lord, something was out there, she was sure of it.

Despair began to descend upon her when all at once it occurred to her: it wasn't fair to be intercepted now.

She'd come all this way with no trouble, and she wanted none. She was making this trip for good reasons, with no intention of hurting anyone. She didn't deserve this, to die out here on the prairie with no one around to mourn her passing.

Why, Gray Hawk might even think she had left him.

She bristled all over again.

256

How dare he! No, there was too much unsettled business between them for this to happen. She couldn't die. Not now.

She had better confront whatever was there. It certainly didn't look as though it was going to go away.

She raised her chin and took a step forward.

But it was just as clear that what was out there advanced toward her. She held back, her knees trembling.

Was it a wolf? A bear? A cougar? Man? A *ca ca boo*?

And then it was there in front of her, not a bear, not a cougar, nor a coyote. It was a man, a tall man, leading a horse behind him.

The man's hair blew back in the breeze, and his muscular figure stood silhouetted against the midnight beams of the moon.

He looked more apparition than real figure, more godly than human flesh.

And she knew him.

"Gen-ee," the phantom said.

She groaned, almost losing her footing. And she didn't know which she felt more, relief or anger.

The apparition kept talking. He said, "I have come for you, Gen-ee. You are my wife. You should be with me. My mother has told me why you left, and I think you should know that I do not intend, and have never intended, to leave you."

She threw back her head. And though there were many things she wished to say, all she was able to utter was, "You have just now scared me."

"I am sorry." He took a step forward.

She backed away. "All right, I—"

"Gen-ee, you are my wife. I would not leave you. I...care for you."

Was that all? She said, "Care? Nothing more?"

"Isn't it enough? It means much to me."

"Does it? Why don't I quite believe that?"

257

He grinned. "I will gladly try to convince you if you will only come closer."

"No," she said. "I...of course, I know you can *convince* me, make me respond to you physically, but I—"

He suddenly swept forward, and, not hesitating a moment, took her into his arms. "But what?"

She tried to take his arms from around her, to back away, but he was too strong, and the pony prevented any movement she would have made.

"Gen-ee," was all Gray Hawk said as his head descended toward hers.

And without warning, the essence of him, that quality that made Gray Hawk who he was, engulfed her. She felt warm all over; she felt loved, wanted. And she could sense herself weakening.

She inhaled, and the scent of buckskin and leather, horseflesh and male essence assailed her. She reached out to touch him, and the warm resistance of his skin fascinated her. She spread out her hands.

The prairie winds caressed them, and the stars, the sky, even the earth beneath their feet, seemed somehow closer, a part of it all.

It was an intoxicating blend and...hard to resist. Still... She turned her head away.

"It is not true," he said, and she could feel the seductive movement of his lips against her cheek, though she tried not to think of it. "I do not know what you heard there in camp, but whatever it was, it is not right. I do not intend to leave you. From the moment I stole you away from the medicine canoe, it has not been so."

"You want your freedom from me, though."

"No," he said. "I want my freedom, but not from you. So that is what you heard, is it?"

She didn't say anything, but her body must have grown stiff in his embrace.

He said, his lips finding and nibbling on her earlobe, "I worry about you, Gen-ee. I know you have problems in your home; I know you need to see your father, and I realize he has reason to speak with me. But I have not been able to give these things to you, and I have worried. When you heard me say I wanted my freedom, I talked about being free of this worry, not from you."

She could feel his grin against her cheek. "I do not wish to worry about you for the rest of my life," he continued. "I would have you settle your problems, my wife, so that we can begin our life together. It was this I meant."

She turned her head back toward him. "But I heard you say '*Nitaakahkayi*' to your friend," she argued. "And that means *I* am going home, not *we*. And then when you did say *we* were going home, you said '*Nitaakitapoohpinnaan ahkayi.*' But that's the exclusive use of *we*, meaning you weren't taking me with you."

Gray Hawk smiled. "You have learned my language well, my wife," he said. "But you forget that '*Nitaakitapoohpinnaan ahkayi*' excludes only the person you are talking to. When I said that, it meant that *my friend* would not be coming home with me, naturally, since he would not be there. I did not mean you."

Genevieve gazed up at him. She said, "Is that what that means?"

He nodded.

Her lips mouthed the word "oh." She paused, regaining her voice, before she said, "Do not mind me, then."

He laughed softly. "But I have something to ask you," he said, his lips a mere hairsbreadth above hers. "Why did you not come and ask me about this? Why did you leave, taking my best pony, to make this trip to the white man's post alone? You have worried me even further."

"Gray Hawk, I—"

"Were you lying to my mother, saying you were doing this only for me? I know that your father is not at that post. Were you doing this to escape me?"

"I..." What could she say? That she would not consider leaving him again? That she loved Gray Hawk more than anything else in her life? That the thought of not seeing him again made her feel slightly ill?

No, she didn't think she could say any of those things. Not when he only "cared" about her.

She tried to back up away from him, but his arms held her tightly to him, and she could do no more than stare at the buckskin shirt at his shoulder.

She took a deep breath. She said, "It is hard to explain what I mean to do."

"I am listening. And as you can see, I have all night."

She sighed. "I am not sure that I want to—"

"We will not leave here until you tell me what you are meaning to do."

"But I—"

"I give you my word on that. We will stay here forever if we have to."

She turned her face slightly in toward him, to give him a "look," but her efforts were wasted. He didn't see, or at least he pretended not to see. Finally, she said, "There is a way my people have of communicating with each other without having to be there. It is called 'writing.'"

"I have seen this," he said. "But it still does not explain—"

"What I meant to do is to write my father a letter once I get to the fort. I have decided to write down, in the letter, all my observations about your people, their language and their customs, and then send it to him. If I could do this, then I will rest easier, knowing my father can finish his book."

She paused, and Gray Hawk said nothing for a long while, not even acknowledging that he had heard her. She felt him breathe deeply once, then again. At last he asked, "Why would you want to do this instead of going back to your home? I know now that you are aware of my intentions to take you to this St. Louis. Do you not wish to see your father?"

"I…" She sighed and rested her forehead on Gray Hawk's shoulder. She said, "Yes, I would love to see my father, but…I am uncertain I wish to… Well, I…may not want to leave just yet. I—"

"And what makes you uncertain of this, my Gen-ee?" His question was just barely whispered. His arms tightened around her.

"Gray Hawk, I…"

"Yes?" He placed a finger under her chin, bringing her face around toward his. "What makes you want to stay with my people for a little longer?"

He stared down into her eyes, his look soft, his gaze inquiring, and suddenly, it was there for her to see: love, his love for her. She could perceive it, read it there on his face, so much so that she felt as though, if she were to reach out, she could touch it.

She shook herself. Back in the Indian camp, he had at times pretended to be the devoted husband, only then to ignore her, to walk away, to leave her alone while he went out on a hunt. How could she be certain if he—

"I love you, Gen-ee," he said as though reading her thoughts. "Until you left tonight, I am not certain that I really knew this. But tonight I have come to realize that I do not wish to live my life without you. Tell me, Gen-ee, is it this that you feel for me?"

She shut her eyes, and very slowly, very slightly, she nodded. It was the first time, outside of a passionate moment, that she had admitted her love to him, and she wasn't certain what to expect.

"I feel it, too, Gen-ee," he said. "If I have been slow to see it for what it is, please believe that it has not been an easy thing for me to accept. I have loved my independent life well, but the thought now of living my life without you has little appeal. I want you with me always."

"Always?"

"Yes, little Gen-ee, always."

She breathed in all at once and shut her eyes, committing to memory this moment: the caress of the wind, the position of the moon and stars, the scent of his skin, the feel of his hair, his arms as he held her.

And her doubts fled, just like that, disappearing into the night as though they were mere shadows.

She stared up at him, his handsome face outlined in the dim, soft light of the moon. She'd known it for quite some time now, that she loved him, but somehow, right here, right now, there was more. She loved this man— totally, completely, without pause.

And suddenly she couldn't get enough of him. She ran her lips over his neck, tasting his clean-scented skin; she pressed her ear to his chest, listening to the sound of his breathing; she placed her hand over his arm, feeling the movement of his muscles.

She wanted him, whatever it was that made him who he was, good or bad, if only because it all was a part of him.

And the weight of her love, the power of it, almost overwhelmed her.

She said, simply, "I love you, Gray Hawk, and I want you to know that you don't have to take me back to St. Louis. I could write this letter at Fort Union, and then we could just go home."

He grunted. He said, "We could, yes. It is good that you will consider this. But if we did not go back, you would never see your father, never know if he received the letter you would write, never know if he survived. You would worry, my wife, and then I would become concerned, and we would most likely have to make the trip later, when it is possible your father might have moved."

"Please, Gray Hawk, I still fear that you might leave me there."

"I will not. Believe me, Gen-ee, I have never intended to do that."

"Yes, of course. I know that now, but still I fear... Gray Hawk, there is more," she said. "I am almost afraid of going back. My society is so different from yours, and I'm concerned that something else might happen... There are few white men who love the Indian. There could be trouble if others discover we are married. It is possible we might be separated."

Gray Hawk shook his head. "Then I would find you and capture you again. You are my wife, Gen-ee, for as long as I will live."

"I am?"

He nodded. "Do your people not mate for life?"

"Yes, but I thought that—"

"Come, Gen-ee. We stand here talking when I have made a camp ahead of us. And while I enjoy the feel of you in my arms, we would be more comfortable elsewhere."

"You have already set up...? But how did you...? I left long before you—"

"Gen-ee, you forget that I know this country well. I have had you in my sight for a while now. Long enough to set up camp in a spot where we should not be disturbed...even when morning comes..."

The intent behind his words, the sensual way in which he said them, was not lost on Genevieve.

She still had her arms around him, her face pressed into the shoulder of his shirt, when she grinned. "You are presuming much, are you not, my husband?"

"I do not think so. You are my wife."

"Prove it."

It was the second time this night that Gray Hawk had been asked to do that.

This particular time, however, he did not object.

"I would be happy to do so," he said as he swept her up into his arms, carrying her as though she were as light as the robe around her shoulders. "I thought you would never ask."

Chapter Twenty-One

*M*oonlight shone down upon the camp, lighting it up as though it were day.

Gray Hawk glanced at the makeshift shelter he had built against a cliff. The front of it leaned up toward the ledge while the back of the tepee-type design was enclosed by a length of buffalo hide. The whole thing disappeared into its surroundings of balsam and pine trees.

If enemies were about, which he doubted, they would have to look closely to find this place, almost hidden from view as it was.

Close by the camp ran a stream that looked as though its bottom were made of gold dust. Moonlight sparkled off the racing water, while the lapping of it provided a sound that was as beautiful as any song he had ever heard.

He took Genevieve first to the stream, and, settling her down upon its bank, cupped his hands to bring water to her. He smiled at her, and she gave him back the same tender look.

He noted almost absently that she had taken to braiding her hair and had even painted a red streak down her center part, as was the style among the Blackfoot women. Her red locks, vibrant with color, glowed here in the moonlight and framed her oval face as though the space around her were alive with red fire.

He touched one of her braids, the texture of her hair as soft as a rose petal, even tied up as it was.

He had always thought his Gen-ee beautiful, but until this moment, he had never admired her so much.

Her skin radiated health; her cheeks were slightly red from the sun, and scattered across her nose was a spattering of freckles.

He ran his hand over her cheek, its feel beneath his fingertips delicate, soft.

He gazed into her eyes, her look slightly shadowed, mysterious. And her womanly scent — sweet, musky, sensual — made him want to hold her and never allow her out of his arms.

Had he known he would feel so possessive of her the first time he had seen her there in the fort, he might have run as far away as he could. But he hadn't.

He had stayed, had even considered accepting her silly proposition, even before she had taken him captive.

She sat before him here, under the moonlight, in a tan Indian dress that was intricately decorated with porcupine quills and beads. On her legs she had tight leggings that reached all the way to her knees, and on her feet she wore moccasins. She looked Indian, yet not.

Her dress was Blackfoot, yes, but her skin, her hair, her eyes...all these things were uniquely hers and not easily compared.

Like her nose. He loved her nose — strong, yet small, the tip of it turning softly up at the end. He ran a fingertip over it and was rewarded with a deep sigh from her.

He groaned.

He loved those little moans. The sounds she made were music to his ears. He listened for them when he made love to her; he gloried in them.

She brought her chin up, and seemed to beg him for a kiss. He didn't hesitate to give it to her.

He almost groaned again. Her lips were sweet and wet from the water. And he wanted so much more.

He deepened the kiss, his tongue sweeping inward to capture even more of her taste.

She pulled her head slightly away from him and grinned at him, her look that of a winsome child.

She drew her shoulders back, her chest automatically going forward, and Gray Hawk's gaze moved downward from her face.

She began to lower the sleeves of her dress, and he gazed back up at her, catching that look in her eyes that was part feline, part minx.

Next came her belt and then her dress. And soon she sat before him, clad only in knee-high leggings and moccasins.

He grinned, and, squatting before her, began the task of removing these last.

She whimpered and made little movements with her legs, with her hips, that would have sent him over the edge if he hadn't realized what lay in store, yet to come this night.

He held himself back.

"You are more beautiful," he said, "than I remember. Perhaps I have been gone too long hunting."

She smiled. "Perhaps."

He was rubbing her feet, and she giggled, sitting forward in a hurry. "That tickles," she said, lying back and sighing.

"What?" He did it again.

"Gray Hawk, stop that."

"Do you mean this?"

She giggled again, sitting up.

Suddenly her face was in front of his. She leaned in toward him, and he drew forward.

"Gen-ee."

"Gray Hawk."

Moonlight shone down on them, bathing their features in the soft rays of silvery beams while the fresh scent of balsam blew around them on the wind.

Caught in the moment, they stared at one another as though unable to believe the beauty of the other: one of them pale, with fiery hair glowing and shimmering with vitality under the waxen light; the other contrastingly dark, his mane of ebony hair glistening with a bluish-black luster.

They were connected, these two, and nothing mattered between them: not race, not culture, not even prejudice.

They loved, pure and simple.

Her lips were only a minuscule distance away from him, yet he didn't touch her, wanting only to admire. He breathed in, and her pure scent, combined with the pine and balsam carried to him on the breeze, reached out to him; her fragrance, her radiance, wrapped around him more tightly than the clothes he wore.

He had never felt this way in his life. Not once. Not ever.

"I love you."

They said the words together, as though their language were perfectly choreographed.

At last he leaned in, closing the tiny gap between them, kissing her with only a hint of sweet passion, yet she swooned forward as though he had given her the world.

His stomach reacted. Ah, his Gen-ee. How he loved her, how he gloried in her response to him.

All at once, her hands came up to his chest, and he felt the effect of her touch all through his system.

He shuddered, but she wasn't done. She kissed her way over toward his ear, and as sensation swept over him again, he heard her say, "One of us has too many clothes on."

He chuckled softly, but at the same time drew his shirt over his head, and, as though it were on fire, tossed it aside.

He felt her fingers at the tie around his waist, at his belt, loosening it.

His breechcloth fell off, leaving only his leggings and moccasins upon him.

And just as he had done with her earlier, she took his feet in her hands, removed each of his moccasins, and massaged first one and then the other foot.

She didn't pay any attention to his leggings since these were only attached to his belt, which was already loosened. Instead she stared at him, at the effect she had on him, and he could feel himself harden even more under her look.

"Gray Hawk, I—"

"Let us swim, Gen-ee."

"No, it is too cold."

"Ah, but it is good for you."

She shook her head and gave him a crooked smile. "Maybe for you," she said. "You are used to it, but I noticed that none of the women in your camp take midnight swims on these cool evenings—only the men. And I must agree with the women. It is too cold."

He splashed a little water up on her.

"Gray Hawk..."

He gave her an impish glance. "Let us wade then, and later we can snuggle underneath one of the robes."

"No, I...wade, did you say?"

He grinned and nodded to her, her face so close to his own.

She said, "I will wade with you, but that is all."

"Good."

He removed his leggings in an instant and stood, offering his hand to help her up.

But she didn't immediately rise.

She just stared at him, her gaze skimming up and down his body, centering in upon that area at the juncture of his legs.

He felt as though his skin tingled under her inspection, and he grew even harder.

"Come," he said, and he pulled her to her feet. "We will wade out into the water, just a little."

He saw her gaze upon his naked body, her glance centering on his chest and his manhood, and he felt his pulse race at her attention. He grinned at her. "You are welcome to do more than look," he said.

She glanced immediately at him, her eyes round.

He merely chuckled and held his hand out toward her. "Come."

He led her out into the stream then, its coolness sending welcome shivers up his spine.

"Gray Hawk, it's freezing."

"Yes, it makes the blood start pounding, does it not?"

"Not, I'm afraid."

He splashed her.

"Gray Hawk, you said you wouldn't…"

"Did I?"

"Yes, well, no, but…" She giggled, and, lunging away from him, splashed him back.

He gave her a stern look. "You know this means a fight to the death, do you not?"

"To the death?"

He grinned. "Perhaps not to the death. Maybe I should say 'to the bed.'"

"Is that what this is? A war over our bed?"

He inclined his head. "It could be. We could wager. If you win this fight, you may order me do whatever you would wish, but if *I* win the fight, *I* will have you…order me to do anything that you wish."

She chuckled and shook her head. "What a fate I must suffer, then. It seems I must order you about no matter the outcome."

He grinned. "Yes," he said. "What terrible things await you." He gave her a deliberate leer, then a tsk-tsk. "Come now. Let us see who is to win this fight." He splashed her.

And she shrieked, but she got him back.

He followed, then she, back and forth.

He held back the full force of his power, seeming to barely keep up his own end, until he had enticed her into the full part of the stream, where he let loose upon her, soaking her entirely.

But she didn't seem to notice. She only laughed and lay back, splashing at him with her feet.

He moved in closer toward her, making a shower with every step he took, until he came right up to her. And there, taking her in his arms and pulling her up to him, he kissed her lips, her cheeks, her eyes, her nose, her lips again.

"I love you," he said. "*Kitsikakomimmo.*" And he began the process all over again.

"*Kitsikakomimmo,*" she said, returning his every embrace.

They stood in the water, only thigh deep.

At first, he wasn't aware of what she did. At first, he was only cognizant that he needed her, that he wanted her.

But she had moved her head slightly downward until she was nibbling on *his* chest, on *his* nipples. Excitement tore through him.

He groaned, the sound deep in his throat. He let her kiss those sensitive spots on his body, over and over, on and on, until he thought he couldn't take it anymore.

And then he brought her back up toward him.

"Do you not like that?" she asked after he had lifted her up to him.

"I like it very much."

"Then why did you have me stop?"

"Because I like it too much," he said, bringing her shivering body in toward his, wrapping her in the warmth of his arms. "I have plans for the night, and I do not wish it to end prematurely."

"Prematurely?" Her gaze at him was one of pure innocence.

He nodded. "Yes. Had you kissed me there too much longer, I would not have been able to stop myself from concluding our love making. I do not wish to do that yet."

"Oh." She mouthed the word.

"Come," he said. "You are shivering. Let us go and find that buffalo robe I promised you."

And with this said, he lifted her into his arms and carried her to the lean-to, not stopping until he had entered the structure and had her…and himself wrapped up in a buffalo robe.

Throwing off the robe, he started a fire, quickly, efficiently, and within minutes, the two of them were warm again, wrapped together within the robe, and staring into the blaze.

"Where will we go, Gray Hawk?" she asked after a while, her body snuggled in closely toward his. "To the fort, or to my father's?"

"To your father's." He didn't look at her. He kept staring into the flames. "It is what I have intended for some time. I see no reason to change my plans now."

She acknowledged his words with a barely-perceptible nod.

"There may be trouble once it is learned that we are married," she warned.

"I anticipate it. It is what I have come to expect since I visited the white man's post. We will have to be strong."

"My father may insist upon my marrying you in our church. He might not feel, until that is done, that we are truly husband and wife."

Gray Hawk said, "Then it will be done."

"There is also the possibility that my father may not recognize our marriage no matter what we do. While he is not prejudiced against other races, he has been exposed to too many primitive people to have much respect for them…as equals."

"What does this have to do with me?"

"He may not understand my wanting to go back to your people with you," she said, not looking at him. "He will think that it is below me, most

271

likely, and may cause us some trouble. He might not accept it altogether, and may insist upon your learning English customs and accompanying us back to our home."

"I will not do this, but you do not answer my question. What does his study of primitive people have to do with me?"

Genevieve gazed around her, at her surroundings before she said, "Nothing, he..."

"Gen-ee?"

She sighed, just barely able to look at him. "He will consider you and your people uncivilized, and he will not understand my returning with you. There will be trouble, Gray Hawk, I just know it. Perhaps it would be better if I simply wrote the letter to him."

"No," said Gray Hawk. "You would always worry, and I would have you free of this. Besides, do I look the kind of man to walk away from trouble?"

"No, it is only that—"

"We will ensure that your father will survive well without you, and then, if we have to, we will sneak away. Some may consider me 'uncivilized,' but I know that I can do this."

"Gray Hawk?" She backed slightly away.

And he gave her an inquiring look.

"I have remembered something."

"Yes?"

"I remembered... I do not believe the Americans think too highly of an Indian man and a white woman together."

He stared at her a moment before he said, "I believe you are right. In truth, it may go beyond even that. I do not think the white man thinks too highly of any other people except his own, but please, go on. What was it you recalled?"

"Gray Hawk, I am white. Do you mean to insult me?"

"No," he said. He paused, but when she didn't say anything further, he went on. "But what did you think of me at first?"

She opened her mouth to speak, yet said nothing. She gazed at him. "Well, I…" She looked away. "I… Gray Hawk, it is only that…I—"

"You do not need to go on, Gen-ee. I know what you thought of me at first, and I am afraid in my trying to have you understand my point of view, I have also caused you to become flustered. It was ill-mannered of me. Please continue. I am interested in what it is you recalled."

"Are you?"

He nodded.

And she said, "When my father and I first came to St. Louis, there was a young boy in the town at the time, a little younger than you. He was half Indian, half white. He became involved with the daughter of a rich fur merchant who did not approve of the boy. When the two young people tried to escape to get married, the father had the half-breed hanged."

Gray Hawk merely shrugged. "What is this 'hanged'?"

"Don't you know?"

"I would not ask if I—"

"It is where a man is put to death by hanging him from his neck."

"I do not understand."

"It is a way of killing a man. It—"

"No, I understand this; what I do not comprehend is why people would kill a man for the simple act of courting a girl in order to marry her. I can see that sometimes there are bad feelings about two people coming together, but once it is done, why would others try to kill him, if this boy had done nothing to them?"

"Because he was Indian."

"And that is the only reason?"

She inclined her head.

"I see," he said. "And this is how a 'civilized people' handle their young?"

"Gray Hawk, not all people are like that. It is only that I remember it now. But I leave the point."

"Then tell me this point."

"If we tell many people in St. Louis that we are married, we may have to acknowledge others' prejudice, and I frankly don't feel like doing it. I believe that we should not let anyone else know we are married."

Gray Hawk shook his head. "It is dishonest. I would never be able to look at your father without the lie being always there, always between us. And I would not live my life that way."

She sat up straighter. "Then we could tell my father and perhaps Robert, too, but only them. They would keep our secret, and—"

"You fear this for me so much?"

Genevieve nodded. "I have observed that the Americans are not too tolerant toward the Indians. In truth, many Americans hate the Indians and would jump at any excuse to do them harm. Now, you will be going into a town where there will be more white men than Indian. You would be unsafe. I only propose that we tell very few people of our marriage and thereby avoid any trouble."

Gray Hawk jerked his head to the left, an emotional expression. He said, "I would not hide from the truth."

"But Gray Hawk—"

"Enough." He gazed over toward her, his stare at her intense, until at last he felt himself relenting. He said, "I may not like what it is that you propose, yet I think you speak wisely. I do not believe you would be so intent upon telling me this if there were not danger. Besides"— he smiled at her— "a man should always listen to the wisdom of his sits-beside-him-wife. Therefore, I will consider all that you ask."

"Good. And your decision? What will it be?"

He grinned. "I do not know. I have not decided yet."

"But you will let me know when you do?"

"I will let you know." He dropped the robe from around their shoulders. "But come now, I did not bring you here to talk of these things.

274

There are many other matters that are more exciting, more interesting to do. In truth, I have other activities on my mind."

She smiled at him. "Such as?"

"Would you like me to show you? Perhaps give you an intimate demonstration of what I have been thinking?"

"I would like that very much, yes."

He laughed. "Come here closer, my sweet Gen-ee, and I will do my best to show you."

And for the rest of the night, Gray Hawk strived to the best of his ability to present to his Gen-ee exactly what he'd had on his mind.

And Genevieve, ever the romantic, relished every moment.

Chapter Twenty-Two

"*Hot* corn! Come gets yer piping hot corn!"

"Fresh milk! Milk here!"

"Aaaaaaaaaples! Fresh aaaaaaaaaples!"

The cries of the street vendors, the tinkling of little bells, the smells of fresh, hot corn, of cinnamon apples, of pies and muffins welcomed Genevieve and her Indian husband into the city of St. Louis.

It had been a long trip to this place. It had been a tiring trip, and it was starting to turn cold.

They walked into the town, no horses in tow, with little more than the clothes upon their backs, having made the journey from the Blackfoot camp almost completely on foot.

It was necessary, Gray Hawk had said. There was always danger, he'd gone on to explain, when one traveled through enemy country on horseback. Horses, found alone, indicated a rider nearby and would always be investigated. It was safer, if not as convenient, to walk and to carry as little as possible.

And so they had left their horses in the care of the orphan boy in Gray Hawk's camp, and with nothing more than a few buffalo robes and several changes of clothing and moccasins in their possession, they had started on their way.

It was not as inconvenient as it might sound, however. Genevieve had already grown used to walking—toes pointed in—and so had found the trek not as daunting as she might have done at some earlier time. She had also

276

grown accustomed to carrying their meager supplies on her back, thus leaving Gray Hawk free to fight any enemy or animal they encountered.

In truth, she'd found that the weight on her back helped her balance. But she hadn't told Gray Hawk this, content to let him believe that she labored under the burden.

When they had first come in sight of white settlements, she noticed that Gray Hawk had taken to making notches on a stick. She had asked him about this and had discovered that he was counting the number of settlements he encountered by putting a scratch on a stick for every home.

But after only a few miles' travel, when he'd found that his entire stick was filled with notches and still he hadn't even begun to include everything he saw, he'd thrown the stick away in disgust.

Genevieve, however, was not at all upset with how numerous the white communities were. She'd already known there were too many to count easily.

No, she was concerned with something else, something that worried her day after day: she did not look Indian.

Despite her clothing, despite her traveling companion, her braids and the load upon her back, she looked exactly what she was: a white woman dressed up in Indian garb.

It wouldn't have been so critical if it weren't for the fact that she wasn't certain what would happen if she and Gray Hawk were sighted as such. What would these people do to a white woman traveling with an Indian? And more importantly, what would they do to Gray Hawk?

She had mentioned her fears to Gray Hawk time and time again. He had listened attentively, and then, only a few days ago, he had acted.

He had taken out the paints that he always carried in a bag with him and had demonstrated his Indian artistry upon her. He'd fussed over her, making designs and patterns all over her body, and within a short time, he had painted the entirety of her face, her hair and any skin visible…red, white and black.

It was an effective disguise. Not too many people would see beyond the surface, even though the paint hadn't entirely covered over the color of her hair, nor had it done anything about the shade of her eyes.

But it didn't seem to matter. The whole effect of it was this: She looked Indian. She looked invisible.

No one paid them any attention.

It wasn't long after they had passed the more numerous settlements that they entered into St. Louis proper, and it was then that Genevieve began to direct Gray Hawk toward her father's home, although Gray Hawk remained always in the lead.

Genevieve had gazed around her as they traveled over the more civilized boulevards of cobblestone, gravel and brick, those streets swarming with pigs.

She'd forgotten how many pigs ran through town, the beasts serving not only to clean up the garbage left on the streets, but also to fill the role of an intelligent household pet.

But besides the pigs, the avenues this day were filled to overflowing with Indians, street urchins, vendors and peddlers, and as she and Gray Hawk passed the vendors selling their goods, Genevieve wished she had the money to purchase something.

She'd practically forgotten about sugar, about its sweet taste, about muffins and scones and breads, and her mouth watered as she sniffed the delicious scents. Funny that she hadn't missed the confections until this day.

They passed all this by, however, Genevieve being content for the moment to do no more than nibble on a piece of dried buffalo meat.

Still, no one paid them the least attention, and at length she and Gray Hawk came to her father's estate, no one having stopped them, no one having demanded that they answer questions, no one having even glanced at them a second time.

She gazed at the place she had called home ever since she and her father had arrived in St. Louis, a little over a year ago.

It was an impressive mansion, at least for this part of the country.

Odd, how her viewpoint had changed.

It looked big now, magnificent. But she remembered the first time she'd viewed this home. Then, having come here directly from England and the grand estate where she had been raised, she had considered this American home, and the grounds that went with it, small and hardly worth the money she and her father had paid for it.

But looking upon it now, it appeared to her as though it were the palace of a king.

It stood three stories tall, its siding painted white; its roof, black; and its shutters and trim, green. It had a wide front porch, perfect for receiving callers, and a curved carriage lane that ran all the way up to the house.

All around the house was acre after acre of rolling hills, where the woods had been pushed back, the lawns carefully cultivated and the bushes cut and trimmed to perfection. Genevieve was amazed that, at this time of the year, her father's lawn was still very green.

Tall trees of maple, oak and birch surrounded the house proper, the leaves beginning to change, and Genevieve, as she gazed out upon it, found that she possessed mixed feelings.

What was wrong with her? Did she have nothing but a flighty disposition?

She must, she decided, for as she continued to stare at her old home, she felt a pang of homesickness, longing to do nothing more than run to the house, go up to her old room and throw herself across its bed, never to come out to face the world again.

But she knew she couldn't do it, and she tried her best to tamp down the urge.

How could she feel this way?

She loved Gray Hawk more than she loved anybody; she wanted to stay with him, live with him. She'd given him her word of honor to return with him, she now remembered. But, goodness, if the sight of all that luxury ahead of her didn't sway her from her intentions—just a little.

Maybe she could persuade Gray Hawk to stay here?

She shook herself physically.

What was she doing? What was she thinking? She couldn't renege on her promise to him. She wouldn't.

It didn't make sense. How could the mere view of a house cause her such doubts, and all within a few minutes?

She didn't know.

But it did.

"That is it," she said. "This is where my father lives."

If Gray Hawk thought anything about it, if he were at all impressed or even daunted by such a show of wealth, he didn't say a word. He merely inclined his head, though when he glanced back at her, his gaze was intent upon her, speculative.

He said, "Come, we had best see him at once."

Genevieve nodded, but then she held back, pulling on Gray Hawk's sleeve.

He turned a sharp gaze on her.

"Have you decided yet what you will say to my father?"

"*Aa*, yes, I have."

"And?"

"You must decide for yourself what you will tell him."

"But I thought that you…"

"He will ask you about what has happened to you, not me. You must tell him what you think is best."

"But I thought you were going to explain matters to him, tell him all about us."

Gray Hawk shook his head. "When I took you to my village, I knew then what would be your fate there, and I made my plans so as to protect you. I do not know your father, and so I cannot make a firm decision one way or the other as to what we will do or say to him. I leave that to you. But know that whatever you decide, he must eventually be told that we are husband and wife, and that you will return with me to my people."

She bowed her head. "Yes," she said. "You are right."

He paused, watching her, though his hesitation was barely perceptible. "Come, then," he said. "I am anxious to meet your father."

****

"Hello, Robert."

Robert, who had answered the door, stared at her, at Gray Hawk, back at her.

"Milady?"

"Yes, Robert, it is I."

"Mistress Genevieve, I...come in at once. I cannot tell you what a pleasure it is to see you." He blocked the entrance to Gray Hawk. "Shall I call the sheriff to put this one away?"

"No, Robert." Genevieve smiled as she strolled into the entryway. "I don't think so. I would not be here if it weren't for him."

"As you say, Mistress Genevieve; however, I—"

"Is my father here?"

"He is."

"And how is he?"

"He is much improved. The medicine the doctor is giving him at last seems to be helping him. He will be even better when he sees you."

"Will you tell him that I am here? I will await him in the parlor. And oh, Robert," she said, before he turned away, "it is so good to see you."

Robert looked momentarily startled. "I had thought to never look upon you again, milady. I have felt it was my responsibility that you were stolen. It was my duty to guard you. I did not do it well. I have not been able to forgive myself for my negligence."

"It had nothing to do with you."

"No, milady." Robert gave Gray Hawk a piercing glare. "I feel I could have prevented it, had I been more careful."

Genevieve touched Robert's arm. "It is no matter. I am here now."

"Yes, milady." He smiled briefly before, with a mere lifting of his chin, he assumed again the role of butler. "I will summon your father."

"Thank you, Robert."

Gray Hawk didn't say a word about her exchange with Robert; he merely watched her closely. He followed her into the parlor, taking up a stance behind her, away in a far corner. Still he said nothing, and Genevieve glanced back at him once, looking to him for direction. Receiving nothing more than stoic scrutiny, she turned her attention to the door.

She didn't have to wait long.

"Genny!" It was her father. "My Lord, Genny, I thought I'd never see you again!"

"Hello, Father."

The elder Rohan limped into the parlor, a cane in hand.

"Father, you are up and walking about. This is wonderful!" Genevieve flew across the room into her father's arms. "Oh, Father, how I have missed you."

"And I, you. Oh," he said, taking her in his arms and hugging her. "Don't you ever do this to me again. Was it terrible? I have worried about you night and day. The Indians didn't hurt you, did they?"

"No, Father, I'm fine, and I have not been hurt at all. As a matter of fact, the Indian standing behind me is—"

"Here for the reward. Yes, I will see to him shortly, but first—"

"He is not here for the reward, and there is something I must tell you…" Genevieve stopped for a moment. "What reward?"

Her father put his arm around her shoulders and escorted her toward the sofa, which was positioned right in the middle of the room. He said, "All in good time, my dear. I'll answer all your questions in good time, but first, won't you sit and have a cup of tea with me?"

"Tea?" Another luxury she hadn't experienced in quite some time.

"Yes, I have ordered the kitchen maid to bring us a spot of tea."

"I would love it, Father. I would genuinely love it."

"Well, come over here, Genny, and sit. Robert, will you see to the maid?"

Robert nodded and left the room, returning shortly with an elderly kitchen maid, who came in wheeling a cart full of tea and cakes. The maid picked up a cup and the teapot.

She took one look at Genevieve, and then at Gray Hawk, who stood over in the corner, spear in hand.

Gray Hawk stared back at the maid, motioning toward her with his spear. The elderly woman backed away, the teacup rattling in her hand while a moan, more resembling a squeal, escaped through her lips. She took another step backward, then another, the cart quite forgotten.

Robert came toward the woman, unaware of her predicament, and was about to dismiss her when the lady suddenly dropped the cup, the teapot still in her hand. Robert had quickly rescued the cup and saucer and was on the verge of grabbing for the teapot when the woman turned, shrieking something about her precious head, and ran from the room as though it, or she, were inhabited by demons.

Tea splattered everywhere.

The elder Rohan didn't notice, being slightly hard of hearing and having his back to the door.

Robert sighed, shaking his head, and went in search of more tea.

"I say, my good man." The elder Rohan glanced toward the door. "Now where did Robert get to?"

"It doesn't matter, Father," Genevieve said, having witnessed the entire affair. "I think there may be..."

The kitchen maid suddenly ran through the hall, crying out something about Indians, tearing at her hair and throwing off her apron as she ran.

"... a problem with the tea," Genevieve finished.

The outer door opened, then closed with a thud, while Robert, his uniform now spotted with tea stains, stepped back into the parlor, a fresh teapot in hand.

"Ah, there you are, Robert. Won't you see to the maid pouring us a bit of tea?"

"Yes, Lord Rohan," Robert said.

Robert finished settling the teapot back on the platter. Wheeling the entire tray over toward the center of the room where the elder Rohan and his daughter were seated, he proceeded to pour the tea.

"Thank you, Robert. But, please, will you fetch the kitchen maid to see to the tea?"

Robert nodded his agreement, serving the tea himself anyway, handing one cup first to her ladyship and then to his master.

"And Robert..."

"Yes, my lord?"

"Won't you see to a new uniform, or mayhap a clean one?"

"Yes, Lord Rohan," Robert said as he straightened, and, proceeding back to the door, again assumed a butler's stance.

But outside of Robert's uniform, the elder Rohan didn't notice anything else amiss. He said, turning to his daughter, "Thank God you are home." He grabbed Genevieve's hands across the center table that separated them, and looked at her, really looked at her. "My, but you surely do resemble an Indian. Did you stay with them long?" He scanned her up and down before he glanced around the room, his gaze coming to light on Gray Hawk. "Did you say that this man with you is here for the reward?"

"No, Father. This is Gray Hawk, and he is here to—"

"Later, my dear. Later. I will see that he gets the reward. But first"— her father again patted her hand—"tell me all about what has happened to you."

"Of course I will, Father, it's just that..." Genevieve glanced up at Robert, who stood at the entrance to the room. If her father thought that Gray Hawk was here for a reward, then Robert must not have told the elder Rohan that Gray Hawk was one and the same man who had captured her. She shrugged and said, "I guess it was quite dramatic. But it's all over now, and it really wasn't so bad. And Father, what reward?"

"I want to hear every detail. Please, Genny, go on."

"I will, Father, but I would feel better if I knew what sort of reward you posted. Did you—"

"Oh, it was just a trivial thing. Nothing, really."

"Father...?"

He took out a handkerchief and coughed into it before he said, into the hanky, "I put up a five-thousand-dollar reward for your return. See? It was nothing."

"Five...thousand..."

"Nothing, you see?" He put the handkerchief away. "Now, tell me, how did you escape? And how were you able to return? Did this man with you hear about the reward and come and steal you away from that demon? Is that how it happened?"

She paused, looking back at that "demon," before she said, "Not quite. I... Father, I have something to tell you, and I think that you..."

Genevieve suddenly rose, brushing down her buckskin skirt as she did so. Why couldn't she say it? It was simple. All she had to do was utter the words, "Father, I'm married." She swallowed. She said, "Would you like some more tea?"

"Not now, dear."

"Well, I believe that I would. Would you excuse me for a moment?"

"Of course, my dear, but..."

Genevieve stepped toward the tea tray, grabbing hold of the teapot as though it were a lifeline. She said, "Robert, would you like some?"

Robert shook his head, giving her an odd look, but her father hadn't seemed to notice anything amiss.

She glanced toward the corner of the room. There stood Gray Hawk, one hand holding on to his spear, the other was resting casually on his hip. He leaned on one foot with the other slightly forward. He looked relaxed, but Genevieve knew it was the exact opposite. He stood alert, poised, ready for action.

"Gray Hawk, would you like a spot of tea?"

"*Saa,*" came the reply from Gray Hawk, and her father looked up suddenly at the man.

"What tribe is he from?"

"The Blackfeet," Genevieve answered.

"The Blackfeet? Oh, my, Genny! You did it!" Her father sat forward. "You have brought back a Blackfoot Indian with you."

"Yes, Father, I—"

"That's my girl. I...tell me, Genny, did he just say 'no'?" And when she inclined her head slightly, her father said, "Algonquian. The Algonquian say 'no' in the same way, as do the Cheyenne."

"Yes, Father," Genevieve said. "I stayed with Gray Hawk's people for a while, and I have come to believe that the Blackfoot language is related to the Algonquian. It could be a significant discovery."

"Oh, Genny." Her father's eyes lit up all at once. "This is something that even our young Mr. Toddman has yet to discover. There may still be hope."

"Mr. Toddman?" She sent a sharp glance to her father. "What has he to do with this?"

"Oh, it's a long and quite boring story, and I'll tell you in more detail later. But first..."

"Father?"

Her father gave her a sheepish regard.

She said, "I thought Mr. Toddman went back to England—that is, after he tried to spend all of our finances."

Her father shook his head. "I'm afraid not. That young man went out and got himself a Blackfoot Indian and is even now, as we speak, writing up all his observations of the fellow in an effort to discredit me. And I'm afraid I haven't been able to do more than stand back and watch. But now that you're back...and you actually spent time with these people... Genny, there is hope!"

"I see. And his father? What does Mr. Toddman's father, the Earl of Tygate, say about all this?"

"I don't think he knows, Genny. If he did, he would be heartbroken. I certainly haven't had the heart to tell the earl. We have been friends for too long for me to do more than watch, but now... now I can outfox that young man, Toddman. We can do it together, Genny. We can finish this book."

Genevieve smiled at her father. "I'm so happy for you, Father, and yes, I will help you, as will Gray Hawk, but there is something else I must tell you."

"Yes, yes, my dear girl. There is so very much you must tell me."

"No, Father, you don't understand. I think this will be a shock."

"It doesn't matter, Genny. I'm so happy you are home again, nothing else matters."

"Yes," she said, "I am home again. But, Father, please, I must tell you that I am not here for long."

"I know, Genny. As soon as possible, we must return to England and — "

"No, Father. I am talking about something else."

"Yes, I — "

"Father," she said, pacing forward to come and sit directly before him. "Father, I am married."

She saw her father's eyelids flicker farther open. "Who..."

"Father, I don't know how else to tell this to you. Please, try to understand. I am married, and...I am married to this Indian who stands behind me. Father, let me introduce you to my husband, Mr. Gray Hawk."

She stood and motioned Gray Hawk to her side. She said, as casually as if she did this every day, "Mr. Gray Hawk, my father."

Chapter Twenty-Three

*G*enevieve Rohan stared out the window, her attention momentarily diverted by a flock of geese flying south in perfect arrowhead order. It was a little late in the season for the birds to be making the trip, she decided, the month being late October, or perhaps because she was farther south, herself, the geese migrated later in the year. She didn't know.

She brought her attention back toward the landscape that surrounded the house. The crisp feel of autumn was definitely in the air, and the leaves here in St. Louis were at their peak for the season, the yellows and golds, oranges and reds reminding her that soon she and Gray Hawk would need to leave here.

She drew in a deep breath.

What was wrong with her? Of course she would leave with Gray Hawk. She loved him. She had given him her promise. It was only that...

A breeze blew in through an open window, bringing with it the fresh scents of grass and fallen leaves. She sniffed. It reminded her of the outdoors, of the prairie, of the open space, of freedom. She had loved it there; she missed it, and yet...

A brief gust suddenly scattered the papers on her desk.

She made a grab for her notes and stood up, shuffling the papers together and placing them out of range of the blowing wind.

Sighing, she stepped to the window, intending to close it, but instead of doing so, watched as a gardener, clippers in hand, strolled past.

Almost a month had elapsed since she had first introduced her father to Gray Hawk—a full month, during which her father had neatly pretended that none of her adventure had happened: not her capture, not her adoption into the Blackfoot tribe and particularly not her union with Gray Hawk.

She might have worried about her father and his mental condition, since he seemed continually absentminded about these things, never quite remembering that she and Gray Hawk were a couple, even to the extent of placing their rooms at completely opposite ends of the house.

But she worried for nothing. In all else, her father appeared to be in full possession of his senses.

She knew what the problem was, of course, and she began to resign herself to the fact that, as far as her father was concerned, her marriage did not exist.

She glanced down toward the notes she was editing.

There was much work that needed to be done on the book even still, so perhaps it was for the best that her father failed to acknowledge the union. Maybe, for the time being, it saved him needless heartache, allowing him to get on with his work.

And he needed to work, just as he needed Gray Hawk. In truth, the two of them had shut themselves behind locked doors, Gray Hawk graciously answering all the questions and inquiries her father had about his tribe, about his beliefs, his customs.

But there would be an end to it…and soon, maybe in only another few weeks. Genevieve could tell from the notes she worked over, that her father was nearing the conclusion of his book.

It was good. She loved the style and flair with which her father imbued his work, making some far-off place come to life. The manuscript was a marvel of information, beauty and historical fact. And…it would be done on time.

But was that enough?

Young Mr. Toddman had already contacted their same publisher and was even now in a race with her father over the publishing date. And worse,

Mr. Toddman had made it appear, to those back in England, that her father would not be able to finish his work.

That might have been true at one point, but it was certainly not the case now.

Still, even if they submitted their manuscript on time, their editor could not accept and release two books on the same subject.

Which book would the publisher choose?

It all seemed so chancy...and unfair.

But this, though it concerned her, was far from her real problem. In truth, not a day went by that she didn't worry about one thing or the other. She felt painfully torn in two directions.

When the book was done, it would be time to leave with Gray Hawk, and she...

Well, was she ready to go? Or more importantly, *could* she go?

She was certain her father would try to stop her, which meant she and Gray Hawk would have to steal away.

Gray Hawk had once mentioned that they might have to do this, and she'd thought nothing of it at the time. But now she wondered.

Could she do this to her father?

She set her lips together. Of course she could; she must.

She had given her vow to Gray Hawk. She wouldn't break it.

She had tried to tell her father of her promise in an attempt to appeal to the viscount's sense of duty; he had merely shrugged and asked if she knew more of the Blackfoot language.

Again she almost hoped it was a matter of absentmindedness on her father's part. Yet she knew better.

But, oh, how she wished sometimes that Gray Hawk would stay here, that her father would accept him, help him to fit into society, honor their commitment. It would solve so many problems, ease so much heartache, if this could be.

Because there was more.

Jumping back into her earlier life had reminded Genevieve of all the luxuries she enjoyed here: a simple bed, a mattress, chiffon and silk clothing, good and varied food — sugar.

Every day she tried to convince herself these riches were not so important that she couldn't give them all up, yet it became harder and harder to do.

She drew herself up and turned away from the window.

She would not think about it any longer. She knew what she had to do — she would do it and stop this continuous ambivalence. It did nothing but confuse her.

She would honor her word to Gray Hawk. It was that simple.

Or was it?

"You do not look as though you are working very hard. Perhaps I should bring a deer or two for you to skin."

Genevieve jumped, swinging her attention back into the room. She put her hand to her chest. "Oh, my, Gray Hawk, you startled me. I didn't hear you enter."

"*Aa*, yes," he said. "I could see that you were thinking deeply. How is your father's work coming?" Gray Hawk moved forward, toward her desk and the papers that were scattered there. He stroked his hands through the notes, his attention seemingly caught on them, but then suddenly he looked up at her, his gaze inquisitive, yet...nonchalant. He asked, "Do you worry over something?"

Genevieve stared at him for a moment without answering.

It seemed that Gray Hawk did not wish to adopt the European style of clothing, despite Robert's attempts to have him do so. And this should have been fine with her, but in a way, it wasn't. In truth, she found it depressing.

Gray Hawk showed no inclination to want to fit into her world.

She had hoped he would. She gazed away as she said, "Yes, I worry."

He nodded. "Is it over your father's accepting me? I think that—"

"No, yes, I mean, not really. I worry about his book. There is another man who is writing a manuscript on much the same thing."

"*Aa*, yes, I know. Your father has told me of this person. Your father has given me to understand that this man was once a member of your household?"

"Yes, he was," she said. "He was an apprentice and worked with my father. It is odd that this Mr. Toddman has turned on us, for he helped my father on so many other projects. But somehow, on this one, Mr. Toddman changed. He...became angry, though my father and I have still not determined why. And Mr. Toddman became convinced that he could do the same thing as my father...only better. He is seeking now to prove it and to discredit us."

"*Nitsikksisitsi'tsii'pa*, I understand. Does this man have with him a Blackfoot Indian to study?"

"Apparently so," she said. "At least, that is what I have been led to believe."

Gray Hawk inclined his head. "Then I can understand your worry." He paused, and when next he spoke, he talked from right behind her. He asked, "And is that all you worry over?"

"Yes, I...no...mostly."

"There is something else?"

She glanced down. "No, not really."

Gray Hawk grunted. "You have yet to tell me, Gen-ee, why the white man lies."

"Gray Hawk, I don't see that this has anything to do with my worries."

Standing behind her, he bent down to whisper into her ear, "You lie. You also do not do it well. I would advise you, therefore, not to do it at all."

She smiled. "You know me so well?"

"I know you so well. What is it, Gen-ee?"

"It is nothing, Gray Hawk. I worry over my father. That is all it is."

Gray Hawk moved out and away from her. He trod on silent feet toward the couch, which was across the room.

But he did not sit.

He paced around it, looking at it, the chairs, the windows, the ceiling, the walls. He stepped to the fireplace and turned back to confront Genevieve. He said, "I do not like these walls. I long for the simple pleasures of the tepee, of my home, where I can feel the wind on my face, taste the sweet air from the mountains. I long to be out on the hunt, on the warpath."

He gestured toward the paintings on the walls. "The white man's dwellings, while impressive, make me feel small and hemmed-in. This is not my home. It is not where I belong." He trod toward her. "But you, Gen-ee, this is your home. Tell me, will you miss it when you leave with me?"

"I don't think I—"

"Do not do that, Gen-ee. Tell me what is in your heart. Say the truth."

She jerked her head away from his gaze. She sighed, and, at length, she said, "I will miss it."

Gray Hawk folded his arms over his chest. "It is as I thought. Do you wish me to let you out of your promise to me?"

"No, I... What do you mean?"

He walked back to her desk, hesitating there and flipping through her papers. He said, "A person is always bound by his word unless the one to which he gave his promise releases him from it. I have the power to allow you to be able to stay here. Do you wish me to release you?"

She didn't say anything for a long while, and Gray Hawk glanced up to her. He said, "I would have you with me because you want to be, Gen-ee."

She jerked her gaze back toward the window, glancing outside, though she registered nothing of what she saw. Her stomach twisted, and her heart seemed to be beating in her throat as she said, "Do you try to rid yourself of me?"

"No, Gen-ee. If I wanted you out of my life, I would not do it this way." He hesitated. "I...feel very deeply for you, my wife. I love you. I would have you happy with me."

She moaned, briefly shutting her eyes. She said, "I love you too, Gray Hawk. I have never lied about that. But...I...love my father, too, even Robert. And my home. I would not leave them. Yet, when I gave you my promise, I knew then what I did. I was aware that it would not be easy to come back here, only to walk away from the life I have known once more. Still, I was willing to do it in order to save my father and his project." She turned her attention back into the room, gazing straight at Gray Hawk. "What sort of person would I be if I gave my promise to someone, and, at the least sign of hardship, I relented?"

"A very warm and loving person, Gen-ee. You feel things so much. It is a part of your beauty, a part of who you are. I would not take this from you."

She lifted her chin. "I thank you, Gray Hawk, but I gave you my solemn oath. I will stand by it."

He leaned away from the desk and strode toward her. "We could live in both worlds."

"What do you mean?"

He shrugged. "My people do very little in the winter. It is always a time of hardship, for not always do the food supplies last. We could winter here with your father."

"My father lives in England."

"Then he could come here every winter."

"No, Gray Hawk, it would not work. He would not do it. Besides, don't you see? My father will never accept our marriage."

"Gen-ee, I think that—"

She held up a hand. "But there is more to it than simply my father. If I were to come back here every winter, I would never want to leave it. I would become more and more attached to my old way of life, much in the same way I am now, and would eventually become unhappy with the way I would live with you in your camp. No, I must live in either one world or the other, not both."

Silence filled the room. Gray Hawk sighed, but at length said, "Rules are not always so stringent. People, like the willow tree, must sometimes bend with the storm. Some think that love is a matter of fate and should never require that they work at it. This is seldom the case. One must always be willing to listen to the other, to bend.

"Yes," he said, "it would be difficult to come back here every winter. It would be a sacrifice. But if it is important, then we should do it. Yes, we would have to solicit your father's cooperation, but have you considered that if you do not do it, if you do not return and visit now and again, you could become unhappy also?"

"He could always come to visit us there. He loves to go among the more…"

"…primitive people?"

"I… Gray Hawk."

He stepped right up to her, taking a lock of her hair into his fingers and twirled it around and around.

He said, "I know you want to stay here. I have seen that this is on your mind. Is there more to it now that you are back in your home? Do you find me primitive, too? Is this why you do not accept any of my proposals?"

He captured the lock of hair in his fingers and pulled it and her toward him. "And now I ask you the same question you asked of me," he said. "Do you wish to be released from me?"

"No, Gray Hawk. I—"

"Gen-ee, I…am glad." His face was only a hairsbreadth away from hers. He kissed first one of her eyelids, then the other. He said, "I know what you want of me, my wife, what you would like to ask me; but understand, I could never leave my home. I have purpose there. I have none here, except helping your father."

"But you could learn a trade, become experienced in something else."

He breathed out deeply and looked up toward the ceiling. "And do you think I would be happy here?"

"You could be."

295

"Gen-ee." He kissed her cheek, her temple, his lips teasing her earlobe as he spoke softly. He said, "Have you not seen how people in this town treat me? It is as though I were less than human. It is the same as it was at the trading post where I lived for a year. To others there, I was always the ignorant Indian, the good-for-nothing. And though I often tried to prove myself, even hunting for the entire post, I was never thought of as an equal, rarely even allowed to eat at the same table as the white men. Your father tries to be different. But it is only here in your house that I experience any sort of respect, and that is more toleration than anything else. I could not live long in a place like this."

Genevieve didn't know what to do. She didn't know what to say. She understood what he said. She even agreed with it. Yet when he was close to her like this, when he spoke so reasonably...

She turned her face toward his, her lips kissing his cheek. "Oh, Gray Hawk, I am so confused. And I am unsure of myself. But of one thing I am certain: I have missed you at night."

"And I, you. I would come to you if I did not care that it would offend your father."

"Gray Hawk, please, I need you here with me. I'm not sure I wish to return with you, but I don't want to lose you, either. Couldn't you try to live here? We could go and visit your family sometimes, perhaps once every few years. You are intelligent. You could learn to—"

He put a finger over her lips.

"I would lose a part of me, Gen-ee, which is why I understand if you would be reluctant to leave here."

"Gray Hawk"—she tried to bring his lips around to hers—"Gray Hawk, please, I... Please, my love. Please, kiss me."

He did, his lips covering hers, his tongue sweeping into her mouth. And she swayed in toward him. "Gray Hawk, couldn't you try it here, at least for a short time?"

He sighed. He lifted his head a little. "I will think on it, Gen-ee. I will think on it. It is as much as I can promise you. At least for now."

****

Two fireplaces had been stoked at both ends of the ballroom, throwing sparks, smoke and the fresh smell of burnt wood into the room. There were three different chandeliers, which, dripping wax alternately onto the hardwood floor or onto some poor, luckless person, lit up the room as though it were daylight.

Torches were burning at every entrance and all around the room. Windows were closed, the evening being a cool one, although the curtains remained open, allowing the ladies and gents to admire their images in the glass as they swirled around and around the ballroom floor.

Now and again a guest left through one of the three balconies, cold air and gusts of wind pouring into the room as the doors opened and closed.

But no one objected. There was too much wine, too much food and too much fun for anyone to take offense.

Guests continued to arrive in a steady flow. This party was, after all, the most major social event in the St. Louis community in quite some time.

Some of the people clung to the sidelines as they entered the room, some rushed toward the wine and the food, while others sped their way onto the dance floor. Wine and whiskey circulated through the crowd as though they were old friends, while a small orchestra played from the minstrel's gallery, situated up high and at the very end of the hall.

Enticing melodies, seductive yet stately, streamed down from the lofty gallery, the strains unfamiliar to one lone Indian, who had never heard them before.

Gray Hawk stood at the edge of the crowd and stared up at the orchestra. He had always known the white man's world was different from his own; he'd simply not imagined how great that difference was. In truth, he couldn't remember ever witnessing such a display of material wealth.

He gazed out upon the dancers, still amazed that white society allowed such a public display of touching.

Still… He grinned to himself. *He* could dance this way with his Gen-ee.

He didn't know why he hadn't thought of it until now. But it occurred to him that he hadn't had much time alone with her these past few days, and this would provide an excellent opportunity to hold her, even if it was in front of other people and only for a little while.

He glanced all through the crowd, looking for his wife, for her father, or any other familiar face, even the brown face of another Indian.

He found nothing.

In truth, besides himself, he saw no other brown-skinned person in the crowd.

He felt a momentary twinge of resentment against such a thing. Why was no other Indian invited here?

He stepped farther into the room.

He heard a giggle. He glanced to his left. A female head turned away.

"Why, I never! A savage!" a feminine voice said.

"What could the viscount be thinking?"

Gray Hawk gazed toward the two young women, both of them staring at him as though he were a sort of particularly distasteful insect.

Was something wrong with him?

He peered down at himself. Had he forgotten to wear some important piece of clothing…his breechcloth, perhaps?

He could see nothing amiss, dressed as he was in his white buckskin breechcloth, leggings and shirt, his very best. His leggings fitted tightly to his calf and thigh muscles, and each article he wore was sewn with porcupine quills and colorful beads. Across his back was his quiver full of arrows, and over his shoulder, his bow.

He looked back up. All his clothing was in order.

The two women were still scrutinizing him, their looks offensive.

And then he understood. He wasn't certain why it had taken him so long to see it. These two women were acting as they were toward him *because he was Indian.*

Gray Hawk raised his eyebrows at the two ladies. Drawing an arrow from his quiver, taking his bow from around his shoulder, and placing it as though he might shoot it at any moment, he grinned widely at them. In truth, he winked.

The two young women gawked, looking more flustered than two prairie hens in a coyote den. One of the ladies flicked her fan open and fluttered it furiously in front of her. The other grabbed her friend and pulled her violently away, the two of them scurrying over to the farthest corner of the room.

Gray Hawk almost laughed aloud.

"Amusing yourself?"

Gray Hawk turned to confront a man he had never before seen: a young man with brown hair and large green eyes, his whole person perhaps not more than twenty-six or twenty-seven winters old.

Gray Hawk didn't answer at once, and the other man went on to say, "I don't know why I am bothering to speak to such an ignorant savage. It is only that I was given to understand that you, my good man, speak English."

Gray Hawk didn't respond, shrugging his shoulders and giving the young man a blank look.

"Leave it to that old gizzard to spread such a tale. Imagine, a Blackfoot Indian who speaks English. What a preposterous fib." Here the other man sneered. "I shall ensure that the proper people know of this lie, and then we'll see whose book will be published and whose will not. I have friends helping me in England, I tell you, and —"

"Ah, Mr. Toddman, I see that you have met my friend." The elder Rohan had come to stand at Gray Hawk's back.

"Yes, quite." Boredom fairly dripped from Toddman's voice. He glanced at his fingernails. "I was just this moment trying to engage the young Indian in a conversation." He fluttered his hand in Gray Hawk's direction, Toddman's gesture being more one of mockery. "I say, old man, the Indian has not said a single word."

"Yes" — the viscount cleared his throat —"well, sometimes my young Indian friend has nothing much to say."

Toddman sneered. "Yes, I daresay. And sometimes the Indian can't speak *English* a'tall."

Gray Hawk raised an eyebrow.

But the viscount barely seemed to notice. "I say, Toddman, so glad you could make it to my party. Wasn't sure you would want to, what with your own book being done and sent off and all. But here I am rambling. Now, has no one made the introductions? Perhaps our Indian here stands on ceremony."

Toddman made to laugh, the action more a ridicule.

"Mr. Toddman," the viscount went on, "I'd like you to meet Gray Hawk, a member of the southern Pikuni tribe of the Blackfeet."

It was only then that Gray Hawk grinned, his look resembling that of a man who had just counted first coup. He said — his speech, his actions exaggerated, English to a flaw —"Pleased, I'm sure," and had the pleasure of watching the pompous Mr. Toddman's eyes pop open.

Gray Hawk turned to the viscount. He said, his English terribly proper, "I am happy to see you, my friend." And here Gray Hawk sent the young Englishman a look that even the devil might envy for its disdain. "I have much news to tell you, Viscount Rohan."

It was the first time Gray Hawk had addressed his father-in-law by his proper aristocratic title. And it might be the only time. It didn't matter. For the moment, it was apt.

Gray Hawk faced the viscount, and, putting a hand upon the older man's back, led him through the crowd, with a certain Mr. Toddman left gaping after them.

"Don't know why the man is here at my party," said the viscount, "but I can't very well throw him out, can I?"

Gray Hawk smiled as he said, "Can't you?"

"Not without causing a scandal."

"Sometimes a scandal is much preferable to the injury a man like that can do. He intends you nothing but the greatest of harm. And I believe he means to discredit you here tonight."

"Can't very well do that. I have your testimonial about your tribe, and I have the same from many others. We'll let the publisher decide whose book is the best. At least now the manuscript is done, and I have fulfilled my contract—and this, despite Mr. Toddman's sabotage. I know you are one of the people I have to thank for that."

Gray Hawk nodded. "It is nothing. You are the father of my wife, and—"

"Mr. Gray Hawk, I really must speak to you privately of that. I—"

"Yes," said Gray Hawk. "I know. But I think now is not the time. By the way, that man, Toddman, said he has friends in England who will help him to publish his book."

Viscount Rohan stopped suddenly. "He told you this?"

"Yes."

"When?"

"Just now. He did not know at the time that I spoke English."

The viscount appeared flustered. "He didn't? But I told him that you spoke it perfectly."

"He did not believe it."

"I see." Viscount Rohan turned to stare at Gray Hawk, having to look up to do so. "Did he say who these men are?"

"No." Gray Hawk returned the elder Rohan's look. "He did not. And in truth, I do not even know what this place, England, is, though I hear much said about it. I was hoping that, if I kept quiet long enough, Toddman would tell me more. But he didn't."

"Yes, well, when I return home, it will be easy enough to determine who this is."

Gray Hawk nodded.

"But come, my friend." The viscount drew his arm through the Indian's. "This is a party of celebration. It is the same sort of party I give every time I finish a manuscript. Whether this one is accepted or not makes no difference. The project is done, and you, my boy, helped me to save it. Come, has anyone shown you how to do these dances?"

Gray Hawk shook his head. "No," he said. "But I would like to learn."

The viscount beamed. "You shall, my boy, you shall."

And without further ado, the elder Rohan led the Indian over into a far corner of a balcony, where, for a moment, no one would see them... dancing.

Chapter Twenty-Four

$\mathscr{G}$enevieve twirled around the room on the arm of the captain of the guard, her antique white dress and her petticoats swirling around her with her every motion. Step, step, sweep, twirl, spin.

She smiled. It had been a long time since she had been to a dance. And she loved it so.

Her partner whisked her around as they neared a corner, and she glanced out into the crowd.

Gray Hawk.

So he had finally arrived. She'd been looking for him all night.

He stood alone within the crowd, seemingly oblivious to the stir he was creating.

He hadn't seen her.

Another rotation and she could see him no longer, though she strained over her partner's shoulder to do so.

There he was. Gray Hawk stared straight ahead of him, seeming not to notice her at all.

But the people around him...

Several women whispered among themselves, their fans held just barely above their mouths. They were each one glaring at Gray Hawk, and some were pointing toward him in mockery, snickering.

The men ignored the Indian, mostly, their backs turned on him, although now and again a mocking chortle could be heard from among them, too.

One of the more daring of the men "stumbled" backward, away from "the group," bumping grandly into Gray Hawk.

Gray Hawk merely snorted and stood his ground.

The men cackled.

Another of the men did the same, then another.

Well, that was it. That did it. Genevieve had seen enough.

Gray Hawk would not defend himself—not here, not at her father's celebration. But *she* would.

She whispered her apology into her partner's ear and left the dance floor, pacing toward Gray Hawk.

And as she made her way to him, she couldn't help but be reminded of the difference between this and the Blackfeet's reception of her, when she'd been a newcomer in their camp.

No one there had made fun of her; no one there had tried to make her feel inadequate. Most had gone out of their way, in fact, to find something of worth she had done that they could praise. And this, though the Blackfeet, as a tribe, had reason to distrust her.

No, they'd adopted her into their tribe; they had even called her "sister."

And yet, as she looked around her, she knew that there were those here tonight who would call those same Indians "savage."

She raised her chin. She might have something to say about that.

While it was true that many people here tonight were dressed in all the finest silk and riches that the European and American civilizations had to offer, beneath that outer finery, there was more savagery here than anything she had ever witnessed in the Indian camp.

She drew in closer toward Gray Hawk, and she could see that he had become aware of her.

His eyes lit up with appreciation, but it was the only form of greeting she would receive from him tonight. She knew it.

He was telling her quite clearly that it would remain up to her as to whether or not she would recognize him here among this crowd of antagonism.

She didn't even hesitate.

She held out her gloved hands toward him. She smiled.

"Gray Hawk," she said. "I thought you would never arrive. I have saved this dance for you."

Gray Hawk nodded, his only acknowledgment. Taking both of his hands into her own, Genevieve led him out onto the dance floor, away from the mob. That she heard tongues wagging didn't matter. These people weren't worth another thought.

She began to move with Gray Hawk, and she led him through the steps, the dance being unfamiliar to him. But he took to the rhythm of it readily, and within minutes he was twirling Genevieve around as though he had done this sort of thing every day of his life.

"Don't pay any attention to those people," she said.

"I was not."

He twirled her around the floor.

"Yes," she said, "I could see that, but what I meant was, please don't think that because these people are so rude, everyone feels this way about you."

"It is not me they mock."

"Oh, I'm so glad you can understand that—"

"It is because I am Indian. These people do not like the Indian as a person."

"Yes, you are right; it is not you personally. It is only that many of these people have relatives who have been killed by Indians. There is much prejudice here because of this. I'm sorry they can't see you for who you are."

He nodded as he whirled her around to the right.

She glanced at him then, and he smiled at her.

His gaze at her was soft and warm as he said, "The antagonism they show me will extend to you if you keep associating with me."

"I do not care. Besides, I have no choice in the matter, since you are dear to me. I would not have you treated badly."

He frowned. "You always have had a choice in what you do, ever since you became my sits-beside-him-woman. I would not force you to do anything."

"No, Gray Hawk. I have given you my word. I will honor it."

He inclined his head and swung her around to the left.

Dip, swing, whirl.

She focused on him, he on her. She beamed at him, and he returned the tender look.

They created quite a sight, the two of them. Both were dressed in antique white, though one's material was buckskin, the other's, silk. They looked as though they belonged together, this white woman and the Indian. Their different nationalities, their different races, didn't matter. Their harmony was as obvious as that of the music filtering down from the gallery.

They loved one another. It was beautiful.

His gaze, sensuous and brooding, centered on her as he led her through a series of turns, looking at her as though she were the center of his universe—and she? She stared up at him, this tall, sleek man, gazing at him as though he were the stars, and she, the moon.

"You cannot stay here in St. Louis," she said at last. "The gossip will only get worse."

"I know this," he said; then he smiled. "And you must stay here."

"Gray Hawk, I—"

"*Maopiit*, shh," he said. "I cannot concentrate on my steps when we speak."

"Gray Hawk, please, I—"

"Shh. It will be all right."

But she knew it wouldn't be.

He whirled her around again in several smooth patterns, and she was certain at this moment that if he hadn't been holding her, she would have collapsed.

"What do you mean?"

"I think you know."

"Gray Hawk, I—"

"Do not say it. I know your heart speaks both ways. You love me, but you also love your father, your society. Therefore, I must do the thinking for us both and decide what is best."

Tears gathered at her eyes, and she struggled to keep them at bay.

"Gray Hawk, I would come away with you."

"And be forever unhappy?"

"I could learn to forget."

"Could you?"

She hesitated. "I...would try."

"And if you had not made this promise to me?"

"I'm sure I would... I... Gray Hawk, I—"

"*Maopiit*, shh. I know your heart. It will be hard only at first. It will get easier with every day."

"Gray Hawk!"

Did she want this? Yes, no, not really, maybe. No, not really. Nor did he. But circumstance demanded that they part. Society commanded it.

"There is a ceremony among my people," he whispered against her cheek. "It is the only way that I can set you free. If I get a stick and throw it away, it is my way of saying that I throw you away. Know that I do not really throw you away. It is the only way I can set you free...as...I would be, too."

A tear rolled down her cheek. "Gray Hawk, I don't—"

"It is the only way."

"No."

"Gen-ee, we are from two different worlds. The only thing we have in common is our love. Is that enough to overcome all the prejudice? Look around you. These people here tonight are only the start. There are also our own personal prejudices. Before we met one another, we neither one thought well of the other person's race. What makes us think that just the two of us can change a lifetime of prejudice? Is love alone enough to do this?"

"Gray Hawk, I don't know. I only know I..." Another tear ran down her cheek.

He whirled her around to the left.

"Tell me you think love is enough."

"I... I... Gray Hawk, I can't just now. But maybe in the future... I...just...my father...my life here. Please, understand."

He sighed. "I do."

Dip, swirl, twirl.

"That is the trouble."

Another tear.

The music stopped, and Genevieve knew she was close to collapsing. She didn't turn to clap, she didn't dare to. She picked up her skirts and ran out of Gray Hawk's arms, out of the circle of dancers and out into the cold loneliness of the night.

And Gray Hawk watched her go, his heart pounding in his throat with every step she took.

****

The sound of Indian drums was the only thing that broke into his mental lethargy.

Gray Hawk glanced around him, toward the center of the room.

There, in the middle of the dance floor, sat Indian men, a buffalo-hide drum set out among them. All three of the men were singing and beating on the drum, keeping time to the song.

Gray Hawk did not know this tribe of Indians, nor could he place them, for he did not recognize their style of clothing, their moccasins, their hairstyle.

He stared, committing to memory what it was about these men that made them different from other Indian tribes of his acquaintance.

And the crowd, as though helping him perceive them, parted back from the center, providing him with a clear view of the three Indians.

What were they doing here?

Gray Hawk heard the whispers in the crowd, the shocked murmurings of the ladies, the gentlemen, even the servants. He also witnessed several people leaving the room by the closest exit.

He was about to take his own leave, too, when suddenly Viscount Rohan appeared in front of the Indian drum. But the singing didn't stop, nor did the drumming, and the viscount raised his voice that he might be heard over the noise.

He said, "And now, ladies and gentlemen, I have arranged a special treat for you tonight. As most of you know, I have recently completed a book on the culture, lore and languages of the North American Indians. In honor of this, I have asked these three men from the Delaware tribe, recently removed to the far western territory, to share their songs with us tonight.

"What some of you might not know," the viscount continued, "is that my book would never have been completed without the help of one man who is in the crowd tonight—my friend Gray Hawk, of the Blackfoot tribe."

The viscount motioned Gray Hawk forward.

"This man has given me his time and attention for an entire month, teaching me his culture and his language. And the only thing he has ever asked for in return was the opportunity to dance and to sing the songs of his people, although I'm not sure he meant in front of an audience."

A few people from within the throng smiled.

"Well, son," the viscount said to Gray Hawk, "I couldn't bring your people here, so I've done the next best thing. I've gathered together these men here tonight so that you might enjoy the dance, too.

"And now," the viscount announced, "Gray Hawk will show us the dances of the Blackfeet."

Crowd or no crowd, Gray Hawk had already started to move in time to the rhythm of the drums. He couldn't help it.

There was a magic to the drumming, a medicine, and he found himself moving in time, as though drawn through the motions.

This was exactly what he needed, he thought, to let the rhythm of the drum, the songs of a people close to his own, wash away any despairing feelings he might have.

Perhaps it would give him the strength to do what he had to do next.

He stepped, he paced, he pranced all around the drum and the men sitting around it, he made his own sacred circle around them. He didn't see the people watching from the sidelines. He became oblivious to them, so focused was he on his movements.

He performed his dance: the dance of the hunt.

He took the bow off his shoulder and held it out away from him as he might when stalking quarry, moving down onto his shins and jumping up suddenly.

He would not dance a war dance. Not this night. Not if there were those here who had lost relatives to some Indian war. Good manners prevented him from doing this.

He paced, he dipped, he tramped, putting his body through terrific contortions.

Down onto his knees, scouting for the game. Up, sprinting to catch it. The drums kept him circling, pacing.

He'd lost himself to the pulse of the dance so completely that he didn't see the figure of another Indian man, a person he did not know, until he had come into the sacred circle.

Gray Hawk did, however, recognize a war dance when he saw one, even when performed by a warrior belonging to another tribe. The brave went through the motions of killing and counting coup upon an enemy.

Gray Hawk stopped and stared.

He couldn't believe it. What was this person doing here?

Suddenly, Gray Hawk let go his war cry, putting an arrow to his bow and pointing it toward his target so quickly that no one in the crowd, not even the other Indian, had any idea what was happening until it was too late.

The other Indian stood still and stared.

"Stop this at once!"

Toddman? What was Toddman doing here?

"What savagery is this, that two men from the same tribe would declare open war upon each other?"

Gray Hawk could not believe what he heard. "This man is not Pikuni."

"Yes." Toddman glanced at his nails in clear disdain. "I realize that, my dear fellow. This man is a Blackfoot Blood Indian. He—"

"Is not."

"I beg to differ, my good man. There are others who say that *you* are not Blackfoot."

Gray Hawk actually laughed, while the other Indian frowned.

"You have been deceived," Gray Hawk declared.

Toddman sneered. "I'm afraid not."

The drums were still beating and the Delaware men were still singing, the accompaniment seeming to be a natural background to what was said between these men.

Viscount Rohan came forward. "William Toddman, what is the meaning of this?"

"I've come to expose you for the fool that you are, Viscount Rohan." His loud voice bellowed through the hall.

The viscount squared back his shoulders and pulled himself up to his full height, which was still a foot short of the other man. "I'm afraid you'll have to leave."

"Not yet," Toddman said. "Not until I reveal to everyone gathered here how completely you have been duped. That man, whom you are parading around as Blackfoot, is not."

Gray Hawk actually laughed, though he didn't lower his aim from the other warrior.

"It is not funny!"

"Is it not?"

"Well, you won't be laughing when you see the sum of money I will be paid from the Duke of Starksboro for my—"

"The Duke of Starksboro?" This from the viscount. "What has that man to do with… He paid you to do this, didn't he? He actually paid you to sabotage my work. He—"

"Does it matter? You're through. You're finished. You sent in a manuscript representing this man as Blackfoot. Well, he is not."

Gray Hawk smiled, never letting down his guard of the other Indian. He said, in pure English, "The man Toddman has been deceived. This warrior whom he has brought here is not Blackfoot. He is not Pikuni, not Blood and not Blackfoot proper. This man is a Snake, a Shoshoni Indian, mine own enemy. Whoever brought this man to you, Toddman, plays a trick on you."

"No! Tell him it's not true." Toddman was addressing the other warrior; then, as though realizing that the Indian could not understand him, he looked to his side. No one was there. His face grew red. "My interpreters seem to have gone. But I will get them back. You wait here."

Gray Hawk ignored the man and suddenly dropped his bow and arrow. Using his hands in the universal language of the plains, he signed to the other Indian, "What game do you play here with this white man?"

The Shoshoni signed back, "The white man wanted an Indian. He got one."

"Did you know he thinks you are Blackfoot?"

The Indian shrugged.

"Tell me the truth, lest the forces of the great mystery strike you dead."

"I know only that this man wants to know everything about my culture and my language. I have been teaching him."

"Did someone bring you to him?"

"Yes," the other Indian signed back. "Two trappers brought me here and gave to my family many items to use if I would stay for a little while."

"And these two trappers, did they tell you that this man thinks you are Blackfoot?"

"No," the other man signed.

Gray Hawk laughed, and, turning toward Toddman, said, in English, "This man that you are calling Blackfoot has just told me that two trappers brought him here in exchange for giving his family many items of use. They did not tell him that he was supposed to be Blackfoot. He has been teaching you, Toddman, the ways of his people, the Shoshoni. Not the Blackfeet." Gray Hawk grinned. "The trappers lied to you."

"No!" Toddman's face contorted. "It is not possible. I wouldn't believe a savage anyway. Nor will anyone else. You cannot speak the truth."

"I do not lie."

"No! No one here would believe you. Not against me. You, a dirty, wild man."

Gray Hawk glanced down at his spotless white regalia. He grinned wider. He said, "Then I challenge you. Take this Indian to any man of knowledge in this part of the country and ask him. Not a trapper. Someone who knows Indians. Is there such a person living here?"

"There is Superintendent Clark," someone from the crowd volunteered. "He knows all Indians. He and Lewis met a lot of 'em thirty years ago."

"Then take this Indian there. You will see."

Toddman drew himself up and squinted his eyes. "I most certainly will. Wait here, you savage. I will, I tell you. Come." He motioned to the Shoshoni Indian, and the warrior, sending Gray Hawk a puzzled glance, followed.

The drums and singing of the Delawares, which had been going all this time, suddenly stopped.

And Gray Hawk glanced to Viscount Rohan.

Gray Hawk said clearly, very distinctly, "You need not fear this other man's work. He has the testimony of a Shoshoni Indian, not a Blackfoot. His are lies." Gray Hawk jutted out his chin. "I have spoken."

The viscount only stared back at Gray Hawk, seemingly at a loss for words, until at last he uttered, "Thank you, son."

Gray Hawk nodded and started to turn away, but Genevieve had come up behind the viscount. Her eyes were red, her face pale.

He stared at her; she, back at him.

He knew what he had to do, for her sake, for his. He hesitated, unwilling to let it happen. But it had to be done.

He picked up his bow from the ground, putting it back around his shoulder. Then he lifted the arrow lying there, too, but instead of replacing it in his quiver, he kept it in his hand.

And then, gradually, so slowly that perhaps no one else, save Genevieve, would notice, he let the stick drop.

He didn't move. Nor did she.

At length, he gave Genevieve one last look before he turned, and then sprinted from the room.

****

Genevieve had watched Gray Hawk's dance from afar.

She'd observed him as he'd jumped, as he'd gone through the motions of a brave out on the hunt.

She was awed by his grace, amazed at his prancing and impressed by his spins as he had hit his knees to the floor, then jumped up. She herself moved up and down to the beat, just as she had been taught in the Indian camp. She couldn't help it.

In the Indian camp.

She caught her breath and glanced around her. This was not the Indian camp.

Yes, there were people here she liked, people here she'd met before and would like to meet again, but they were all mere acquaintances. None of them had ever come as close to her as her three Indian sisters.

Her sisters. She loved them.

It was an odd thing to realize out here in the middle of a posh, European-style dance floor. She would miss the company of her Indian sisters.

Yet *this* was her world, not the prairie.

Or was it?

Was her heart here? Or out there?

She grimaced. She'd been fighting it ever since she'd arrived back home. Yes, there were amenities here that she'd begun to think were necessary, riches she couldn't do without, and yet the happiest she had ever been was out there on the prairie — with Gray Hawk.

She'd been trying to deny it, hoping she wouldn't have to confront it, but something had happened to her out there. It was as though, out among the open spaces, she'd found herself. Not the Lady Genevieve others knew her to be, not the devoted daughter, nor any other image she might have given of herself. She'd been able to simply be herself.

She sighed. It was true. Her happiness did not lie here. It was with Gray Hawk, and perhaps it had been that way ever since the first time she had seen him. She didn't know.

But it didn't matter. At last, she knew what to do.

Perhaps it had taken the threat of loss to bring her to her senses.

Perhaps not.

Karen Kay

Whatever it was, Genevieve knew her life would be a bleak, miserable existence if Gray Hawk weren't in it.

She didn't know why it had taken her so long to see it: that Gray Hawk was a man of honor, a man of integrity and a man of sensitivity. Here was someone a person would be proud to call friend...a man that a woman would be lucky to find in her lifetime.

She would tell him, somehow. She must. Before it was too late. Before he threw her away.

This decided, she slowly stepped toward him. She would join the dance with him. She would show him that nothing mattered, not her society, not his. They loved. Somehow they would solve their problems...together.

She had just started to advance toward him, into the sacred circle, when suddenly another Indian stepped forward, an Indian she did not recognize.

She saw Gray Hawk stop. She heard his war cry, listened to what he said.

She watched as he communicated with the other Indian in sign language. She read the signs herself, she and her father having learned the language long ago.

What was this? The other Indian openly admitting to not being Blackfoot?

Could this be true? If it were, it meant...

Her spirits soared, and she almost laughed.

Her father would have no further competition from Mr. Toddman, nor the Duke of Starksboro.

It was incredible.

She had to find her father. She had to tell him, if he didn't already know. She peered through the crowd, looking for her father. Once finding him, she fought her way toward him, coming up behind him.

But her father didn't notice her. He was staring straight ahead of him, staring at Gray Hawk. And Gray Hawk peered back.

316

Gray Hawk's gaze, of a sudden, switched to her. She opened her lips to say something. But before she could do a thing, Gray Hawk frowned at her. She froze.

No, it couldn't be. Not now, not when she had just discovered the truth of her feelings.

But she was too late.

Gray Hawk had already opened his hand, and, as she watched, as though from afar, a stick — one of his arrows — hit the ground.

She jerked her gaze back up toward him.

Their glances met, hers tortured, his resigned. One second ticked by, and another, and then he was turning aside. Before she could let go of her lethargy and run to him, he was already sprinting away.

"Gray Hawk," she said, too late, her voice barely audible. Then, more distinctly, "Gray Hawk!"

"Genny!" It was her father speaking.

"I love him, Father. I don't know —"

"Go to him. Go on, before he gets away forever. We'll work things out later. Go on, now. I've been a fool, Genny, to separate the two of you. I could see only what *I* felt, never considering you...or him. I was wrong to put prejudice before intelligence. You've a fine man there; don't let him get away. Go on, now. Get him before he's gone."

She gave her father a tortured glance.

"There's still time. I'm sorry I ever stood in your way. You belong with him. Go."

"Oh, Father." She flung her arms around him. "You've truly accepted this? You'll still love me?"

"I'll love you no matter what. Now get, Genny, before he's forever gone. Just come and visit once in awhile."

She didn't wait another second. Lifting her skirts, she ran through the crowd of people as fast as she was able. She didn't care what anyone said; she didn't care what anyone thought. These people's opinions were based on prejudice. Hers were founded on love.

"Gray Hawk!" she called out, running through the hall and straight out onto the porch. "Gray Hawk, wait!"

There was no sign of him.

"Gray Hawk! Please, don't go!"

But there was no one there to hear.

How could he have disappeared so quickly?

She had to act, and fast. The man could run as swiftly as the wind.

She ceased thinking. She grabbed a horse, still saddled and tied to the hitching post outside the house. And even though the animal was not her own, she didn't think twice about what she did. She would return the animal.

Hopping up into the saddle, she straddled the horse. She didn't even consider protocol and the correctness of riding sidesaddle. She didn't have time to consider it.

She urged the animal forward down the carriage lane, nudging it to a gallop, then into a run.

Dear Lord, she didn't see Gray Hawk anywhere. Where could he have gone? Wait! What was that up ahead of her?

A man sprinting through the street?

She urged the horse on even faster.

Yes, it was. It was a man dressed in white, a man tearing down the road as though he were a thief escaping a crime. A man dressed in white buckskin.

"Gray Hawk!"

He didn't stop.

"Gray Hawk, wait!"

He slowed, looking back over his shoulder. All at once, he stopped and turned back to face her.

"Wait, Gray Hawk, please!"

He shook his head as she approached, throwing his hair back behind his shoulders, and he braced his hands on his hips.

She rode right up to him.

"Gen-ee, it is no use. I have already thrown you away."

She stared down at him, not bothering to dismount. "It doesn't matter. I did not agree. It's not valid."

"You did not stop me."

"I am now."

"It does not matter. Genny, how could we live together? I could not keep you in my camp forever, and there is too much prejudice here. It is not an easy thing to experience. I would not have you feel this too because of me."

"I don't care."

"I do. I would protect you."

He turned away from her as though he would leave again.

"Wait, Gray Hawk. What do you mean, protect me? Who are you 'protecting' me from? You?"

He spun around. "Yes. I would not have you experience this prejudice."

"I already have. It doesn't matter to me."

"It does to me. I would die a little every time someone said something bad about you."

"Even in your own camp?"

"Yes, in my own camp...what do you mean?"

"I mean that I am going with you."

"But your father?"

"He will come and visit, or we can always journey here to see him or travel to England if he returns. You were right, Gray Hawk. Sometimes, you have to work at these things; sometimes, you have to bend."

He hesitated. "You would give up all this?"

"Yes," she said. "But not forever. We can live in both worlds. It will not be easy, but life without you would be misery. I would rather be fighting the

319

prejudice than always remembering—with regret—the love that we had. I would have your children, Gray Hawk."

Still, he didn't seem convinced. "You are certain?"

"I am certain. I don't know why I didn't see it before. My place is not here just because I was raised here. My place is where my heart is. It is with you."

He grinned. He let go a cry. He spun around in a circle and walked a short distance away.

But before he had a chance to step more fully away, or even to return, Genevieve took hold of a lasso that had been tied onto the horse. Setting the animal to walk up to Gray Hawk, she dropped the rope around him.

She said, "I'm not letting you go away without me. Know now that the first time I captured you, I had to do it for my father. This time, Gray Hawk, I do it for me. And don't you dare dispute a sits-beside-him-wife."

He smiled; he chuckled, his teeth gleaming white and straight under the streetlight torches. He said, "I would not even attempt it."

She smiled then, too, her laughter mixing with his as she dismounted and fell into his waiting arms.

"Oh, Gray Hawk," she said. "Forever I will love you. And yes, I can answer your question now. Love is enough. We will make it so."

He jerked his head to the left, smiling and laughing with her. But when he spoke, all he seemed able to utter was, "Oh, my sweet, courageous Gen-ee."

And he picked her up, swinging her round and round until, at last, he carried her quietly away, into the night.

A little farther back, a man stood with his best friend, one who posed as his servant. Slowly, this first gentleman lit a cigar, unable to keep the tears from his eyes, nor the smile from his face.

Quietly, he said, "We'd best go bring the horse home, what do you say, Robert?"

When his friend acknowledged him, Viscount Rohan defiantly raised his cigar in the air. And, beaming, said, "Here's to my grandchildren."

And with that, with the horse's reins grasped firmly in hand, the Viscount Rohan and his good friend, Robert, strolled leisurely back toward the house.

About the Author

Multi-published author, Karen Kay, has been praised by reviewers and fans alike for bringing the Wild West alive for her readers.

Karen Kay, whose great grandmother was a Choctaw Indian, is honored to be able to write about a way of life so dear to her heart, the American Indian culture.

"With the power of romance, I hope to bring about an awareness of the American Indian's concept of honor, and what it meant to live as free men and free women. There are some things that should never be forgotten."

Stay in touch with Karen Kay by signing up for her newsletter;

https://signup.ymlp.com/xgbqjbebgmgj

Find Karen Kay online at www.novels-by-karenkay.com

Enjoy this excerpt of

The Eagle and the Flame

By

Karen Kay

The Wild West Series

Book One

A vision foretold his tribe's doom. Is the flame-haired beauty the trickster or his true love?

Lucinda Glenforest's father, a general who'd fought in the Indian Wars, taught his flame-haired daughter to out-shoot even the best men the military could put up against her. When Luci's sister is seduced and abandoned, it's up to Luci to defend her honor in a duel. Although she wins, the humiliated captain and his powerful family vow vengeance. The sisters' only hope is to flee and hide until their father returns from his overseas mission. Out of money, Luci hatches a plan to disguise herself as a boy and use her sharpshooting skills in Buffalo Bill's Wild West Show.

The chief of the Assiniboine tribe has a terrifying vision: that someone called the deceiver, or trickster, spells doom for the children of his tribe. He enlists Charles Wind Eagle to join Buffalo Bill's Wild West Show in hopes of appealing to the President of the United States for help, and to find and stop the deceiver. When Wind Eagle is paired with a girl whom he knows is disguised as a boy, he believes she might be the deceiver. Still, she stirs his heart in ways he must resist, for he has a secret that can never be told, nor ignored. And Luci can never forget that her father would destroy Wind Eagle if she were to fall in love with him.

Forced to work together, they can't deny their growing attraction. Will Luci and Wind Eagle find a way through the lies to find true love? Or will they be consumed by the passion of deception and slander?

Warning: A sensuous romance that might cause a girl to join the rodeo in order to find true love.

Prologue

The Assiniboine Sioux Reservation

Northeastern Montana

May 1884

"*R*un! Run to them! Help them!"

Ptehé Wapáha, Horned Headdress, couldn't move. It was as though his feet were tied to the ground with an invisible rope. He attempted to lift his feet one at a time. He couldn't. Bending, he struggled to remove the shackles that held him prisoner. It was impossible.

Straightening up, he looked down into the Assiniboine camps from his lofty perch upon a hill, and he watched as a cloud of dust and dirt descended from the sky to fall upon the children of the Assiniboine. Helpless to act, he stared at the scene of destruction as each one of the children fell to the ground, their bodies withering to dust. Still, he stood helpless, unable to act in their defense. He heard their cries, their pleas for aid. He reached out to them, he, too, crying. But he couldn't move; he couldn't save them.

The cloud lifted. The children were no more; their bones had returned to the earth. Instead, in their place arose a people who appeared to be Assiniboine outwardly, but within their eyes, there showed no spark of life.

They appeared to be without spirit, without heart; they were broken—mere slaves.

From the cloud of dirt came the sound of a whip as the people cowered beneath its assault. Then arose the lightning strikes and the thunder. One by one even those soulless people fell to their knees—a conquered people, their heads bowed in fear.

And, then they were no more. All was lost; all was gone.

What force was this? Who or what was this faceless power that had killed the Assiniboine people and their children? He knew it not.

He cried, his tears falling to the ground, but even the essence of this, his body's grief, was barren. His proud people were no more.

Jerking himself awake, Ptehé Wapáha, Horned Headdress, chief of the Rock Mountain People, sat up suddenly. His sleeping robes fell around him and sweat poured from his body. Tears fell from his eyes as he came fully into the present moment.

At once, he realized that what he had seen had been a mere dream, and, while this might have comforted a lesser being, Horned Headdress knew that there was more to the nightmare. It was a vision, a warning from the Creator: this was what would come to pass if he and his people didn't act. And now.

But, what was he to do? He didn't know who this enemy was.

It was then that, wide awake, he beheld a vision unfolding before him as the Creator spoke to him in the language of the sacred spider. And, as the spider weaved his web, pictures of a future time appeared upon that maze, as though it were a backdrop for the images.

Astonishment and fear filled his soul. But, he soon came to realize that the Creator had not warned him in vain, for, upon that same web appeared visions of deeds that would thwart that future evil, if he could but do them.

He must act, and with speed. This he vowed he would do. But how? He was no longer a young man, conditioned to the rigors that would be required. He could not perform the skills necessary to accomplish what must be done.

But there are two youths among our people who can. The thought came to him as though it were his own, but he realized that the words were from the Creator. Moreover, he saw with his mind's eye, that there were, indeed, two young men who were strong enough and proficient enough to undertake this task.

With a calmness of purpose, Horned Headdress knew what he would do, what he must do....

Chapter One

May 1884

"*Our* way of life is endangered, and our people might well be doomed, I fear—all our people—unless we act."

Twenty-year old, Waŋblí Taté, Wind Eagle, of the *Hebina*, the Rock Mountain People of the Nakoda tribe, listened respectfully to his chief, Horned Headdress. The chief held an honorable war record, was honest beyond reproach and was known to be wise at the young age of fifty-two years. On this day, Wind Eagle and his *kóla*, Iron Wolf, were seated in council within the chief's spacious sixteen-hide tepee. There were only the three of them present: Horned Headdress; himself, Wind Eagle; and Macá Mázasapa, Iron Wolf, the chief's son.

"The White Man is here to stay," continued Horned Headdress. "Many of our chiefs speak of this. Already we have seen changes that are foreign and confusing to us, for their customs are not ours. I have asked you both to this council today because I have dreamed that our people will not long exist if we do not act as a united people. But allow me to explain.

"As you both are aware, the annuities, promised so easily in treaty by the White Father, did not arrive this past winter to replace the hundreds-of-years-old food source, the buffalo. Because of this, too many of the young and the old did not survive the harsh snows and winds that inflicted wrath upon this country; a worse winter cannot be remembered, not even by the very old. All our people are grieved, for every family amongst us lost loved ones, and, I fear that if we do not become like the beaver and act in a fast and well-organized manner, we, as a people, will perish from the face of this earth.

"The Indian agent is partly to blame for this; he put us at a terrible disadvantage, for our men of wisdom and experience, who have always ensured that our people remain alert to future dangers, were rounded up and placed in an iron cage that the agent calls jail. He used Indian police to do this; they were young men from our tribe who listened to this agent's poisonous tongue, and, feeling they knew best for our people, acted for the agent and not us. They helped him to disarm us, not realizing that their people had need of their guns and their bows and arrows not only to defend their families, but to hunt for food. Later, these same young men lamented their actions, for they learned too late that the Indian agent is not our friend.

"Some of our young men, like yourselves, escaped by hiding until the danger passed. Then, stealing away into the night, these men left to find food and bring it back to supply us with needed rations. But in many cases, the food arrived too late, and the evil face of starvation caused the death of too many of our people.

"We have heard this agent laugh at our plight, but what are we to do, for we have no one else to speak for us to the White Father? We chiefs have spoken often of this matter and have pondered who among us might seek out the White Father and express our grievances.

"Recently I received a vision from the Creator. I have now seen that the danger is not in the past; I have learned that our children have a terrible fate and we might lose them all if we remain here and do nothing to change our future."

Wind Eagle nodded solemnly; no words were spoken, as befit the purpose of this council.

"I believe I know what must be done," continued Horned Headdress. "I have seen in vision that there is a white man whose name is Buffalo Bill Cody, who is now visiting our Lakota brothers to the southwest of us. I am told that this man, Buffalo Bill, is not a bad man, though he pursues fame and approval, as well as the white man's gold. Further, I am told that he searches for those among us who can perform feats of daring, because he would take the best that we have and parade those youths before the White Man. It is said to me that this is the manner in which this man purchases the necessities of living.

"I have discovered that he offers a home for those whom he chooses, as well as the white man's gold and silver which can be traded for clothing, food and other comforts. He is soliciting youths who can perform trick riding, or who can run as fast as the wind or those who can shoot with precision. He also is asking for young men who are unparalleled in tests of strength and brawn. Wind Eagle, you have proven yourself to be unequalled in shooting the arrow straight, accurately and with a speed that no one in all the nations can match."

Wind Eagle nodded silently.

"And you, Macá Mázasapa, my son, are the best horseman in all the Nakoda Nation, performing tricks that even the finest riders of the Plains, the Blackfeet, admire."

Iron Wolf dipped his head in acknowledgement.

"I am now asking you to act for me on behalf of your people; humbly, I would implore you both to travel to the Lakota people on the Pine Ridge Reservation and enter into those contests sponsored by this man, Buffalo Bill." Horned Headdress paused significantly as though he were choosing his next words with care. "I have seen in vision," he continued, "that the White Father, or a man representing him, will attend one of Buffalo Bill's Wild West shows. If I could, I would go in your place, but there are reasons why I cannot. I am no longer a youth who might compete against other youths. Also, I am needed here to counsel our sick and our needy and to act against this Indian Agent on behalf of our people, for this man is still here, is still corrupt, and every day denies our people the food and supplies that have been promised to us by treaty."

As was tradition in Indian councils, neither young man spoke, both kept their eyes centered downward, in respectful contemplation. Not only was it the utmost in bad manners to interrupt a speaker, but it was a particular taboo to volunteer one's opinions with an elder of the tribe unless asked to do so. At length, Horned Headdress continued, saying, "I have seen into the future, and I believe that both of you will be accepted by this showman. I ask you this: when the White Father or his representative comes to this show, ask for a private audience with this man, who I believe will grant your request. But beware. I have also seen that all will not be easy for you, for there is a deceiver there. You may come to know this person by being part of Buffalo Bill's show. Have a care, and do your work well, for this deceiver might be the greatest threat to all the Indian Nations. This trickster, if not recognized and stopped, may bring about death and destruction to our children in ways that our minds do not comprehend. Look for this person, discover who it is, man or woman. Be alert that if we do not learn from what tribe he or she hails, this deceiver could bring disaster not only to us, but to all the Indian Nations, and we, as an Indian people, might die in spirit forever. Identify this person as quickly as you might and disarm him or her, for I do not speak lightly that the fate of our children rests with you."

He paused for a moment. "And now," he continued, "I would hear what you wish to say about this burden I ask you to shoulder, for I would know if each one of you stands ready to pit your skills against this ill wind of tragedy for our people."

Now came the chance for each young man to speak, and they both agreed that they would be honored to bear this responsibility. They would go at once to their Lakota brothers in the south, and yes, they would use all their cunning and strength to prevent any future harm that might befall their people.

Horned Headdress nodded approval. "It is good," he acknowledged, before adding, "Seek out another young man from your secret clan, the Wolf Clan, once you have been successful in joining Buffalo Bill's show. Take him into your confidence, for I have also seen that three is oftentimes better protection against evil than two."

Both young men nodded.

"*Wašté*, good. Now, listen well, my young warriors, and I will tell you what I wish you to say to the white man's representative, and what I wish you to do...."

***

Wind Eagle looked out from his lofty perch upon a stony ridge, which sat high above the winding waters of the Big Muddy, or as the white man called it, the Missouri River. He faced the east, awaiting the sunrise, his face turned upward, his arms outstretched in prayer. Below him unfolded numerous pine-covered coulees and ravines, jagged and majestic as they cut through the mountains, a range which appeared to never end. The huge rock beneath his moccasined feet felt solid and firm, and, as he inhaled the moist air of the morning, he gazed outward, welcoming the beauty of the Creator's work.

He sought a vision to guide him on this vital quest for his people. Also, he hoped to ease his troubles, for as Horned Headdress had so elegantly said, the shared tragedy that had destroyed so many of their people had also struck Wind Eagle personally.

It was true that starvation had been the ultimate weapon employed by rogue forces within and without the tribe. Because both the Indian Agent and the Indian police had acted against the people, Wind Eagle's grandfather had died in those cages the white man called jails. At the time, Wind Eagle and his father had been gone from the village on the hunt for food. But game was scarce, causing his own, and his father's, absence to extend for too long a time. When they had returned to their village, they had found that many of their friends were now gone. Even his beloved grandmother — the woman who had raised him — had been weak when Wind Eagle and his father had returned. For a short while, it had appeared that she might recover, but it was not to be. Too soon, she had left this life to travel to the Sandhills, where she would join her husband. At least, they would journey on that path together.

It was only a few days past that Ptehé Wapáha, Horned Headdress, had spoken to himself and Iron Wolf, setting the two of them into action. Quickly, they had made their plans and had talked of nothing else for the past two days, and, if they were both picked by the Showman to be a part of the show, each individually knew what his part would be in this vital task. Failure was no option; the life of their people must continue.

Because no delay could be spared, they were to leave this very night to set out upon the trail to the Pine Ridge reservation. They would travel by horseback, the both of them taking two or more of his ponies with him.

But no such journey could commence without first seeking a vision, for only in this way could a man communicate with his Creator. And so Wind Eagle began with a prayer:

"*Wakaṅtanka*, hear my plea. I come before you humble, having given away my best clothing to the needy. As is right for my appeal, I have bathed myself in the smoke of many herbs, and have spent many days in prayer. Show me, guide me, to see how I might best aid my chief and my people."

Then he sang:

"*Wakaṅtanka, wacéwicawecioiya,* (Creator, I pray for them)

Wakaṅtanka, wacéwicawecioiya,

Wakaṅtanka, ca jéciyata, (Creator, I call thee by name)

Wakaṅtanka, ca jéciyata,

Wakaṅtanka, unkákí japi. (Creator, we suffer)

Wakaṅtanka, oićiya. (Creator, help me)

Wakaṅtanka, oićiya."

He closed his eyes, inhaling deeply as the sun peeped up from above the horizon. Already, he could feel the sun's warming rays, and he sighed. It was good, and he became quiet, merging himself with the spirit of Mother Earth, hoping that he might be gifted a vision. Perhaps Wakáŋtaŋka was attuned to the cries of His people, for Wind Eagle was not left long to linger. As he opened his eyes, he beheld a pair of bald eagles—his namesake— dancing in the cool drafts of the air. Beautiful was their courtship ritual as they climbed ever higher and higher into the airy altitudes of the sky.

Then it happened, the dance of love: locking talons, they spun around and around, spiraling down toward the earth in what might seem be a dive to their death. Still, neither let go of the other, embracing and holding onto each other in their twirling spectacle until the very last moment. From that courtship dance, the pair would mate and form a union that would last their lifetime, and out of that union would appear a new generation of bald eagles. So it had been for thousands of years past; so it was now.

Entranced by the exquisiteness of this show of nature, he didn't at first see what was before him, didn't realize the two eagles were now hovering in the air, within his reach. The sound of their flapping wings, however, was loud in the cooling mountain breeze, and, lifting his vision to encompass them both, they spoke to him:

"We, the eagle people, are sent here from the Creator to tell you that He has heard your plea. He has told us to say this to you.

"Learn from us, for we, the eagle people, marry but once, and for all our life. Heed the advice of your heart, since it will lead you on a path that will ensure the well-being of your people. Beware the past mistakes of others. Beware also the one or the many who would hide within the cloak of deceit. Be strong, remain alert, for the way to help your people will be fraught with great danger.

"Opportunity will soon be yours, for your skill is the best in all the Nations. Use this to learn about your peoples' secret enemy, for it will be through this venture that will appear the chance to free your people from a coming darkness. If you are successful, your acts of valor will be spoken about throughout the Indian Nations.

"Trust your heart, for there is one there who might help you to find peace within your mind and spirit.

"We have spoken."

Wind Eagle outstretched his arms toward the eagles, and he might have sung his song back to them, but the two birds had already lifted away from him, soaring higher and higher into the sky. Once more, the eagles locked talons, repeating the ancient courtship ritual dance.

Breathing deeply, he watched their magnificent show with respect, until at last the eagles plummeted to the earth, breaking away from one another before striking the ground. Coming together again, they climbed high over the rocks, alighting at last upon their nest. Here, they would love, ensuring that their species survived well into the future.

What was the meaning of their verse? He would relay his vision to his chief, of course, for only in this way could he assure the success of his task. But, before he left, he sang out his thanks in prayer, saying:

"Wakaṅtanka, I thank you for the vision you have given me.

"Wakaṅtanka, I honor you. I honor your messengers.

"And now I would seek out my chief that I might ensure I understand fully your instruction to me."

So saying, Wind Eagle stepped back from the ridge and retraced his steps to his camp. The day was still young, and he felt renewed with purpose.

Chapter Two

An infamous dueling field outside Bladensburg, Maryland

May 1888

$\mathcal{T}$he early morning's cool, gray mist hung low over the dueling field's short grass and the woods that surrounded it. The lawn and woods-scented air was heavy and moist here at the Bladensburg contesting grounds; and, because this notorious spot lay only a few blocks from Washington DC proper, the atmosphere was further flavored with the scent of smoke from the fires and the wood-burning stoves of the numerous houses in the city. The earth felt mushy and wet beneath her footfalls, and the grass both cushioned and moistened the leather of her boots, as well as the bottom edge of her outfit. There was a chill in the air, and Lucinda Glenforest wore a short jacket of crushed velvet gold over the flowery embroidered skirt of her cream-colored, silky dress. Her bonnet of gold and ivory velvet boasted a brim that was quilled, and the satin bow that was tied high on top, fell into inch-wide strings that tied under her chin. The color scheme complemented her fiery, golden-red hair that had been braided and tied back in a chignon that fell low at the back of her neck. The entire ensemble had been strategically donned in the wee hours of the morning to allow for freedom of movement, which might be more than a little required for the sedate "battle" which was to take place.

Beside her reposed Lucinda's fifteen-year-old younger sister, Jane, whose condition being only a few months in the making, was, for the moment, hidden. But soon, in less time than Lucinda liked to consider, the consequence of Jane's ill-fated affair would become evident.

"Don't kill him, Luci."

The words served to irritate Luci; not because of Jane's concern for the swine who had done this to her, but because of Luci's involvement in a situation that should rightly involve male members of their family. But their father, General Robert Glenforest, had left for the Island of Hawaii on the urgent business of war, and this, because their family had no brother to uphold its honor, left only Luci to contend with the problem. The fact that she possessed the skills to tackle the dilemma was hardly the point.

Being the eldest child in a military family, Luci had been fated to mimic her father's profession, for General Glenforest had made it no secret that he had hoped his firstborn would be a boy. To this end, he had carefully schooled Luci into the more male occupations of war, of shooting, of defense and of strategic planning. Luci's own inclinations—which had included dolls and pretend dress-up—were of no consequence to her father. With the feminist movement in full swing, General Glenforest had found favor in openly proclaiming that he hoped Luci would follow in his footsteps, or if this weren't quite possible, to marry a soldier as like-minded as he. He went further to state that he hoped his daughter would thereafter advise her husband wisely.

As Luci had grown older, she had protested, of course, but it hadn't done her any good, especially since she enjoyed and stood out in the sport of the shooting gallery. Her prowess in these matches had earned her many a trophy over her male counterparts, and, as time had worn on, she had gone on to win and win and win, even those matches where the man she was pitted against was years older than she.

Now, while it might be true that Luci enjoyed the thrill of shooting matches, it was not factual that she shared other traits of the male gender.

After all, she was well aware that she was not a man, and outside of the marksmanship that she excelled in, she held few common threads with the male of the species. Indeed, she often found a boy's rather crude sense of humor extremely gross and very unfunny.

So it was that she had mastered a defense against her father, her resistance being to dress up and to act in as ladylike a manner as possible. Indeed, she flaunted her femininity, had done so even as a child, especially when her father was in residence. Her rebelliousness had earned her a treasure, though. She had come to love the manner in which she adorned herself. Even her day dresses protested the current trend of the dark colors of black, brown and gray; none of that for her. Her clothing consisted of vivid hues of blue, coral, pink, yellow, green and more. Indeed, she flaunted the style of the walking dress, cutting her version of that style low in the bodice. Tight waists, which hugged her curves, ended in a "V" shape over her abdomen in front and the beginning arc of her buttocks in back. These and other attributes of her clothing asserted her female gender quite vividly. Her bustles were soft and feminine, and were generally trained in back, adding to the aesthetic allure of her costume, while the overall effect of her skirts, draped in gatherings of material, fell like a soft waterfall to the floor.

That this style was considered to be a woman's attire for only evening gatherings bothered her not in the least. Although she had often heard the whispered gossip doubting the truth of her maidenhood, no one dared to repeat such lies to her face.

Her father, when he was in residence, accused her of playing up her feminine assets too well. But when he had gone on to criticize her too greatly, Luci had merely smiled at him; revenge, it appeared, was sweet. Truth was, left to her own devices, Luci might have made much of her own inclinations, for her heart was purely girlish. Indeed, secretly at home, she enjoyed the more womanly chores of baking, cooking and sewing.

It did bother her that her abilities with a gun appeared to frighten suitors, for at the age of nineteen, she had never known the amorous attentions of any young man; no boyfriends, no male interest in her as a young woman. She'd not even experienced a mild flirtation with a member of the opposite sex. Indeed, it might be said that she was nineteen and ne'er been kissed.

So it was with reluctance that Luci answered her sister's plea to "not kill him," saying, "I promised you that I wouldn't, Janie, and that's all I can assure you. You must admit that the brute deserves no consideration whatsoever. If father were here, you know that he would demand a Military Tribunal for that man, since both our father and that viper are military. Even a firing squad would be too good, I'm sure. To think, that skunk told you he wasn't married—"

"He did propose to me."

"How could he? Janie, he was married when he proposed to you. He's nothing but a lying thief."

"He's not a thief!"

"He took your maidenhood, didn't he?" Lucinda whispered the words. "Once lost, it's gone forever. You must see that he deserves to be killed."

Jane blushed. Still, she persisted, entreating, "Please don't do it, Luci. Please. I love him so."

This last was said with such urgency and dramatics, that Luci's only response was a sigh. If it were up to her...

She still remembered back to a few weeks ago, and to Janie's confession.

Luci had found her blond and beautiful fifteen-year-old sister locked in her room, grieving. On enquiry, Jane had confessed her problem. "I'm pregnant, Luci. We had planned a June wedding. But now?..."

"Pregnant? Had planned a June wedding?"

"He's married. I didn't know. I swear I didn't. He told me he loved me, and that we would be married in June. But when I came to him to tell him of the child, he laughed at me."

"He laughed? You're telling this to me truly? He honestly laughed?"

Jane cried and seemed unable to speak. She nodded instead.

"Who is this man?"

Jane hiccupped. "I...promise me that you won't kill him."

"How can I say that to you in view of what has happened? And with Father gone. Now, tell me, who is this man? You know I'll find out one way or the other."

"I suppose you will. But please, I can't reveal his name to you unless I have your word that you won't kill him."

Luci paused. She could force the issue, but she would rather not. Perhaps it was because Jane was more like a daughter to her than a sister, for Luci had taken on the role of "mother" at the age of four, when their own mother, shortly after giving birth to Jane, had passed on to the heavenly plane. Plus, their father had never remarried. Luci uttered, "I will do my best not to kill him, Janie. But that's all I can promise."

Sniffing, Jane blew her nose on the dainty handkerchief in her hand, then at length, she admitted, "I guess that's good enough. I think you might know him. It's Captain Timothy Hall. But please, don't be angry at him. I love him so."

Of course Luci knew the worthless snake. He had once courted Abagail Swanson, one of her best girlfriends, who also had been underage at the time. Luckily for her friend, she had discovered the truth of Hall's marital state before he'd been able to inflict permanent damage on her.

What was wrong with the man? Was his twenty-year-old wife already too old for him? Was he a pervert?

Oh, what she would like to do to him if the society around them would only allow it....

Well, that was all in the recent past; what was done was done. Today was the day he would pay. Today, that no-account slime would contend with her, and Luci pledged to herself that her sister's honor, as well as that of their family, would be avenged.

Once again, she thought back to the last few weeks. In less than twenty-four hours after her talk with Janie, Luci had challenged the bearded, black-haired degenerate, and had done so in as public a place as possible, a garden party. He had laughed at her, of course, when she had confronted him, and, using her gloves, she had slapped his face.

"You're a two-timing scoundrel, Captain Hall, and I challenge you to a duel. Make no mistake, I will protect and defend my family's honor."

"You? A woman? Dueling me?" He snickered. "I wouldn't stoop so low."

"Low? Are you a coward, then? Is your problem that your spine runs yellow? You know that no man has ever bested me in the skill of the shooting gallery."

His answer was nothing more than a loud hiss.

"My second will act at once, setting the time and place of the duel. And hear me out, if you don't show, I will ensure that all the country in and around Washington DC, as well as your wife, will know not only of your misdeeds, but also of your cowardice. And this, I promise."

Still, she thought, he might not come. For now, she awaited her second, as well as those in Hall's party. She picked up her pistol—a Colt .45—checking it over carefully, swearing to herself what she would do to him if the wicked man didn't show....

***

"The rules for this duel are as follows," declared Sergeant Anthony Smyth, a tall, dark-haired gentleman, who was Luci's second. Smyth was an excellent marksman in his own right, which was one reason why Luci had picked him to preside over the duel. That both he and his wife were close family friends had aided Luci in making the choice. But Smyth was continuing to speak, and he said, "The match continues to first blood, and, regardless of how minor the injury, the match then ends. No further shots are legal, and will not be tolerated. The twenty paces, which were agreed upon in writing, have been marked out by a sword stuck in the ground at each side of the field. When I drop the handkerchief that I hold in my hand, you may each advance and fire. Lieutenant Michaels is on duty as the official surgeon." Sergeant Smyth glanced first at Luci, then at Captain Timothy Hall. "Are there any questions?"

When neither she nor Captain Hall spoke up, Sergeant Smyth continued, "Then it is begun."

Luci glanced down the field, estimating her distance, as well as determining where exactly she would place her shot. Having already decided that a shoulder injury would be the easiest to heal, she calculated the precise angle that would be required to obtain that "first blood," and end the match. Next to Captain Hall stood his older brother, James Hall, his second.

Behind Luci, well to her rear and out of shooting range, sat Janie, who had brought a blanket to cushion the soft ground upon which she sat. Refreshments of cinnamon rolls and coffee, with plates and coffee cups, decorated a table next to Janie. As was expected by the rules of conduct for all matters concerning dueling, both Janie and Luci had brought the refreshments for the participants today, including that serpent, Captain Tim Hall.

Luci hadn't easily consented to the early morning snack, but her friend, Sergeant Smyth, had already determined that the duel would follow the rules of personal combat exactly, making her obligated to provide the food and drink.

She sighed as she awaited the signal to begin, but she never once glanced away from her target. To do so might be fatal.

Smyth dropped the handkerchief, and both duelists fired at will. Luci's shot hit Hall in the shoulder, as she had intended, while Hall's volley missed her entirely.

"First blood has been taken," called out Sergeant Smyth. "The match now ends as formerly agreed upon. All participants are to put down their weapons, and all are invited to coffee and rolls, which they will find at the far side of the field. A surgeon is on hand to deal with your wound, Captain Hall."

Luci turned away, setting her gun down on the table next to her.

Blast!

The explosion was unexpected. The match was finished, wasn't it? If so, why was Captain Hall still firing at her?

Boom!

Hall's next shot hit her in her left upper arm.

"Stop this at once!" shouted Smyth. "Halt! This is illegal!"

But Luci ignored her second in command; she was in a gun fight and under attack; his words didn't even register with her. With the quick reflexes of one who is in command of her weapon, she grabbed hold of her Colt, turned, and carefully aimed her shot to do the most damage to Captain Hall without killing him.

Blast!

She sent her answering bullet at Captain Timothy Hall, placing the slug high up on his thigh, intending the bullet to miss, yet graze his masculine parts. His loud cry indicated she had been successful. She turned her pistol on Hall's second—James Hall—who had picked up his own gun, as though he might consider using it against her, also, illegal though it was.

"Captain Hall, you and your brother must cease this at once. You will be reported. You and your second will likely be court martialed if you continue firing," Sergeant Smyth yelled, as he hurried toward Luci, his own Colt drawn and aimed at the two culprits. But his threat fell on deaf ears. Hall had fallen to the ground, his shrieks indicating he was in too much pain to be of any more use in a gunfight. Hall's brother, James, however, looked ready to continue the match, except that when he espied Luci's Colt pointed directly at him, as well as Smyth's drawn weapon, James Hall instead dropped his gun and held his hands up in surrender.

Luci nodded. But that was all that she did. Without letting her guard down, she kept her weapon trained on both the Hall brothers as she paced to where Jane sat at the side of the field. Bending, Luci grabbed hold of her sister by the arm and pulled her up. Then, without turning her back on Captain Hall and his brother, she made her retreat toward the street, where her coach awaited.

"Make a report of this at once," she instructed Smyth, as well as Lieutenant Michaels, the military surgeon. "Let all know what a cowardly slime Captain Hall truly is. My father must be informed, and he will thank you both for doing so."

Without cause to do more at the moment, Luci and Jane slowly withdrew, Jane leading the way to their coach, for Luci never once turned her back on her opponent. That the screams of Captain Timothy Hall wafted through the air was music to Luci's ears. By measured retreat, they gained the street and the carriage, and Jane practically flew into her seat within.

"Driver!" yelled Luci as she quickly followed her sister into the conveyance. "Take us to the army telegraph office as quickly as possible!" Seating herself with care, she continued, declaring to Jane, "We must send Father word of this at once."

"Why, you're hurt!"

It was true. The exact extent of the damage was yet to be determined, and it was only now, within the relative safety of their coach, that Luci realized her arm hurt unbearably.

Yet, to Janie, all she said was, "It is only a scratch, soon healed. But come, Jane, please tear off a part of my petticoat, and give it to me to tie, that I might stop this bleeding, for I fear it is staining my blouse."

"Leave it to you to consider only the damage to your clothing," scolded Jane as she did as instructed. It was also she who tied the tourniquet. "As soon as we arrive at our home, I will summon our surgeon to attend to you at once."

"After we send that telegraph to father," amended Luci. "I fear we have not heard the last of Captain Hall and his brother. Though I feel assured that Mr. Smyth will also telegraph word to our father on any channel available to him, he may not be able to do this at a speed that could be required to ensure our good health."

"What do you mean?"

Luci sent her sister a cautious glance. With the duel having gone as badly as it had, it was not in Luci's nature to instill even more alarm in Jane, especially considering her delicate condition. Nevertheless, a word of attentiveness might be in order.

To this end, she patted Jane's hand, smiled at her and said, "When Captain Hall heals from the wound I inflicted upon him, he might feel compelled to seek us out for daring to expose his base nature to his fellow military officers. A man who would flaunt the rules of honor cannot be trusted. And I fear—"

"Luci, please," Jane cried, tears in her eyes. "What he has done is wrong, so very, very wrong, but please do not keep degrading his character to me. A scoundrel he is, I have no doubt, and I feel terrible that he has hurt you, but I am, after all, carrying his child. I wish I weren't, Luci, but it is done, and I must bear the consequences of my actions. However, I fear that, as he is the babe's father, he may have rights that even I don't understand. I should try to discover a good trait he might possess, for I fear that I may have to deal with him in the future." She pulled out a hanky from her purse and blew her nose. "Is it possible that he might have some logical reason as to why it was necessary to continue to fire at you when he should have stopped? Perhaps it was a reaction he could not control?"

"He fired two illegal shots at me, Janie, not one."

"Oh, how hard it is to love a man so much," Janie uttered with so much heartfelt passion that Luci was reminded of her sister's youth—and the hardship of being pregnant at so young an age. "I know it's true enough that he lied to me, but that doesn't make him all bad, does it? I once found good in him. It must still be there. Oh, Luci, it hurts to love him so. It hurts."

Momentarily, Luci felt at a loss for words. She made up for that lack by patting Jane's hand instead.

"It will get better," she assured Jane at last. "I know it might seem now as though the hurt will never heal. But it will." She sighed. "It will. And perhaps you are right. Maybe in the future we might be dealing with a good man. I guess one could say that only the future will declare the truth of his character. We can hope, Janie, we can hope."

Luci averted her gaze to stare at the closed, royal blue curtains that fell down over the windows of the carriage. Enough said. She would send this telegram to their father, then wait and see what might unfold. Reaching over to pull that blue, velvet curtain away from the window, she watched as the sun came up in the east.

ISBN 979 8 54370 0 259

Made in the USA
Columbia, SC
14 July 2022

63481296R00209

DU MÊME AUTEUR

Aux Éditions Gallimard

LA PROIE DES FLAMMES

UN LIT DE TÉNÈBRES

LA MARCHE DE NUIT

LES CONFESSIONS DE NAT TURNER

LE CHOIX DE SOPHIE

CETTE PAISIBLE POUSSIÈRE ET AUTRES ÉCRITS

Du monde entier

WILLIAM STYRON

FACE
AUX TÉNÈBRES

CHRONIQUE D'UNE FOLIE

Traduit de l'anglais par
Maurice Rambaud

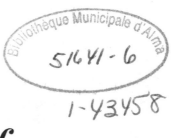

GALLIMARD

Titre original :

DARKNESS VISIBLE — A MEMOIR OF MADNESS

NOTE DE L'AUTEUR

Ce livre a pour origine une conférence que je fis à Baltimore en mai 1989 à l'occasion d'un symposium sur les troubles de l'affectivité patronné par le Département de psychiatrie de la Faculté de médecine de l'Université John Hopkins. Considérablement étoffé, le texte devint un essai publié en décembre de la même année dans Vanity Fair. *Je m'étais tout d'abord proposé de commencer par le récit d'un voyage que j'avais jadis fait à Paris — un voyage pour moi particulièrement important sur le plan de l'état dépressif dont je souffrais depuis un certain temps. Mais malgré le format exceptionnellement substantiel que m'avait consenti la revue, il y avait inévitablement des limites, et je fus contraint de renoncer à cette première partie en faveur d'autres problèmes que je tenais à aborder. Dans la version actuelle, cette partie a retrouvé sa place au début du texte. A l'exception de quelques modifications et additions relativement mineures, le reste du texte est conforme à ce qu'il était à l'origine.*

W.S.

A Rose

C'est que tout malheur dont
j'avais peur fond sur moi,
et ce que je redoutais
vient m'assaillir.
Je ne connaissais plus ni paix,
ni sécurité, ni repos;
enfin les tourments m'envahirent.

Job, *ch.3/25.26*

I

En 1985 à Paris et par une soirée fraîche de la fin octobre, je pris pour la première fois conscience que la lutte contre le trouble dont souffrait mon esprit — une lutte qui m'accaparait depuis plusieurs mois — risquait d'avoir une issue fatale. La révélation survint alors que la voiture où j'avais pris place descendait une rue luisante de pluie non loin des Champs-Elysées et longeait la lueur rougeoyante d'une enseigne au néon qui annonçait : HÔTEL WASHINGTON. Il y avait près de trente-cinq ans que je n'avais vu cet hôtel, en fait depuis le printemps de 1952 où, durant plusieurs nuits, il avait été mon premier gîte parisien. Au cours des tout premiers mois de ma *Wanderjahr*, j'avais quitté Copenhague pour gagner Paris par le train, et la décision saugrenue d'un agent de voyage new-yorkais m'avait valu d'échouer à l'Hôtel Washington. En ce

13

temps-là l'hôtel était l'un de ces nombreux établissements humides et frustes destinés aux touristes, en majorité américains, disposant de modestes ressources, qui s'ils étaient dans mon cas — c'est-à-dire affrontaient pour la première fois et non sans appréhension les Français et leurs mœurs bizarres — n'oublieraient jamais comment l'exotique bidet trônant dans la morne chambre, ni les toilettes situées tout au bout du couloir chichement éclairé, définissaient virtuellement l'abîme qui sépare la culture française de la culture anglo-saxonne. Mais je n'avais séjourné que peu de temps au Washington. Quelques jours plus tard à peine, et sur les instances de quelques jeunes Américains avec qui je m'étais lié d'amitié, j'avais déménagé pour m'installer dans un hôtel de Montparnasse plus minable encore, mais néanmoins plus pittoresque, situé à deux pas du Dôme et autres hauts lieux littéraires. (J'avais dans les vingt-cinq ans et venais de publier un premier roman qui avait fait de moi une célébrité, bien que d'un rang très modeste dans la mesure où parmi les Américains de Paris, fort peu avaient entendu parler de mon livre et moins encore l'avaient lu.) Et les années aidant, l'Hôtel Washington disparut peu à peu de ma mémoire.

14

Il réapparut, pourtant, par cette nuit d'octobre alors que je longeais la façade de pierre grise sous un petit crachin tenace, et le souvenir de mon arrivée tant d'années auparavant resurgit soudain, suscitant en moi le sentiment que, et ce pour mon malheur, la boucle était bouclée. Je me rappelle m'être dit que, lorsque le lendemain matin je quitterais Paris pour regagner New York, ce serait pour toujours. Je fus secoué par cette certitude que déjà je me résignais à l'idée de ne jamais revoir la France, et aussi de ne jamais recouvrer une lucidité qui me fuyait à une vitesse terrifiante.

A peine quelques jours plus tôt, j'avais abouti à cette conclusion que je souffrais d'une grave maladie dépressive et que tous mes efforts pour en venir à bout se soldaient par un échec lamentable. Je ne tirais aucun réconfort de l'heureux événement qui me valait de me trouver en France. Entre autres atroces manifestations de la maladie — tant physiques que psychologiques — l'un des symptômes les plus universellement répandus est un sentiment de haine envers soi-même — ou, pour formuler la chose de façon plus nuancée, une défaillance de l'amour-propre — et à mesure qu'empirait le mal, je m'étais senti accablé par un sentiment croissant d'inutilité. Ma languissante morosité était en conséquence d'autant plus ironique que j'avais pris l'avion pour passer quatre brèves journées à Paris afin de me voir décerner un prix qui aurait dû me galvaniser et me réconcilier avec moi-même. Au début de ce même été, m'était parvenue la nouvelle que j'avais été choisi pour recevoir le Prix Mondial Cino del Duca, décerné chaque année à un artiste ou à un savant auteur d'une œuvre reflétant des thèmes ou principes empreints d'un certain « humanisme ». Le prix avait été fondé à la mémoire de Cino del Duca, un immigrant d'origine italienne, qui à la veille et au lendemain de la Seconde Guerre mondiale, avait amassé une fortune en éditant et commercialisant des magazines bon marché, en particulier des illustrés, ce qui ne l'avait nullement empêché de se consacrer par la suite à des publications de qualité ; il était devenu propriétaire du quotidien *Paris-Jour*. Il était également producteur de films et propriétaire d'une célèbre écurie de courses, qui s'enorgueillissait de compter de nombreux gagnants tant en France qu'à l'étranger. Aspirant à de plus nobles satisfactions, il se mua en un philanthrope célèbre et, ce faisant, fonda une maison d'édition qui ne tarda pas à publier des œuvres d'un

16

grand mérite littéraire (par pur hasard, mon premier roman *Lie Down in Darkness* fut l'une des premières réalisations de del Duca, dans une traduction intitulée *Un lit de ténèbres*) ; lorsque survint sa mort en 1967, cette maison, les Editions Mondiales, était devenue une entité respectée d'un empire aux ramifications multiples, suffisamment prestigieux malgré sa richesse pour que se fût estompé le souvenir de sa vocation première, la publication d'illustrés, quand la veuve de del Duca, Simone, créa une fondation dont la principale fonction était l'attribution annuelle du prix éponyme.

Le Prix Mondial Cino del Duca s'est acquis un immense respect en France — un pays aimablement entiché de prix et récompenses d'ordre culturel — non seulement en vertu de son éclectisme et du mérite dont témoigne le choix des récipiendaires, mais pour la générosité du prix lui-même, qui cette année-là se montait à environ vingt-cinq mille dollars. Au nombre des élus au cours des vingt dernières années, figurent Konrad Lorenz, Alejo Carpentier, Jean Anouilh, Ignazio Silone, Andreï Sakharov, Jorge Luis Borges et un Américain, un seul, Lewis Mumford. (Pas la moindre femme jusqu'ici, avis aux féministes.) En ma qualité d'Américain tout particulièrement, il m'eût été difficile de ne pas me sentir honoré d'être inclus dans leur cénacle. Alors que l'attribution et la réception de prix littéraires suscitent d'ordinaire et de toutes parts une vague malsaine de fausse modestie, de médisances, de misérabilisme et d'envie, je considère pour ma part qu'il peut être fort agréable de se voir décerner certains prix même s'ils ne sont aucunement indispensables. Le prix del Duca fut pour moi et d'emblée un événement à ce point agréable que tout délai de réflexion paraissait absurde, et j'acceptai donc avec gratitude, précisant dans ma réponse que je serais heureux de souscrire à l'obligation fort raisonnable d'assister à la cérémonie. A ce moment-là, j'envisageais et avec joie la perspective d'un voyage de détente, et non d'un aller-retour précipité. Eussé-je été capable de prévoir mon état d'esprit à l'approche de la cérémonie, je me serais récusé.

La dépression est un dérangement de l'esprit si mystérieusement cruel et insaisissable de par la manière dont il se manifeste au moi, à l'intelligence qui lui sert de médium — qu'il échapperait pour un peu à toute description. Aussi demeure-t-il pratiquement incompréhensible pour qui ne l'a pas lui-même subi dans ses manifestations extrêmes, même si la tristesse, « le cafard » qui épisodiquement nous accablent et que nous attribuons à la tension de la vie quotidienne, sont à ce point répandus qu'ils permettent en réalité à beaucoup de se faire une idée de la maladie dans sa forme la plus catastrophique. Mais à la période dont je parle, j'avais déjà sombré bien au-delà de ces crises de cafard banales et supportables. A Paris, je le comprends maintenant, je traversais une phase critique dans l'évolution de la maladie, qui se situait à un stade intermédiaire et lourd de menaces entre les vagues remous survenus au début de l'été et le dénouement frisant la violence qui en décembre m'envoya à l'hôpital. Je tenterai par la suite d'évoquer l'évolution de cette maladie depuis ses origines les plus lointaines jusqu'à mon hospitalisation ultérieure et ma guérison, mais le voyage à Paris a gardé à mes yeux une signification toute particulière.

Le jour de la remise du prix, qui devait avoir lieu à midi et être suivie d'un déjeuner officiel, je me réveillai au milieu de la matinée dans ma chambre de l'Hôtel Pont-Royal en constatant que je me sentais raisonnablement en forme, une bonne nouvelle dont je m'empressai de faire part à Rose, mon épouse. Avec l'aide de l'Halcion, un tranquillisant anodin, j'étais parvenu à vaincre mon insomnie et à goûter quelques heures de sommeil. Aussi me sentais-je raisonnablement optimiste. Mais ce genre de fragile allégresse était une affectation désormais habituelle qui, je le savais, ne signifiait pas grand-chose, car, et j'en avais la certitude, je me retrouverais plongé dans un affreux marasme avant la tombée de la nuit. J'en étais arrivé à un stade où j'enregistrais minutieusement les moindres phases de mon état et de sa dégradation. Mon acceptation de la maladie faisait suite à un refus de l'admettre qui plusieurs mois durant m'avait tout d'abord poussé à attribuer mon malaise, mon agitation et mes brusques crises d'angoisse au manque provoqué par mon renoncement à l'alcool : brutalement au mois de juin j'avais banni le whisky et toute autre boisson alcoolisée. Tandis que mon climat affectif allait en empirant, j'avais lu un certain nombre de choses sur la dépression, tant des livres spécialement destinés au profane que des ouvrages professionnels plus érudits, entre autres la bible des psychiatres, *DSM, Diagnostic and Statistical Manual of the American Psychiatric Association.* Tout au long d'une grande partie de ma vie, je me suis vu contraint, peut-être imprudemment, d'être autodidacte en matière de médecine, ce qui m'a valu d'accumuler des connaissances bien supérieures à celles de l'amateur moyen dans le domaine médical (auxquelles nombre de mes amis, sans nul doute imprudemment, se sont souvent fiés), aussi constatai-je avec stupéfaction que je frisais quasiment l'ignorance quant à la dépression, qui autant que le diabète ou le cancer est souvent un problème médical d'une extrême gravité. Vraisemblablement, en tant que sujet prédisposé à la dépression, j'avais toujours inconsciemment rejeté ce qu'il importait de savoir ou n'en avais tenu aucun compte ; cela frôlait de trop près le psychisme et je l'avais écarté comme une adjonction importune à mon savoir.

De toute manière, j'avais tout récemment comblé cette lacune par des lectures assez substantielles, durant les quelques heures où l'état dépressif me laissait un répit suffisant pour me permettre le luxe de me concentrer, et j'avais assimilé nombre de faits fascinants et perturbants dont, cependant, je ne pouvais tirer parti. Les spécialistes les plus honnêtes reconnaissent franchement qu'une dépression grave se prête mal à un traitement aisé. Au contraire, disons, du diabète, dont avec des mesures immédiates prises pour corriger l'accommodation du corps au glucose, il est possible de renverser de façon spectaculaire et finalement de maîtriser une évolution dangereuse, il n'existe, dans les phases critiques de dépression, aucun remède efficace à court terme : cette impuissance à soulager le mal est l'un des facteurs les plus pénibles de la maladie à mesure que la victime en prend conscience, un facteur qui en outre la situe sans ambiguïté dans la catégorie des affections graves. Sauf dans le cas de maladies définies catégoriquement comme malignes ou dégénératives, on garde espoir en un *certain* type de traitement et d'éventuelle amélioration, que ce soit au moyen de drogues, d'une thérapie, d'un régime ou d'une intervention chirurgicale, le tout assorti d'une progression logique allant de l'atténuation des symptômes à une guérison définitive. De façon effrayante, le profane en proie à une grave dépression, s'il vient à feuilleter certains des livres dont regorge le marché, constatera qu'il existe une abondante information en matière de théorie et de symptomatologie, mais fort peu de choses qui légitimement pourraient suggérer une guérison rapide. Quant à ceux qui assurent qu'il existe des solutions faciles, ils sont spécieux et vraisemblablement malhonnêtes. Il existe d'honnêtes ouvrages de spécialisation qui, avec intelligence, indiquent les voies possibles de traitement et de guérison, expliquant comment certaines thérapies — la psychothérapie ou la pharmacologie, ou leur éventuelle association — ont en effet le pouvoir d'apporter la guérison hormis dans les cas extrêmement tenaces et irréductibles ; mais les plus judicieux de ces ouvrages soulignent cette cruelle vérité que les graves dépressions ne sauraient disparaître du jour au lendemain. Tout cela tend à mettre en évidence une réalité fondamentale quand bien même navrante, mais qu'il convient, je crois, de mentionner au début de ma chronique : dans sa forme pathologique, la dépression demeure un immense mystère. Elle a livré ses secrets à la science avec infiniment plus de réticences que nombre d'autres maux graves qui nous assaillent. L'intense esprit de secte, parfois d'une virulence comique, qui caractérise la psychiatrie de notre époque — le schisme entre les adeptes de la psychothérapie et les tenants de la pharmacologie — évoque les querelles médicales du dix-huitième siècle (saigner ou ne pas saigner) et suffit presque en soi à définir la nature de la dépression et la difficulté de toute guérison. Comme me le dit un jour en toute honnêteté un spécialiste en la matière, avec à mon avis, un don remarquable de l'analogie : « Si l'on compare notre savoir à la découverte de l'Amérique par Christophe Colomb, l'Amérique demeure inconnue ; nous sommes toujours échoués là-bas sur la petite île des Bahamas. »

Au cours de mes lectures j'avais, par exemple, appris que d'un certain point de vue digne d'intérêt, mon cas était atypique. Aux tout premiers stades de la maladie, les gens se sentent particulièrement mal le matin, une sensation tellement maléfique qu'ils n'ont pas le courage de sortir du lit. Ils commencent seulement à se sentir mieux à mesure que la journée avance. Dans mon cas, c'était exactement l'inverse. Tandis que j'étais capable de me lever et de vivre de façon presque normale lors de la première partie de la journée, je commençais en milieu d'après-midi ou un peu plus tard à sentir les symptômes revenir à l'assaut — la tristesse m'assaillait, ainsi qu'un sentiment de peur et d'aliénation et, par-dessus tout, une angoisse étouffante. J'ai dans l'idée que, fondamentalement, il est indifférent de souffrir davantage le matin que le soir : à supposer que ces états d'atroce quasi-paralysie soient similaires, comme ils le sont sans doute, le problème de chronologie paraîtrait académique. Mais ce fut sans nul doute parce que les habituels symptômes quotidiens faillirent à se manifester, que ce matin-là à Paris je pus me rendre sans encombre, plus ou moins maître de mes moyens, jusqu'au merveilleux palais baroque de la Rive droite qui abrite la Fondation Cino del Duca. Et ce fut là, dans un salon rococo, que je me vis décerner le prix en présence d'une petite foule distinguée de représentants de la culture française, et prononçai mon discours de réception avec, me sembla-t-il, une relative assurance, annonçant que si je faisais don de la plus grande partie du montant de mon prix à diverses organisations vouées au développement de l'entente France-Amérique, dont l'Hôpital Américain de Neuilly, l'altruisme a ses limites (cela sur le ton de la plaisanterie) et j'espérais que personne ne s'offusquerait de me voir garder pour moi une modeste partie de la somme.

Ce que je ne disais pas, et qui n'avait rien d'une plaisanterie, c'était que la somme que je prélevais pour mon usage personnel était destinée à régler le prix de deux billets sur le vol Concorde du lendemain, de manière à pouvoir regagner de toute urgence avec Rose les Etats-

Unis où, à peine quelques jours plus tôt, j'avais pris un rendez-vous pour consulter un psychiatre. Pour des raisons qui, j'en ai la certitude, découlaient de ma répugnance à accepter une réalité qui se dissolvait dans mon esprit, j'avais évité de recourir à l'aide d'un psychiatre au cours des dernières semaines, alors que s'intensifiait ma détresse. Mais je le savais, je ne pourrais remettre indéfiniment la confrontation, et lorsque en fin de compte je me mis en rapport par téléphone avec un psychiatre qui m'avait été chaudement recommandé, il m'encouragea à me rendre à Paris, en s'engageant à me voir sitôt mon retour. J'étais très impatient de rentrer, au plus vite. En dépit de l'évidence que j'étais en proie à de graves difficultés, je m'obstinais à voir la situation en rose. Une grande partie de la documentation disponible sur la dépression est, je le répète, d'un optimisme désinvolte, professant l'assurance qu'il suffirait que soit mis au point l'antidépresseur adéquat pour que la grande majorité des états dépressifs puissent être stabilisés ou guéris ; naturellement le lecteur se laisse facilement influencer par les promesses de prompte guérison. A Paris, alors même que je formulais mes remarques, j'avais hâte que la journée se termine et ressentais un désir dévorant de m'envoler pour rejoindre l'Amérique et le cabinet de mon médecin qui, grâce à ses drogues miraculeuses, dissiperait comme par enchantement mon mal. Je me souviens maintenant clairement de cet instant, et ai peine à croire que j'étais alors en proie à un espoir tellement naïf, ou que j'étais à ce point inconscient du problème et du péril qui m'attendaient.

Chose compréhensible, Simone del Duca, une forte femme brune au port de reine, se montra tout d'abord incrédule, puis furieuse, lorsque la cérémonie terminée, je lui annonçai que je ne pourrais assister au déjeuner qu'elle donnait au premier étage de la grande demeure en l'honneur de la douzaine de membres de l'Académie française qui avaient choisi de m'attribuer le prix. Mon refus était à la fois catégorique et piteux ; je lui annonçai sans ambages que j'avais modifié mes projets pour déjeuner au restaurant en compagnie de mon éditeur français, Françoise Gallimard. Naturellement, une telle décision de ma part était scandaleuse ; ainsi que toutes les personnes concernées j'avais été informé des mois auparavant qu'un déjeuner — qui plus est, un déjeuner en mon honneur — figurait au nombre des festivités de la journée.

Mais en réalité mon comportement était imputable à ma maladie, qui avait évolué au point de révéler certaines de ses caractéristiques les plus connues et les plus sinistres : confusion, impuissance à se concentrer et trous de mémoire. Lors d'une étape ultérieure, mon esprit tout entier serait assujetti à des incohérences anarchiques ; je l'ai dit, j'en étais a un stade qui n'allait pas sans évoquer une bifurcation psychique : une forme de lucidité au cours des premières heures de la journée, une confusion grandissante au cours de l'après-midi et de la soirée. Sans doute était-ce sous l'empire de ma morne hébétude de la soirée précédente que j'avais pris rendez-vous pour déjeuner avec Françoise Gallimard, oubliant mes engagements à l'égard de Mme del Duca. Une décision qui continuait à conditionner ma pensée, m'enfermant dans une obstination telle que je me trouvais soudain capable d'insulter carrément la digne Simone del Duca. « *Alors* ! » me lança-t-elle, son visage s'empourprant de fureur tandis qu'elle exécutait une volte-face hautaine, « *au... revoir* ! » Tout à coup je me sentis sidéré, hébété d'horreur à l'idée de ce que je venais de faire. Je me représentai une table où étaient installés l'hôtesse et les gens de l'Académie française, l'invitée d'honneur à la

Coupole. J'implorai la secrétaire de Madame, une dame à lunettes au visage blême d'humiliation et munie d'un écritoire, de tenter d'obtenir mon pardon : il s'agissait d'une affreuse erreur, une confusion, un *malentendu*. Sur quoi, je lâchai quelques mots qu'une vie tout entière marquée par un relatif équilibre et une foi béate dans l'invulnérabilité de ma santé mentale, m'avaient prémuni contre l'idée que je risquais un jour de prononcer ; ce fut avec un frisson que je m'entendis les adresser à cette parfaite inconnue : « Je suis malade, dis-je, *un problème psychiatrique*[1]. »

Magnanime, Mme del Duca accepta mes excuses et le déjeuner se déroula sans autre crise, quand bien même je ne pus me défaire tout à fait du soupçon, tandis que nous bavardions de façon plutôt guindée, que ma bienfaitrice demeurait perturbée par mon comportement et me prenait pour un drôle de numéro. Le déjeuner fut long, et à peine fut-il terminé, je sentis que je réintégrais les ombres de l'après-midi lourdes d'angoisse et de terreurs menaçantes. Une équipe de télévision envoyée par l'une des grandes chaînes attendait (elle aussi je

---

1. En français dans le texte (*N. d. T.*).

29

l'avais oubliée), prête à m'emmener au musée Picasso depuis peu ouvert au public, où j'avais accepté de me laisser filmer en train d'admirer les œuvres et d'échanger quelques commentaires avec Rose. Ce qui s'avéra être, comme je l'avais prévu, non une promenade captivante, mais une lutte exténuante, une épreuve majeure. Le temps que nous arrivions au musée, et par suite des embarras de la circulation, il était quatre heures passées et déjà mon esprit était assailli par ses habituels tourments : panique, désintégration, sensation que mes processus mentaux sombraient peu à peu dans un flot délétère et innommable qui oblitérait toute réaction agréable au monde et à la vie. Cela pour dire de façon plus explicite que loin d'éprouver du plaisir — le plaisir qu'assurément aurait dû m'inspirer ce lieu fastueux dédié à une œuvre de génie — j'éprouvais dans mon esprit une sensation proche, bien qu'indiciblement différente, de l'authentique douleur. Ce qui m'amène à évoquer de nouveau la nature insaisissable de ce mal. Que le terme « indicible » s'impose à mon esprit n'est nullement fortuit dans la mesure où, il convient de le souligner, s'il était aisé de décrire la douleur, la plupart des innombrables victimes de ce fléau séculaire seraient capables de décrire sans réticences à leurs amis et leurs proches (et même à leurs médecins) certaines des dimensions réelles de leur tourment, provoquant peut-être ainsi une compréhension qui, dans l'ensemble, a toujours fait défaut ; une telle incompréhension relève en général non d'une absence de compassion, mais de l'incapacité fondamentale où se trouvent les gens bien portants de se représenter une forme de tourment totalement étrangère à l'expérience quotidienne. Pour ma part, cette douleur s'apparente très étroitement à la noyade ou à la suffocation — mais même ces métaphores sont loin de la vérité. William James, qui pendant de longues années lutta contre la dépression, en vint lui aussi à renoncer à cette quête d'une représentation adéquate, dont il suggère la quasi-impossibilité lorsque dans *Les Variétés de l'expérience religieuse* il écrit : « Il s'agit d'une angoisse positive et active, une sorte de névralgie psychique totalement étrangère à la vie normale. »

Au musée, la douleur persista durant toute ma visite et atteignit son paroxysme au cours des quelques heures qui suivirent lorsque, de retour à l'hôtel, je m'affalai sur mon lit et restai là les yeux fixés au plafond, virtuellement paralysé par une transe marquée par une extrême souffrance. D'ordinaire en de pareils moments, toute lucidité désertait mon esprit, d'où le terme de *transe*. Je ne vois pas de mot plus pertinent pour qualifier cet état, un état d'hébétude impuissante dans lequel la conscience faisait place à cette « angoisse positive et active ». Et l'un des aspects les plus intolérables de tels intermèdes était l'impossibilité de trouver le sommeil. Tout au long de ma vie, pratiquement, j'avais eu pour habitude, comme un nombre considérable de gens de m'octroyer une petite sieste lénifiante en fin d'après-midi, mais il est notoire que toute perturbation du cycle du sommeil naturel est un trait dévastateur de la dépression ; à la dangereuse insomnie dont depuis longtemps je souffrais chaque nuit, s'ajoutait l'outrage de cette insomnie de l'après-midi, par comparaison négligeable, mais d'autant plus affreuse qu'elle me frappait pendant les heures où ma détresse était la plus intense. Il était désormais clair que jamais ne me seraient octroyées fût-ce les quelques minutes de répit qui m'eussent permis d'échapper à mon épuisement de tous les instants. Je me souviens nettement de m'être dit, allongé sur mon lit, Rose assise à mes côtés et plongée dans un livre, que mes après-midi et mes soirées empiraient de façon presque mesurable, et que cet épisode était jusqu'à présent le pire. Je parvins néanmoins à me secouer suffisamment pour sortir dîner avec — qui d'autre ? — Françoise Gallimard, covictime au même titre que Simone del Duca de l'affreux contretemps du déjeuner. Il faisait une nuit âpre et venteuse, avec des rafales froides et humides qui balayaient les avenues, et lorsque Rose et moi retrouvâmes Françoise, son fils et un de leurs amis à la Lorraine, une brasserie scintillante de lumières située non loin de l'Etoile, le ciel vomissait une pluie torrentielle. Quelqu'un de notre petit groupe, devinant mon état d'esprit, déplora le temps affreux qu'il faisait, mais je me souviens de m'être dit que même s'il avait fait une de ces nuits embaumées, chaudes et romantiques qui font la renommée de Paris, je n'en réagirais pas moins comme le zombie que j'étais devenu. Le climat de la dépression est dépourvu de nuances, sa lumière est un camouflage.

Et tel un zombie, approximativement au milieu du dîner, j'égarai le chèque du prix del Duca, un chèque de vingt-cinq mille dollars. J'avais fourré le chèque dans la poche intérieure de ma veste, et comme machinalement j'y glissai la main, je constatai qu'il avait disparu. Avais-je eu « l'intention » de perdre cet argent ?

Depuis quelque temps j'étais harcelé par la pensée que je n'étais pas digne de ce prix. Je crois en la réalité des malheurs qu'inconsciemment nous perpétrons sur nous-mêmes, aussi était-il facile que cette perte ne fût pas une perte, mais une forme de répudiation, une conséquence de ce dégoût de moi-même (le premier signe distinctif de la dépression) qui m'avait persuadé que je ne pouvais pas mériter le prix, qu'en réalité je ne méritais aucun des hommages à mon talent dont j'avais fait l'objet depuis quelques années. Quelle que fût la raison de sa disparition, le chèque n'était plus là et sa perte concordait tout à fait avec les divers autres fiascos du dîner : mon impuissance à faire honneur au grand *plateau de fruits de mer*[1] placé devant moi, mon impuissance à m'arracher le moindre rire et, enfin, une impuissance quasi totale à parler. En l'occurrence, la féroce *intériorité* de la souffrance engendrait en moi une immense inattention qui m'empêchait d'articuler et d'émettre autre chose qu'un murmure rauque ; je me rendais compte que mes yeux louchaient, que je parlais par monosyllabes, et me rendais compte aussi que mes amis français commençaient non

1. En français dans le texte (*N. d. T.*).

sans embarras à remarquer mon fâcheux état. Au moment précis où je suggérais qu'il était temps de partir, le fils de Françoise découvrit le chèque qui, je ne sais comment, avait glissé de ma poche pour échouer sous une table voisine, et nous nous mîmes en route dans la nuit pluvieuse. Ce fut alors que dans la voiture qui m'emportait, je me mis à penser à Albert Camus et à Romain Gary.

II

Alors que j'étais tout jeune écrivain, j'avais traversé une phase où Camus, davantage peut-être que toute autre figure littéraire contemporaine, avait radicalement influencé ma conception de la vie et de l'histoire. J'avais lu son roman *L'étranger* plutôt tardivement et le regrettais — j'avais alors dépassé la trentaine — mais quand je l'eus terminé, je ressentis cette impression fulgurante d'adhésion instinctive qu'engendre la lecture de l'œuvre d'un écrivain qui a su allier à la passion morale un style d'une grande beauté, et dont l'imperturbable lucidité a le pouvoir de terrifier l'âme jusqu'au tréfonds d'elle-même. La solitude cosmique de Meursault, le héros du roman, me hantait au point que lorsque j'entrepris d'écrire *Les confessions de Nat Turner*, je ne pus m'empêcher d'utiliser la technique de Camus en présentant l'histoire du point de vue d'un narrateur isolé dans la cellule de sa prison au cours des heures qui précèdent son exécution. Dans mon esprit, il existait un rapport d'ordre spirituel entre la solitude glacée de Meursault et le triste sort de Nat Turner — son précurseur par une bonne centaine d'années dans l'histoire de la rébellion — comme lui condamné et abandonné des hommes et de Dieu. L'essai de Camus *Réflexions sur la guillotine* est un document virtuellement unique en son genre, empreint d'une terrible et ardente logique ; il est difficile de concevoir le plus vindicatif des partisans de la peine de mort se cantonnant dans la même attitude après avoir affronté de cinglantes vérités exprimées avec tant de fougue et de rigueur. Je le sais, ma vision personnelle des choses fut à jamais influencée par cette œuvre, qui non seulement bouleversa complètement mon optique et me persuada de la barbarie fondamentale de la peine de mort, mais également imposa à ma conscience de substantielles exigences quant au problème de la responsabilité en général. Camus contribua grandement à purifier mon esprit, en me débarrassant d'innombrables idées faciles, et, par le biais d'un pessimisme perturbant comme jamais je n'en avais connu, en m'incitant à me passionner de nouveau pour l'énigmatique promesse de la vie.

La déception que j'ai toujours éprouvée de n'avoir jamais rencontré Camus, était indissociable du fait qu'il s'en était fallu de peu. J'avais fait le projet de le rencontrer en 1960, alors que je partais pour la France et j'avais été informé par une lettre de l'écrivain Romain Gary que durant mon séjour à Paris, il se proposait d'organiser un dîner où je ferais la connaissance de Camus. Gary, cet écrivain à l'immense talent, que je ne connaissais que vaguement à l'époque et qui par la suite devint un de mes amis très chers, m'avait informé que Camus, dont il était un intime, avait lu *Un lit de ténèbres* et avec une grande admiration. Naturellement je me sentis très flatté et eut le sentiment que cette rencontre serait un événement magnifique. Mais avant même mon arrivée en France, tomba la consternante nouvelle : Camus avait été victime d'un accident de voiture et, à quarante-six ans, soit cruellement à la fleur de l'âge, il était mort. Je n'ai pratiquement jamais ressenti avec autant d'intensité la perte de quelqu'un que je ne connaissais pas. Sans relâche, je méditais cette mort. Bien que Camus ne conduisît pas la voiture, on pouvait supposer qu'il savait que le conducteur, le fils de son éditeur, était un fanatique de la vitesse ; aussi y avait-il dans l'accident un élément de témérité qui suggérait un comportement quasi suicidaire, au moins un flirt avec la mort, et il était inévitable que les conjectures suscitées par l'événement n'en reviennent au thème du suicide dans l'œuvre de l'écrivain. Une des professions de foi intellectuelles les plus célèbres de notre siècle se situe au commencement du *Mythe de Sisyphe* : « Il n'y a qu'un problème philosophique vraiment sérieux : c'est le suicide. Juger que la vie vaut ou ne vaut pas la peine d'être vécue, c'est répondre à la question fondamentale de la philosophie. » En lisant pour la première fois ces lignes, je me sentis perplexe et ma perplexité persista pendant la plus grande partie de l'essai, dans la mesure où malgré sa logique et son éloquence persuasives, beaucoup de choses m'échappaient aussi, et toujours j'en revenais à affronter vainement l'hypothèse initiale, incapable que j'étais de m'accommoder de ce postulat selon lequel chacun devrait d'emblée éprouver l'envie de se suicider. Je lus une de ses œuvres ultérieures, un court roman, *La chute*, que j'admirais également mais non sans quelques réserves ; le remords et l'autocondamnation du narrateur-avocat, qui

40

débite lugubrement son monologue dans un bar d'Amsterdam, me paraissaient quelque peu outranciers et excessifs, mais à l'époque j'étais incapable de me rendre compte que l'avocat était en réalité plongé dans les affres d'un grave état dépressif. Telle était mon innocence, j'ignorais jusqu'à l'existence de cette maladie.

Camus, me dit Romain, faisait de temps à autre allusion au profond désespoir qui l'habitait et parlait de suicide. Il en parlait parfois en plaisantant, mais la plaisanterie avait un arrière-goût de vin aigre, qui n'allait pas sans perturber Romain. Pourtant il n'avait apparemment jamais attenté à ses jours, aussi n'est-il peut-être nullement fortuit que malgré la constance de la tonalité mélancolique, un sentiment du triomphe de la vie sur la mort soit au cœur du *Mythe de Sisyphe* et de son austère message : en l'absence de tout espoir, nous devons néanmoins continuer à lutter pour survivre, et de fait nous survivons — de justesse. Il me fallut quelques années de recul pour trouver crédible que la déclaration de Camus sur le suicide et l'intérêt obsessionnel qu'il portait au sujet, aient pu découler tout autant d'une perturbation mentale chronique que de ses préoccupations d'ordre éthique et épistémologique. De nouveau en août 1978, Gary exposa à loisir ses hypothèses quant à la dépression qui avait frappé Camus ; je lui avais alors prêté le pavillon que je réserve à des amis dans le Connecticut, et avais quitté le temps d'un week-end ma maison d'été de Martha's Vineyard pour lui rendre visite. Tandis que nous bavardions, j'eus le sentiment que certaines des hypothèses de Romain, quant à la gravité du désespoir qui assaillait Camus, se trouvaient renforcées par le fait qu'il avait, lui aussi, commencé à souffrir d'un état dépressif, ce qu'il reconnut franchement. Un état qui n'entravait en rien son travail, affirmat-il, et qu'il parvenait à contrôler, quand bien même il l'éprouvait de temps à autre, cet état d'âme pesant et délétère, couleur vert-de-gris, tellement incongru dans la luxuriance de l'été de la Nouvelle-Angleterre. D'origine juive et né en Lituanie, Romain m'avait toujours paru marqué par une mélancolie très Europe de l'Est, aussi n'était-il pas facile de s'y retrouver. Néanmoins, il souffrait. Il m'avoua qu'il était capable de percevoir la lueur vacillante de ce désespoir que lui avait décrit Camus.

La situation de Gary n'était guère rendue moins pénible par la présence de son ex-épouse l'actrice Jean Seberg, originaire de l'Iowa ; ils étaient divorcés et, du moins le croyais-je, brouillés depuis longtemps. Elle était là, appris-je, parce que leur fils Diego passait quelques jours dans la région à l'occasion d'un stage de tennis. En raison de leur brouille supposée, je fus surpris de voir qu'elle vivait avec Romain, et surpris également — non, pas surpris, choqué et attristé — par son aspect : tout ce qu'autrefois sa beauté blonde pouvait avoir de fragile et de lumineux avait été englouti par un masque de bouffissure. Elle se déplaçait comme une somnambule, parlait peu, et avait le regard vide de quelqu'un qui à force de tranquillisants (ou de drogues, voire les deux) est à deux doigts de sombrer dans la catalepsie. Je compris qu'ils demeuraient très attachés l'un à l'autre, et me sentis ému par la sollicitude qu'il lui témoignait, à la fois tendre et paternelle. Romain me confia que victime des mêmes troubles que lui, Jean suivait un traitement, et il fit allusion à certains antidépresseurs, sans d'ailleurs que j'y prête grande attention, ni que cela m'évoque grand-chose. Ce souvenir de ma relative indifférence a son importance, dans la mesure où ce genre d'indifférence illustre avec force l'incapacité, pour qui est extérieur au problème, de mesurer l'essence du mal. La dépression de Camus et maintenant celle de Romain Gary — de toute évidence aussi celle de Jean — étaient pour moi des maux abstraits, en dépit de ma compassion, et à l'instar de la majorité de ceux qui jamais n'ont personnellement fait l'expérience de la maladie, je n'avais pas la moindre idée de ses véritables dimensions ni de la nature de la souffrance qu'endurent tant de victimes à mesure que l'esprit poursuit son insidieuse déliquescence.

A Paris par cette nuit d'octobre, j'étais, et je le savais, moi aussi en proie à la déliquescence. Et tandis que la voiture me ramenait à l'hôtel, j'eus une révélation limpide. Une perturbation du cycle circadien — les rythmes métaboliques et glandulaires qui commandent notre vie de tous les jours — serait, semble-t-il, en cause dans nombre d'états dépressifs, sinon dans la plupart; c'est pourquoi, si souvent, de brutales insomnies se produisent et c'est pourquoi très vraisemblablement le schéma quotidien de la maladie est marqué par une alternance relativement prévisible de périodes de paroxysme et de soulagement. Pour moi, le soulagement de la soirée — un répit incomplet mais sensible, pareil à la transition entre une averse torrentielle et une petite pluie fine — survenait entre la fin du dîner et minuit, lorsque la douleur refluait un peu et que mon esprit retrouvait assez de lucidité pour se concentrer sur des sujets transcendant le cataclysme immédiat qui bouleversait mon organisme. Naturellement j'attendais ce moment avec impatience, car il m'arrivait parfois de me sentir raisonnablement sain d'esprit, et cette nuit-là, dans la voiture, j'eus le sentiment de retrouver un semblant de lucidité, en même temps que la capacité de rationaliser les choses. Cependant, après avoir pu évoquer le souvenir de Camus et de Romain Gary, je constatai que les pensées qui me venaient n'étaient guère réconfortantes.

Le souvenir de Jean Seberg m'accablait de tristesse. Moins d'un an après notre rencontre dans le Connecticut, elle prit une overdose de drogue et fut retrouvée morte dans une voiture garée au fond d'une impasse donnant sur une grande avenue de Paris, où son corps était resté longtemps abandonné. L'année suivante, je déjeunais un jour en compagnie de Romain chez Lipp, un long déjeuner au cours duquel il me confia qu'en dépit de leurs différends, la perte de Jean avait aggravé sa dépression au point que, de temps à autre, il s'était retrouvé virtuellement dans l'incapacité de rien faire. Pourtant, même alors, j'étais incapable de percevoir la nature de son angoisse. Je me souvenais que ses mains tremblaient et, bien qu'il n'eût certes rien d'un retraité — il avait la soixantaine passée — sa voix avait l'essoufflement de l'extrême vieillesse qui, je m'en rendais maintenant compte était, ou pouvait être, la voix de la dépression ; emporté par le tourbillon de mon extrême souffrance, j'avais commencé à adopter moi aussi cette voix de vieillard. Jamais je ne devais revoir Romain. Claude Gallimard, le père de Françoise, me raconta par la suite comment en 1980, quelques heures seulement après un autre déjeuner durant lequel les deux vieux amis avaient parlé de tout et de rien sur un registre calme, voire enjoué, en tout cas nullement lugubre, Romain Gary — par deux fois lauréat du prix Goncourt (dont l'une sous un pseudonyme, il avait allègrement mystifié les critiques), héros de la République, valeureux titulaire de la Croix de Guerre, diplomate, bon vivant, homme à femmes par excellence — regagna son appartement de la rue du Bac et se tira une balle dans la tête.

Ce fut je ne sais trop quand au cours de ces rêvasseries, que l'enseigne HÔTEL WASHINGTON surgit dans mon champ de vision, ravivant le souvenir de ma lointaine arrivée dans la ville, en même temps que la brusque et féroce certitude que jamais je ne reverrais Paris. Une certitude qui me laissa en proie à la stupéfaction et à une frayeur nouvelle, car si des idées de mort avaient souvent été mon lot depuis le début de ma maladie, balayant mon esprit comme les rafales d'un vent glacé, elles étaient les formes informes du destin qui, je suppose, hante les rêves de quiconque est aux prises avec une maladie grave. La différence cette fois tenait à la certitude que demain, lorsque la souffrance m'accablerait de nouveau, ou le jour suivant — en tout cas dans un avenir pas tellement lointain — je me retrouverais contraint de juger que la vie ne valait pas la peine d'être vécue et du même coup de répondre, pour moi-même du moins, à la question fondamentale de toute philosophie.

III

Pour beaucoup d'entre nous qui, comme moi, connaissions Abbie Hoffman ne fût-ce que peu, sa mort survenue au printemps de 1989 fut un événement affligeant. A tout juste cinquante ans, il était trop jeune et apparemment trop plein de vitalité pour faire ce genre de fin ; dans la plupart des cas la nouvelle d'un suicide suscite un sentiment de détresse et d'horreur, et la mort d'Abbie me parut particulièrement cruelle. J'avais fait sa connaissance en 1968 à Chicago lors des journées et nuits folles de la convention démocrate où je m'étais rendu pour écrire un article destiné à la *New York Review of Books*, et par la suite, je fus l'un de ceux qui, lors du procès, également à Chicago, en 1970, déposèrent en sa faveur et en celle des autres prévenus. Au milieu des hypocrites folies et des infâmes corruptions de la vie américaine, son style bouffon était vivifiant, et il était difficile de ne pas en admirer le panache et le brio, l'individualisme anarchique. Je regrette de ne pas l'avoir fréquenté davantage ces dernières années ; sa mort brutale me laissa un sentiment de vide très particulier, comme en général tout le monde en éprouve à l'annonce d'un suicide. Mais le caractère poignant de l'événement fut encore exacerbé par ce que l'on doit se résoudre à interpréter comme une réaction prévisible de la part de beaucoup : la négation, le refus d'accepter le fait même du suicide, comme si l'acte volontaire — au contraire d'un accident, ou d'une mort due à des causes naturelles — était entaché d'une faute qui, en un sens, discréditait l'homme et sa réputation.

Le frère d'Abbie parut à la télévision, bouleversé et éperdu de chagrin ; comment ne pas éprouver de compassion à le voir s'efforcer d'infléchir la thèse du suicide, en affirmant qu'Abbie, après tout, s'était toujours montré imprudent avec les drogues, et n'aurait jamais volontairement plongé sa famille dans le deuil. Pourtant, le coroner confirma que Hoffman avait absorbé l'équivalent de cent cinquante phénobarbitals. Il est parfaitement naturel qu'en cas de suicide, les proches de la victime s'empressent si souvent et si fiévreusement de nier la vérité ; le sentiment d'être soi-même impliqué, d'être personnellement coupable — l'idée que peut-être l'on aurait pu empêcher l'acte en prenant certaines précautions, en se comportant de façon quelque peu différente — est sans doute inévitable. Néanmoins, la victime — qu'elle ait véritablement mis fin à ses jours ou simplement tenté de le faire, ou se soit bornée à en formuler la menace — se trouve souvent, par suite des dénégations de tiers, injustement présentée comme coupable d'un méfait.

Un cas similaire est celui de Randall Jarrell — un des meilleurs poètes et critiques de sa génération — qui par une certaine nuit de 1965, non loin de Chapel-Hill en Caroline du Nord, fut renversé par une voiture et tué sur le coup. La présence de Jarrell sur cette portion de route, à une heure insolite de la soirée, tenait quelque peu d'une énigme, et dans la mesure où certains indices permettaient de supposer qu'il s'était délibérément laissé heurter par la voiture, les conclusions du premier verdict imputèrent sa mort à un suicide. Ce fut ce qu'entre autres publications affirma *Newsweek*, mais la veuve de Jarrell protesta dans une lettre adressée à ce magazine ; il s'ensuivit un tollé général chez beaucoup de ses amis et partisans, et une commission d'enquête judiciaire finit par conclure à une mort accidentelle. Jarrell souffrait depuis déjà un certain temps d'une grave dépression et avait été hospitalisé à plusieurs reprises ; quelques mois à peine avant son accident sur la grand-route et pendant l'un de ses séjours à l'hôpital, il s'était tailladé les poignets.

Il suffit d'être informé de certaines particularités chaotiques de la vie de Jarrell — entre autres ses violentes sautes d'humeur, ses accès de sombre désespoir — et, en outre, d'avoir une connaissance élémentaire des signaux de danger qu'émet la dépression, pour éprouver des doutes sérieux quant au verdict du coroner. Mais le stigmate d'une mort volontaire représente pour certains une tache odieuse qu'il convient d'effacer à tout prix (plus de deux décennies après sa mort, dans le numéro de l'été 1986 de *The American Scholar*, un ancien étudiant de Jarrell, chargé de commenter un choix de lettres du poète, tira de son commentaire moins un bilan littéraire et biographique qu'un nouveau prétexte pour persister à exorciser le fantôme ignoble du suicide).

Il est pratiquement certain que Randall Jarrell mit fin à ses jours. Il le fit non parce qu'il était lâche. ni en raison d'une quelconque faiblesse de caractère, mais parce qu'il était affligé d'une dépression tellement dévastatrice qu'il n'avait plus la force nécessaire pour en endurer la souffrance.

Cette ignorance largement répandue de ce qu'est en réalité la dépression, se manifesta avec force tout dernièrement dans le cas de Primo Levi, le remarquable écrivain italien rescapé d'Auschwitz qui, en 1987 à Turin, à l'âge de soixante-sept ans, se précipita du haut d'un escalier. Dans la mesure où environ une année plus tôt, j'avais moi-même survécu à une attaque de dépression quasi fatale, la mort de Levi avait suscité en moi un intérêt tout particulier. et ce fut ainsi que lorsque, à la fin de l'an dernier, je lus dans le *New York Times* le compte rendu d'un symposium consacré à l'écrivain et à son œuvre, organisé par l'Université de New York, je me sentis fasciné, mais davantage encore terrifié. Car, selon l'article, nombre de participants, tous écrivains et érudits de grand renom, paraissaient mystifiés par la mort de Levi, mystifiés et déçus. On eût dit que cet homme auquel tous avaient voué une admiration si fervente, et qui avait enduré tant

53

d'épreuves aux mains des nazis — un homme d'un ressort et d'un courage exemplaires — avait, en se suicidant, révélé une faiblesse, un effritement de son caractère qu'ils répugnaient à admettre. Confrontés à un absolu atroce — l'autodestruction — ils réagissaient par un aveu d'impuissance et (comment le lecteur eût-il pu l'éviter?) avec une pointe de honte.

Si intense fut l'irritation que j'éprouvais, qu'elle m'incita à rédiger un court texte pour la page éditoriale du *Times*. L'argument que je choisis d'avancer était relativement simple: la souffrance occasionnée par une dépression grave est tout à fait inconcevable pour qui ne l'a jamais endurée, et si dans de nombreux cas elle tue, c'est parce que l'angoisse qui l'accompagne est devenue intolérable. Tant que la nature de cette souffrance n'aura pas fait l'objet d'une prise de conscience généralisée, la prévention du suicide demeurera souvent entravée. La guérison qu'apporte le temps — et dans bien des cas le recours à la médecine ou à l'hospitalisation — permet à la plupart des gens de survivre à une dépression, ce qui peut-être en constitue l'unique rédemption; mais quant aux innombrables infortunés que la tragédie contraint à se détruire, ils ne devraient pas davantage que les victimes d'un cancer incurable encourir le moindre blâme.

J'avais exposé mes pensées dans ce texte du *Times* de manière plutôt précipitée et spontanée, mais la réaction fut tout aussi spontanée — et énorme. Il ne m'avait fallu, l'idée m'en vint alors, ni originalité, ni hardiesse particulières pour m'exprimer avec franchise au sujet du suicide et de l'impulsion qui y mène, mais apparemment j'avais sous-estimé le nombre de ceux pour lesquels le sujet était resté jusqu'alors tabou, un problème auréolé de secret et de honte. Eu égard à la réaction dominante, il m'apparut que, par pure inadvertance, j'avais contribué à déverrouiller un placard d'où, nombreux, des êtres aspiraient à s'échapper pour proclamer qu'ils avaient, eux aussi, éprouvé ce que j'avais décrit. C'est la seule et unique fois où j'eus le sentiment que d'avoir ainsi violé ma vie privée, et pour la livrer au public, en valait finalement la peine. Et l'idée me vint que, compte tenu de cet élan, il pourrait être utile de relater brièvement divers aspects de mon expérience de la dépression, et ce faisant, d'esquisser un système de référence d'où il serait peut-être possible de tirer une, voire plusieurs conclusions de quelque intérêt. Des conclusions de cet ordre, il convient de le souligner, doivent néanmoins se fonder sur les événements vécus par une personne déterminée. En consignant ces réflexions, je n'ambitionne pas à présenter mon épreuve comme un exemple de ce qui arrive, ou risque d'arriver aux autres. De par ses causes, ses symptômes et son traitement, la dépression est beaucoup trop complexe pour qu'il soit possible de tirer des conclusions formelles d'une expérience isolée. Quand bien même, en tant que maladie, la dépression s'accompagne de certaines caractéristiques immuables, elle est en même temps marquée de nombreuses particularités ; j'ai été stupéfait de constater certains phénomènes bizarres — jamais relatés par aucun autre malade — qu'elle provoqua dans les méandres du labyrinthe de mon esprit.

La dépression accable directement des millions de personnes, et des millions d'autres qui sont parents ou amis des victimes. D'un démocratisme aussi péremptoire qu'un poster de Norman Rockwell[1], elle frappe sans discrimination des gens de tous âges, toutes races, toutes

1. Norman Rockwell : artiste graphique contemporain, attaché au *Saturday Evening Post*, spécialiste des personnages de l'Amérique « profonde » (*N.d.T.*).

croyances et toutes classes, bien que les femmes soient considérablement plus menacées que les hommes. La liste par professions de ses victimes (couturières, chefs mariniers, cuisiniers de restaurants japonais, membres du Cabinet) serait trop longue et fastidieuse ; il suffit de dire que rares sont ceux qui ne courent pas le risque d'être en puissance victimes de la maladie, du moins dans sa forme mineure. En dépit du champ d'action éclectique de la dépression, il a été démontré de façon relativement convaincante que les gens de tempérament artistique (surtout les poètes) sont particulièrement vulnérables à ce type de mal — qui, dans sa manifestation clinique la plus grave prélève vingt pour cent au moins de son tribut par le suicide. Quelques-uns de ces artistes disparus, tous des modernes, suffisent pour constituer un triste mais brillant tableau d'honneur : Hart Crane, Vincent Van Gogh, Virginia Woolf, Arshile Gorky, Cesare Pavese, Romain Gary, Vachel Lindsay, Henry de Montherlant, Sylvia Plath, Mark Rothko, John Berryman, Jack London, Ernest Hemingway, William Inge, Diane Arbus, Tadeusz Borowski, Paul Celan, Ann Sexton, Sergei Essénine , Vladimir Maïakovski — la liste n'est pas close. (Le poète russe Maïakovski avait sévèrement jugé le suicide de son célèbre contemporain Essénine quelques années plus tôt, ce qui devrait être un avertissement pour quiconque se sent enclin à condamner l'auto-destruction.) Lorsque l'on pense à ces créateurs, ces hommes et ces femmes dotés de tant de talents, et voués à la mort, on est amené à s'interroger sur leur enfance, l'enfance où, tout le monde le sait, les germes de la maladie plongent leurs racines; se peut-il que certains d'entre eux aient eu, alors, une intuition de la nature périssable de la psyché, de sa subtile fragilité? Et pourquoi eux furent-ils détruits, tandis que d'autres — frappés de façon simi-laire — parvinrent à s'en sortir?

IV

A peine eus-je pris conscience d'avoir été ter-
rassé par la maladie que j'éprouvai le besoin,
entre autres, d'élever une protestation énergique
contre le mot « dépression ». La dépression, la
plupart des gens le savent, était jadis appelée
« mélancolie », un mot qui apparaît en anglais
dès l'an 1303 et resurgit à maintes reprises chez
Chaucer, lequel, à en juger par l'usage qu'il en
fait, avait conscience de ses connotations patho-
logiques. Le mot « mélancolie » continuerait à
paraître plus approprié et évocateur des formes
les plus noires du mal, s'il n'avait été supplanté
par un substantif à la tonalité insipide et, en
outre, dépourvu de toute dimension doctorale,
indifféremment utilisé pour décrire une période
de déclin économique ou une ornière dans le sol,
un mot parfaitement invertébré pour qualifier
une maladie d'une telle gravité. Il se peut que le
savant auquel on en attribue généralement

l'usage courant à l'époque moderne — un professeur d'origine suisse de la John Hopkins Medical School et objet d'une légitime vénération — n'ait pas eu l'oreille assez musicale pour percevoir les consonances plus subtiles de l'anglais et, par conséquent, n'ait pas soupçonné les dégâts sémantiques qu'il avait perpétrés en proposant le mot « dépression » comme substantif apte à décrire une maladie à ce point horrible et dévastatrice. Néanmoins, et pendant plus de soixante-quinze ans, le mot s'est faufilé à travers la langue comme une inoffensive limace, ne laissant que peu de traces de sa malveillance intrinsèque et empêchant, en raison de son insipidité même, une prise de conscience généralisée de l'intensité atroce de la maladie dès lors qu'elle se déchaîne.

Comme tous ceux qui ont connu toutes les phases de la maladie, même les plus extrêmes, et pourtant ont émergé pour en faire le récit, je serais enclin à préconiser une formulation saisissante. « Tempête sous un crâne », par exemple, a malheureusement déjà été utilisé pour décrire, de façon plutôt facétieuse, l'inspiration intellectuelle. Mais quelque chose de cet ordre s'impose. Informé que les troubles psychiques dont souffre quelqu'un ont dégénéré en tempête — une authentique tempête déchaînée dans le cerveau, car c'est là en réalité ce qu'évoque le plus fidèlement une dépression clinique — même le profane serait enclin à manifester de la compassion plutôt que la classique réaction suscitée par le mot « dépression », quelque chose du genre de « Et alors? », ou bien « Vous finirez par vous en sortir. » Ou encore « Tout le monde a ses mauvais moments ». L'expression « dépression nerveuse » semble en passe de disparaître, assurément à juste titre, pour ce qu'elle sous-entend de mollesse de caractère, mais il semble toutefois que nous restions voués à traîner « dépression » en attendant qu'un nouveau substantif, plus juste et plus vigoureux, voie enfin le jour.

La dépression qui me submergea n'était pas du type psychose maniaque dépressive — le type accompagné par de grandes périodes d'euphorie — qui selon toute probabilité se fût manifesté plus tôt dans ma vie. J'avais soixante ans lorsque la maladie me frappa pour la première fois, dans sa forme « unipolaire », qui précipite une chute brutale. Jamais je ne saurai ce qui a « causé » ma dépression, de même que jamais personne ne le saura en ce qui concerne la sienne. Parvenir à le savoir s'avérera probable ment à jamais impossible, si complexes sont les facteurs indissociables de la chimie, du comportement et de la génétique de l'anormal. Manifestement, de multiples composantes interviennent — trois ou quatre peut-être, très probablement davantage, au gré d'insondables permutations. C'est pourquoi la plus grande illusion à propos du suicide réside dans cette croyance qu'il existe une réponse clef, unique et immédiate — voire même un faisceau de réponses — quant aux raisons susceptibles d'expliquer l'acte.

L'inévitable question, « Pourquoi a-t-il (ou elle) fait ça ? » conduit en général à de bizarres spéculations, qui pour la plupart ne sont elles-mêmes qu'illusions. Nombre de raisons furent aussitôt avancées pour expliquer la mort d'Abbie Hoffman : le contrecoup de l'accident de la route dont il avait été victime, l'échec de son tout dernier livre, la grave maladie de sa mère. Dans le cas de Randall Jarrell, furent évoquées une carrière à son déclin, cruellement résumée par un livre malveillant, et l'angoisse qu'il avait suscitée. Primo Levi, à en croire la rumeur, avait été accablé par la charge que représentait pour lui sa mère paralytique, une charge psychologiquement plus lourde pour lui que son expérience d'Auschwitz elle-même. Il se peut que l'un ou l'autre de ces facteurs ait été incrusté comme une épine dans le flanc de ces trois hommes, et leur ait été une torture. Des circonstances aggravantes de ce type peuvent se révéler cruciales et ne sauraient être méconnues. Mais dans l'ensemble, les gens endurent avec sérénité l'équivalent de blessures, carrières sur le déclin, critiques malveillantes de leurs œuvres, maladies au sein de leur famille. Dans leur immense majorité, les rescapés d'Auschwitz ont tenu le coup plutôt bien. Le corps en sang et écrasé par les atrocités de la vie, la plupart des êtres humains poursuivent cependant en titubant leur chemin, et la véritable dépression les épargne. Pour découvrir pourquoi certains sont engloutis par l'abîme de la dépression, il convient de chercher au-delà des symptômes manifestes de la crise — sans pour autant jamais aboutir à autre chose qu'à de doctes hypothèses.

La tempête qui s'abattit sur moi en décembre 1985 et me conduisit à l'hôpital, se manifesta tout d'abord au mois de juin précédent, comme un nuage à peine plus gros qu'une coupe à vin. Et le nuage — les symptômes manifestes — était en rapport avec l'alcool, une substance dont je n'avais cessé d'abuser depuis quarante ans. A

63

l'instar de tant d'autres écrivains américains, dont le penchant pour l'alcool est devenu légendaire au point d'engendrer un flot d'études et de livres, j'avais eu recours à l'alcool comme à la voie magique qui mène à l'imaginaire et à l'euphorie, et à l'exaltation de l'imagination. A quoi bon me repentir ou m'excuser d'avoir eu recours à cette substance lénitive et souvent sublime qui toujours contribua grandement à mon œuvre; bien que jamais je n'aie écrit une seule ligne sous son empire, j'en usais de façon différente — souvent conjointement avec la musique — comme d'un moyen pour permettre à mon esprit de concevoir des visions auxquelles le cerveau non dopé par l'alcool ne saurait avoir accès. L'alcool fut toujours un associé inestimable et privilégié par mon intellect, sans compter qu'il était un ami dont chaque jour je recherchais les secours — et qu'aussi je recherchais, je le vois maintenant, comme un moyen de calmer l'anxiété et la peur naissante que j'avais si longtemps dissimulées quelque part dans les oubliettes de mon esprit.

Le problème, au début de cet été-là, c'était que je me retrouvais trahi. Cela me frappa tout à fait inopinément, quasiment du jour au lendemain: je ne pouvais plus boire. C'était comme si mon corps s'était révolté pour protester, en même temps que mon esprit, et avait conspiré pour rejeter ce bain quotidien de mon âme après lui avoir si longtemps fait fête, qui sait, avoir peut-être même fini par en éprouver le besoin. Maints buveurs ont fait l'expérience de cette intolérance à mesure qu'ils prenaient de l'âge. J'ai dans l'idée que la crise était, du moins en partie, un problème de métabolisme — le foie qui se rebellait, comme pour dire : « Assez, assez » — mais quoi qu'il en soit, je constatai qu'absorbé en quantités minuscules, fût-ce une simple gorgée de vin, l'alcool provoquait en moi des nausées, une hébétude intense et désagréable, une sensation de vertige, et en fin de compte, une nette répugnance. L'ami secourable m'avait abandonné, non point insensiblement et à regret, comme l'eût fait un véritable ami, mais d'un bloc — et je me retrouvais échoué et, bien sûr, au sec, et dépourvu de gouvernail.

Ni par volonté ni par choix je n'étais devenu abstinent ; la situation me plongeait dans la perplexité, mais elle était également traumatique, et selon moi les premiers symptômes de mon état dépressif coïncident avec les débuts de ce sevrage Logiquement, on devrait être transporté de joie que le corps ait, et de façon si expéditive, banni une substance qui minait sa santé ; on eût dit que mon organisme avait engendré une forme d'antidote qui aurait dû me permettre de continuer tout heureux mon chemin, convaincu qu'un caprice de la nature m'avait arraché à une néfaste dépendance. Mais, au contraire, je ne tardai pas à éprouver un malaise vaguement inquiétant, la sensation que quelque chose avait dérapé dans l'univers familial que j'habitais depuis si longtemps, si confortablement. Quand bien même la dépression n'est nullement un phénomène inconnu pour qui en vient à renoncer à la boisson, elle se manifeste en général sur une échelle qui n'a rien de menaçant. Mais il convient de ne pas oublier à quel point les visages de la dépression reflètent des idiosyncrasies particulières.

Tout d'abord cela n'eut rien de vraiment inquiétant, dans la mesure où le changement était subtil, mais je constatais cependant que le décor qui m'entourait à certains moments se parait de tonalités différentes : les ombres du crépuscule semblaient plus sombres, mes matins étaient moins radieux, les promenades en forêt se faisaient moins toniques, et il y avait maintenant un moment en fin d'après-midi pendant mes heures de travail où une sorte de panique et d'angoisse me submergeait, le temps de quelques minutes à peine, accompagnée par une nausée viscérale — des manifestations pour le moins quelque peu inquiétantes, somme toute. Tandis que je consigne ces souvenirs, je me rends compte qu'il aurait dû m'apparaître évident que déjà je me trouvais aux prises avec les premiers symptômes de graves troubles psychiques, mais à l'époque, j'ignorais tout de ce genre d'affection.

Lorsqu'il m'arrivait de réfléchir à cette étrange altération de ma conscience — ce que ma perplexité m'incitait à faire de temps à autre —, je supposais que, d'une manière ou d'une autre, tout cela était en rapport avec mon abstinence forcée de tout alcool. Et, bien sûr, dans une certaine mesure, c'était vrai. Mais je suis aujourd'hui convaincu que l'alcool me joua un tour pervers du jour où nous nous dîmes adieu : quand bien même, comme chacun devrait le savoir, l'alcool est un dépresseur majeur, jamais il ne m'avait véritablement déprimé au cours de ma carrière de buveur, opérant au contraire comme un bouclier contre l'anxiété. Disparaissant brusquement, le grand allié qui si longtemps avait tenu mes démons en échec, ne se trouvait plus là pour empêcher ces mêmes démons d'envahir en masse le subconscient, et émotionnellement, j'étais nu, vulnérable comme jamais encore je ne l'avais été Aucun doute, il y avait des années que la dépression rôdait autour de moi, guettant le moment propice pour fondre sur sa proie. Désormais j'étais dans la première phase — prémonitoire, pareille à la lueur vacillante d'un éclair de chaleur à peine perceptible — de la noire tempête de la dépression.

Au cours de cet été exceptionnellement beau, je me trouvais à Martha's Vineyard, où depuis les années soixante je passe toujours une bonne partie de mon temps. Mais déjà j'avais commencé à accueillir avec indifférence les plaisirs qu'offrait l'île. J'étais en proie à une sorte d'engourdissement, d'apathie, mais plus spécifiquement de bizarre fragilité — comme si mon corps était véritablement devenu frêle, hypersensible et, d'une certaine façon, mal articulé et gauche, privé de coordination normale. Et bientôt, je me trouvais dans les affres d'une hypocondrie diffuse. On eût dit que tout allait de travers dans mon moi physique ; il y avait des douleurs et des élancements, parfois intermittents mais le plus souvent apparemment constants qui semblaient présager toutes sortes d'infirmités redoutables. (Compte tenu de ces symptômes, on comprend mieux maintenant comment, au dix-septième siècle déjà, — dans les notes de médecins de l'époque, et dans les diagnostics de John Dryden et de tant d'autres — un rapport est établi entre la mélancolie et l'hypocondrie; les mots sont souvent interchangeables, et furent utilisés ainsi jusqu'au dixneuvième siècle, par des écrivains aussi différents que Sir Walter Scott et les sœurs Brontë, qui eux aussi voyaient un lien entre la mélancolie et une peur obsessionnelle de troubles physiques.) Il est aisé de voir comment cet état est inséparable du système de défense de la psyché: répugnant à se résigner à sa dégradation menaçante, l'esprit annonce à la conscience qui l'habite que c'est le corps, le corps avec ses défauts peut-être corrigibles — et non le précieux, l'irremplaçable esprit — qui menace de se détraquer.

Dans mon cas, l'effet global fut extrêmement alarmant, exacerbant l'anxiété qui désormais ne me quittait pratiquement plus durant mes heures de veille et en outre, alimentait un nouveau schéma de comportement — une agitation inquiète qui me tenait constamment en mouvement, à la perplexité de ma famille et de mes amis. Un certain jour, à la fin de l'été, à bord d'un avion qui m'emmenait à New York, je commis l'erreur téméraire d'avaler un scotch-soda — ma première goutte d'alcool depuis des mois — qui ne tarda pas à me précipiter dans un gouffre, provoquant en moi une sensation de maladie et de délabrement à ce point horrifiée que, dès le lendemain, je me précipitai chez un spécialiste de médecine organique de Manhattan qui entama une longue série d'examens. Normalement, j'aurais dû me sentir rassuré, voire ravi, lorsque au terme de trois semaines d'investigations très poussées et extrêmement onéreuses, il décréta que j'étais en grande forme ; et c'est vrai *je me sentis heureux*, pendant un jour ou deux, jusqu'au moment où, une fois encore, reprit l'érosion quotidienne et rythmée de mon moral — angoisse, agitation, craintes diffuses.

J'avais alors regagné ma maison du Connecticut. Nous étions en octobre et l'une des particularités pour moi inoubliables de cette phase de mon déséquilibre est la façon dont ma vieille ferme, depuis trente ans ma maison bien-aimée, prenait à mes yeux, au moment où en fin d'après-midi mon moral était immanquablement au plus bas, un caractère sinistre et menaçant quasi palpable. La lumière du soir à son déclin — analogue à cette célèbre « lumière rasante » chère à Emily Dickinson, qui lui parlait de mort, de froide extinction — avait dépouillé son habituel charme automnal, mais me prenait au piège de ténèbres oppressantes. Je me demandais comment ce lieu familier et aimable, débordant de souvenirs, par exemple (dans ses poèmes encore) « Jeunes gens et jeunes filles », « des rires, des talents, des soupirs/ des robes et de jolies boucles », pouvait de manière presque perceptible paraître si hostile et menaçant. Physiquement, je n'étais pas seul. Comme toujours, Rose était sans cesse présente et avec une patience inlassable prêtait l'oreille à mes doléances. Pourtant j'étais en proie à une solitude immense et torturante. Je me trouvais désormais incapable de me concentrer pendant ces heures de l'après-midi que, des années durant, j'avais consacrées à mon travail, et l'acte d'écrire lui-même devenant de plus en plus pénible et épuisant, l'inspiration se ralentit, et finit par se tarir.

Il y avait aussi d'affreuses, de brutales crises d'angoisse. Par une journée radieuse alors que je me promenais dans les bois en compagnie de mon chien, un vol d'oies du Canada passa très haut en cacardant au-dessus des arbres qu'embrasaient leurs frondaisons, un spectacle et une musique qui d'ordinaire m'eussent mis la joie au cœur, le passage des oiseaux me fit m'arrêter net, cloué par la peur, et je restais là figé, impuissant, frissonnant, conscient pour la première fois d'avoir été frappé non par de simples angoisses dues au manque, mais par une maladie grave dont j'étais capable, et ce également pour la première fois, de m'avouer le nom et la réalité. En regagnant la maison, je ne parvins pas à chasser de mon esprit la phrase de Baudelaire, exhumée d'un lointain passé, qui depuis plusieurs jours rôdait à la lisière de ma conscience : « J'ai senti passer sur moi le vent de l'aile de l'imbécillité[1]. »

Ce moderne besoin compréhensible peut-être que nous éprouvons de rogner les dents acérées de ces multiples calamités qui sont notre lot, nous a amenés à bannir les mots rudes désormais désuets : maison de fous, asile, aliénation, mélancolie, dément, dingue, folie. Que jamais pourtant il ne soit mis en doute que la dépression, dans sa forme extrême, est folie. La folie découle d'un processus biochimique anormal. Il a été établi avec une certitude raisonnable (non

---

1. Baudelaire, *Journaux intimes* (Hygiène) (*N.d.T.*).

sans une résistance acharnée de la part de nombreux psychiatres, et il n'y a pas si longtemps d'ailleurs) que ce type de folie est chimiquement provoqué parmi les neurotransmetteurs du cerveau, probablement du fait d'un stress systémique, qui pour des raisons inconnues déclenche une déplétion de substances chimiques, la norépinéphrine et la sérotonine, et l'augmentation d'une hormone, le cortisol. Conséquence de ces perturbations dans les tissus du cerveau, de l'alternance d'imprégnation et de privation, il n'est pas surprenant que le cerveau en vienne à se sentir blessé, accablé, et que les processus confus de la pensée témoignent de la détresse d'un organe en convulsions. Parfois, pas très souvent cependant, un esprit à ce point perturbé nourrira des idées de violence à l'égard d'autrui. Mais en raison de cette effroyable tendance à l'introversion, les victimes de la dépression ne sont en général dangereuses que pour elles-mêmes. La folie de la dépression est, en règle générale, l'antithèse de la violence. Certes c'est une tempête, mais une tempête des ténèbres. Bientôt se manifestent un ralentissement des réactions, une quasi-paralysie, une diminution de l'énergie psychique proche du point zéro. En dernier ressort, le corps est affecté et se sent miné, drainé de ses forces.

Cet automne-là, tandis que peu à peu les troubles prenaient le contrôle de tout mon organisme, l'idée s'imposa graduellement à moi que mon esprit lui-même était pareil à ces vieux standards téléphoniques de petites villes qui insensiblement se retrouvent inondés en période de crue : un à un les circuits normaux commencent à se noyer, et en conséquence, certaines fonctions du corps et presque toutes celles de l'instinct et de l'intellect se déconnectent lentement.

Il existe un répertoire fort connu de certaines de ces fonctions et de leurs défaillances. Les miennes tombèrent en panne pratiquement selon les prévisions, beaucoup d'entre elles selon le schéma classique des crises de dépression. Je me souviens en particulier de la lamentable et quasi totale disparition de ma voix. Elle subit une étrange transformation, au point de devenir par moments faible, poussive et spasmodique — la voix d'un nonagénaire, comme le fit observer par la suite un de mes amis. La libido ne tarda pas elle aussi à défaillir, comme presque toujours dans les cas de maladies graves — c'est le besoin superflu d'un corps aux abois. Beaucoup de gens perdent tout appétit ; le mien était relativement normal, mais j'en étais à ne plus manger que pour survivre : la nourriture, comme tout ce qui est du ressort de la sensation, était totalement dépourvue de saveur. La plus lamentable de toutes ces débâcles instinctuelles était celle du sommeil, en même temps qu'une totale absence de rêves.

Allié à l'insomnie, l'extrême abattement est une torture suprême. Les deux ou trois heures de sommeil que je parvenais à trouver chaque nuit, étaient toujours déclenchées par un tranquillisant anodin, l'Halcion — un point qui mérite d'être souligné. Depuis maintenant un certain temps de nombreux spécialistes en psychopharmacologie laissent entendre que les tranquillisants de la famille des benzodiazépines, à laquelle appartient l'Halcion (et entre autres le Valium et l'Ativan[1]), risquent d'avoir un effet dépressif et même de provoquer de graves dépressions. Plus de deux ans avant ma maladie, un médecin désinvolte m'avait prescrit de l'Ativan pour faciliter mon sommeil, m'affirmant d'un ton dégagé que je pouvais en prendre sans appréhension, comme de l'aspirine. Comme le

1. *Ativan* : équivalent américain du Témesta ou du Tranxène (*N.d.T.*).

75

révèle le manuel intitulé *Physicians'Desk Reference*, la bible pharmacologique, le médicament que j'avais absorbé à l'époque, était : a) trois fois plus puissant que la dose normalement prescrite ; b) déconseillé comme médication au-delà d'un mois environ ; c) à utiliser avec une prudence toute particulière par les gens de mon âge. A l'époque dont je parle, je ne pouvais plus me passer d'Halcion pour m'endormir et j'en ingurgitais de fortes doses. Il paraît raisonnable de penser que c'était là un autre facteur qui contribuait au trouble dont j'étais accablé. Assurément, voilà qui devrait servir de leçon à tout le monde.

De toute façon, mes rares heures de sommeil étaient généralement interrompues à trois heures du matin, et je restais alors là, le regard perdu dans les ténèbres béantes, à réfléchir torturé par une souffrance intolérable aux ravages qui s'opéraient dans mon esprit, et à attendre l'aube, qui, d'habitude, me valait de sombrer un temps dans un sommeil fiévreux et sans rêves. J'en suis pratiquement convaincu, ce fut pendant l'une de ces crises d'insomnie que me vint la certitude — une bizarre et affreuse révélation analogue à celle d'une vérité métaphysique longtemps occultée — que si la maladie suivait son cours, il m'en coûterait la vie. Cela se situe sans doute juste avant mon voyage à Paris. La mort, je l'ai dit, était désormais une présence quotidienne, dont le souffle déferlait sur moi en rafales glacées. Je ne me représentais pas avec précision comment surviendrait ma fin. Bref, je m'obstinais à repousser toute idée de suicide. Mais manifestement, la possibilité rôdait autour de moi, et je ne tarderais plus à l'affronter.

Ce que j'avais commencé à découvrir, c'est que, mystérieusement et par des voies aux antipodes de l'expérience normale, le petit chagrin gris de l'horreur qu'induit la dépression peut s'assimiler à la douleur physique. Pourtant ce n'est pas une douleur immédiatement identifiable, comme celle qui accompagne la fracture d'un membre. Peut-être serait-il plus exact de dire que le désespoir, par suite de quelque mauvais tour joué au cerveau malade par la psyché qui l'habite, finit par être semblable à l'épouvantable et diabolique malaise que l'on ressent à être claustré dans un local férocement surchauffé. Et comme aucune brise ne vient agiter cette fournaise, comme il n'existe aucun moyen d'échapper à cette réclusion étouffante, il est tout à fait naturel que la victime en vienne à penser sans trêve à la plongée dans le néant.

V

L'un des moments les plus mémorables de *Madame Bovary* est la scène où l'héroïne implore le prêtre du village de lui venir en aide. Bourrelée de remords, éperdue, en proie à un désespoir pitoyable, Emma l'adultère — qui déjà tend vers un suicide inéluctable — s'efforce maladroitement d'inciter le prêtre à l'aider à trouver une issue au malheur qui l'accable. Mais le prêtre, un homme simple et pas des plus malins, se borne à tirailler sa soutane souillée de taches, à interpeller d'un air éperdu ses acolytes, et à offrir des platitudes très chrétiennes. Sans rien trahir de sa frénésie, Emma reprend sa route, au-delà de tout réconfort de l'homme ou de Dieu.

Je me sentais un peu comme Emma Bovary quant à ma relation avec le psychiatre, je l'appellerai le docteur Gold, que je commençai à consulter aussitôt après mon retour de Paris, alors que déjà le désespoir me soumettait chaque jour à son implacable martèlement. Jamais jusqu'alors je n'avais éprouvé le besoin de consulter un psychothérapeute, et je me sentais embarrassé, et aussi vaguement sur la défensive ; ma souffrance était devenue si intense que j'estimais tout à fait improbable que de quelconques entretiens avec un autre mortel, même quelqu'un de professionnellement expert en matière de troubles mentaux, puissent soulager l'affliction. C'était en proie à ce même mélange d'hésitation et de doute que Madame Bovary était allée consulter le prêtre. Pourtant, notre société est ainsi faite que le docteur Gold, ou l'un de ses homologues, est l'autorité à laquelle l'on est contraint de s'adresser quand survient la crise, ce qui d'ailleurs n'est pas totalement une mauvaise idée, dans la mesure où le docteur Gold — formé à Yale, hautement qualifié — du moins représente un point de convergence vers lequel diriger des énergies agonisantes, offre la consolation sinon beaucoup d'espoir, et devient un réceptacle propre à accueillir l'épanchement de vos malheurs pendant cinquante minutes qui d'ailleurs apportent un répit mérité à votre femme. Néanmoins, bien que jamais je n'irais mettre en doute l'efficacité possible de la psy-chothérapie dans les manifestations initiales ou les formes bénignes de la maladie — ou peut-être même dans les séquelles d'une crise grave —, il convient de dire que son utilité au stade avancé qui était le mien, fut virtuellement nulle. Mon objectif spécifique en allant consul-ter le docteur Gold était de recevoir l'aide de la pharmacologie — ce qui, hélas, était également une chimère pour une victime qui, comme moi, se trouvait au creux de la vague.

Il me demanda si j'étais suicidaire et, avec répugnance, je lui avouai que oui. Je ne m'éten-dis pas sur les détails — dans la mesure où cela me semblait inutile — et ne lui dis pas davan-tage qu'à la vérité, nombre des objets qui peu-plaient ma maison étaient devenus de possibles instruments pour mettre fin à mes jours ; les poutres du grenier (et dehors un ou deux érables), un moyen de me pendre, le garage, un lieu idéal pour respirer l'oxyde de carbone, la baignoire, un récipient pour recueillir le flot de sang de mes artères ouvertes. Pour moi, les couteaux de cuisine rangés dans leur tiroir n'avaient qu'une seule raison d'être. Une mort consécutive à une crise cardiaque me sem-blait particulièrement tentante, en ce qu'elle m'aurait absous de responsabilité directe, et j'avais également caressé l'idée d'une pneumonie autoprovoquée — une longue promenade en bras de chemise dans le froid par les bois détrempés par la pluie. Par ailleurs, je n'avais pas manqué d'envisager un simulacre d'accident, à la Randall Jarrell, en me jetant sous les roues d'un camion sur l'autoroute voisine. Peut-être trouvera-t-on ces pensées bizarrement macabres — une plaisanterie forcée — mais elles sont authentiques. Nul doute qu'elles ne paraissent tout particulièrement répugnantes aux Américains débordants de santé et soutenus par leur foi dans le surpassement de soi. Pourtant, il est vrai que ce genre d'horribles fantasmes, qui font frissonner les gens bien portants, sont, à l'esprit plongé dans la dépression, ce que les rêveries libidineuses sont aux personnes dotées d'une robuste sexualité. Le docteur Gold et moi prîmes l'habitude de bavarder deux fois par semaine, mais je n'avais pas grand-chose à lui raconter, et ne pouvais que tenter, en vain, de lui décrire mon désespoir.

De son côté il n'avait pas grand-chose à me dire. Bien que ses platitudes ne fussent pas chrétiennes, elles étaient en fait tout aussi inefficaces, des citations directement puisées dans les pages de *The Diagnostic and Statistic Manual of the American Psychiatric Association* (dont j'avais d'ailleurs lu une bonne partie), et en guise de réconfort il me gratifia d'un antidépresseur appelé Ludiomil. Le médicament me mit à cran, me poussa à une déplaisante hyperactivité, et lorsqu'au bout de six jours on augmenta la dose, j'eus la vessie bloquée pendant plusieurs heures au cours de la même nuit. Lorsque j'informai le docteur Gold de ce problème, je m'entendis répondre qu'il faudrait attendre dix jours pour purger mon organisme avant de passer à une autre médication. Dix jours pour quelqu'un ainsi cloué sur un chevalet de torture équivalent à dix siècles — sans même prendre en compte le fait que lorsqu'on passe à une nouvelle drogue, il faut plusieurs semaines avant qu'elle commence à faire de l'effet, un résultat qui d'ailleurs est loin d'être garanti.

Ce point soulève le problème de la médication en général. Il convient de rendre à la psychiatrie l'hommage qu'elle mérite pour s'être obstinée à traiter la dépression par la pharmacologie. L'utilisation du lithium pour stabiliser les états psychiques en cas de troubles maniaco-dépressifs constitue une grande prouesse médicale ; la même thérapeutique est également utilisée avec de bons résultats de façon préventive dans de nombreux cas de dépression unipolaire. Il ne fait aucun doute que dans de nombreux cas bénins et certaines formes chroniques de la maladie (les pseudo-dépressions endogènes), les drogues se sont révélées inappréciables, capables souvent d'infléchir de façon spectaculaire l'évolution de troubles graves. Pour des raisons qui persistent à ne pas me paraître claires, ni les médicaments ni la psychothérapie ne parvinrent à enrayer mon plongeon dans l'abîme. A supposer que l'on puisse ajouter foi aux affirmations de spécialistes qui font autorité en la matière — dont des assertions émanant de médecins que j'en suis venu à connaître personnellement, et à respecter — la malignité croissante de ma maladie me mettait au nombre d'une minorité distincte de patients, gravement atteints, dont l'état ne relève d'aucun traitement. Par ailleurs, je ne voudrais pas paraître insensible au fait qu'en définitive et dans la plupart des cas, les traitements suivis par les victimes de la dépression sont couronnés de succès. Surtout dans les premières phases, la maladie réagit favorablement à certaines techniques, par exemple la thérapie cognitive — utilisée seule ou associée à des médications —

ainsi qu'à d'autres approches psychiatriques en perpétuelle évolution. La plupart des malades, somme toute, n'ont pas besoin d'être hospitalisés et ils ne se suicident pas, ni même tentent de le faire. Mais jusqu'au jour où une substance à action rapide aura enfin été mise au point, la confiance que l'on peut accorder aux cures pharmacologiques en cas de dépression grave doit s'assortir de réserves. Leur impuissance à agir de façon rapide et positive — un échec qui est désormais la norme — est en un sens analogue à l'impuissance de la plupart des drogues, pendant des années, à enrayer les infections bactériennes majeures avant que les antibiotiques deviennent un remède spécifique. Ce qui d'ailleurs peut être tout aussi dangereux.

Ce fut ainsi que j'en vins à ne pas attendre grand-chose de mes entretiens avec le docteur Gold. Lors de mes visites nous continuions à échanger des platitudes, les miennes désormais débitées d'une voix hésitante — dans la mesure où mon élocution, imitant mon allure, s'était ralentie à ne plus être que l'équivalent vocal d'une démarche traînante — et j'en jurerais, aussi ennuyeuse que la sienne.

En dépit des tâtonnements persistants des traitements, la psychiatrie a, sur le plan analytique et philosophique considérablement contribué à la compréhension des origines de la dépression. Il reste manifestement bien des choses à apprendre (et il ne fait aucun doute que bien des choses demeureront un mystère, du fait du caractère idiopathique de la maladie, de l'interchangeabilité constante de ses facteurs), mais on ne peut nier qu'un élément d'ordre psychologique ait été établi de manière indubitable, à savoir le concept de perte. Le sentiment de perte, dans toutes ses manifestations, est la clé de voûte de la dépression — en ce qui concerne l'évolution de la maladie et, très vraisemblablement, ses origines. Par la suite, je devais peu à peu acquérir la conviction que dans certaine perte accablante éprouvée lors de mon enfance, résidait vraisemblablement la genèse de mon mal ; en attendant, et tout en mesurant la dégradation de ma condition, j'éprouvais à propos de tout un sentiment de perte. La perte de tout respect de soi est un symptôme bien connu, et pour ma part, j'avais pratiquement perdu tout sens de mon moi, en même temps que toute confiance en moi. Ce sentiment de perte risque de dégénérer très vite en dépendance, et la dépendance risque de faire place à une terreur infantile. On redoute la perte de tout, les choses, les gens qui vous sont proches et chers. La peur d'être abandonné vous étreint. De rester seul dans la maison, fût-ce quelques instants, me plongeait dans une panique et une agitation intenses.

Des quelques images de moi-même en cette période dont je garde le souvenir, la plus bizarre, et aussi la plus décevante, demeure celle de moi, à l'âge de quatre ans et demi, traversant un marché dans le sillage de mon épouse à l'inaltérable endurance ; et pas un seul instant, je ne pouvais perdre de vue cet être d'une patience infinie qui était devenue nourrice, maman, consolatrice, prêtresse et, plus important encore, confidente — une conseillère d'une inébranlable centralité dans mon existence, et dont la sagesse dépassait de loin celle du docteur Gold. Je serais enclin à prétendre que nombre de désastreuses séquelles de la dépression pourraient sans doute être évitées si les victimes bénéficiaient d'un soutien analogue à celui qu'elle me dispensait. Mais entre-temps, mes sentiments de perte s'aggravaient et proliféraient. Il est indubitable que du moment où l'on frôle les ultimes abîmes de la dépression — c'est-à-dire juste avant cette phase où l'on commence à passer à l'acte du suicide au lieu de se borner à l'envisager —, le sentiment aigu de perte est inséparable de l'intuition que la vie s'enfuit à une vitesse croissante. On se découvre alors des fixations farouches. Des choses ridicules — mes lunettes de lecture, un mouchoir, un certain instrument pour écrire — polarisèrent ma possessivité démente. Égarer provisoirement l'un d'eux me remplissait d'un désarroi frénétique, chacun de ces objets étant le rappel tactile d'un monde voué à bientôt s'effacer.

Novembre s'écoula, lugubre, âpre et froid. Un certain dimanche, un photographe et ses assistants se présentèrent pour faire des photos destinées à illustrer un article à paraître dans un grand magazine. De cette séance, je ne garde que peu de souvenirs, sinon celui des premiers flocons qui piquetaient l'air au-delà des fenêtres. J'eus l'impression de me prêter à la requête du photographe qui me demandait de sourire souvent. Un ou deux jours plus tard, le rédacteur en chef du magazine téléphona à ma femme, pour lui demander si j'acceptais de me soumettre à une nouvelle séance. Il avança comme raison que toutes les photos prises de moi, même celles où je souriais, « reflétaient trop d'angoisse ».

J'avais maintenant atteint cette phase de la maladie où tout vestige d'espoir avait disparu, en même temps que l'idée d'un possible futur ; mon cerveau, esclave de ses hormones en folie. était devenu moins un organe de la pensée qu'un simple instrument qui, au fil des minutes, enregistrait les variations d'intensité de sa propre souffrance. Les matins étaient plutôt pénibles, tandis qu'émergeant de mon sommeil artificiel, je traînais, léthargique, mais le pire, c'étaient les après-midi, qui commençaient à partir de trois heures environ, quand je sentais l'horreur, tel un banc de brouillard délétère, déferler sur mon esprit, au point que j'étais contraint de m'aliter. Je restais là couché parfois pendant six heures, abattu et virtuellement paralysé, les yeux rivés au plafond dans l'attente de ce moment de la soirée où, mystérieusement, le supplice se ferait moins cruel, juste assez pour me permettre d'ingurgiter un peu de nourriture avant, tel un automate, de chercher à nouveau quelques heures de sommeil. Pourquoi n'étais-je pas hospitalisé ?

VI

Pendant des années, j'avais tenu un calepin —
pas à strictement parler un journal, les nota-
tions étaient irrégulières et rédigées au hasard
— dont je n'aurais guère apprécié que le contenu
tombât sous d'autres yeux que les miens. Je
l'avais caché en lieu sûr dans un coin de ma
maison. Je ne suggère rien de scandaleux ; les
observations étaient beaucoup moins obscènes,
ou perverses, ou révélatrices que mon souci de
ne pas révéler l'existence du calepin aurait pu le
dénoter. Néanmoins le calepin était une chose
que j'avais la ferme intention d'utiliser professionnellement, puis de détruire avant le jour
lointain où le spectre de la maison de retraite se
ferait par trop menaçant. Ainsi, à mesure
qu'empirait ma maladie, je me rendis compte,
non sans une sensation de nausée, que si jamais
je décidais de me débarrasser du calepin, ce

moment coïnciderait inévitablement avec ma décision de mettre fin à mes jours. Et un soir au début de décembre, ce moment survint.

Cet après-midi-là je m'étais fait conduire en voiture (je n'étais plus capable de conduire moi-même) au cabinet du docteur Gold, qui m'annonça sa décision de me prescrire un nouvel antidépresseur, le Nardil, une drogue plus ancienne qui présentait l'avantage de ne pas provoquer de rétention d'urine, au contraire des deux autres drogues qu'il m'avait précédemment prescrites. Toutefois, il y avait des inconvénients. L'effet du Nardil ne commencerait probablement pas à se manifester avant quatre à six semaines — j'eus du mal à en croire mes oreilles — et je devrais observer scrupuleusement certaines règles alimentaires, par bonheur plutôt épicuriennes (ni saucisse, ni fromage, ni pâté de foie gras), de manière à éviter un conflit entre enzymes incompatibles qui risquerait de provoquer une attaque d'apoplexie. En outre, annonça le docteur Gold, le visage impassible, il était possible qu'à dose optimale et entre autres effets secondaires, le médicament entraînât l'impuissance sexuelle. Jusqu'à cet instant, bien qu'il me fût parfois arrivé de ne guère apprécier sa personnalité, jamais je ne l'avais jugé totalement dénué de perspicacité : cette fois, je n'en aurais pas juré. Me mettant dans la peau du docteur Gold, je me demandais s'il pensait sérieusement que ce semi-invalide ravagé et sans énergie, qui se traînait et soufflait comme un vieillard, pût émerger chaque matin de son paisible sommeil Halcion en proie au démon de la chair.

Ce jour-là notre entretien eut quelque chose de si désolant que je rentrai chez moi dans un état particulièrement lamentable et me préparai pour la soirée. Nous attendions quelques invités pour dîner — une perspective qui ne m'effrayait pas davantage qu'elle ne me souriait, ce qui en soi (c'est-à-dire vu mon apathie) révèle un aspect fascinant de la psychopathologie. Il s'agit là non du seuil familier de la souffrance, mais d'un phénomène parallèle, à savoir l'impuissance probable de la psyché à assumer la douleur au-delà des limites temporelles prévisibles. Dans l'expérience de la souffrance, il existe une aire où la certitude d'un éventuel soulagement permet une endurance surhumaine. Au fil des jours, on apprend à vivre avec la souffrance à des degrés variables, ou sur de longues periodes de temps, et par bonheur, le plus souvent, elle nous est épargnée. Lorsque nous endurons une souffrance intense de nature physique, notre conditionnement nous a depuis l'enfance appris à nous adapter aux exigences de la douleur — à l'accepter, que ce soit crânement ou en pleurnichant, selon notre degré personnel de stoïcisme, mais en tout état de cause à l'accepter. Sauf en cas de douleur intraitable au stade terminal d'une maladie, il existe presque toujours certaines formes de soulagement : nous comptons sur ce soulagement, qu'il soit dû au sommeil, au Tylenol, à l'hypnose ou à un changement de position ou, plus souvent, aux pouvoirs d'auto-guérison dont est doté le corps, et nous accueillons ce répit à venir comme la récompense naturelle qui nous échoit pour nous être montrés, provisoirement, tellement braves, beaux joueurs et vaillants dans l'épreuve, tellement optimistes et fanas de la vie.

Dans les cas de dépression, cette foi dans la délivrance, dans un ultime rétablissement fait défaut. La souffrance est implacable, et ce qui rend cette condition intolérable est de savoir à l'avance qu'aucun remède ne se matérialisera — fût-ce dans un jour, une heure, un mois, ou une minute. C'est l'absence d'espoir qui plus encore que la souffrance broie l'âme. C'est ainsi que les décisions à prendre dans le quotidien n'impliquent pas, comme dans la vie courante, le passage d'une situation exaspérante à une autre moins exaspérante — ni de l'inconfort à un relatif confort — mais le passage d'une souffrance à une autre souffrance. On n'abandonne jamais, pas même un instant, sa planche à clous, l'on reste couché dessus, où que l'on aille ; ce qui aboutit à une extraordinaire expérience — une expérience que, puisant dans la terminologie militaire, j'ai appelée la condition de blessé ambulatoire. Car dans pratiquement toute autre maladie grave, un patient à ce point affligé serait cloué dans son lit, probablement sous l'effet de calmants et branché aux tubes et fils des respirateurs artificiels, mais en tout cas dans une posture de repos et dans des conditions d'isolement. Son invalidité serait inévitable, incontestée et nullement déshonorante. Cependant, la victime d'une dépression n'a pas ce genre d'option et en conséquence se retrouve, à l'instar d'un blessé de guerre ambulatoire, plongée dans d'intolérables situations sociales et familiales. Et là il lui faut, malgré l'angoisse qui dévore son cerveau, offrir aux autres un visage analogue à celui que l'on associe aux circonstances et aux relations de la vie normale. Il lui faut s'efforcer de parler de tout et de rien, de réagir aux questions, de hocher la tête et froncer les sourcils d'un air entendu et, même, que Dieu l'aide, de sourire. Pourtant c'est pour lui une épreuve atroce que de s'arracher quelques simples mots.

Cette soirée de décembre, par exemple, j'aurais pu rester dans mon lit comme je le faisais d'ordinaire dans les pires moments, ou choisir d'assister au petit dîner que ma femme avait organisé en bas pour quelques invités. Mais la simple idée d'une décision à prendre était théorique. L'une comme l'autre, les deux perspectives étaient une torture, et je choisis d'assister au dîner non parce qu'il présentait le moindre intérêt à mes yeux, mais par indifférence à ce qui, je le savais, serait une série d'épreuves noyées dans une brume d'horreur. Au dîner je fus à peine capable de parler, mais les invités, tous de bons amis, étaient au courant de mon état et feignirent par courtoisie de ne pas remarquer mon mutisme catatonique. Puis, après le dîner, assis au salon, je ressentis une bizarre convulsion intérieure que je ne saurais décrire autrement que comme une désespérance au-delà de toute désespérance. Elle surgit de l'air froid; jamais je n'aurais cru possible une telle angoisse.

Pendant que mes amis bavardaient paisiblement devant la cheminée, je m'excusai et regagnai l'étage, où j'allais extirper mon calepin de sa cachette. Après quoi je me rendis à la cuisine et avec une aveuglante lucidité — la lucidité de quelqu'un qui se livre à un rite solennel et le sait — j'enregistrai dans mon esprit les slogans publicitaires des divers articles courants que j'entrepris alors d'assembler dans le but de me débarrasser du calepin: le rouleau tout neuf de serviettes-papier Viva que j'ouvris pour envelopper le livre, le papier collant Scotch que j'enroulai autour, la boîte vide de céréales Post Raisin Bran où je glissai le paquet avant de sortir pour aller le fourrer au fond de la poubelle, qui serait vidée le lendemain matin. Le feu l'eût détruit plus rapidement, mais le livrer aux ordures impliquait une annihilation du moi appropriée, comme toujours, à l'autohumiliation féconde de la mélancolie. Je sentais mon cœur battre follement la chamade, comme celui d'un homme face au peloton d'exécution, car, je le savais, je venais de prendre une décision irréversible.

Un phénomène que beaucoup de gens en proie à une grave dépression ont pu constater, est la sensation d'être en permanence escorté par un second moi — un observateur fantomatique qui, ne partageant pas la démence de son double, est capable d'observer avec une curiosité objective tandis que son compagnon lutte pour empêcher le désastre imminent, ou prend la décision de s'y abandonner. Il y a là quelque chose de théâtral, et pendant les quelques jours qui suivirent, tout en m'employant avec flegme à préparer ma disparition, je ne parvins pas à me défaire d'un sentiment de mélodrame — un mélodrame dont moi, la victime potentielle d'une mort volontaire, j'étais à la fois l'acteur solitaire et l'unique spectateur. Je n'avais toujours pas choisi les modalités de mon trépas, mais, je le savais, cette étape surviendrait, et très bientôt, inévitable comme la tombée de la nuit.

Je m'observais avec un mélange de terreur et de fascination tandis que j'entreprenais les indispensables préparatifs : une visite à mon avocat dans la ville voisine — afin de réécrire mon testament — un ou deux après-midi en partie consacrés à une tentative brouillonne pour gratifier la postérité d'une lettre d'adieu. Il s'avéra que la rédaction d'une lettre de suicide, qu'une forme d'obsession me contraignait à vouloir composer, était la tâche d'écriture la plus dure à laquelle j'avais jamais été confronté. Il y avait trop de gens à saluer, à remercier, auxquels léguer d'ultimes fleurs. Et en fin de compte, je ne parvins pas à assumer la lugubre solennité de la chose ; je trouvais quelque chose de comiquement choquant à la pomposité de, par exemple, ce genre de remarque : « Depuis quelque temps déjà, je décèle dans mon travail une psychose croissante qui, sans nul doute, est le reflet de la tension psychotique par laquelle est infectée ma vie » (une des rares lignes dont je me souvienne mot pour mot), en même temps que quelque chose de dégradant dans la perspective d'un testament, auquel j'aurais souhaité insuffler du moins un peu de dignité et d'éloquence, réduit à un bégaiement débile tissé d'inadéquates excuses et de plaidoyers pro domo. J'aurais dû choisir comme exemple le texte lapidaire de l'écrivain italien Cesare Pavese, qui en guise d'adieu se contenta d'écrire : *Assez de mots. Un acte. Jamais plus je n'écrirai.*

Mais même quelques mots finirent par me paraître trop prolixes, et je déchirai le fruit de mes efforts, en me promettant de faire ma sortie en silence. Tard par une nuit d'un froid âpre, alors que, je le savais, je n'aurais pas la force de me traîner jusqu'au terme du jour à venir, je m'assis dans le salon, tout emmitouflé pour me protéger du froid ; la chaudière était tombée en panne.

Ma femme était montée se coucher, et je m'étais fait violence pour regarder une vidéo-cassette dans laquelle une jeune actrice, qui avait joué dans l'une de mes pièces, tenait un petit rôle. A un moment donné du film, qui se situait à Boston à la fin du dix-neuvième siècle, les personnages s'avançaient dans le couloir d'un conservatoire de musique, tandis qu'au-delà des murs, parmi un groupe de musiciens invisibles, montait une voix de contralto, la soudaine envolée d'un passage de la Rhapsodie pour contralto de Brahms.

Cette mélodie, à laquelle comme à toute forme de musique — en fait, comme à toute forme de plaisir — j'étais dans ma torpeur resté insensible depuis des mois, me transperça le cœur comme une dague, et dans un flot de souvenirs rapides, je repensai à toutes les joies qu'avait connues la maison ; les enfants qui jadis gambadaient à travers les pièces, les fêtes, l'amour et le travail, le sommeil honnêtement gagné, les voix et le brouhaha plein d'allégresse, l'éternelle tribu des chats, des chiens et des oiseaux, « des rires, des talents, des soupirs, des robes et de jolies boucles ». Tout cela, soudain je m'en rendais compte, était trop pour que jamais je puisse y renoncer, tout comme ce que j'avais entrepris de faire si délibérément était trop pour que je puisse l'infliger à ces souvenirs, et à ceux, si proches de moi, auxquels s'attachaient ces souvenirs. Et tout aussi intensément, je me rendis compte que je ne pouvais perpétrer cette profanation sur ma propre personne. Je fis appel à quelques ultimes lueurs de bon sens et mesurai les dimensions terrifiantes du mortel dilemme dont j'étais prisonnier. Je réveillai ma femme et bientôt les coups de téléphone se succédèrent. Le lendemain j'entrai à l'hôpital.

VII

Ce fut le docteur Gold, qui en qualité de médecin traitant, fut appelé pour organiser mon admission à l'hôpital. Chose curieuse, c'était lui qui à plusieurs reprises lors de nos entretiens (et lorsque, non sans hésitation, j'eus suggéré l'éventualité d'une hospitalisation) m'avait assuré que je devrais m'efforcer à tout prix d'éviter l'hôpital, en raison des stigmates que je risquais d'en garder. Un commentaire qui m'avait paru alors, comme il me paraît toujours, des plus malencontreux ; j'étais convaincu que la psychiatrie avait suffisamment évolué pour dépasser le stade où des stigmates s'attachaient à tous les aspects des maladies mentales, y compris l'hôpital. Ce refuge, bien que loin d'être un lieu plaisant, est une solution vers laquelle peuvent se tourner les malades quand les drogues se révèlent inefficaces,

103

caces, comme par exemple dans mon cas, et un lieu où le traitement dispensé pourrait être considéré comme un prolongement, dans un contexte différent, de la thérapie inaugurée dans des cabinets comme celui du docteur Gold.

Il est impossible de dire, bien sûr, quelle approche aurait eue un autre médecin, et si lui aussi se fût prononcé contre la solution de l'hôpital. De nombreux psychiatres, pour la simple raison qu'ils semblent incapables de comprendre la nature et la profondeur de l'angoisse qui accable leurs malades, s'accrochent à leur foi dans les produits pharmaceutiques avec la conviction que tôt ou tard les drogues se décideront à agir, feront de l'effet, que le malade réagira, et que le cadre sinistre de l'hôpital lui sera épargné. Le docteur Gold était ce genre de médecin, de toute évidence, mais en l'occurrence il se trompait ; je suis convaincu que j'aurais dû être hospitalisé des semaines plus tôt. Car, en réalité, l'hôpital m'apporta le salut, et plutôt paradoxalement ce fut dans ce lieu austère aux portes verrouillées et blindées et aux mornes couloirs peints en vert — avec jour et nuit neuf étages plus bas le hurlement des ambulances — que je trouvai le repos, l'apaisement de la tempête déchaînée dans mon cer veau, que je n'avais pas réussi à trouver dans ma paisible maison de ferme.

Cela est en partie dû à la séquestration, à la sécurité, à la soudaine transplantation dans un univers où le besoin impérieux d'empoigner un couteau pour se le plonger dans le cœur, disparaît dans cette conscience nouvelle, qui bientôt s'impose au cerveau désorienté du malade, que le couteau avec lequel il tente de couper son steak trop cuit est en plastique souple. Mais l'hôpital apporte aussi le traumatisme relatif, bizarrement satisfaisant, d'une brusque stabilisation — un transfert hors du cadre trop familier de son chez-soi, où tout est anxiété et chaos, dans une détention disciplinée et bienveillante où l'unique devoir est d'essayer de guérir. Pour moi, les vrais guérisseurs furent la solitude et le temps.

VIII

L'hôpital fut une étape, un purgatoire. Lors de mon arrivée, ma dépression paraissait à ce point profonde que, de l'avis de certains des médecins, je relevais d'une électrothérapie — le traitement de choc, selon l'expression courante. Dans de nombreux cas, c'est là un remède efficace — le traitement a été amélioré et a retrouvé sa respectabilité, débarrassé pour l'essentiel de la réputation de barbarie quasi médiévale qui jadis lui était attachée — mais incontestablement, il s'agit là d'une procédure draconienne qu'il est naturel de vouloir s'épargner. Elle me fut épargnée car je commençai bientôt à aller mieux, insensiblement mais de façon régulière. Je me rendis compte avec stupéfaction que les fantasmes d'autodestruction disparurent presque tous dès les premiers jours qui suivirent mon arrivée, un témoignage supplémentaire de l'apaisement que peut apporter l'hôpital, de sa capacité immédiate à opérer comme un sanctuaire où l'esprit est à même de retrouver la paix.

Il convient d'ajouter une ultime mise en garde, pourtant, au sujet de l'Halcion. J'ai la conviction que ce tranquillisant est responsable d'avoir au minimum exacerbé jusqu'à les rendre intolérables les idées de suicide qui m'obsédaient avant mon entrée à l'hôpital. La preuve empirique à laquelle je dois cette certitude découle d'une conversation que j'eus avec un psychiatre de l'établissement quelques heures à peine après mon admission. Comme il me demandait ce que je prenais pour dormir, et à quelle posologie, je lui répondis : 75 mg d'Halcion ; son visage aussitôt s'assombrit. et il fit observer d'un ton catégorique que cela représentait le triple de la posologie hypnotique normalement prescrite, de plus une dose particulièrement contre-indiquée pour une personne de mon âge. On me mit sur-le-champ au Dalmane, un autre hypnotique de la même famille mais à action sensiblement prolongée, qui pour m'aider à m'endormir se révéla tout aussi efficace que l'Halcion ; plus important, je constatai que peu après le changement, mes idées suicidaires diminuèrent pour bientôt disparaître.

Nombre de témoignages accumulés ces derniers temps accusent l'Halcion, (dont le nom chimique est Triazolan) d'être un facteur déterminant dans l'apparition d'obsessions suicidaires et autres aberrations mentales chez des sujets fragiles. Compte tenu de ce type de réactions, l'Halcion a été catégoriquement banni aux Pays-Bas et il est souhaitable qu'ici, son usage fasse l'objet d'un contrôle plus strict. Je ne me souviens pas d'avoir jamais entendu le docteur Gold s'interroger sur la dose indûment forte qu'il savait pertinemment que je prenais, sans doute, n'avait-il pas lu la notice relative aux contre-indications figurant dans le *Physicians' Desk Reference*. Bien que je fusse moi-même coupable par imprudence d'avoir ingéré des doses à ce point excessives, j'attribue mon imprudence aux assurances désinvoltes que l'on m'avait prodiguées quelques années plus tôt, lorsque j'avais commencé à prendre de l'Ativan sur l'ordre d'un médecin expéditif m'affirmant que je pouvais, sans risques, prendre autant de comprimés que je voudrais. L'on frémit en songeant aux préjudices que la prescription de tranquillisants potentiellement dangereux risque d'occasionner à des malades un peu partout dans le monde. Dans mon cas, bien sûr, l'Halcion n'était pas seul en cause — j'avais déjà mis le cap vers l'abîme — je crois néanmoins que sans lui, je n'aurais pas touché le fond.

Je restai à l'hôpital pendant près de sept semaines. Tout le monde, cela va sans dire, ne réagirait pas nécessairement comme je le fis ; la dépression, il convient d'insister constamment sur ce point, présente tant de variations et est dotée de tant de facettes subtiles — dépend tellement, en bref, du potentiel de motivation et de réaction de chacun — que ce qui pour certains serait une panacée, risque d'être un piège pour d'autres. Mais indiscutablement l'hôpital (bien sûr, je parle des bons hôpitaux, qui sont nombreux) devrait être dépouillé de sa réputation, ne devrait pas si souvent être assimilé au traitement du dernier recours. L'hôpital certes n'a rien d'un lieu de vacances ; celui où je fus hébergé (j'eus le privilège que ce soit dans l'un des meilleurs du pays) n'échappait pas au morne ennui qui caractérise tous les hôpitaux. Si en outre se trouvent réunis au même étage, comme par exemple au mien, quatorze ou quinze hommes et femmes entre deux âges en proie aux affres d'une neurasthénie à tendances suicidaires, il est facile de se représenter un environnement d'où le rire est en général banni. Une situation que dans mon cas n'amélioraient en rien la nourriture, plus médiocre encore que sur les lignes aériennes, et les aperçus que j'avais du monde extérieur : *Dynastie* et *Knots Landing*[1] et le bulletin d'informations du soir sur CBS qui chaque jour défilait dans le foyer aux murs nus, et avait du moins parfois le pouvoir de me faire sentir que le lieu où j'avais trouvé refuge était une maison de fous d'un genre plus aimable, plus bienveillant que celui que j'avais quitté A l'hôpital, je bénéficiai de ce qui est peut-être l'unique bienfait qu'à contre-cœur dispense la dépression — sa capitulation finale. Même ceux pour qui une thérapie fut une épreuve inutile, peuvent se réjouir à la perspective de voir un jour se dissiper la tempête. S'ils parviennent à survivre à la tempête elle-même, presque toujours sa fureur décroît et finit par s'éteindre. Mystérieux au moment de son flux mystérieux au moment de son reflux, le mal suit son cours, et l'on trouve la paix.

A mesure que s'améliorait mon état, je trouvais certaines formes de distractions dans la

1. *Knots Landing* : feuilleton télévisé très populaire, genre *Santa Barbara* ou *Dallas* (*N.d.T.*)

routine de l'hôpital, lui aussi doté de ses comédies de situation. La thérapie de groupe, paraît-il, a ses mérites ; pour rien au monde je ne voudrais dénigrer un concept qui pour certains se révèle efficace. Mais la thérapie de groupe n'eut sur moi d'autre effet que de me mettre en fureur, peut-être parce qu'elle était animée par un jeune psychiatre d'une suffisance odieuse, à la barbe noire taillée en forme de pique (*der junge Freud ?*), qui dans ses tentatives pour nous faire expectorer les semences de notre détresse, oscillait entre la condescendance et la tyrannie, et réduisait parfois quelques-unes de ses infortunées patientes, pathétiques à voir avec leurs kimonos et leurs bigoudis, à ce qui était à ses yeux, j'en jurerais, des larmes satisfaisantes. (En raison de leur tact et de leur compassion, les autres membres de l'équipe psychiatrique me parurent exemplaires.) Le temps se traîne dans un hôpital, et tout ce que je peux dire concernant la thérapie de groupe, c'est qu'elle aide à tuer le temps.

L'on pourrait dire plus ou moins la même chose de la thérapie par l'art, qui est de l'infantilisme organisé. Notre classe était dirigée par une jeune femme délirante qui arborait un sourire figé et infatigable, et manifestement, sortait

d'une école spécialisée dans les cours de pédago-
gie de l'art pour malades mentaux; pas même
un enseignant spécialiste pour enfants retardés
d'âge tendre, n'aurait pu se voir contraint de
dispenser, sans directives précises, tant de
gloussements et roucoulements orchestrés.
Déployant de longs rouleaux de papier mural
lisse, elle nous invitait à prendre nos fusains
pour faire des dessins illustrant des thèmes de
notre choix. Par exemple: Ma Maison. En proie
à une fureur humiliée j'obéis, et dessinai un
carré, pourvu d'une porte et de quatre fenêtres
de guingois, coiffé d'une cheminée d'où sortait
la fioriture d'une fumée Elle m'accabla de
louanges, et tandis qu'au fil des semaines mon
état s'améliorait, mon sens de la comédie en fit
autant. Je me mis à tripoter avec enthousiasme
les pâtes à modeler de couleur, sculptant tout
d'abord un horrible petit crâne vert aux babines
retroussées que notre professeur salua comme
une splendide réplique de ma dépression. Au fil
des phases intermédiaires de ma récupération,
je m'attelai à une tête rosâtre et angélique qui
arborait un sourire style « Bonne Journée A
Vous ». Coïncidant de fait avec le moment de ma
libération, cette création transporta littérale-
ment de joie mon professeur (que malgré moi

j'avais fini par trouver sympathique), dans la mesure où, à l'en croire, elle était le symbole de ma récupération et en conséquence une illustration supplémentaire du triomphe remporté sur la maladie par la thérapie par l'art.

Nous étions désormais au début de février, et si j'étais encore chancelant, j'avais, et le savais, retrouvé la lumière. Je n'avais plus l'impression d'être une gousse vide, mais un corps dans lequel de nouveau frémissaient certaines des délicieuses pulsions du corps. Je fis mon premier rêve depuis bien des mois, un rêve confus mais aujourd'hui encore impérissable, avec quelque part une flûte, une oie sauvage et une jeune danseuse.

IX

Dans l'ensemble, la grande majorité des gens qui font une dépression, même très grave, survivent et, par la suite et jusqu'à la fin de leurs jours, vivent au moins aussi heureux que leurs semblables épargnés par le mal. Exception faite du caractère horrible de certains souvenirs qu'elle laisse, une dépression aiguë n'inflige que peu de blessures permanentes. Qu'un grand nombre — la moitié en fait — de ceux qui sont un jour terrassés, soient condamnés à l'être de nouveau tôt ou tard, est un tourment de Sisyphe ; la dépression a coutume de récidiver. Mais la plupart des victimes surmontent ces rechutes, et même les assument mieux, car psychologiquement leur expérience antérieure les a préparées à affronter l'ogre. Il est d'une extrême importance que ceux qui subissent un accès de dépression, peut-être pour la première fois, soient avertis — soient persuadés, plutôt — que la maladie suivra son cours et qu'ils s'en sortiront. Une rude tâche que de lancer : « Courage ! » quand on est en sécurité sur le rivage à quelqu'un qui se noie, ce qui équivaut à une insulte, mais, et la preuve en a été faite à d'innombrables reprises, si l'encouragement est suffisamment opiniâtre — et le soutien également fervent et impliqué — la personne en péril peut dans la grande majorité des cas être sauvée. La plupart des gens en proie aux affres de la dépression se trouvent, on ne sait pour quelle raison, plongés dans un état de désespoir irréaliste, déchirés par des maux exagérés et des idées de mort sans rapport avec le réel. Cela peut exiger de la part des autres — amis, amants, famille, admirateurs — un dévouement quasi religieux pour convaincre les victimes que la vie vaut la peine d'être vécue, ce qui souvent est en conflit avec le sentiment qu'elles ont de leur propre inutilité, mais ce genre de dévouement a empêché d'innombrables suicides.

Au cours de ce même été et tandis que se poursuivait mon déclin, un de mes proches amis — un célèbre journaliste — fut hospitalisé pour cause de psychose maniaque dépressive. Alors que l'automne arrivé je commençai à dégringoler la pente, mon ami avait récupéré (dans une large mesure grâce au lithium, et aussi, par la suite, à la psychothérapie) et nous nous entretenions presque chaque jour au téléphone. Son inlassable soutien m'était précieux. Ce fut lui qui me rappela sans relâche que le suicide était « intolérable » (il avait été obsédé par des tentations suicidaires) et ce fut également grâce à lui que la perspective d'entrer à l'hôpital cessa de m'apparaître comme une affreuse menace. C'est avec une immense gratitude que je repense encore aujourd'hui à sa sollicitude. L'aide qu'il m'apporta, me confia-t-il plus tard, avait été pour lui une thérapie constante, démontrant ainsi que, du moins, la maladie peut être source d'amitiés durables.

Lorsqu'à l'hôpital je commençai à récupérer l'idée me vint de me demander — pour la première fois avec un intérêt authentique — pourquoi j'avais été frappé par ce genre de fléau. Il existe, sur le sujet de la dépression, une littérature psychiatrique énorme, avec d'innombrables théories concernant l'étiologie de la maladie, proliférant avec autant d'exubérance que les théories sur la mort des dinosaures ou l'origine des trous noirs. Le nombre même des hypothèses témoigne du mystère quasi impénétrable de la maladie. Quant au mécanisme qui la déclenche — ce que j'ai appelé les symptômes manifestes —, puis-je véritablement me satisfaire de cette idée que le renoncement brutal à l'alcool a précipité le plongeon? Que penser des autres possibilités — le fait incontournable, par exemple, qu'à peu près au moment où je fus frappé, j'eus soixante ans, soixante ans, cette énorme borne de notre mortalité. Ou bien se pouvait-il qu'une insatisfaction vague quant à la façon dont mon travail avançait — les prémices de cette inertie qui tout au long de ma vie d'écrivain s'était de temps à autre emparée de moi, et me laissait hargneux et morose — m'eût également harcelé plus férocement que jamais au cours de cette période, amplifiant d'une certaine manière mon problème d'alcool? Quel rôle pouvait jouer l'accoutumance à un tranquillisant? Autant de questions impossibles à résoudre, que mieux valait ne pas tenter de résoudre.

De toute façon ces problèmes m'intéressent moins que la quête des origines de la maladie. Quels sont les événements oubliés ou enfouis dans la mémoire qui peuvent apporter une ultime explication à l'évolution de la dépression et, par la suite, à son épanouissement dans une

118

forme de folie ? Jusqu'à l'offensive de ma propre maladie et à son dénouement, jamais je n'avais tellement réfléchi à la dimension inconsciente de mon travail — un champ d'investigation réservé aux détectives littéraires. Mais lorsque j'eus recouvré la santé et fus de nouveau capable de réfléchir au passé à la lumière de mon épreuve, je commençai à voir clairement à quel point la dépression était, de nombreuses années durant, restée tapie à la périphérie de ma vie. Le suicide a toujours été un thème persistant dans mes livres — trois de mes personnages majeurs ont mis fin à leurs jours. Relisant, pour la première fois depuis des années, des extraits de certains de mes romans — des passages où mes héroïnes avancent en titubant par les chemins qui les mènent à l'abîme — je fus abasourdi de constater avec quelle minutie j'avais créé le paysage de la dépression dans l'esprit de ces jeunes femmes, décrivant avec ce qui ne pouvait être que l'instinct, jailli d'un subconscient déjà agité par des perturbations de l'esprit, le déséquilibre psychique qui les entraînait vers leur perte. C'est ainsi que la dépression, quand finalement elle me frappa, n'était nullement en fait une étrangère pour moi, pas même une visiteuse

119

survenue inopinément : depuis des décennies elle grattait à ma porte.

La condition morbide découlait, j'en suis venu à le croire, de mes premières années — de mon père qui durant une grande partie de sa vie combattit lui aussi la Gorgone, et dans mon enfance avait dû être hospitalisé au terme d'une plongée dans le gouffre du désespoir qui, je le voyais avec le recul, présentait de grandes analogies avec la mienne. Il semblerait que les racines génétiques de la dépression soient maintenant établies au-delà de toute controverse. Mais je suis également convaincu qu'un facteur plus signifiant encore fut la mort de ma mère alors que j'avais treize ans, ce type de catastrophe et de deuil précoce — la mort du père ou de la mère, avant ou pendant la puberté — revient dans la littérature consacrée à la dépression comme un traumatisme capable parfois de provoquer des dégâts émotionnels virtuellement irréparables. Le danger est particulièrement évident si de jeunes êtres sont affectés par un phénomène que l'on a qualifie de « deuil avorté » — ont en réalité, été incapables de procéder à la catharsis du chagrin, et portent donc enfoui en eux au fil des années un intolérable fardeau dont la colère et le remords, pas seulement le chagrin refoulé, sont des composantes, et deviennent des semences potentielles d'autodestruction.

Dans un livre récent et d'une grande pertinence consacré au suicide, *Self-Destruction in the Promised Land* (Rutgers), Howard I. Kushner, qui est non pas un psychiatre mais un spécialiste de l'histoire des sociétés, défend de façon fort persuasive cette théorie du « deuil avorté » et choisit pour illustrer sa thèse l'exemple d'Abraham Lincoln. Tandis que les terribles accès de mélancolie dont souffrait Lincoln appartiennent à la légende, il est beaucoup moins connu que pendant sa jeunesse il fut souvent la proie de tendances suicidaires et se retrouva plus d'une fois à deux doigts d'attenter à ses jours. Or il semblerait que ce comportement soit en relation directe avec la mort de la mère de Lincoln, Nancy Hanks, alors qu'il avait neuf ans, et à un chagrin demeuré refoulé et exacerbé par la mort de sa sœur dix années plus tard. Tirant ses conclusions de la chronique du succès de l'âpre lutte de Lincoln pour échapper au suicide, Kushner démontre de façon convaincante non seulement la thèse qu'un deuil précoce précipite un comportement autodestructeur, mais également, et c'est de bon augure, que ce même comportement peut se muer en une stratégie qui permet à la personne impliquée d'affronter son remords et sa fureur, et de triompher d'une mort délibérément choisie. Il se peut que cette forme de réconciliation soit inséparable d'une quête d'immortalité — dans le cas de Lincoln, tout autant que dans celui d'un auteur de fiction, une lutte pour vaincre la mort grâce à une œuvre honorée par la postérité.

Si donc cette théorie du deuil présente quelque validité, comme je le crois, et si en outre il est vrai que dans les ténèbres les plus secrètes du comportement suicidaire, le malade demeure inconsciemment aux prises avec une perte immense quand bien même il s'efforce d'en surmonter tous les effets et les ravages, dans mon cas personnel le fait que je parvins à échapper à la mort fut peut-être un hommage tardif que je rendis à ma mère. Ce que je sais en tout cas, c'est que durant ces ultimes heures avant que j'entreprenne mon sauvetage, tandis que j'écoutais le fragment de la Rhapsodie pour contralto — que jadis elle avait un jour chanté en ma présence — elle n'avait cessé d'obséder mon esprit.

X

Presque à la fin de l'un des premiers films d'Ingmar Bergman, *A travers le miroir*, une jeune femme qui se débat dans les affres de ce qui paraît être une grave psychose, est l'objet d'une hallucination terrifiante. Alors que, pleine d'espoir, elle s'attend à ce que se produise une vision transcendante et salvatrice de Dieu, elle voit surgir la forme tremblotante d'une monstrueuse araignée qui tente de la violer. Un instant d'horreur et d'atroce vérité. Pourtant, même dans cette vision de Bergman (qui lui aussi souffrit cruellement de la dépression), on a le sentiment que malgré son talent artistique accompli, il se révèle, en un sens, impuissant à rendre fidèlement l'horrible fantasmagorie de l'esprit qui se noie. Depuis l'Antiquité — dans la complainte torturée de Job, dans les chœurs de Sophocle et d'Eschyle — les chroniqueurs de

123

l'esprit humain ne cessent de se mesurer à un vocabulaire capable d'exprimer de façon adéquate la désolation de la mélancolie. A travers toute la littérature et l'art, le thème de la dépression court comme une veine indestructible, la veine du malheur — du monologue de Hamlet aux vers d'Emily Dickinson et de Gerard Manley Hopkins, de John Donne et Milton à Hawthorne et à Poe, de Camus à Conrad et Virginia Woolf. Dans nombre des gravures d'Albrecht Dürer, il est de déchirantes représentations de sa propre mélancolie : les astres tourbillonnants et déments de Van Gogh présagent la plongée de l'artiste dans la démence et l'extinction de son moi. C'est une souffrance analogue qui souvent colore la musique de Beethoven, de Schumann et de Mahler, et imprègne les cantates les plus sombres de Bach. L'immense métaphore qui représente avec le plus de fidélité cette insondable épreuve, cependant, est celle de Dante, dont les vers hélas trop familiers ne cessent de frapper l'imagination par leur présage de l'inconnaissable, du ténébreux combat à venir :

Nel mezzo del cammin di nostra vita
mi retrovai per una selva oscura
chè la diritta via era smarrita.

Au milieu du chemin de notre vie
je me retrouvai dans une forêt obscure,
car j'avais perdu la voie droite.

On peut être assuré que ces mots ont été
maintes fois employés pour évoquer les ravages
de la mélancolie, mais les noires prémonitions
qui les marquent ont souvent éclipsé les derniers
vers de la partie la plus célèbre du poème,
empreints de leur hymne d'espoir. Pour la plupart de ceux qui l'ont connue, l'horreur de la
dépression est à ce point accablante qu'elle en
est inexprimable, d'où le sentiment frustré de
relative impuissance qui se décèle dans les
œuvres des plus grands parmi les artistes. Mais
dans le domaine de la science et de l'art, il ne fait
aucun doute que se poursuivra la quête d'une
représentation claire de sa signification, qui
parfois, pour ceux qui en ont fait l'expérience,
est une image des maux de cet univers qui est le
nôtre : la discorde et le chaos de notre quotidien,
notre irrationalité, la guerre et le crime, la torture et la violence, l'impulsion qui nous précipite vers la mort et l'élan qui nous pousse à la
fuir, réunis dans l'intolérable et délicate balance
de l'histoire. Si nos vies n'avaient d'autre confi-
guration que celle-ci, nous souhaiterions fatale-

ment mourir, peut-être le mériterions-nous ; si la dépression n'avait pas de dénouement, alors dans ce cas le suicide, certes, serait l'unique remède. Mais il n'est nul besoin d'entonner une note forcée ou inspirée pour souligner cette vérité que la dépression n'est pas l'annihilation de l'âme ; les hommes et les femmes qui ont surmonté la maladie — ils sont légion — portent témoignage de ce qui est sans doute son unique côté rédempteur : il est possible de la vaincre.

Quant à ceux qui ont séjourné dans la sombre forêt de la dépression, et connu son inexplicable torture, leur remontée de l'abîme n'est pas sans analogie avec l'ascension du poète, qui laborieusement se hisse pour échapper aux noires entrailles de l'enfer et émerge enfin dans ce qui lui apparaît comme « le monde radieux ». Là, quiconque a recouvré la santé, a presque toujours également recouvré l'aptitude à la sérénité et à la joie, et c'est peut-être là une compensation suffisante pour avoir enduré cette désespérance au-delà de la désespérance.

E quindi uscimmo a riveder le stelle.

Et là nous sortîmes pour revoir les étoiles.

Composition Eurocomposition.
Impression S.E.P.C.
à Saint-Amand (Cher), le 21 mars 1991.
Dépôt légal : mars 1991.
Premier dépôt légal : septembre 1990.
Numéro d'imprimeur : 763.
ISBN 2-07-072105-1./Imprimé en France.